THE MAGIK SCARF

Book One
of
The World of Daegries Series

M. K. Browning

Howling Wolf Press
www.howlingwolfpress.com

The Magik Scarf

Alyssa's Map

N
W E
S
BLIGHTED VALE
SNOWCLIPS
WELLSPRING
DRAGON
HALDOR
NEEDLEMOUNT CASTLE
WOLVES
YETI MOUNTAINS
HEIGHTLANDS
HALFMOON MANOR
FOREST OF SHADOWS
SILK SEA
MERMAID
MARKETPLACE
OLD STONY
MEADOWLANDS
GRYPHON
OLD STONY
FARMLANDS
MAZE
MUDDEN
SWAMP LANDS
HOME

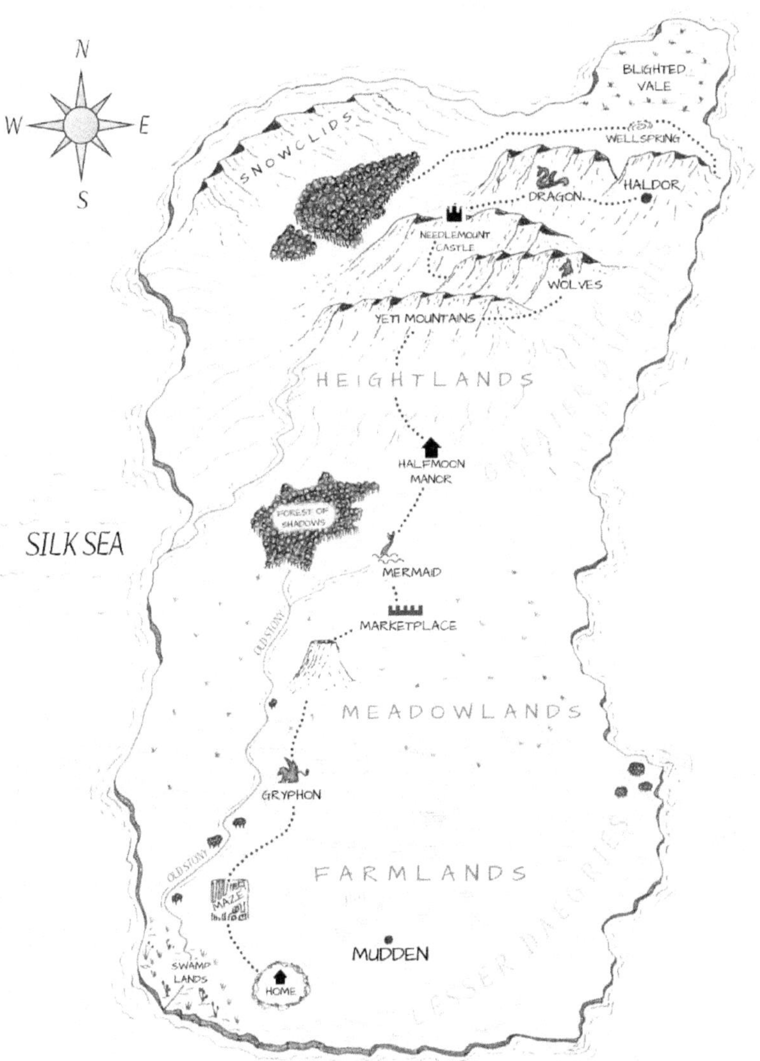

This book is dedicated to…

My grandchildren

Acknowledgements
This book would not have been possible without ….

Ellen Holder, who helped with editing.
My beta readers, thank you!
Quills to Computers, for your critiques!
My husband and kids who give me love.

____

CREDITS

Map by Alyssa Hurlburt (the name of main character is the
same by a twist of fate!)
https://www.youtube.com/@Alyssahurlbert
Cover design by Miblart.com

Prologue

Sixty years earlier...

A fresh snowfall encompassed the wizard's gathering in Knowledge Mountain Hall, a fortress hidden deep within the Snowclid Range. The place felt cold and unforgiving but the residents, the wizards, didn't even notice the inhospitable conditions anymore. Instead, they wore heavier cloaks, warmer undergarments, hats that kept their heads warm, and gloves with the fingers cut out.

A young and inexperienced mage had stumbled upon the fortress during a blinding snowstorm that day. Disoriented, hungry, and fearful, the mage came in and took food and drink, then endured a bit of questioning. He called himself Pappy Oh, and they assisted him to find a suitable sleeping place in the fortress keep, which consisted of little more than a few robes on the ground. He accepted this gratefully and once his snores rose and fell, they left him there.

The wizards joined together to discuss what to do with Pappy Oh.

"He's a rube," Crunas the Blue announced, brushing dust from his long robe. Crunas was an important figure at the keep for his knowledge about star formations and how to follow them. "Completely untried."

"Cru, don't be unkind," Pridalf begged. Pridalf, an elixir sorceress and potions master, tried to keep the peace. "It isn't his fault he's untried. He's just young."

Crunas drew his cloak tighter about himself and fell silent.

Trudor stood away from the rest, hands behind his back, pacing, listening. Finally, he paused and said, "There will be many we must trust and not on their merit or skills. And we must decide tonight." Trudor, the eldest of those gathered, had mastered all subjects in which the others were still specializing.

"You're our leader and the wisest among us. I will do whatever you believe to be best," Pridalf replied. Her answer met with much nodding of heads among the other seven wizards gathered there.

"What say you?" Trudor asked, turning to the rough-hewn table where everyone sat on cut logs. "This mage, Mr. Oh–he is untried as Crunas has said, but he is also cunning and smart for one so young. I say we send the Book with him south. The Malevolent One will never suspect we would do such a thing."

"And what man of us is going to be the one delegated to travel south to keep up with Oh and our precious Book?" an older wizard named Sinster asked. He wore a shimmering golden cloak such as had never been seen away from the Desert Lands. He oftentimes refused to tell anyone of his magik. He could create many things from thin air.

"Excellent question," Trudor replied. "Would you do it? I am needed here. Consider it an adventure before age and time prevent you from ever enjoying such again."

Sinster peered down at his blue-veined hands gripping a staff made from oak. He had been south a few times in his life. This wouldn't be a stretch for him. At least it wouldn't have been a few years ago. Now… uncertainty filled him.

"What's in this for me?" he asked, piercing blue eyes boring into Trudor. "I cannot go there and stay, as you know. This will require someone to follow behind me one day. Time and age have already taken their toll, I am afraid. It isn't like the Book is going on holiday and returning to us any time soon. Someone will be required to check on it at times."

"Why don't you train Mr. Oh? He's going to have possession. He should certainly learn how to use it," Crunas said. This sounded like good thinking to several who nodded at his words.

"Train him? To what end? For the Malevolent One to appear one day and torture him for his use of it?" the elder wizard asked. "Nay, brother Crunas. Nay."

"Sinster, it's not going to be a pleasant journey, we all know this. Likely fraught with danger and trouble. But with your devotion to the men of the south, which you have proven before now, you will be the absolute best person for this. If you do this, I will appoint you the keeper of the raven's loft on your return. You will never have to work another day."

"If I live through this *adventure* as you call it," Sinster the Gold replied dryly. He rose to his feet and went to the door, holding his bent back with one hand. "Fine. I'll go. But only to prove to you all that an old wizard is still a viable one." He paused and added with a nod to Trudor. "Nevertheless, best be electing my successor, Tru."

After he left, conversations went late into the night about the Book and how to prepare Mr. Oh for his impending part in a game that would prove dangerous to every man in the entire world of Daegries. And later, once alone to pace his own solar, the place where he slept, Trudor the White thought about a successor for Sinster the Gold.

In fact, he thought of a young man about the same age as Mr. Oh. Someone who was heir to the silver scepter of the wise. His own son.

Chapter One

The Spell

Losing a loved one to death is terrible. Bringing them back has other assorted issues. And when it's your own flesh and blood... well, necromancy has limits.

Alyssa Chance Oh tensed against the problems before her. She stood in her family's log house in her bedroom, turning about once or twice, trying to assess things.

The house stood like a pinprick on the river's edge. A mere smudge in the grand scheme of the whole of Daegries. But it was her entire world, the only home that ever mattered. And her family, grown even smaller recently, needed her to take charge.

Alyssa sighed, staring at items strewn on her bedroom floor. She'd been up early, studying spells, trying to figure out what wasn't working. "Why do I have to jump up and down on the bed? This incantation sounds like something a fool would say."

Alyssa had tried the spell twice, spouting different words and performing various actions as she saw fit, but nothing had happened. No flash of light, no smell of sulfur... no risen grandfather. Nothing. And she desperately wanted her grandfather back on this side of the dirt.

She sat absently flicking at the petals of a sundew plant sitting on the scuffed wooden desk. Magik usually kicked in at sixteen, and her birthday had been a few months ago. But apparently, that wasn't a sure-fire win at spell casting.

Bitterly eyeing the thick book she'd been using for the spell, Alyssa grabbed it, and her deep blue eyes darted back and forth over the text written in tiny script. "I have to get this done."

The book had been filched from the personal library of her late grandfather, Pappy Oh, a mage of considerable renown in their region of the Lesser Daegries, a small rural town called Mudden. Unwanted fame clouded his name because of journeys he'd made outside of the Lesser Daegries. Journeys that always made townspeople whisper behind their hands. They said normal folk didn't take off from their family and stay gone for long periods. It just wasn't done. But in Alyssa's family it *was* done and done often.

And being witnessed in the company of mysterious strangers didn't help matters, either. True enough, mages often kept strange company. But Pappy Oh entertained folks that caused women to yank their children inside their homes and lock the door. Strange folks dressed in cloaks and hoods that came in the dark of night and left the same way. These happenings brought a lot of fear to townsfolk, and they talked about it endlessly.

Probably why Alyssa's family had moved closer to the river and farther from town.

Maybe now that Pappy lay on the other side, they would hush their gossiping. She'd find a way to keep him hidden. *If I could only get this spell to work…*

With a heavy sigh, Alyssa ran her fingers down the illuminated text on the tattered spine of the book.

The Grimoire of Necromancy, or simply *The Grim*, contained reference material for conjurers to raise the dead in times of need and for more assorted reasons including discussion of magik and spells. Alyssa hoped to bring her grandfather back to the side of the living for reasons of her own, including the ones listed. *The Grim* also spoke of necessary items required to keep the risen going once they arrived, and she made a mental note about those.

There were many other spells and items of interest in the great tome, but Alyssa focused on reanimating and had never examined anything else. She promised herself, "When I have time, I'm going to try some of this."

Her lips moved silently, forming unfamiliar words as she read each line of the spell. "I still don't understand a lot of these supernatural references," she muttered.

Frustrated, she rose from her chair, eyes still riveted on the feathery script. Her left hand tapped the worn pages of another book lying open on her other side, titled *Huckleberries, Follygrass, and other Healing Plants*. That book gave information about poultices for rotting flesh. That didn't bother her. She'd helped Granny Gert wrap hot rags around old Mrs. Slumtuggle's boil. No decomposition would ever be as bad as that oozing sore.

"How can you raise the dead and bring them back to life without something alive being in the mix?" she asked, her gaze landing on the sundew plant nearby. Impulsively, the girl grabbed the plant in its clay pot for use in the spell. As she lifted it, a jagged piece of pottery cut the side of her hand. She winced as she placed the pot into the assortment of items gathered there. The nick on her hand bled a little more than expected, and blood spattered one petal on the plant at her feet.

Alyssa lifted her hand to her mouth and wished the bleeding to stop. While she stood there trying to decide what to do next, the candle's flame on the desk danced like a shadow puppet against the wall of the small room. It closed in on her and she took a deep breath.

With a sigh, she let her hand fall by her side. She must get busy!

Her injury sufficiently soothed, Alyssa began again. *Why can't I do it my way and see what happens?* So, instead of jumping on and off the bed, she spun five times counterclockwise, arms outstretched, reciting the words from the spell. Dizzy, she fell against her bed in a puddle of giggles.

"Pappy Oh?... A little help here?" she asked as she slid to her backside on the floor.

No answer.

She giggled again. "Okay, time to get serious. Follow the rules, finish the spell."

This time she carried the plant back to the desk, careful to avoid the gouged-out part of the pot, and she gave the old book's pages another perusal. "Stay *inside* the circle, huh? I didn't do that..." It also didn't call for her to spin around. Alyssa huffed softly and was stricken with a sneeze. The spell was pretty simple. All she had to do was follow directions!

Through watering eyes, she read the incantation's requirements again and turned around to glare at her window.

It should be much darker.

She hastily crossed the room, stood on a three-legged stool, and pressed hard against the makeshift curtain where it met with the window frame. Unable to stop the sun's bright rays from peeking around the edges of the covering, she grabbed two heavy amethysts from her stone collection and used them to secure the fabric to the windowsill.

The curtain, an abandoned horse's blanket she found in her grandparents' barn, draped across the wooden rod which was crudely fastened to the wall with nails. Alyssa gazed at it.

If only it was a little wider...

She preferred one of Granny Gert's handmade quilts, but its disappearance would rouse too many questions. And questions now would spoil her surprise later, when she presented the risen Pappy Oh to his wife.

No, Alyssa would rather not answer questions yet. She would make do with the scratchy horse blanket with its faint smell of horse manure and stale hay.

She tugged at the blanket, stepped down, and studied the effect. "That'll have to do."

Once back at the desk, Alyssa scooted the candle closer to the back edge, to illuminate the area marked for Pappy Oh's re-entry into her world. "I sure hope he recognizes me," she said, running a hand through her long hair. She pulled it together and tucked the thick rope of hair into the back of her tunic to keep it out of her way.

Pappy had always been fond of her hair, commenting on how the color changed depending on what light hit it. Moonlight turned it more silver. Sunlight turned it more gold. Either way he had told her she looked like her mother, and that thrilled her. Her memories of her mother were tender kisses and gentle laughter and a profound love. She couldn't remember incidents, being too young when her parents left the farm and never returned.

Alyssa sighed at these thoughts, missing Pappy even more. He and Granny Gert had been her parents and grandparents. They had made mistakes, but they always showed love. She gave her hair one last swipe out of her eyes and focused again. Her appearance hadn't changed since they had buried the old man. Surely, he would know her.

She surveyed the crude circle drawn on the wooden boards of her floor with a chip of chalk she'd stolen from Granny Gert's kitchen slate. She'd opened and closed the circle a couple of times and needed to redraw it. *First, it needs to be bigger.*

It had to include her bed if that was a part of the spell. No wonder it hadn't worked! She grabbed a container of salt from the desk and poured it out to extend the chalk circle under her bed, a small wooden-framed sleeping box with a featherbed tucked inside.

Magik, once released, had a mind of its own, *The Grimoire* had said. Magik cared not about circles fashioned from chalk or the finest of paints, so long as it contained within it the conjuring elements required. Salt would be fine.

"Pappy Oh's staff, pipe, cloak, and notebook," Alyssa muttered aloud, mentally ticking off everything gathered inside the circle. "I sure hope this is enough. Granny'll get suspicious if I go around pulling out all of his things."

The Grim said the spell required darkness and focus above all. She would concentrate on that rather than her lack of skill. *This has to work. My intent is solid. It is sound.* She took a few deep breaths and focused but kept an ear out for Granny. If the old woman came in at the wrong time, it would be a spell disaster and end up a failed attempt.

Granny Gert had been gardening since sunrise. Alyssa hoped she would be away long enough for the spell to take effect. Pappy Oh's untimely demise had left the old woman with a vast hole in her life she kept trying to fill with chores. She toiled tirelessly, from sunup to sundown. Alyssa believed bringing Pappy back would be a great surprise, and it might even heal her Granny's broken heart.

Time to go to work.

With the heavy book open on the desk, she went to the circle situated close beside her bed and decided to follow the spell to the letter. After smudging a small space for an entrance, she stepped inside and sprinkled a line of salt to close the circle. No fudging this time. No more fooling around.

She closed her eyes and recited from memory.

"Sprinkle bits of bread." Alyssa took from her pocket another piece of dried bread she had filched from dinner a few nights ago and crumbled it on top of the dark cloak. Thankfully Granny didn't care that she took food to her room. This trial spell had used most of the bread in her possession, so it had to work this time.

"Jump upon the bedstead." She climbed onto her feather mattress and jumped up and down. The bed had no headboard or footboard, so Alyssa took care not to send the mattress flying off onto the floor.

"Tell the time of days, from death 'til raised," she recited. She slowed here. Pappy Oh had died a month ago. They had buried him up on Kudzu Hill right after that. It had been hot work clearing vines and making a resting place. The memory of clods hitting his wooden box sent a shiver through her.

"One month. Thirty days, from death until raised," she chanted, jumping higher and faster.

"From bread comes life, from life comes death, from death comes—"

"—Alyssa!" Granny Gert called from the kitchen.

Oh no. Not now!

"From bread comes life, from life comes death, from death comes Pappy Oh!" she cried out, breathless from her exertions. "Come on, Pappy!"

She soared from the bed into the circle as the spell required. But her aim was distorted after so much jumping up and down, and her feet landed on the curved end of the old man's staff. The other end flew up and thwacked her right on the nose.

"Alyssa!" Granny Gert hollered, her voice closer.

"Ow," she moaned, as blood trickled down through her fingers. The droplets fell into the circle, and she sank to her knees in pain. Unbidden tears streamed down her cheeks.

Alyssa tried to keep focus like the book required, but her thoughts only flew back to her throbbing nose. Tilting her head back to stop the blood flow, she wiped one palm on her britches.

Her room remained quiet; nothing moved. She glanced around. Pappy Oh had not materialized.

Nothing. At all.

Drops of blood ran down her wrist, and she tipped her head back again. This wasn't what she had wanted. No sir, not at all. She had hoped for something, anything, even a rattling of her desk drawers. But not this… silence.

Granny Gert tapped on the bedroom door, opened it a tiny slit, and let sunlight from the sitting room edge in. She had always been the type to give Alyssa privacy, so she wouldn't come right in.

"Alyssa," she said around the doorframe. "Why didn't you come when I called you?"

The girl moaned again, partially from her throbbing nose, and partly from her disastrous attempt to raise a dead person.

"I hit myself in the nose, and it hurt so badly I couldn't answer you right away," she tried to say, although it came out more like, "I hit myself in the naws and it hurt so baddy I couldn't ahnser you wight away."

"You're a calamity fixing to happen. Come on out here and let me see you."

Alyssa assessed her condition. The blood flow had stopped. She stood and then hesitated. Her hands and face must be a mess. She stared at the cloth hanging from her porcelain washstand. No way to get it from here.

She slowly lowered her head and peered around at the circle and its contents. Everything remained. Alyssa had used the right words, straight from the book, but nothing, not a single thing, had happened.

She had failed.

She wanted to cry for real but figured that would be as useless as the spell had been. What had she been thinking? It took years of practicing magik and heavy research for things like this to work. Alyssa couldn't even be called a magik-user yet.

The magik work she had done in her life included handing Pappy Oh items for spells and helping Granny with her healing art. Maybe the spell didn't perform for beginners like her. This sort of magik meddling would be exactly what Granny had warned her about.

"Don't go messing in magik and think you can whip up a spell on a whim, gal," Granny Gert had said. "That's why the townsfolk hate us so much. They see us as a passel of trouble. Our ways have sure enough brought us trouble, no doubt."

Alyssa had lowered her eyes and said, "Yes, ma'am."

She certainly didn't tell Granny that she snuck into town on a regular basis. Properly hidden under her cloak, or behind a fan in the summer heat, of course. But no one seemed to pay her any attention. No one cared about a lonely girl living at the edge of the land.

She stared hard at the room's corners, trying to see something, anything. A wisp of fog… a shiny spot… a dull flash… a sign that would blossom into her grandfather.

The book talked little about what reanimated people looked like, other than you might face smelly, gross flesh on them. So far, this attempt had failed.

Granny Gert called to her again, impatiently. The old woman permitted privacy, but at some point, she'd be too aggravated to care.

Better get a move on, else she'll be in the middle of this silly experiment asking questions.

Alyssa wiped her eyes with the back of her hands. When she glanced at her tunic, it was smeared with blood, too. She cringed at what her grandmother would say about that.

She moved gingerly inside the circle, hesitant to leave if it could still be used. Did it have a second chance? Alyssa sighed. She would have to go back to the book again and find what she'd missed, left out, or didn't do.

Maybe find a chapter on what to do with a failed reanimating or a way to reuse the spell. The girl wanted to stamp her foot, but she cast a glance at the staff and thought better of it.

Granny tapped again, this time forcefully enough to show she meant business. "Quit dawdling, now. Get out here where I can see you. Are you bleeding? What are you doing in there, anyway?"

"Nothing, Granny. I'm coming."

Jumpy from the intrusion into her thoughts, Alyssa scuffed out part of the circle to permit her exit. She would leave it open in case Pappy Oh materialized by some twist of magik and needed to get around.

She had learned about the magik circle from Pappy Oh after interrupting one of his "experiments." You had to open the circle before leaving it, like a door to a room. And of course, if you wanted to contain the contents, you had to redraw the circle before leaving it alone. "Wouldn't want the wrong thing to enter your world," he'd said. But Alyssa didn't have time to redraw.

To her knowledge, Pappy Oh had been the singular presence called for, and he possibly had been delayed in making his way back from the other side. What possibly delayed a person from coming back? She shrugged. Only a wizard knew the answers to such a question, and she didn't have access to one of those.

As for other things—unplanned-for spirits—if they used her botched spell to appear, well, they would have to sit down and wait. Her Granny remained a force to be dealt with on a good day.

Better not keep her waiting.

Chapter Two

Pappy Oh

Alyssa strolled into the sitting room and blinked at the bright afternoon sunlight pouring in through the window. Pappy Oh had been lucky enough to get panes of glass in a frame to use for the sitting room. Windows were important and showed a person's status. The Ohs were not rich folk, but they had style.

Granny Gert examined Alyssa's injured nose. She braced herself for a thorough fussing over.

"Not broken," her grandmother declared, finally handing her a dampened dish towel. "Take this wet towel and clean yourself."

The girl complied, wordlessly. The white flour sack towel turned pink from her blood. She also wiped at her tunic and britches and determined they needed to be scrubbed.

"Don't fret over that," Granny said, taking the bloodied rag. "I'll give it a good beating with well water."

Alyssa didn't say anything. If she intended to be good and behave like Pappy had asked, she'd be the one beating the cloth with lye soap, relieving Granny from the task.

"Listen, we have a real situation out in the garden," Granny Gert said. The old woman grabbed her hand and led her past the sitting room fireplace, still warm from when Alyssa built the blaze to heat some stew for breakfast.

Her stomach rumbled again, and she thought she might eat more stew before dinner.

Her grandmother pulled on the wooden handle of the door, letting Alyssa go before her. They entered the yard, Granny in front and Alyssa following behind.

She kept waiting for Granny to give her a speech about playing with magik, but it never came. Perhaps her grandmother hadn't seen much from her vantage point outside the bedroom. Or maybe the garden happenings took her full attention, because the old woman moved with quick steps for the first time in a while.

Granny took the middle of three dirt paths, which all led in different directions. Alyssa followed her bent back and caught a glimpse of her granny's blue-gray fly-away hair tied into a knot at the nape of her thin neck. The strands had accumulated sticky sap, leaves, and twigs. Granny wore a pair of Pappy's old pants, two sizes too long for her and rolled up to her knees.

"What is it, exactly?" Alyssa asked, struggling to breathe through her swollen, stuffy nose.

"It's something unexpected and brilliant, but well, you'll have to see for yourself."

"But what is it?"

Granny Gert waved off her questions and strode by sunflowers proudly showing off their colorful yellow faces under the broiling late summer sun. On either side, they passed rows of autumn root vegetables like beets and carrots and the thick leaves of hardy collards that had begun to grow, although the fall season was still on the horizon. Some of the plants looked starved for water due to a dry spell they'd been having, but the land oozed life beneath her feet, and Alyssa breathed in the scent of it.

The path ended at a pond where a bridge made from flat rocks arched over it. The bridge had no handrails or supporting timbers and did not appear exactly safe in its current state. Beyond the bridge, tall, lush plants waved majestically, blocking the view of a high hedge planted there. The sun stood in the sky over it all like a massive golden sentry burning down on them.

The hedge had blocked the way to the outside world ever since her childhood, with the exception of her finding places to slip through. It had never been blocked like this before.

"There." Granny Gert pointed to the bridge's other side. "Do you see those big green plants?"

"Yes," Alyssa answered, squinting in the sunlight, her nose throbbing again. "Where did they come from? They weren't there yesterday."

"My theory is, it's the garbage I hauled up here from the swamp."

Granny Gert had been carting refuse from the backwater of Old Stony, the river to the west of them. Alyssa's grandmother forbade her to go into the backwater or the swamp, as most Mudden folks called it. Strange tales came from there about will-o'-the-wisps and body snatching. Alyssa didn't know the truth about it and assumed it was a tale to keep children out of harm's way, but when her parents disappeared and never returned, she agreed that it would be better if she didn't try to find out.

But Granny went into the swamp often, and recently took scummy clumps of leaves and decomposed water plants back to their pond to use as filler to dam it up until she could finish the bridge and the path she intended to make. Alyssa still had no solid answer as to what this path would lead to or why Granny even believed it necessary.

"That composted stuff had massive properties in it, I'm thinking. I remember tossing some of it over that way thinking it might help me kill back the hedge a mite. The big old things popped up almost before my eyes. Least, I didn't see them at all, and then there they were, presto change-o! Well, maybe the swamp goop *and* the heat brought them on. Winter's nearly on us and this heat won't quit," she said, mopping at her brow. "Do you know what they are, girl?"

"No. Never seen them before. They're awful green though, Granny."

"Oh, that green is just their way of lookin', I'll warrant. Something that shows up perhaps since these are new, babies really. That might be it. They ain't had a chance to get sunburnt yet."

Alyssa thought about the herb and healing book she had been reading. "Swamp grass?" she asked, dredging up the first plant that came to mind.

"Uh-uh. They are *Putridaficationaconacus*. And a healthy lot of them, too."

Alyssa scratched her thinker, that name unrecognizable. "What's that again? Say it slower."

"Putrid-afication-acon-acus. Flesh-eating plants."

"Ugh. Good name for them," she said, observing their barbed mouths opening to catch insects nearby. They eerily resembled the sundew plant sitting on her desk.

"Don't be so quick to judge, now. They serve a purpose."

"What? Eating creatures for their flesh? That would be okay if they only ate snakes," Alyssa said with a shudder.

"Not exactly, except that might be true, right enough. They do eat reptiles and insects and anything else that happens along their way. The old books say that *Putridificationaconacus* plants are the protectors of portals."

"Portals? What kind of portals?"

"The kind that open up a sort of rift when the right magik is used. Your Pappy used to strive to create them. He never got one to open and go anywhere though. I always said he lacked a certain ingredient needed to get the magik to... you know, go." She waved her hand outward. "Out there. Off into the Great Beyonder."

"Magik you say?" Alyssa stood straighter. "What sort of magik?"

"Some dark art or other. Your Pappy dabbled a little in it there at the end. Might have been what ended him."

Alyssa winced. Had she created a rift back there in the circle? Opened a portal leading into the faraway plane of everlastingness? Brought about these hungry snapping plants before her?

"And these plants popped up out of nowhere, just now?" she asked.

"Like that," her grandmother said with a snap of her fingers. "Seems like they grew a mite while I idled inside collecting you to come to see them."

"Well, how do you know that Pappy Oh's rifts, or whatever you call them, didn't go anywhere? Did you try them out? What if something rattled one of them and made the plants grow?"

"Of course, I tried them out, girl. Certainly. They went nowhere, and they never developed into anything. They never had one of those gargantuan beasties dangling out at their doorway either, I might add." She pointed at the massive stalks again. "The things are man-eaters, is what they are. Big, green, gloppy man-eaters."

This was news!

"Granny, I've got to get back. I left something burning in my room," Alyssa said in a rush, as she turned and jogged back the way they'd come.

"Hey, wait a minute! We have to figure out how to keep these things over there and not over here where we are," her grandmother yelled at her.

Alyssa did not slow at her words, her mind consumed with wonder. What if she had opened the portal? What if her spell had brought the plants? Which spell variety had done this thing? She'd switched it up so many times!

But if true, didn't that mean her spell, at least one version of it, had been successful? Had she been too injured to notice the raised Pappy Oh? Maybe he showed as a shade of himself, or maybe she needed more than simple candlelight to illuminate him. Maybe it took a bit of time to get from there to here. The idea made her short legs pump harder. Her mind careened forward in time. What if…

She flew into the house and skidded to a halt at her bedroom doorway. The circle remained as she had left it. Nothing had moved, nor roamed about.

Alyssa edged around the circle and made for the window. With a few hard tugs, she yanked down the blanket. Sunlight poured into the small room, sending dust motes dancing.

The candle burned happily as if nothing had happened. Well, at least she had not lied. She had left something burning. The scent of melted wax rose to greet her nose as she turned and stared at the area where she'd attempted the spell.

The circle's contents had not moved, except for the staff, which now lay pointing in a completely different direction after she had been so dumb as to land on it. She perused the crimson drops gelling on her wooden floor where she had given her blood for the whole debacle.

She cleared her throat.

"P-Pappy Oh? Are you here? I sure tried to bring you back to be with us again. I'm tired of learning this magik stuff on my own. I need your skill."

Silence returned.

"Ah, rats," she said in disgust. Maybe the swamp garbage had bred the monster plants. Maybe her spell had nothing to do with it at all. Whatever made her think she could pull off such a thing? Who did she think she was?

She leaned against the old desk, crossing her arms in dejection, and said, "You're a big, fat loser with a capital L; that's what you are, Alyssa Chance Oh."

The thought of failure made her want to cry, but when she squeezed her eyes shut, it made her nose wrinkle, and the pain sent all other thoughts catapulting away. She opened her eyes.

Crying is not an option today. Failure is not an option either, any day. But still… I've failed to bring Pappy Oh back. I didn't create a rift or open a portal any more than he did. Maybe Granny Gert's interruption stopped things at a critical point… Maybe I should try again?

Thinking aloud, she said, "No wonder it's so hard to become a wizard. You've got to know what you're doing and have a little bit of prior success to prove your skill. Not to mention own a magik item. I don't have even a hint of what I'm doing and never mind the rest. I failed the whole thing."

Alyssa shivered as cold, clammy air crept up her legs and blew straight into her face, sending her hair spraying backward and extinguishing the candle.

"Ah. This is much nicer," a gravelly voice said with a sigh.

"P-Pap…?"

"Over here, Lys."

She turned toward the bookcase along the wall. "Where?" she asked.

"Here," the voice said. It sure sounded like Pappy.

"Here where?"

In a heart-stopping motion, the crank turned on her old jack-in-the-box sitting on a bookcase shelf and, when the music reached its crescendo, the clown's head snapped out and the voice shouted, "Surprise!"

"Pappy! You made it!" Her heart sang with joy. "I missed you, Pappy Oh!"

"You did? Well, it's nice to be missed."

Then her joy turned to despair. "Did it hurt you to come back through?" She moved to the toy box and touched it softly.

"Pappy Oh? You're a toy? Boy, could I mess this up any worse?"

Pappy Oh said, "Now Lys, don't you fret none."

As thought after thought tumbled through her mind, she asked, "Do I need to do anything for you? How will I feed you?"

"Nah, girl. Spirits don't eat."

"Do they sleep? And gosh, is there any chance the rest of you will appear?"

"Don't know about sleeping, but they do get quiet. Don't worry about getting the rest of me here. This is fine for now. Glad to have my voice. Oh, and my spirit too. Ha, otherwise, the voice would be a little useless. Who needs a body?"

"Me." Alyssa sank onto the rickety cane-bottomed chair at the desk, deflated. "I wanted you to come back intact. Granny Gert will be madder than a poked wasp's nest when she finds out what mischief I've been up to."

"You let me worry about Gert. She's my old lady, and she's used to strange happenings around here. So, what did I miss?"

Alyssa dropped her chin and stared at her crossed arms. A full-fledged pout neared explosion level. "Nothing. I worked the spell, Granny called for me, I smacked my nose on your staff, and she made me go out in her garden to see some new plants. You didn't miss a thing."

"If that were so, you wouldn't be sitting there with your face all a-droop. What's the matter? I'm not mad at you about the partial return. Heck, I'm proud of you for trying. I won't ask why. I'm sure you have your reasons. We'll get the rest of me here, eventually. Magik is not an exact art, much like medicine isn't. That's why doctors say they are practicing medicine, and why magik users are practitioners of the art. Takes a powerful lot of experience and the right… ah, cachet."

"I wanted you to be back," Alyssa said, her lip quivering. "We need you here. Granny Gert is working herself to death in the garden, and Pappy, it's like when Mommy and Poppy ran off. She won't stop and rest. And, well, I know it's selfish, but… I need you. I want to learn spells and things and…" She let her voice fade away. She pushed her hair back from her face and tried not to look sad.

He didn't reply, but the jack-in-the-box rattled a little, so she sighed and stood. "Granny Gert might need to know about your return or… w-whatever this is. I'll run and get her."

"Hey now. Take me with you. I'm as portable as a handful of peanuts."

She lifted the toy from the shelf and headed out of the bedroom.

"Point the face of this silly thing forward so as I can see where I'm going," Pappy Oh told her.

"You can see?" She silently rejoiced and did as he asked. Soon, they strolled along the garden path in search of Granny Gert.

"The sunflowers sure are pretty. Y'all ain't got much rain, huh?"

"Not much. Not since the night after you crossed over. What was that like for you?"

"Dark as Moody's goose."

"Who's Moody?"

"It's a saying, child. Keep walking."

"Did it hurt?"

"What? Crossing over? Nah. Didn't feel like nothing, kind of calm and peaceful. Like sitting on the back porch with nothing but stars overhead. Coming back… hit me different. Kind of like being sound asleep and somebody yanking the covers off and turning the oil lamps up."

"I'm sorry, Pap. I didn't know. We missed you. Granny cried a lot."

Pappy Oh chuckled. "Oh my. Won't she be tickled about this?"

But Alyssa saw the ruckus up ahead, and she didn't think Granny would be too thrilled about anything for a while. One monster plant had wrapped around the old woman's legs and yanked her toward the side of the bridge.

Cavernous mouths opened and closed inside the plant like the maw of a gigantic spider.

"What in tarnation is *that*?" Pappy Oh asked, seeing the situation playing out before them.

"Oh, my Billy goat's beard! Those evil weeds have got Granny. I've got to go help her. Sit here!" She hastily settled the jack-in-a-box beside the path and ran for the bridge.

Granny Gert struggled with the beastly plant, pounding it with her fists. When she caught sight of Alyssa running toward her, she screamed, "Bring that scythe over there. Chop it off!"

Alyssa darted to the edge of the bridge where it met the path and scooped up the scythe. She ran forward, watching for an opportunity to slice into the long arms. They swung wildly back and forth. One nearly took her off her feet. She danced away barely in time.

"Get it off!" Granny Gert yelled, slapping against the creature's opening mouth.

Alyssa took a deep breath and darted dangerously close to the plant, lifted the scythe, and brought it down hard on the moving arms, lopping off three. This damage sent the entire plant springing back toward the hedge side, releasing Granny Gert.

Alyssa tossed the scythe to the ground, threw her arms around her grandmother, and rushed off the bridge, out of immediate danger.

When they drew close to the jack-in-the-box, Granny collapsed to the ground, breath heaving. "They got me good,

Lys. You're going to have to go to the barn and bring the wheelbarrow to get me back to the house. Holler for Tony; he's working out in the back pasture. Tell him we need his help. We got us a disaster."

"Yes, ma'am, but first, there's something I got to tell you," Alyssa said.

"This ain't no time for telling stories, now. This poison's done eat away all my pants, and the longer it sits on my skin the more like a sponge I'm getting. It won't be a pretty sight when it gets finished."

"But Granny—"

"Run on, Lys."

"But Granny—"

"Did you hear me, girl? I'm lying here dying and you're standing there mouthing at me!"

The jack-in-the-box bounced up and down, and Pappy Oh finally spoke.

"Gertrude, you always were hard on that child."

Granny Gert stared at the box, realized whose voice she had heard and fainted.

Like a fire whirl, Alyssa took off to find Tony. Behind her, she heard Pappy say, "Well, at least she won't feel any pain."

Chapter Three

Granny Gert

Later, Alyssa and Tony worked together to get Granny Gert into her bed. Tony carried the old woman up to the house; they didn't have time to go collect the wheelbarrow. Alyssa pulled the quilt, sheets, and pillows off the bed before Tony placed Granny atop it. Tony seemed to be embarrassed to be in the healer's bedroom and whispered to Alyssa that he needed to step outside. With a quick nod, Alyssa moved aside for him to go, and she replaced the bedcovers.

Granny could be a hard woman to contend with. In pain, she would not control her word-whipping ability. Tony knew better than to get in the old healer's way when her mood soured. He was safer outside than in.

Tony lived in Muddentown proper. The news about the plants, and especially their attack on Granny Gert, might make the *Mudden Herald* if he blabbed about it. That would not be good for Alyssa's family. They still grew herbs and raised their food, doctored themselves, and others who had the bravery to ask. They lived a rural farm life, without any of the perks of smithy-made tools like most of the Muddentown folks had. It made life harder for Alyssa's family, but they didn't mind. Even her education consisted of mostly healing and farming science, not reading, writing, and arithmetic, although she knew all that too.

When her parents went on an errand to the next region and never returned, the Mudden folks had gotten involved. They tried to force her family to change to a more up-to-date ideology, using modern ways, but it had failed as soon as they went back to minding their own business, as usually happens.

Except that Alyssa had learned about town life, and the desire to see more had begun to grow. She had never even tasted bakery-made goods until then. That was what sent her sneaking back into town more often.

These thoughts brought her back to the present.

Muddentown. If this news was told in the Mudden Herald, people would come around again. *Our lives will be affected by town folks even worse than before. Granny, without Pappy Oh, couldn't stand up against such a force.*

Alyssa didn't know whether to rejoice in the freedom to go into town, or to shrink away from the thought. It would not sit well with her grandparents either way. *Granny ain't fit to fight, and Pappy is in no shape to be among people yet.*

Tony had to keep their business to himself. *He had to.*

And they had to get Granny better fast.

While these thoughts flitted through Alyssa's mind, Granny's moans as she regained consciousness sounded like a disturbed bumblebee humming in distress.

Alyssa got the old woman undressed and into a soft, pale-yellow nightgown. Granny Gert winced in pain from being shifted around. Alyssa turned her attention to the wounds that draped across her grandmother's legs in hot red stripes.

Alyssa had carried Pappy Oh in his tin box back to the house ahead of Tony and Granny. Now he spoke up from his vantage point on the chair beside the bed. "Them welts... kinda like having candy cane legs."

"That's strong poison in those plants for sure," Alyssa agreed, assessing the damage.

Granny attempted to rise and fell back in pain. "What in thunder have you done bringing your Pappy Oh back like this? Don't you know that's a crime against nature?"

"Ain't a crime against nature if it's done properly. I thought I would surprise you by bringing him back. I thought you were lonely," Alyssa answered as she dabbed at the stripes with cool water. Fear of her grandmother dying made her hands shake. "What am I supposed to use to treat this? Will Mercurochrome hurt too much?"

"Now you're *trying* to make her look like a candy cane," Pappy Oh commented.

"Keep your tongue, old man," Granny said.

"Now, Pappy, try to be helpful. Put your thinking cap on because I ain't never seen these plants before. And I ain't never read about stopping poison from any such thing either," Alyssa said. "I've got to do something."

She stared into the pain-wracked eyes of Granny Gert. "You're the healer, Gran. What do you think? I recently read about poultices for rotting flesh, but that's for raising dead folk and giving them a normal appearance. Don't think they had this in mind in that book."

The old woman gazed around the room. "There ain't nothing here in this house that will fix this mess. I guess I'm going to die."

Alyssa set the bowl and rag on the floor and fought back tears. "No, you most certainly are not. And if you think I won't bring you right back, you have another think coming. I have Pappy Oh to help me with reanimating now, and you won't even be dead long enough to get stiff. So, you better plan on staying right here on this side of the dirt, if you know what's good for you."

Granny gazed at her for a moment. "Don't get all sassy on me, Lys. I'm only griping from the pain. If you want to help me, then you're going to have to do what I tell you. Let me warn you, it ain't going to be no fun at all. The best remedy is to get me some gryphon tears."

"Where do you keep those?" Alyssa took a step away from the bed. "In the kitchen?"

"No, now Lys, you ain't listening. Pay attention, girl. Gryphon tears. Do you even know what a gryphon is?"

"How could she know?" Pappy Oh asked. "You never let her go outside our little plot of land. How would she ever find out what's on the other side of that hedge?"

"Keep quiet, old man."

Alyssa lowered her gaze at this. She had most certainly been outside their land, all the way into Mudden. But she had never seen any gryphons. "No, ma'am. I don't know what a gryphon is."

"Then you ain't likely to know where to find it either." Granny Gert moaned as she tried to sit up. "Gryphons are near extinct, and even if you happen upon one, you'll never get it to give up a tear for an old grump like me."

"Extinct? Now I'm curious. So, what are they?" Alyssa put a pillow under her grandmother's shoulders to prop her up. Maybe if Granny kept talking about gryphons, she would stop talking about dying.

"There's a book called *Critters, Some to Cook and Some to Keep* over in my bookcase. Pull it down and bring it here. I'll need for you to read some things to me."

Alyssa padded barefoot out into the hallway and fumbled through the strange collection of books. She found the one she wanted, and another one called *Magikal and Mythical Creatures*, and carried them to Granny Gert, but the injured woman waved her away.

"Don't give me anything to focus on too hard; the pain's mighty awful," Granny Gert said. "Find a remedy in there for poison. And soon as you can, get me a cup of willow bark tea."

Alyssa set the books aside and hurried to the kitchen. She pulled a corked container marked "willow bark" from the old shelf over the stove. She threw a stick of wood on the fire to get it going again and poured water in a pot from a pitcher nearby. She hung the pan from the hook over the fire and waited for it to boil. It didn't take long. Then, once the water was hot, she took a pinch of the powder, dumped it into the pan, and stirred it around.

Finally, she poured a mug of the willow bark tea for her granny and took it back to the bedroom. Once her grandmother had taken a few sips of the tea, grimacing fiercely at the taste, Alyssa settled down beside the bed to read the books.

She opened the one that appeared to be a schoolbook. "Oh, okay. Let me read… table of contents…"

"Page 199," Pappy Oh told her. "Under Fevers, Poisons, and Remedies."

"Ah, so you can remember things?" Alyssa asked, flipping to page 199. "That's a comfort. Here it is."

Granny frowned at the clown's face. "I thought you never read books to help in your magik. Least, you acted like reading books was of no use when I sat down with one."

"I read when necessary. Getting a handle on fevers and such falls under that category," he replied dryly.

Alyssa stopped to glance at her grandmother. She hoped they would not break into one of their famous arguments. The last one, before Pappy Oh passed away, had been a doozy, whereby one of Granny Gert's best mortar and pestle sets got broken after being flung simultaneously, one piece in each hand, at Pappy Oh.

But trapped in his silly toy body, her grandfather did not take the bait and remained mute.

Alyssa read out loud. "Here it is. 'Gryphons. Gryphons are old-world creatures like winged horses with heads and chests like eagles and hind parts like goats or sometimes lions.' Wow. That's a strange creature."

"What else does it say?" Granny asked.

"Says… *'they have been known to give up their tears, which are reported to have healing properties in them, for medicinal purposes.'*" She skimmed down the page. "The catch is, they ain't easy to convince to let loose of those tears, it sounds like."

"Yep. Although I ain't never been privileged to see one," Pappy Oh said.

"Does it say where to find one?" Granny Gert asked.

Alyssa read the line. She blinked and read it again.

"Yes, ma'am. Says they live in the Meadowland." She paused and gazed at her grandmother. "Wild animals fill the Meadowland, you always said. Dangerous wild animals and… I shouldn't ever go hunting over there." She bit her lip. She had honored that request and never gone into the wilderness beyond their land.

"It is. Wild with gryphons and such. As I said, I guess I'm going to die."

"Granny don't give up yet," Alyssa told her. "I'm good with a bow and arrow, ain't I? Didn't I bring home that turkey for Samhain dinner? I can go get one of these gryphon things and bring it back here. We'll make him cry, won't we, Pappy Oh?"

"Indeed," he replied. "If you can convince one to squeeze itself into our house, my presence in this toy box will be enough to scare him into a crying fit."

"Well, then." Granny closed her eyes. "Here's the rub. When your mom and pop vanished into the wild out there, I raised us a great big old bunch of boxwoods. You know the hedge? That's a part of it. Then, I made them into a garden maze. I figured if my own kin didn't come back—as well trained as they had been in magik and other stuff, well, there weren't no hope. They probably got eat up. No sense in painting a rosy picture here, Lys. They didn't come back. You know that well as I do. I've done my best to keep you contained on the farm and out of harm's way. Now, it's going to be downright tricky to teach you the maze route to get out on the other side. I'm not sure I should even try." Granny Gert paused here and grimaced at the clown's face before moving her gaze to meet Alyssa's. "You're all I got left."

Pappy Oh made a sputtering noise. "What about me?"

"You're dead and buried, old man," she said. She took Alyssa's hand. "I'm leaving it up to you. Go if you want to. Stay if you don't. Just know, there's critters out there. There's so much bad out in the world of Daegries, that I can't bear to think of it all where you're concerned."

Alyssa thought a moment before replying. "I can get my bow and arrows and take along a drinking horn to catch those tears up in. I reckon I'm going, Granny. Tell me how to get there."

"That's my pupil," Pappy Oh said.

Alyssa thought she saw a glimmer in the eyes of the jack-in-the-box.

Granny squeezed Alyssa's hand and let it go to hiss at the pain throbbing in her legs. Finally, she said, "Go out the back door, and turn left, and start walking. You'll find the maze easy enough. But don't start walking down the row of hedges thinking you'll miss them mean old plants, 'cause you won't. I don't think there's many holes in my hedge, but there might be. You don't need to go getting yourself lost."

"Okay, so turn left, keep going straight." Alyssa recounted the instructions.

Granny fixed her gaze on her only grandchild. "Lys, you sure about this? What if something happens and you need me? I can't come. Not in this condition."

"I'll be fine, Granny. I can take care of myself."

"Yeah, Gert, she's old enough to go out into the world. Fight wild gryphons, best the elements, sleep under the stars." Pappy's voice sounded teasing like he aimed to get the old woman's fire to rage.

It worked.

"Pappadopolis Andromeda Oh," she grumbled. "Don't you tell me what my grandchild can do or can't do. I'll decide that for my own self."

"You ain't never decided without consulting me in your adult life," the mage replied from the tin box. "Why start now? I say let her go."

"I've got a good mind to *not* allow her to go because you said that."

Alyssa's shoulders drooped. "Y'all," she began, trying to get them to quit baiting each other. "While we sit here with you two deciding if I should or shouldn't go, that poison is getting more and more of a hold. Granny'll be unconscious before I can get back now."

Pappy Oh fell silent with a grunt.

Granny turned back to Alyssa and squeezed her hand. "The directions are in my recipe chest, child. I update them when I can. Need to go out there and check on my markings anyway, so you can do it for me now. Let me know if I need to fix anything when you get back. Follow them directions exactly. Once you get out of that maze, don't stop walking. You'll be in a big old meadow. There won't be nothing around for a long way but tall green grass. The gryphons eat grass all the livelong day. They're monstrous big, but they hunker down in that tall grass, so you'll have to keep walking until you come upon one. I ain't never had the pleasure, only read about them, so be careful."

Chapter Four

King Hubert the Gryphon

Alyssa slung the bow by its strap over her shoulder and adjusted the arrows in their quiver over her back. She double-checked the drinking horn's security on its cord tied to her belt.

Ready as I'll ever get, I guess.

Her grandmother had given her directions and warnings and a good dose of scare tactics before she'd left the bedroom where the old woman lay. Alyssa went to her room and gathered Pappy's old travelling pack, then filled it with items she might need. Once done, she trudged back for one last hug.

Pappy Oh promised her he'd manage if they needed help.

"Now, how are you going to do that, Pappy?"

"I'll yell and scream until I get Tony's attention."

"Pappy, you can't get anywhere in that tin can, and especially not close enough to a door or window to do any good."

"Don't you worry about me, gal. I'll make enough racket to bring back more dead folks. I've got this covered, tin box, and all."

Unconvinced, she stared at her Granny Gert.

"I'll be here when you get back," the old woman said. "Don't you stray off that path, though. You hear me? We'll be fine, Alyssa. I'm putting my trust in you."

Alyssa nodded and gazed at the toy jack-in-the-box.

"Are you sure, Pappy? I'm awful worried."

"Yes, child. Haven't I labored with you all these years? You can do this. Now get on over there and bring us them tears." He strained the clown's neck toward her and added in a whisper,

"Don't dawdle though, Lys. Her time is probably shorter than either of us wants to admit."

No pressure, Pappy.

She patted the clown's head, said goodbye to her grandparents, and trekked down the rock-strewn path that wound left from the back porch. The path went down a short hill and through Granny Gert's wisteria bower.

The bower, a wild place of gnarled vines and dried-up purple blossoms, leaned inward and seemed to want to totter over onto an unsuspecting visitor at any moment.

She loved the smell of the light purple blossoms and the wild honeysuckle that wove itself through the bower's vines in the spring. She sniffed the faded late summer fragrance recalling her childhood. The bower had been a perfect place for her imagination to flourish.

As a child, she had dodged through the spaces between the woody stalks, never even caring about the scratches she got. Her mother would douse her skinned arms and legs with poultices and wraps and laugh at her romping around.

But when her parents had disappeared, her Granny Gert had let the entire area fall into disarray. They didn't tend the flowers, or the roots, or the other invading plants, and Alyssa always supposed they had done it out of anger or spite. Nevertheless, the disarray of the bower and path had halted her childish attempts to find her parents.

It nearly halted her now. After much effort, she pushed through the foliage and plants. Hot and disheveled, she moaned at the sight on the other side.

The path ended at the side of the high hedge. The same hedge where the Putrid Plants had erupted farther down, over by the bridge.

A strong aversion to going forward struck her.

As a child, she had once seen a snake slithering into the hedge and had always feared to go that way. And to be honest, she didn't like poking around unknown places. Especially as a beggar hunting for gryphon tears, but she had no choice.

She stood there weighing her options: to go or not to go. She snapped off a few leaves from the nearest branch and debated this foolhardy trip.

At one time, a path or trail had led through the hedge to the Meadowlands, because her parents had traveled down it, never to return. The fear that a terrible fate awaited her also climbed up her chest and wrapped its gnarly fingers around her neck until she had trouble breathing.

"You best quit that right now, Alyssa Chance Oh. There ain't nothing for it this time. You've got to go," she said aloud, taking a deep breath to steady her nerves. If she happened upon a snake, she would scream. Not that anyone would come running to save her, but maybe it would scare the creature away. And if a terrible fate awaited her on the other side, well, she would've at least given it her total focus and tried.

She consulted Granny's directions written on a small piece of parchment and squeezed through the hedge. The branches clung to her. She twisted around sideways to disengage them.

Her determination tested, she said to the wicked limbs. "Y'all ain't going to trifle with me now."

After a few more moments of struggle with the offensive greenery, she shoved forward, using her bow as a tool to spread thick branches apart. Soon, the fight with the foliage faded, and she moved ahead easier.

The hedge grew thinner now, and she saw where weeds had grown up beneath them. She heard rustling nearby and held her breath until a crow flew out and overhead, cawing madly. *No snakes. No snakes*, Alyssa thought.

She pushed outward with all her might on the hedge branches into space beyond. This sent her tumbling onto a dusty path with even higher hedges all around. This had to be the garden maze! She gazed at Granny's spidery handwriting on the card she carried. The way through the maze looked like a combination of turns. You had to go left and right and left again in particular sets of numbers, with certain things as landmarks.

"When you first get into the maze, you'll be in hedges thick and high," Granny's note read. "Turn left at the end of the first row. Go straight sixteen paces. Watch for the cut-out."

Well, maybe for me it will be twenty. I have short legs.

She strolled and counted but came up short. No sort of cut-out emerged.

"What kind of cut-out does she even mean?" Alyssa asked aloud. Assessing herself to be in the right area, she pushed her hands through the brush to see what appeared. Nothing did. Had time caused the cut-out to grow back together?

She wandered around. It had to be there, not on the other side. It had to be there… *there*.

And then, feeling slightly silly, she realized that her Granny's idea of a cut-out had not been a cut-out place in the hedge, but a cut-out scarecrow made from old bed linens. It had seen better days. The ragged creation leaned crazily backward.

"Guess I better let Granny know this old thing needs fixing," she said as she patted the stick figure on its arm on her way past. "Thanks, Charlie, or whatever she named you."

On and on she went until Alyssa had a good idea of what the maze's end would be like. She followed a row of yellow daisies, faded and dying. Then she turned right at the end of the row and searched for jays and their nests. She almost missed those, as wild plum and sumac had taken over.

Eventually, she found the last landmark—a stack of flat rocks like what the bridge had been built of—and turned left following the hedges until they thinned out and vanished entirely.

When she stepped out from the labyrinth, she found herself in the Meadowland. But instead of tall green grass greeting her, it was dry and wispy like wheat stalks. The grass stood taller than Alyssa.

The sky whirled, overcast and gloomy, and she wrinkled her nose at the smell of rain. It did not smell fresh or pleasant like in her favored farmland. But maybe the Meadowlands were different.

She bit her lip as worry crept up. This trip might be pointless if she didn't find the gryphon. And what would she do if she didn't find it? She refused to go back to the farm to her grandmother and watch her die. She would certainly bring her back, even half-way, as she had done with Pappy Oh. She would work her heart out to save her Granny Gert.

She ventured forward, tugging her bow from her shoulder, and nocking an arrow. The grass met the sky on the horizon, and it blew back and forth as gusts of wind howled down ahead of a massive storm.

Alyssa glanced up at the gray clouds swirling overhead. If the weather held, then she might find this creature and get her job finished. If the storm broke, flattening herself in the grass with her head covered would be her only option.

A rust-colored flash in the field ahead stopped her cold. It leaped into the air a short way and then down again, over, and over.

She eased forward, never letting her eyes move from her target. When the creature flapped giant wings and squawked, it became apparent that she'd never encountered such as this before. The sound it made hurt her ears.

When it leaped again, she saw the beak. Long and wicked sharp, it could tear prey to pieces. No common bird jumped or squawked like that.

Then she remembered what *Magikal and Mythical Creatures* had said about the gryphon. Part bird, part lion, all dangerous.

Fear-fueled thinking made her cower a little. *It's not too late. I can still run home. That maze didn't kill me coming into the Meadowlands; it won't kill me going back.*

Remembering her reasons for being there, she stood straighter and shouldered her responsibility. "I ain't no coward, and Granny Gert is counting on me."

She had no time for being a scaredy cat. She crept forward. Closer, closer until she stood a few paces away, separated by the few blades of grass, wilted, and withered after the pounding the gryphon had given it.

"Hey! Hey, you!" she shouted at the creature. "I need to talk to you."

Angry, black eyes flashed at her. Another half-squawk. The creature rose to its full height, only to be overcome with curiosity and lower its head to peer at her.

"Yes, you," she told it, hoping the sounds it made equaled communication of some sort. She inched forward. The creature didn't move, only continued to watch her approach.

Alyssa assessed the creature. Head of an eagle, pointy beak, big flappy wings covered by hideously long rusty-red feathers, an entire body of a lion, complete with a lion's tail. Likely speedy as the book's description said it would be, if you believed such a manual when faced with one in real life.

I ain't in the Farmlands anymore.

She stood before a mythical creature in a place she'd never been before. Could this all be make-believe?

She pulled herself together and gave herself a good shake.

You ain't dreaming. You're truly here, and you're truly seeing this.

Her bravery deflated a little when she saw what the creature resisted under its paw. A squirming rabbit wriggled to get free. When the gryphon saw her staring at his prize, he shifted his gaze also, an amused glint in his eyes. A heavy golden medallion hung around the bird-like neck, and it moved against his powerful muscles as he toyed with the animal.

Incensed, Alyssa's temper erased all her fears. "Now you let that go! Ain't no reason for anyone to be done like that, least of all an innocent bunny."

The paw lifted slightly.

"I need a moment of your time, Mr. Gryphon. I have a matter of importance, and I'm in a powerful hurry," she said, motioning for the rabbit to be freed.

"You address me without kneeling? How impudent!" He patted the rabbit a little to make it squeak. "Would you rather I held you captive instead of this wild hare?"

Alyssa's mouth gaped open, and the bow lowered. "You can speak?"

"Yes, is that so surprising? Far more unnatural for a girl human to be in the Meadowlands."

"Is this your meadow, sir?" Alyssa took a more pronounced approach via politeness and manners. "I'm sorry to bust in."

"Kneel, Human! You are in the presence of His Royal Highness, King Hubert the Gryph, Seventh of His Lineage, First Son of Gregory," he told her, releasing the rabbit.

The terrified bunny scampered away while Alyssa knelt on one knee, placing her bow and arrow before her.

"Alyssa Chance Oh, apprentice to—"

"Withdraw your weapon, Subject. This is my kingdom, but we have no war here." He flicked the medallion around his neck with a claw.

Squinting, Alyssa made out words about nonviolence and kingdom on the medallion.

"While you are in my territory, you will abstain from such evilment."

She nodded and put the arrow away and slung the bow over her shoulder again. "I don't want to do battle, King Hubert. I'm in dire straits. I need your tears to heal my grandmother."

He waved for her to rise. She complied.

"Impertinence!" He flapped his wings, creating an even greater wind than had been blowing from the approaching storm. "Punishment is nigh! Make yourself presentable, Subject! I am a king, not a field mouse! Brush your knees off. Has no one taught you how to address a royal?"

She peered at her knees and did as he asked. "No, sir, Your Royal-ness. But please, sir. I need to get those tears and get back home before this storm breaks. Can you put them in here?" She pulled at the drinking horn she had brought along for the purpose.

"Do you take me for some simpleton?" the gryphon roared. "My tears are the most valuable substance in the Grasslands. I do not eke them out for little snips like you."

Thunder rumbled across the far side of the meadow and an even larger black cloud moved toward them.

Alyssa doubted his tears were as valuable as he stated, as he seemed like a sort who embellished a little. But since she came seeking his tears, she thought it best not to mention it. "I appreciate that, I really do. And I promise to treat them as precious, but this storm is about to fall from the sky, and it might slow down my return even more. Can you please tell me what I need to do to get your tears for my grandmother?"

The gryphon drew itself up and faced her.

"Well, now that you've asked," he stated. "I believe I have something in mind. There's a certain scarf that I've had my eye on. If you will retrieve it for me, then perhaps giving you my tears would be worthwhile."

"Oh, yes sir, Your Majesty." Alyssa curtsied slightly. "And where would I find this scarf?"

"Ah, that is the question."

She lifted her head and eyed him squarely. "You mean you don't know where it is?"

He shook his head and flapped his wings. "Of course not, silly girl. If I could find out its location, I wouldn't need *you.*" He emphasized by pointing at her with one of his talons.

"How can you have your eye on something that isn't even around?" Alyssa asked.

"Kings can do many things."

"Something tells me that this is going to be harder than it sounds," she said with a sigh.

Chapter Five

A Gryphon's Tears

While they stood there, the storm raged overhead with lightning and thunder.

When a few raindrops fell, Alyssa said, "It ain't real smart to stand around in an open meadow in poor weather. Is there somewhere we can get out of the rain and talk?"

Hubert nodded. "Follow me." He flapped his wings until he lifted from the ground.

She ran along beside him as he half-flew, half-galloped through the tall grass. Too short to see where they were headed, Alyssa stumbled to a sudden stop at the steps of a stone pavilion which showed up unexpectedly in front of them.

Hubert squawked, scaring off three massive crows with bright yellow beaks. "Begone, you slowcoaches!"

Alyssa sat on a log under the pavilion's eave and listened for a time to the miniscule raindrops dripping down. Too few to make a dent in the dry spell. She pulled the bow from her shoulder and set it beside her.

The gryphon strutted back and forth in front of her, flapping his wings and making a lot of noise like a bird enjoying its birdbath. Finally, he said, "You are a brave girl to come here armed with a bow and arrows. What do you intend to do with those? Shoot me? King of the Grassland? Why, I would have flown away before you even pulled the string back."

"I didn't mean to be impertinent, Sire. I had to prepare for whatever might come at me. I've put them aside, see?"

She motioned to the quiver and bow sitting by her feet, hoping they seemed innocent and nonviolent. Not knowing what else to say, she fell silent. Her nerves pinged around the massive animal for fear he would pounce on her like he had done the rabbit. She listened to his pompous outbursts about her kind's rude behavior until the rain tapered off.

The rain stopped, and she said, "Your Highness, I'm sorry for coming here armed and all. I meant no disrespect. Can you please tell me where to find this scarf? I'll do whatever's necessary to help my Granny. I've failed on a few things today already, and I ain't feeling special about my chances at getting that scarf for you. But I guess I've got to try. Anything to save Granny Gert. My Pappy told me to hurry and get back. She might not be with us for long. I'm afraid for her life." Her voice lowered as she realized how true those words were. "I'm afraid of almost everything right now."

He stopped fluttering about and stared at her with his beady eyes. "Being afraid is a good thing. It builds fierceness. You can easily see that I am fierce. And that is because fear has given me wisdom."

He preened, too long in her opinion, and she assessed him to be a braggart. But then he took a different turn, and her attention focused on what he said.

"But ahem, yes, about the scarf… it's made from follygrass, you know."

"No, I didn't know."

He bent a little to peer into her face. "Follygrass doesn't grow in the Grassland."

"You mean the Meadowlands."

"I mean what I mean. We call it what we call it, and you can call it what you will." This brought a new squawk from him.

"How odd."

"Rude!"

"I'm not saying *you're* odd, King Hubert. I'm saying it's odd that the scarf is made from follygrass. It doesn't grow here from what I've heard."

Her limited knowledge about follygrass consisted of how tall it grew, how thick its leaves blossomed, and how one could weave it into many things. But the most interesting part of its lore stated it had magikal properties. Follygrass could be used for spells, and like a bit of clear quartz, would work with any other material to bring the desired result.

Wonder where it does grow? Guess I skipped that part.

"Follygrass is only found in the Greater Daegries," he told her, as if reading her mind. "And of course, that scarf could be anywhere now, even back where it came from. It has been missing for quite some time."

"The Greater Daegries? How in the name of bears do you expect me to get the scarf if it's in a place as big as that? And even if I could get there, which I can't without wings, I don't have time to hunt for it high and low. I have to get back home! Granny Gert's going to die if I don't get your tears to her fast!" Her heart thrummed in her chest. If she refused to seek the scarf, would he withhold his tears? How could she save Granny?

The shiny bird eyes glanced at her, then flicked away. "Ahem. I've not been entirely truthful. The scarf has been stolen. Someone stole it from me, and I want it back. They took it into the Greater Daegries. You must go abroad. There is no other way."

Apparently, gryphons are liars. That fact wasn't in the book.

Soon, filled with curiosity and a little trepidation, she interrupted his utterings and asked, "Why did you keep the truth from me? Are you always dishonest? My Pappy warned me about liars and thieves. Maybe I shouldn't even agree to such a—"

With a mighty squawk, he puffed out his chest and made the medallion move. "Yes, I did, didn't I? Let that be a lesson. Never let your offender know everything about your business until it is time. Lies can be useful until the truth is necessary."

She lifted an eyebrow. "Oh, so a kind of test? A ruse to test me. Fine then. By fudging the truth about the scarf, I've learned a lesson about gryphons."

The truth isn't in them. And apparently the ability to find their own belongings isn't either.

"Why don't you just go and get the scarf for yourself?"

He looked abashed and pawed at the dirt. "I'm a king. I cannot rule my kingdom from all over the realm! If I had a knight at the ready, I would send him. As it is… you have asked for a favor from me. I am asking for something in return," he paused. "If this does not meet with your agreement, you are free to go."

At that, he turned away. Her throat closed and tears flowed down her cheeks.

When he glanced at her again, she dashed at the tears. He had asked the impossible. "King… sir… that's so far…"

Understanding crossed his face. He tapped on the dirt with his claws making scratches that soon turned into a crude drawing of the Lesser and Greater Daegries. "Put your attention here now. We are here… your farm is somewhere around here… and the border of my land butts up against the edge of the Greater Daegries… near here. Do you see?"

She swiped at her eyes again and leaned over the stone seat sideways to squint down at the dirt drawing. "Yes, I see. What about it?"

"To aid in the relocation and recovery of my property, what if I went with you to your house and tended your grandmother's hurts, then flew you out of the Lesser Daegries to get you started on this… eh… adventure. Would that help?"

She brightened and leaped to her feet. "Why, yes, that way I could take all the time I need to find your scarf! Provided my Granny is okay and all." She paced for a moment, thinking.

I could collect some follygrass for myself while I'm there. Perhaps I could learn how to make my own magikal scarf while I'm at it.

"Yes, that would be perfect," she finished with a bright smile, her fears abating. "If that is okay with you, of course."

The Gryphon King chirruped to himself and wouldn't meet her eyes.

While he collected himself, Alyssa reseated herself on the bench and appraised the situation at hand.

"Now, what's your plan for taking care of Granny Gert? She's bedridden. I don't even know how she'll let anyone in."

"You concentrate on how you will find my scarf. I'll accomplish this task. Tending to your grandmother will be my job. I am a king, after all. I am used to getting others to do my bidding."

"Well, let's get on with it. I should get back." She pulled her quiver over her shoulder and slung the bow over her other. "Granny's waiting."

He fidgeted, annoyed. "Silly girl. You cannot travel alone in the rain through the Grassland. It isn't safe."

Sorry excuse for a rain, she thought, and sat again. "So, I see." *It ain't safe in this place with creatures who think they're the ant's pants, either.*

As the thought of other creatures in the Meadowlands occurred to her, she gazed far into the distance through the high grasses. How were other creatures faring with such an overblown king?

The Gryphon King babbled, mostly to himself. "It would be difficult to accomplish this mission on a clear day, but today, with the rain, it will be impossible."

Alyssa's heart fell. She pulled her drinking horn out and thrust it at him. "Just put the tears in there. I'll tend to my kin alone. You'll have to manage that scarf business on your own too, though. I don't have time to keep playing games."

He puffed out his feathers and quipped, "Do not be so quick to decide your fate, Snippet. A king ponders about all situations. I have now decided what to do. There is always more than one way to accomplish a task." He stepped to the edge of the stone pavilion's overhang and gazed at the sky. "Solly, Solly, where have you gone, my friend?"

At this, the gray cloud hovering over them moved away. Traces of sunlight lit the cloud's dark edges until the golden orb beamed down once more.

"Ah. See? My good friend, Solly, the sun, has not forgotten me."

Marvel of marvels! Gryphons have powers to call on the sun, maybe even the whole of nature! That surely wasn't in any book.

"Surely you don't have power to control the sun?" Alyssa asked, amazed.

The gryphon waved it off. "I am something of a weather predictor, but no, I do not have *that* ability. The clouds were blowing away anyway," he told her. Then, looking up at the sky, he added, "It's been doing a lot of that threatening rain but not delivering it these days."

She grinned at the thought that a lion-bird could even know what weather was and that there had been any sort of lack.

"Come, girl. Climb upon my back. We shall fly to your grandmother and see to her needs, and then you will fulfill your promise to me to find my scarf. Be sure, your grandmother's life is ransom until you return it to me."

Alyssa gasped. *What did he mean?* The Gryphon King altered his mind so fast, exasperation filled her.

"Ransom? What does that mean?"

"Trade for a trade. You collect my magik scarf, and I will help your grandmother."

"How do you know it's magik?" she asked, lifting an eyebrow. No mention by the gryphon of anything unusual about the scarf until now. She already knew it probably had been imbued with some sort of magik, but she hadn't planned on telling him.

"Because it belongs to me. Didn't I tell you? The scarf is mine. Handed down from one generation of gryphon to another. The magik is old and special."

Curiosity filled her and she suspected he was lying about something. "What does the magik do exactly?"

"Do? Why, it doesn't do anything. It simply is."

Alyssa shook her head. Talking with the gryphon made little sense sometimes. "But magik is active. I've been studying it. I'm sort of a newcomer to it, but I'm trying to learn. And what I know is this: magik does *magikal* acts. It changes or grows. Items open and close. It's glimmer and glint, like your wings. They fan out, they fold up, and they flap and lift you. So magik doesn't sit like a toad on a rock. It does... things."

"Yes, yes. But I am not inclined to share all my information with you, remember? It is not good to discuss all possibilities when the most important item is still missing. Suppose I told you what I know about the magik in the scarf, and you decide to use it and never bring it to me? Futility is not in my blood."

She sighed, exasperated. "What happens if I don't make it back? What if I get eaten by lions or something?"

"That is a good question. I must have some assurances of your commitment. I have decided that your grandmother's life and your family farm will suffice as collateral in this endeavor. You cannot promise to come back, as there are many things between you and my scarf. But we shall see what we shall see in good time. In the event that you do not return, your home and family will be my payment."

"So, I get Granny whole and healthy, and you get your scarf, or I end up dead and you get all of everything? Except the scarf, because I will likewise not have it to give. And that's the whole deal?"

"And, as a bonus, do not forget, I will be the one to carry you on my wings as far as the edge of the Greater Daegries. You are receiving free air carriage to the edge of your journey." Then, he added, as an afterthought, "But no farther. I am a king, not a carrier pigeon. Once I release you in that land, finding your way through whatever perils may befall you is on your head. This I so decree."

He knelt on his hind legs and flattened out his surprisingly dry wings to allow her to climb onto his back. Once there, she groped for a handhold, and finding nothing, grasped his medallion rope, checking to make sure she didn't choke him.

He flapped his wings, and soon they lifted off. Solly sent the last bits of rain cloud scurrying across the sky, making the day bright. Alyssa felt her heart nearly leave her chest as they rose higher and higher.

This has certainly been an adventurous day and may not end anytime soon. What if I don't make it back? What will happen to Granny and Pappy?

These dark thoughts only made her shake her head, even more determined to see the task through and come out on the other side as a winner.

The land below them turned into one more recognizable as she viewed the maze's dark area and the light area of the sunflower patch. Soon, Alyssa pointed out the tiny farmhouse below, and the gryphon landed beside the backdoor pathway.

She slid from his back, rearranging her bow and arrows. "I'll go in and let her know you're here. I wouldn't want her to be frightened."

"Yes, yes. Do prevent an alarm. I will work on bringing forth tears."

Alyssa didn't want to know what a gryphon had to do to make itself cry. She didn't wait around to watch, either. Instead, she dropped her belongings on the porch and fled into the house's safety. The moaning of her grandmother filled the farmhouse's interior, and Alyssa quickened her steps.

The sight that greeted her in Granny Gert's bedroom sent waves of revulsion bubbling up from her gut as she slogged through a smelly liquid that dripped down the bedside and pooled on the floor.

"Ew, gross! What is this?"

"The plants are called putrid for a reason," Pappy Oh commented from his place. "The poison turns its victims into a liquid that the plants can feed on."

"Will it hurt me if it gets on me?"

"No. It's the result of the poison, not the poison itself," he answered.

Granny Gert spoke in a weak, pain-filled voice. "Did you find the gryphon, Lys?"

Alyssa moved to her bedside. Her shoes slurped in the vile substance—a close relative of snot—and the sucking noises made her gag.

She drew closer to Granny Gert so she could hear her. "Yes, ma'am. He's outside about ready to come in."

"Did he agree to cry?"

"Yes, ma'am." Alyssa didn't know if she should tell her grandmother that the Gryphon King's tears came at a price.

"Bring him in then. Let's get this over and done."

Alyssa turned to go back to the door, but King Hubert saved her the trouble. He poked his sharp beak into the room and took in the surroundings, blinking rapidly, his black eyes curious.

When Pappy Oh exclaimed something about a real gryphon and bounced up and down in his tin box, the creature jumped at the shock of it, squawking.

"What in the name of Strange addresses a king from such a contraption as you have there?" King Hubert asked, wrapping a wing over his chest. "I've nearly gone extinct in shock."

"Oh, that's my grandfather. Well, leastways, it's what's left of him. I sort of failed at necromancy," Alyssa replied.

"Ah. So, you're into magik, wizardry, and other assorted tinkering?" King Hubert stared at her, those beady eyes seeing far too much.

She squirmed. "Um. Sort of. I told you; I've been learning."

"You didn't say *what* you were learning, however," he retorted.

Alyssa smiled. "You told me not to give out all my information to anyone at one time, remember? Just following orders, Your Majesty."

The Gryphon King, nonplussed, grunted.

"Can we get started? She's in a bad way," Alyssa asked, turning back to her grandmother. "Hold on Granny. This might hurt a little."

She pulled the sheets back and exposed her grandmother's legs. King Hubert moved beside the bed.

"Out upon a moonlit night, while I girded up my might, came a witch across the sky, evilness that made grass die. Voice of metal, eyes of steel, one who caused a king to kneel, now visits me to break my

will, and must need tears to heal this ill," King Hubert recited, somberly. As he finished, he leaned over Granny Gert and directed his tears to fall onto her legs.

Steam rose.

She hissed and balled the coverlet in her hands against the pain.

"The salt in my tears is tremendous for healing but terrible for irritating what ails the patient," the gryphon said when he was finished.

"Has Tony been back?" Alyssa asked Pappy as she looked at dirty towels lying on the floor.

"Yep. He's been nursing Granny with cool rags. They're over here."

Alyssa slopped over to the other side and pulled out a clean rag from a pile on the floor. Then, she took a bowl of water from Granny's washstand, dumped it outside, refilled it from the well, and returned to place a dampened rag on her grandmother's forehead. "How are you now?" she asked, worried.

"I can't feel my legs," Granny Gert replied. "And I'm powerful tired, too. Maybe I'll have a little shuteye for now."

Alyssa nodded and turned to address the gryphon. "What now?"

"Healing will begin now, but it might be a few days before the numbness leaves her. And a few more before she can stand on her legs. Often, recovery is a long process."

"In the meantime, who's going to take care of her while I go and…" Alyssa's voice trailed off as she realized Pappy Oh listened to every word.

"Ahem, yes. I desire to see the rest of this quaint little farm, now. I think I shall stay here for a time. After dropping you off, I will collect one of my subjects on the return flight. To aid with healing and such."

Suspicion tinged his words as Pappy Oh asked, "Where are you going to now, Lys? Is this great brute sending you off somewhere? And why is he coming back here with a healer?"

Alyssa's gaze went from the gryphon to the toy, where something flickered behind the painted-on eyes. She remained desperate to do the right thing, although she knew no one would like it.

She leaned toward the clown's face and whispered, "I sort of struck up a bargain with the King here, Pappy. I'm going to go run an errand for him in trade for those tears. It won't take long, and he's going to be around to care for Granny Gert. You two won't be alone. He's even bringing back a healer. Isn't that great?"

"Not in this lifetime!" Pappy Oh exclaimed.

"Shh," she warned, with her index finger against her lips and a tilt of her head toward the sleeping Granny Gert.

"You're either going to take me with you on this errand, or never be allowed to go. I have spoken," Pappy said in a hushed voice.

Alyssa pictured the old man jutting his chin out and crossing his arms in determination.

"Please Pap," Alyssa said. "You can't do that. A bargain's a bargain. This seemed the best way to get Granny Gert the help she needed. Now what kind of person would I be if I didn't keep my word? I have to go."

She didn't mention the fact that the Gryphon King had the power to control the sun, the weather, and maybe all of nature. His powers could kill them all.

Pappy persisted. "There's no telling what he might be up to, girl. What makes you so sure he won't do more damage?"

"Well, he's kept up his end so far, Pappy. I have to do likewise."

"You might need my help."

"I might, but you can't be much help in that little box you're stuck in—"

"Come on, Lys. Do it for me. Do it for Gert. No telling what he might conjure up as retribution if you don't come back. I suspect he'll incorporate our farm into his land and take it over. We'll be slaves. If he even lets us live…"

Alyssa stared at the jack-in-the-box. That disembodied voice belonged to her grandfather, someone helpful to her if he could remember some spells and such.

She gazed at King Hubert. "Can I take him?" she asked. "He'll weigh next to nothing and might be more useful to me than to you. He can be a little mouthy."

The gryphon tapped his talons on the hardwood floor. "I suppose so. I've little patience for tinny voices in a can."

Alyssa restrained herself from asking how many tinny voices in a can he had ever heard before. Instead, she patted the clown's head.

"Okay then, looks like we're ready to go, Your Highness."

"Excellent. Let's go outside."

"Do you think we should leave Granny a note?" Alyssa asked Pappy.

"No. She'll be better off not knowing that we both went off on an adventure."

"Shouldn't we tell Tony, at least? What if Granny needs something before someone gets back here?"

"No. Afraid old Tony will blab to the town about this. Bad enough as it is—"

Hubert interrupted. "No time anyway. You must leave now. Besides, my tears also have sedative effects. She'll sleep for some time."

Alyssa nodded, hoping this to be true. Her Granny, the highest order of healer, would know what to do for herself when she woke up. The gryphon's helper could take up the slack her own absence would create.

The old woman would know right away when they both went missing that something had happened, but the two of them could not avoid it. Granny would badger Hubert until he gave up the story.

Alyssa gave her grandmother a last glance and trudged out of the room with Pappy Oh in her arms. She set him down by her bow and arrows outside and waved to the gryphon to wait a moment while she packed a bag.

She grabbed a pack that she found in the loft where Pappy kept his winter clothes. The pack had been used when he went on his journeys, rare occasions these last few years. She pulled her tunic and britches off and replaced them with a long-sleeved shirt and coveralls. She tossed in clean clothes along with a few foodstuffs and a scant few coins. She immediately felt guilty for taking them, knowing how hard they were to come by. Finally, she carried the pack outside and rejoined the gryphon and her pappy.

She struggled to climb onto the big, winged body with a jack-in-the-box, a pack on her back, and her weapons, but she managed with a huff and a puff.

King Hubert gave them a moment to settle in before flapping his giant wings and taking off. He soared over the pond and the bridge where the deadly plants waved beyond it. Alyssa peered down at them, hoping they hadn't gotten any bigger, or bossier. She would make sure they were destroyed as soon as she got back. They would not ever attack her family again if she had any say about it.

The jack-in-the-box's top sat closed. Pappy Oh didn't want to see how high they got. His digestion wasn't quite what it used to be, he had said. And he worried he might throw up a screw or a bolt if he got nervous.

Alyssa believed he jested but didn't press him on it. They climbed into the now sunlit sky. Solly shined down on her. The sun's rays became almost too warm for the coveralls she now wore.

The vista sprawled out below and came into view with every downward sweep of the gryphon's wings. They flew past craggy mountains on either side of Old Stony that flowed right outside her grandparents' farm. Just past the plants. Her heart soared.

No wonder those nasty creepy vines want to keep everyone from going that way! It's the most beautiful trail ever made!

The river twisted snake-like, rising until it met a bowl-shaped mountain. One side of it had four ravines running from top to bottom like someone's giant claw had ripped the ground from it, leaving deep gullies.

King Hubert fluttered to the ground on the mountain, into a small clearing. The trees towered taller than Pappy and Granny's silo, and in full leaf, spreading lush scents of pine and juniper with it. King Hubert did a fine job avoiding a collision with any of them. Alyssa marveled that where the farmland was withering under the lack of rain, this area still showed life and growth.

"This is where I leave you," the gryphon said, flattening out his wings for them to slide down. "I have a kingdom to attend to." He turned to go.

"Hold on, now!" Alyssa carried the toy box by its crank and struggled to stand under the weight of the pack and the weapons. Firmly on the ground, she turned to King Hubert for final instructions.

"Which way do I go, and what am I hunting for, aside from a follygrass scarf? Did you see the person who took it?"

He squawked, fluffed his feathers, and pinioned her with a stare. "You are the most annoying girl I have ever met. The person was a thief—do you know what a thief appears like?"

She frowned. "I suppose like anyone else."

"Exactly. Now go find him."

"What if it ain't a 'him' but a… her—a girl instead?"

"Then find her if you wish. Him or her, it matters little to me. I desire my scarf."

About that time, strange music churned out of the little box. Alyssa let go of the crank, palmed the box, and on the crescendo, Pappy Oh—in the clown form's head—popped out. "What did I miss?"

King Hubert, caught off-guard, took three steps backward and stumbled onto his hindquarters. "I wish you would learn to control that thing!"

"Watch yourself, King. That's my Grandpappy you're mean-mouthing."

The gryphon took a deep breath and tried for a majestic stance. Then, in a strangled voice, he said, "My apologies. Ahem. Now, you girl—"

"Alyssa," Pappy Oh interrupted. "Her name is Alyssa."

"Ahem. Yes. Now Alyssa. If you would be so kind as to remember our agreement, you will have until sunset of the round moon."

"What?" she exclaimed. "You didn't say anything about a time limit!"

"Mute your impudence. It isn't my time limit. It is the time when the scarf will permit a new owner to take it over. The time of Luna, the round moon. When Luna's entire face is seen, there are a lot of magikal properties in the world that become active. Abilities become heightened. Abilities such as taking over the scarf to steal it and return it to me, the rightful owner."

"So, I have to find it, take it from the thief, and make it back home to our farm by the day of the full moon?"

"Well, no. I intend to be here in this clearing on the last day, holding court until *sunset*. If you do not arrive by *then*, I will assume you have failed and take the next measure."

"Which is?" Pappy Oh asked.

"I will lay siege to your farm, Sir, and if your lady wife does not cede the residence, I shall take it by force. But first, my helper will be happy to burn that hedge-maze and open a passage between our lands."

"Don't you ever worry, King Hubert; we'll be back long before then," Pappy Oh said with certainty Alyssa didn't share.

Annoyed, she placed Pappy Oh on the ground, pulled her gear off, and set it alongside. "Can you tell me anything to help find the thief or scarf? I don't know where to begin." While she waited for the King's answer, Alyssa settled Pappy Oh in his metal box into the top of her pack. "I don't know which way to go, what I'm seeking, or even who might have it."

It rankled her. This pompous creature who insisted on her help couldn't instruct her in the slightest. He must imagine her to be a first-rate magik-maker who needed no help.

King Hubert readied himself to take off. He peered at her over his shoulder. "The thief is a human, like you. A sword-seller. Of which I had no use at all, of course. But this man—yes, a man—who likened himself to be a warrior, listened not at all. When I refused his goods, he stole my scarf. I am sure he does not know the value of it. Nor of the potential dangers involved with considerable magik unleashed improperly, should that occur, of course."

"Did this sword-seller give you a name by any chance?" Pappy Oh asked.

"Pryon. Lord Pryon, he called himself. Of course, I believed not a word of it. No one as base as he could be lord over anything." He ruffled his wings. "No, more like a common merchant stealing and reselling. I wish you well with this endeavor, Alyssa Chance Oh. Fail me not."

Alyssa's heart sank. No wonder the gryphon had been so shady. Finding the scarf would be difficult if not impossible.

The gryphon jogged forward. The wind filled his wings and lifted him into the air. She wanted to call him back but found it would be pointless and utterly exasperating.

When he disappeared behind a far hill, she grumbled, "He's the most aggravating critter ever to walk this planet. Said it might be a girl, then said it wasn't. Ain't sure he knows up from down and down from up."

"Some critters are full of themselves, is all," Pappy said. "Better not to understand them. You'll strain your thinker."

"Why won't he go and get the scarf all by his lonesome self?" she asked. "He can fly, for goodness sakes."

"He's a king, ain't he? Maybe he thinks it's beneath him. Besides, magik can be mysterious. The scarf might not want him to show up as its wearer again. Maybe somebody else has to get it for him so he can take it over again."

Alyssa didn't bother telling him that the king had mentioned his status as a ruler exactly as Pappy had said.

"Well, I sure hope that scarf takes a hankering to us," she muttered, trudging forward. "I'll be mighty upset if it refuses me."

She checked Pappy Oh's positioning, riding in the top of her pack, and made sure he could see. He assured her it seemed like being a child on a piggyback ride.

They walked through the clearing, going west, following Solly as he made his trek across the sky.

Pappy Oh sang a funny little tune he liked to yammer out sometimes. It kept their journey from being such a chore as they trod along.

Have you ever been a' walkin' on a warm summer's day?
Have you ever stopped to stare deep into the bay?
Put your hands in the air while you do a little prance,
turn around and 'round and do a jiggle giggle dance!

They climbed through a small glade of trees, pulling, and pushing at the thick branches and underbrush. Ahead, they heard the faint sounds of metal striking metal.

"I think it's someone playing horseshoes," Alyssa said, holding back a slender sapling branch.

"More like a barn-raising," Pappy Oh commented, when the branch snapped back into place over his head.

As they drew nearer, shouts and the sound of pounding horses' hooves rang out. The clamor grew louder, more insistent.

Pappy still sang his silly song until Alyssa put her hand over the painted-on mouth of the clown's face in the jack-in-the-box.

"Shh," she told Pappy Oh. "Ain't horseshoes or barns being raised. That's men fighting."

When he fell silent, she removed her hand and eased forward. Quietly, she pulled an arrow from her quiver, and lowered her bow into her hand. She loosely nocked the arrow and used it to push back the immediate foliage in front of her. Every fiber of her being readied for danger. She'd never shot a person with an arrow before, only deer. She shook her head at such scary thoughts and peered through the trees.

The sight made her gasp.

Chapter Six

Lord Bryon

Alyssa had stumbled upon a marketplace or an outdoor bazaar where swordplay came from a group of men who thrust and parried and yelled at each other close to the edge of the tree line. A little farther away, some were on horseback, clashing lances as their opponents approached. Massive oaks surrounded the area in a semicircle, and mountain peaks glimmered over the treetops, snow coloring their tops. No immediate danger appeared to her, but Alyssa kept her bow handy.

She eased away from the protecting oaks and moved toward the nearest two men, arriving just as the taller of the two disarmed his opponent. The loser held up his arms in surrender, and the other laughed as he picked up the fallen blade.

"You should protect yourself better, George."

"Excuse me, sir," Alyssa said to the victor, a broad-shouldered man with a leather vest over his long-sleeved tunic. "Can you point me in the direction of the sword-seller's tent?"

He hefted both swords, glaring at her nocked arrow. "I believe the good mistress means business, George," he threw over his shoulder. "Careful with that arrow, milady. Lest you accidentally let it fly." Then, smiling, he pointed with his sword's end to the left of where they stood. "Go to the last row of tents down there."

"So sorry," she said, realizing how she must appear to a stranger, armed to the teeth. She tucked her arrow into its quiver and slung her bow over her back, thanked him, and jogged along the woodlands' southernmost edge. Best to move along before the two men could get a glimpse of the jack-in-the-box in her pack.

The tan tents were various sizes with pegs, ropes, and turnbuckles that gleamed in the sun. The banners of each who transacted business inside them were colorful and varied. She tried hard to make out what each one signified.

A pale lemon-colored banner with a slice of watermelon on it probably meant a fruit stand, and a gray banner with a hammer and blade would most likely be a tool-seller's tent. When a wagon rolled past in front of her, and she saw two children in the bed of it fighting over a large striped melon, she trusted her instincts.

She walked on. When she spied a sea foam banner with a pair of black, crossed swords on it, she sighed in relief. Either some sailors plundered for gain, or she had found a sword-seller's tent. Whether the tent belonged to this Lord Pryon remained to be discovered. She paused and considered how to proceed.

This place holds nothing to fear, I hope.

Few customers stood around this tent—open on all sides—and her curiosity piqued when she finally stepped under the awning.

A man with a scruffy beard sat on a three-legged stool behind a sturdy wooden table of knives, swords, leather scabbards, belts, and whetstones.

"Hello," she said, interrupting his steady sharpening of a blade.

He laid the blade and whetstone aside and wiped his hands on a dirty apron around his middle before rising and coming over to greet her.

"May I help you, Miss?"

"Not too certain, but maybe. I'm seeking Lord Pryon. He's said to be some sort of sword-seller, and I'd like to speak to him."

The fellow stared at her as if she'd slapped his face. His ice-blue eyes were twin slits separated by a furrowed brow.

"Well, that would be pretty impossible now, wouldn't it?"

Alyssa heard Pappy Oh grunt at the man's rudeness.

"I'm awful sorry, sir, but I'm not from around here. Why is it impossible?"

"Because Lord Pryon died last week in a mysterious battle up in the Heightlands. Guess you didn't know about that either?"

Alyssa shook her head. His face clouded like he didn't believe a minute of it.

Just my luck. Found the right tent, got the wrong man. Now, what do I do?

Things might have gone along a little smoother if Pappy Oh hadn't made his presence known.

"Who'd he do battle with?" he asked, his voice a tinny squeak.

The man moved from behind the table. "Who said that?" he asked.

"Who's asking?" Pappy Oh came back.

The man's eyes narrowed, and he shifted to one side of her, staring at the jack-in-the-box. "Is that box talking?" he asked.

Alyssa shook her head. "Of course not. Don't be silly. It's a toy. Toys can't talk."

Pappy Oh must have realized his mistake and fell silent.

The man sidled up to Alyssa, touched the clown's head, pushed it down into the box, and slammed the lid shut.

"What's your name again?" Alyssa asked nervously, seeking something to turn the subject to.

"Lord Bryon, son of Lord Pryon, of Half Moon Manor. And your voice and that other voice are not the same. How are you doing that? And who are you?"

"Alyssa Chance Oh, of the lands beyond the forest. I learned how to throw my voice from a man at a festival."

"And why would a girl such as yourself want my father?" His gaze strayed to the toy box to see if it answered.

Alyssa backed away. "He had a sword I've heard about. I wanted to have a word with him."

She glanced at a knife nearby on the table, avoiding his gaze. The lie had escaped her lips easily. Habitually honest, she wondered how had she had gotten that way so quickly?

Lord Bryon moved back to the seller's side of the table. "His blades are mine now, and everything else you see here. Ask me what it is you wish to know."

Alyssa took her time, trying to think of a plausible story to tell that would complement her falsehood. "I heard he used a follygrass scarf to protect his blade. I wanted to see it."

The man paused. He placed a hand loosely over the hilt of his short sword. His fingers tapped against it suspiciously. "Are you interested in my father's sword or his sash? You've said you have questions about the blade, yet you seem equally informed about his belongings. I wish to know how you came by this information and why it is of any importance to you."

The crank on the toy box turned, and the odd music played, muffled by the pack.

If I don't answer him, in a moment or two, Pappy Oh is going to jump up and say something that might get my throat cut...

"Lord Pryon has been accused of a crime concerning the scarf, and I have been given the task of clearing his name. Will you help me?" she blurted out.

"If you was smart, you'd do what she asks," Pappy Oh exclaimed as the clown's head popped out.

Bryon jumped at the suddenness of the toy's movement and proclamation. Precious seconds given to the man's surprise gave Alyssa time to dart out of sword striking range if he had that on his mind.

She shimmied her bow into her hand. If he wanted to go hand-to-hand, she would be ready.

Bryon slid the sword from the table and gestured at her with it. "There is something quite unnatural about you and that box. I want answers and I want them now. If you won't give them, I shall call for the ranger in the shade of yon trees," he pointed over her shoulder, "and have you bound until you can answer truthfully."

"Pappy do be quiet," Alyssa urged. Do I tell him my story? Will he believe me? I need answers as much as he does. We sure can't stand here the livelong day, sparring. To the lord's son, she said, "I'll tell my business if you swear to help me." She stood unmoving.

A man with broad shoulders came into her line of sight. He meandered down a path toward the tent. There wouldn't be much time before he arrived.

"How can I swear to that if I don't know what I'm swearing to?" Lord Bryon asked.

"I'm telling you the truth. Your father's been accused of stealing that scarf, and I've been sent to find it. If he's dead, then it should be your duty to honor his name by clearing it of wrongdoing."

He contemplated her words before changing the subject. "What manner of mischief is that box?"

"I'll tell you later. I've been warned about telling all my business before it's time. Also, a man is coming up behind you, and he's going to be mighty curious what our standoff is about."

And to the perusing eye, they were tensely standing apart, bodies humming with a threat, nothing but a collection of weapons between them.

Bryon slid the sword back onto the table. "Right. That would be Lando, my kinsman. I'll agree to help you only as far as your story goes. Should you be false, I'll retract my agreement and turn you over. Your fate, your hand. If you threaten my life, I'll have you killed unless I kill you myself."

She gulped the gall that rose to her throat. To settle the contract, she walked up to the table and stuck her hand out. He paused, sighed disagreeably, and then shook it once, roughly. She shouldered her bow and nodded in agreement.

Amusement lifted the corners of the young lord's mouth.

… little snips like you… the Gryphon King's voice played in her head. What would he say about her now?

Lando arrived at last and spoke in a deep voice to Lord Bryon, explaining the lateness of his arrival. Alyssa wandered through the tent, handling items as though shopping for something. Bryon set Lando to work on the blade he'd been sharpening.

"I'll be going now. There are things to attend to that won't keep, including my lady mother and her ill health. Perhaps I can return tomorrow," he told Lando as he prepared to leave. He pulled a long knife from the table and inserted it into a sheath on his belt.

He caught Alyssa's eye and tilted his head to show she should follow. She moved out into the sunlight, drifting away as if she was no longer interested in the merchandise.

They walked apart for a time, following the tree line. He thrust back the nearest branches and showed her a well-worn dirt path on the other side. Alyssa trusted he knew which way to go. They halted by a gurgling river.

Bryon motioned for her to sit upon a moss-covered boulder. "Now, I'll have the complete story, beginning with that box."

She pulled the bow from her shoulder and leaned it against the boulder. "Fine. It ain't a happy tale, though, if that's what you're thinking. I'm from Mudden, the land on the other side of the Meadowlands. We're farmers and builders and mostly poor. My parents went missing when I was a *betot*, and my grandparents raised me. Granny Gert, and Pappy Oh..." She paused and Pappy rattled the box. "Now, he's living as a voice in this toy box."

"How that happened is a tale unto itself, I'll warrant," Bryon replied. "Please continue."

She stared at him for a moment, gauging his sincerity, and related all that had happened with her attempt at necromancy and Granny's run-in with the plants. Finally, she said, "The rest of this tale is what you're waiting to hear. It might take a few minutes. Why don't you have a seat?"

Bryon, who had been standing still, glanced at her, and nodded. He seated himself next to her and waved for her to finish.

"I had to go find the gryphon and get his tears to heal up Granny Gert. He didn't give them to me without cost, as they say. He wants his scarf back. Someone from here took it. He named your father. That scarf has some special meaning for him, and, well, he intends to do some mighty nasty things to my family if I don't bring it along in a hurry."

Bryon frowned at that. "What things?"

"Take over my family farm, put my Granny in servitude, maybe worse. I have one moon cycle to find that scarf, retrieve it, and take it to him."

"There's a bit you should know from me," Bryon said. "A terrible land baron named Madrid has taken over the realm you find yourself in. He has exacted payments from every citizen once every moon phase. These payments are preposterous. No one can afford them. He's taking whatever he pleases in exchange for the payments, and that includes lives. I believe either he or his son, Ragon, killed my father."

"What makes you think that?"

"A battle ensued on the flat land surrounding Needlemount. That's the tall thin mountain you see there." He pointed ahead of them at a sheer mountain peak with a castle perched at the summit. "Someone slaughtered my father and his page."

Alyssa shivered.

"When they didn't return as expected, I scoured the land for them. I found them almost buried in the snow, their retinue and accouterments gone. Father had been hoping to discover more about Madrid. Half Moon Manor, my home, is not exempt from these payments. Our land is at the lowest level of the Heightlands surrounding Needlemount, and Madrid usurped power as some sort of overlord. My father feared what might transpire if Madrid, or his son in his stead, should attempt to exact money from the aristocrats in the region, as threatened. My lord father tried to avoid war."

"Why are you a sword-seller in a common market? You seem to be highborn to me."

"It was a hobby of my father's to make weapons and sell them to his friends. He thought it would be a good outlet for his sons instead of falling into trouble. We were not always highborn."

Nodding, Alyssa paused before asking, "Did your father steal King Hubert's scarf?"

"Yes, I confess, he did. He heard from a court singer while visiting the Meadowlands that the Gryphon King's scarf would protect whoever wore it from being killed in battle. Father intended to oust Madrid and save the realm. He thought wearing the scarf in battle would bring success."

"So, that's what that lion with the eagle head kept hiding," Pappy Oh said in his tinny voice. "Up to something underhanded after all. He knew the scarf would protect its wearer. A mage such as me, or an apprentice such as you, Lys, might find that scarf equally as handy. But he didn't want us to know that little tidbit."

"Now Pappy, I promised that gryphon I'd bring it back to him. I ain't got no designs on that thing. I'll admit, the magik must be mighty strong to protect someone, though." Alyssa studied Bryon's face. "I guess your father, Lord Pryon, didn't have it with him on that trip up the mountain?"

Bryon's eyebrows lifted. "Oh, yes, he did. My father wore that scarf as a part of his armor. It never left him, not even in sleep. But when I found him up on Needle Flats, no scarf could be found anywhere. Needle Flats is a level rise in the land before you start truly climbing up into the mountains surrounding Needlemount.

"I'm positive that whoever killed my father took his hunting party as slaves and now has the scarf in their possession. Whether or not they know it has any power, I cannot say. I wish to gather information from the folk up on Needlemount. Someone knows something about that battle and what happened. I'll find out, even if it is with the end of my sword."

"Wait," Pappy Oh interrupted. "How'd your father get killed if he wore the scarf?"

"He must have removed it."

"But why?" Alyssa asked.

Bryon shrugged. "I can only assume. The magik did him no good. Nor any of them." He glanced at the mountain. "I'll have my chance to find out what this Madrid knows, though.

My time to take payment from them has come. I intend to go seeking answers."

"I'd like to have a stab at that old, wicked Madrid my own self," Pappy Oh said, voice trembling with anger. "Lys, we're going along."

"Yes sir, Pappy."

"We'll need a plan," Bryon said, blue eyes darkening. "Anyone who would come upon my father's armed men, take them, and either slay them or enslave them must have unimaginable power."

"True. But I have an idea coming together." Pappy answered. "Let me sit and think for a minute, and then we'll have another confab." And with that, the clown's head went down, and the trapdoor closed.

Chapter Seven

The Siren's Stream

While they waited for Pappy Oh to figure out the plan, they lounged by the stream and got to know one another.

"It isn't far to Half Moon Manor from here," Lord Bryon told her. "Perhaps a few hours' walk. Tell me about your land in the Lesser Daegries. What did you call it? Muddy?"

"Mudden," Alyssa corrected. "It's made up of mostly mud and clay. We grow a lot of things down there, thanks to the nearness of Old Stony. That's the river. We call it Old Stony because of some big stone spires growing alongside it."

"Stone spires? What's that about?"

She shrugged. "No one remembers. They're from some ancient village way back when the town became Springdale."

He paced a few feet away and glanced at the sky. "My lord father would know all these answers. He traveled widely."

Alyssa, sensing his sadness, cast about for a new topic. "What is this land called where we now sit?"

"We are on the outskirts of the Forest of Shadows. My liegemen made the trail through here since it is near the market and on the way to the manor. As you can see, it is quite fair and cool beneath the trees' covering."

"Do your liegemen live at your house? We have a few hired hands back home, my Granny and me. And well, now Pappy, or well, some of him."

He smiled. "Some do. The manor can host hundreds of men and riders. We rarely have that many any longer. My father is gone, and his kinsmen left for their own lands rather than taking up his battle. I still do not know what happened to his entourage."

"Sorry to remind you of your loss so often," Alyssa said, mentally kicking her own shins. "My folks are gone too. Dead."

Grief left fine lines under his eyes. "Ah, must everything these days be reminders of loss?"

"Been a long time for me."

"I tied my loss to the treachery of Madrid. He will get paid at the end of a sword one day."

"What will you and your folks do now? Declare war?"

"Not at this time. We have barely gathered ourselves together again since losing my lord father. We, the aristocrats and I, have a long road ahead to plan for the future of Half Moon Manor and the surrounding land. And until we sort out Madrid and his evil seed, we cannot truly be solid in any plan. No, I believe something different should transpire for the troubles on the mountain," he replied.

"Do you worry about leaving home to go sell swords in the market? And also, if you go ahead up the mountain, don't you fear what might happen to the folks at home at the manor? I believe I heard you say your mother's ailing?"

He pursed his lips and shook his head. "No. I am not afraid. My retainers and my household are safe and well-protected, even with fewer men there. They are well-trained and strong."

Too trusting. His unquestioning attitude and limited numbers might mean disaster if a stealthy attack came.

"What numbers are we talking about here, Lord Bryon?" she asked, trying not to sound impertinent.

"At midsummer, when festivities are going on in celebration, the household numbers swell to full. Such a gatherment brings in more butchers, bakers, and candlestick makers. But it is not midsummer now. And until I can bring in kinsmen from around the land, we host about a third of that number. Still, it is enough for now. Yes, I believe it to be so."

His voice faded, and his face belied the sorrow and concern for his homeland. Alyssa stared at the ground and fell silent. She had asked enough.

Finally, Bryon tapped his knife with his index finger and glanced at the toy box. "Excuse me, my lady. I will depart to scout out the trail ahead while we await the plan."

Alyssa nodded. He would find a place to work out his feelings. Maybe not a crying type, but he might use his knife on a dead limb somewhere. At least that's what she would have done.

She rose from the rock to stretch. A nap appealed to her but might not be appropriate given the company she traveled with.

She glanced once at the bow and arrows, but as Lord Bryon had talked, she believed him to be an honorable man and had no reason to fear him.

The stream, peaceful and lazy, sluiced along the rocky bed beside her. She pushed her britches legs above her knees and took advantage of the freedom to walk along the stream barefoot, admiring the water.

Although a smaller branch of a river, it built strength and depth as she went along it. Lost in thought, she didn't realize how far from Pappy and Lord Bryon she had wandered until Lord Bryon shouted.

She jerked out of her reverie and peered to where he stood waving his arms, alarmed. The distance prevented her from hearing what he said.

Then, out of the corner of her eye, she saw movement in the water to her right. A water creature swam toward her with a giant fin that flipped up and down propelling it forward, faster and faster. It had the face and body of a beautiful woman. Her glossy raven hair flowed around her like a floating scarf.

Alyssa, enchanted, and more than a little amazed, heard music playing nearby. The lilting sound pulled her to the water's edge. Melodic and sweet, the tune stirred something deep inside of her.

The icy touch of water on her feet brought her back to herself mere seconds before the dark-haired creature grabbed her legs and pulled her in. She didn't have time to do more than gasp air into her lungs as her feet flew out from under her and she plunged into the midst of the now rushing tributary.

At first, she flailed her arms and tried to grab a rock as it whisked past, but the slimy surface prevented her from gaining any purchase.

Then Alyssa lost her ability to fight. The song had stolen her entire will. Her arms floated uselessly, and the siren pulled her by the leg toward the far bank. And as they neared it, the blackness of a cave yawned menacingly. The water flowed into the cave and went who knew where.

Alyssa observed all of this in a state of stupor and without resistance. The creature let Alyssa go. The siren's song filled her mind, and the siren's dangerous intent showed in her mysterious eyes.

Then, through a fated moment, old Solly beamed down and struck the glittering scales, blinding Alyssa and breaking the spell.

Her instincts kicked in.

… must swim away. Now!

Alyssa fought to rise to the surface. She flapped her arms and kicked her feet and strove upwards. Her clothing became like weights, preventing her from making any upward movement.

She unfastened three buttons, tugged the coveralls off her shoulders, and let the material fall to the bottom. Dressed now in her chemise, she fled for the surface.

The siren floated nearby, watching her, laughing at her troubles.

The sun's cheerful face struck the water, guiding her up and up.

With her lungs near bursting, her head finally broke through the water, and she inhaled a great gasp of air.

Nothing had ever felt as wonderful as the breath of life going into and out of her panicked body. But the challenger returned. Hands grasped her legs, yanking her under once again.

Alyssa struggled, went under, popped out again, gulped air, and went down once more.

The fishy tail flipped powerfully as the siren tugged on her. Alyssa kicked at the creature's head, trying to disentangle herself, determined those eyes would not mesmerize her again.

It bared long wicked teeth at her as it captured both feet, threatening. Alyssa didn't want to be bitten. Losing this fight wouldn't be an option either. She twisted like a fish on a line, getting one foot free. She pummeled the creature on its head and face with her heel. The siren screamed in frustration, her voice, a terrible rattling deep under the water. The sound sent nearby fish fleeing in all directions.

Oxygen. Air!

Alyssa fought for her life. She bent at the waist as far down as possible and punched at the sinewy hands and arms that grasped her. She bent one of the long fingers back until it should have broken and then it grew shorter and webbed. This new appendage clutched even tighter.

Alyssa punched, pinched, scratched, and kicked over and over. Until the creature let go of her in self-defense.

Her lungs ached from her held breath, and she sensed blackness approaching.

She lunged at the violent fish-woman and tried to throttle her. But the creature realized Alyssa's intention and floated backward and away. Wisely considering the validity of a continued battle, it fled in the opposite direction, allowing Alyssa to escape.

Alyssa didn't wait to find out if the creature recoiled to return or not. Near to fainting, she swam hard for the surface.

This time, when she broke through the top of the water, she took in large gulps of air, choking and spewing as some water came with it. She didn't stop swimming for the shallow water either. Another bout with the siren and all would be lost.

Alyssa saw Lord Bryon with the jack-in-the-box standing by, waiting for her to make it to shore. Lord Bryon cupped his hands around his mouth and shouted for her to swim harder.

Alyssa threw herself into the task until she finally scrambled through the slippery rocks and fell to her knees before Lord Bryon on the bank.

He grabbed her under the arms and pulled her further onto the shore, propping her against a large rock nearby. He stood beside her with grave concern on his face, as she bent double and heaved water up from her stomach. She struggled to breathe.

"Was that a… a…?" the young manor lord asked, turning away to stare at the water.

Alyssa didn't have the breath to reply. She closed her eyes and rested and tried to stop her heart from beating so erratically. When she placed her hand on her heart, she realized she wore no proper clothing.

Lord Bryon's back straightened. "My lady, you—"

"I need clothes from my pack," Alyssa replied in a broken voice. "Could you…?"

He lifted a hand and hurried away. When he returned, she had covered herself as best she could with her shift pulled down over her knees that were now pulled tightly to her chest.

He pulled his apron from around his middle and handed it to her, along with her pack, before jerking away. "That could not have been. My eyes play tricks."

"Oh no. It's exactly what you thought," Alyssa replied through chattering teeth.

"A siren, merwoman, Lorelei? Something terrible has befallen us," he said, voice sputtering.

"Don't know about that," Alyssa answered, examining her legs before drying them with the scratchy apron and slipping into a pair of britches. "But it had these long, awful teeth and sticky webbed hands. I declare I'll get back in there if she bit me." She examined her arms and hands. No skin was broken. She pulled a tunic top out of the pack and slipped it on. "Lucky for her," she muttered, tossing her blond braid over her shoulder.

"The bite of a mer-creature is said to be deadly." Bryon's voice trembled with wonder.

Alyssa took another deep breath. "You can, er, turn back around. I'm clothed." And then she glanced at Pappy's toy box. "Pappy?"

The box didn't move.

"He didn't come out with his plan, I take it?" she asked, pulling the strings tight on her britches. Bryon shook his head in answer, so she stalked to where they had been earlier, snatched her shoes up, and pulled them on her now dry feet.

"I sure do hate losing my overalls," she said. "Those were nice and handy with all their pockets and such."

"You will not go back into the water to find them," Bryon commanded, striding to her side. "I forbid it."

She tilted her head and gave him a stare. "No fear. I won't. My Granny can sew me a new pair. Not worth another scrap with that water-cat."

Relieved, Bryon spoke, staring out again over the bubbling stream. "Sir Oh has not come back to us with a plan, and his inattention aided in your attack. I thought a mage, a sorcerer might conjure up something to save you."

Alyssa picked up the toy box and walked away from the water with it. "Why didn't you save me?"

He moved to join her, then paused. "I confess, I never learned how to swim. I would have been no help to you."

Alyssa silently questioned how anyone grew up without swimming. Her father had taught her at the shore of Old Stony before he went missing.

"I'm not hurt," she told him, attempting to be light-hearted. "Wouldn't have been much good for anybody if we both drowned."

Lord Bryon's gaze fell to his feet. "I am truly sorry for my unchivalrous act."

"Staying alive ain't exactly unchivalrous, Lord Bryon. Anyway, I'm fine as peach wine, and Pappy will show up when he's ready. His plan is more important than some old fish-girl and her dunking me."

"You're a brave lass, young miss. I would not have been so lion-hearted under those conditions," Lord Bryon said before he plucked something from her sleeve. "Ah, a gift from the mer-creature, perhaps?"

Alyssa glanced at his outstretched palm where he pinched an iridescent scale between his thumb and forefinger. He dropped it into her hand. She turned it over and marveled at the way the colors transformed into many hues. The sun glistened off it. She shoved it into the pocket of her trousers. "A keepsake, for sure," she said.

Bryon smiled. "I believe you will be relating the tale of your battle with the siren many times to come. That small scale will aid in your retelling, methinks. Few have ever lived to tell such a story, so yours will be interesting to listeners far and wide."

The toy box shook, and the crank on the side turned. The eerie music issued out and the clown's face inside popped out.

"What did I miss?" Pappy Oh asked, turning the clown's face toward them. "Girl, you been out there swimming? Well, it sure is hot enough, I suspect."

"No, Pappy. Not swimming. Not for fun, not voluntarily."

"Did you fall in?" The clown's head bent over slightly, staring at her feet.

"No. I got pulled in by a… a…"

"A siren, Sir Oh," Bryon finished.

"Well, I'll say! Haven't had the pleasure of seeing one of them before. They say they're common in the Silk Sea. 'Course an old farmhand like me never gets out that way much no more."

Alyssa drew a deep breath to calm herself. The talk about the siren made the event more real to her.

"What did it pull you in for?" Pappy asked.

"Never mind, Pap. What plan have you come up with for us? This whole siren thing has romped on my temper, and I ain't in much of a mood to discuss it."

Pappy Oh cleared his throat. "Before I get to that, Lys, did you see that creature's purse?"

"What purse?"

"Ain't sirens supposed to have gold and such in their purses?" Pappy Oh directed this to Lord Bryon.

"Some rumors say so, but no one in my realm has ever seen such. I do not think any of us have ever seen a siren, to be honest. I cannot believe one was found here in a freshwater stream so far from the sea."

"It's the drought," Pappy told him, thoughtfully. "Something's wrong with the weather. Ain't supposed to be this hot this late in the year. That siren might be lost out here, swimming around to find a cool spot and took the wrong turn up the channel. Might have come up from the sea."

"What about the purse?" Alyssa asked, trying to bring his original question back to the conversation before they went too far off course.

Lord Bryon shrugged. "Perhaps. Historical maps have shown where sirens have sunk merchant ships and taken their gold and treasures and put them on faraway islands."

"Ain't likely this one brought none of that with her, eh?" Pappy asked. "Reckon we'd have to go diving to find out."

Now, Alyssa did shudder. "Well, I'm not jumping back into that water to go find out. Not for my coveralls and not for any old treasure."

Lord Bryon frowned at the toy box. "I cannot swim, sir, so I also say no."

"Fine," Pappy Oh said with a sigh. "Might be good to have gold coins or something to barter with along the road, but if neither of you is interested, then we better move on."

"What about the plan?" Alyssa asked. Bryon nodded, apparently thinking the same thing.

"We're going to the manor house, tend to his sick mother, get some men to go with us, load up some horses and food, because I know how much you eat, Lys. Then I reckon we're going to go mountain climbing and see what we see."

"Not much different from what we talked about earlier, Pappy. What have you been doing? Napping? What are we going to do once we get to the top of the mountain? The men who live up there are planning something terrible for these folks and have already begun it with the killing of Lord Pryon. You planning to conjure up something to help us fight the men who have the scarf?"

"Oh yeah, sure will. Plan to mix up the spell while at that Half Moon house."

"What kind of spell?"

"One to give us an edge."

"Anything else?" Bryon asked, hope etched in the way his shoulders lifted.

"Don't need nothing else," Pappy answered.

"What if they use the scarf's magik?" Alyssa asked. "Will your spell be able to work against it?"

"Can't we handle magik? Ain't we magik-wielders? Ain't we healers? Why I remember a time when my magik swarmed a whole crop of weeds and yanked them right outta their—"

"Well, yes, but—"

"No buts, Lys. You need to learn to trust yourself, and me a little here. We'll do what needs doing when the time comes." The disembodied voice sounded peeved.

She shrugged and looked at Bryon. He shook his head. Heeding a voice in a tin box, let alone planning potential battle strategies with one, needed no discussion.

They followed the stream back awhile until it became narrow enough to cross. Then they trekked northeast until they picked up the dirt trail again.

The land, desolate with withered trees and dry underbrush, sometimes rustled with small wildlife. Alyssa stopped walking to watch a gray squirrel scurry across her path.

The recent drought that had stricken the whole of the Daegries was evident in the many barren places they crossed. It had been bad in Mudden but not this bad.

Alyssa relied upon Lord Bryon to get them to his manor and lands, as she had no idea where they were and even less of where they were going. She wished for a map once again.

They passed around a stand of evergreens and found themselves in a sunny glade.

She repositioned her bow. "How far, Lord Bryon?"

"Oh, not far now at all, my lady. The manor house is on the other side of this clearing."

They trudged through dried grasses, each blade making a swishing sound against their legs. The wind picked up somewhat and blew a breeze into their faces.

Alyssa, carrying Pappy Oh in his box, asked, "So, Pappy, what are we going to do about the scarf?"

"I'll let you know when it's time. It ain't time yet. These things need to sprout like Gert's herb garden in the spring. Can't rush it."

Alyssa figured her grandfather studied on a magik spell and didn't want to talk about it in front of Lord Bryon. She didn't ask any more questions about it.

In a short while, they were through the other side of the glade and found themselves in a valley with rolling hills. On the near horizon, Half Moon Manor stood in the waning sun, its four turrets rising above the landscape and a drought-shrunken body of water surrounding it.

"Is that a lake around your house?" she asked Bryon.

"No, my lady. That is called a moat. It is to protect us from attack. We have lost most of it in this dreadful heat of late."

She realized then that Lord Bryon had a title and lands, and she revised how she thought of him. A lord, not simply a swordsmith, although his renown alone impressed her. A lord with liegemen and everything associated with a title and deserving respect and appreciation for his kindness as well.

When they reached the bridge crossing the moat, a rider rode out on a large prancing pony. Concern lined Bryon's face until he recognized who approached. The hand behind his back had grasped a sword, but when he relaxed, that hand came forward and sheathed the blade.

"Hail, Lord Bryon," the man shouted, kicking his horse to make it hurry.

"Galdron has certain peculiarities, my lady," Bryon told Alyssa, conspiratorially. "Overlook him." And then to his man, he said, "Hail and well met, Galdron. What news?"

Galdron, wearing a brown tunic and soft doe-skin boots that were tied up to his hose-covered knees, replied as he clasped his liege's hand. "The aristocrats are in a quandary over the gossip about the Silk Sea and an apparent portal."

"What do you say?" Bryon answered, incredulous. "A *portal*?"

"Aye, my liege. They believe something has happened, the opening of a portal or another evilment that has brought about villains of yore. Evil sea-witches have been seen near yon river. Gods only know what someone else may see soon. I've sent a company of men to talk to them to get the whole story."

Bryon shot a warning glance at Alyssa for her to remain quiet. She took the action in stride. No way did she want to have to explain her tussle with the raven-haired water woman again. But a portal? Where had she heard that before? Her mind, still foggy from the events of the day, strained to grasp all that had happened to her in the recent past.

As she listened to the two men discuss happenings in the realm, she thought maybe Bryon hadn't given Galdron a fair assessment. There *had been* a siren in the stream who shouldn't have been there according to Pappy Oh. Maybe the older man knew more than Bryon did about some things.

She pulled her pack forward and readjusted Pappy in his box. She had placed him at the top of it, and he had been quiet since the happening at the stream. Whether he remained silent conjuring up something, or sat in there sulking, she didn't know.

It would be nice if he came up with a solution to their dilemma with the men of Needlemount. But at this moment, conjuring spells in his present condition remained in doubt. Anxious thoughts assaulted her.

She trudged forward with the others across the bridge, through the courtyard, and toward the houses of Half Moon Manor. She wore a scowl on her face and held dark thoughts in her heart.

Lord Bryon offered Alyssa and her jack-in-the-box grandfather a comfortable room in which to sleep and refresh. Not knowing what else to do, she accepted the offer for them.

"There ain't time for all this sleeping and eating and so on," she muttered aloud as she paced in the room's expanse.

Banners, more like tapestries hung on the walls, their appearance official and rich like a wealthy lord might own. Alyssa fingered one as she wandered past for the tenth time. Uncovered twin window slits allowed the breeze to enter unimpeded. She wandered over to one and peered down into the courtyard. Men and horses wandered back and forth from the stables to the entrance.

Pappy still hadn't come out of his box, and she wondered if he'd fallen asleep. She wanted to go over and turn the crank and pop his silly head up and make him reveal what his thoughts were.

"Pappy?" she called out. "You ever going to come out of that thing? We only have a week to work that spell you're cooking up." She said it louder than necessary in case he didn't hear her through the tin box walls.

Finally, the box rattled and shook, the crank turned, and the clown's face popped out.

"Yep, I got a plan," Pappy Oh said. "Got us a goodie."

"Well, spill it. Time's a' wastin'."

"We're going to go up to that old castle and we're going to search high and low until we find that scarf."

"That's not a plan. We're already going to do that. And don't forget, castles are mighty big, Pappy."

"Yeah, but we're going to go to that castle, and my spell is going to help us find the scarf. Don't you worry, Lys. You're going to do fine. I'm going to walk you through this conjure. You'll find what you're seeking."

Alyssa grimaced. "The last time I tried magik on my own, I managed to get you partly here. You trust me?"

"As sure as sunrise. You didn't have everything going right at the same time. I'm studying on that spell you were trying to work on to get me back. I'll figure it out. First things first, though. With this spell, you'll be able to find all the magik items in that castle on top of the mountain. This spell will turn 'em all as green as your granny's garden in the spring."

"But how can we do that, Pappy?" Alyssa asked, a frown crossing her brow. "I didn't bring any spell-making stuff with me. No books, no candles, no nothing."

"Yeah, well. About that…" Pappy hesitated, and the clown twisted a little. "We're going to need a few things. We might have to improvise a little."

"Are you sure? Half Moon Manor might have ample supplies and such. They might have whatever we have at home. Herbs, water, moonlight. That sort of thing."

Pappy Oh cleared his throat. "It ain't like that, Lys. This spell will be um… dark."

"Oh," she said in a small voice as her heart leaped in her chest. Granny had told her Pappy had been playing around with some magik that didn't include healing.

"What does dark magik call for?"

"Blood," came the reply.

Chapter Eight

Pappy's Spell

Blood? Did he just say blood?

Alyssa's mind raced, and she drew a deep breath. "Whose blood?"

"Fee, fi, fo, fen, I need the blood of a little siren," he answered, his sing-song voice soft.

"Oh, no you don't! I ain't going back and doing battle with that wicked thing ever again!"

"Come on, Lys. It's for your Granny Gert. She needs us to come through. This spell will give us a leg up, so to speak."

"Why do I have to be the one to do it?" Alyssa asked, plopping down on the floor, arms crossed, and a pout on her lips. "I don't have mage knowledge like you do."

"Well, as you can see, I ain't in no shape to go swimming with a siren. I can see you ain't confident about this, but nobody said this would be easy. Remember, you were the one who signed us up for this. Now you gotta see it through. Besides, I might not be able to go the full trip, anyway. We still don't know the ramifications of your bringing me back. I mean, I ain't all here, yet. So, I can't be the one to do the siren thing. I can't be in the scarf-stealing business either. It's gotta be you."

"There has to be another way to do this without using the blood of a siren," she persisted, frustration full-blown.

He fell silent.

"Oh, Pappy. I'm tired. Let's go to bed for the night and figure it out in the morning. It has been a day to remember, and I reckon more's ahead."

"Just so you know, the siren's blood would enable us to find her purse and all her gold. We would be rich," Pappy said.

"Most magik creatures get enslaved to a magik-user if they take their blood from them, even accidentally."

"I don't want to take blood from anyone and enslave them. No, way. We don't need it. What in the world of Daegries has happened to you, Pap? You didn't use to talk like this."

He snuffled. "I guess being dead made me realize some stuff, Lys. Gold and riches would sure help your Granny Gert out if I should... you know… fade away."

Alarmed, Alyssa crawled over to the box and picked it up. "I can't really see you, Pap. You're just a silly clown's face. But I know it's you in there. Even if you're saying scary stuff. Are you okay? What makes you talk about fading away?"

"You used magik, Lys. Gert was right. It ain't natural. Magik shifts the structure of things. Sometimes the stretching, well, it goes the wrong way."

Tears welled in her eyes. "Please don't leave me, Pappy Oh. I can't get the scarf by myself. I'll get the siren's blood. I'll get whatever it takes!"

"Good girl," he said. "Now here's the plan…"

"Wait. Don't we need to get Lord Bryon in here? Don't we need him to be in on this?"

"I'd rather not," Pappy said. "The less folks in these parts know about our art, the better."

"But what if something goes wrong? I mean we're talking about me going bare knuckles with a siren. Again." Alyssa closed her eyes and shuddered. "What if I drown?"

"Do you think I'd ever let that happen?"

"Well, you didn't poke your nose underwater earlier when she hexed me plumb dumb. And what can you do to stop it?"

Silence.

She closed her eyes and let out a breath. "Okay, fine. I guess you know what you're doing. I sure hope you do. My life depends on it. But how are we going to get out of this place and back to the stream without raising a ruckus?"

Pappy Oh answered, "Don't worry none. We'll tell them guards we're on Lord Bryon's business. He'll have told them all about us and what we're here for by later tonight. I figure midnight might be a good time to go out."

"Well, I best get some shut eye then," Alyssa said, pulling herself up and scooping the toy box into her arms. "And you too, if you're even tired after all the resting you've been doing."

He made some muttering sounds, the clown's head went down, and the top of the jack-in-the-box closed with a snap. The box shook for a moment, then went still.

The grounds and moat around the manor house sat silent, save for the sound of the jingle of the chains on the bridge moving periodically from a breeze. Occasionally a frog croaked, or a fish splashed nearby, but these interruptions were faint and few.

Alyssa feared getting lost. They traveled by the light of the dim quarter moon. Thankfully, no clouds scudded overhead to block the sliver of light. And no rumblings or lightning meant the weather would not interfere either. She had the forethought to bring a candle stub with them and juggled the toy box and the stub as she eased out of the manor house.

The thin nightgown she wore (shorter at the bottom since she had grown taller) would hardly weigh her down in the water if she had to go deep-diving after the siren. Over the gown, she wore a dark wine-colored shift. That would keep her hidden as she slithered along the drawbridge. The bridge remained open, permitting their passage. As she marveled at their good luck, a voice called out in the dark.

"Who goes there?"

She stopped and stared in the direction the voice came from. "Alyssa and Pappy Oh."

Shuffling footfalls sounded, hurrying toward them on the wooden slats of the bridge. Alyssa shoved the stub of the candle under her arm, hiding it. She waited for the guard to reach them. Once he slid to a stop in front of her, he lifted a candle in a beaten metal holder to see them more clearly.

"Oh. My lady, I do apologize. One cannot be too certain in this evil time what is real and what is a vision," the white-haired gentleman said. "I am Sir Hyer, one of Lord Pryon… er… Lord Bryon's kinsmen. So difficult to think of my lord as passed on."

"Oh, yes. I'm sorry for your loss. I'm on an outing for the good lord. It won't take long," Alyssa said with a smile, sliding past the old man.

"Take your time, my lady. I will be on duty until sunrise. Forgive me if I inquire after you on your return. Lord Bryon's request of anyone who comes or leaves, you know."

She nodded and turned to go, before remembering the candle. She pulled it out and asked the old man if he would light it for her. He complied, and they parted ways. Surprised he didn't ask about her business, she smiled at her luck.

She didn't know how to get back to the stream they had found, nor even the path they'd trod. Once they reached the glade, she stopped to get her bearings.

"Pappy," she whispered to the box. "You awake in there?"

No answer.

She sighed and peered at the trees standing around her like ghostly sentries in the half-light. She had never been good at directions in the dark on the farm, even when her memory of familiar buildings and landmarks acted as her guide. Here, nothing reliable guided her, not even her senses.

"If I've said it once, I've said it a dozen times. I need a map! Nothing for it but to plunge on ahead and deal with whatever falls out," she said aloud, tucking the toy box under her arm and holding the candle aloft.

She chose an overgrown dirt path, hoping it would be the right one. After a short time, she brushed her bangs back and examined her scratched arms. She felt ready to pop open the tin box and yank her grandfather out by the clown's neck. She stared into the gloom. What would happen if this path turned out to be the wrong one?

When she stumbled into a small clearing, she set the box down—a little roughly, and demanded Pappy Oh come out.

Nothing happened. The box didn't rattle or shake. The crank didn't turn, and the clown's head didn't appear. Pappy's words returned to her, and Alyssa panicked. "Pappy! You better get on out here now," she said in a loud voice. "You better not be faded away!"

No answer issued forth from the jack-in-the-box.

"Pappy Oh," she said. "Come on out here now. I ain't playing."

Only the sound of crickets chirping in the night returned to her.

"Pappy?" she dropped to her knees, set the candle between two rocks, and lifted the tin box to shake it. "Pap?"

Her heart throbbed, making her pant. Why didn't he answer?

Terror seized her. Something was wrong. Pappy would never ignore her like this, alone and in need of him.

What do I do?

She shook the jack-in-the-box again, harder this time, and then with trembling hands turned the crank.

"Pappy, I'm sorry if this hurts you, but if you are still with me, you need to wake up and say so!" And she swiveled the crank until the music reached a crescendo and the clown's head popped up with a snap of the lid. She pulled on the clown gently, the springs rigid beneath the ruffled shirt.

"Pappy Oh," she said, her voice choking. No sound, save for the weird music that came from the tin box. "Pappy... Pappy... no!"

She sat on the cold ground, hugging the box to her, weeping. The longer she thought about her missing grandfather, the harder she cried, and muffled screams wrenched from a place deep inside. A place of loss that came roaring back from the time when her parents went missing.

"No! No! I can't lose you again!"

She crouched low, head to the ground, mourning her grandfather. How long, she didn't know, but when she could not cry anymore, she pulled the box into her chest and wrapped herself around it.

Eventually, she fell into a troubled dream. In it, she sat at a table with her parents and grandparents. Food was spread out before them in platters and bowls. So much food, in fact, that no one had space to put their plate. Smells of dishes she missed from younger days filled her nose. Squash baked with sweet onion in a brick oven, green tomatoes fried into crisp pinwheels, and field peas seasoned with salt pork steaming in the pan made her mouth water. When someone prepared to cut into a hot pan of cornbread, golden brown from the fire, she woke up.

Still half-asleep and trying to recapture those heavenly scents, she heard a whisper of something moving behind her. Instinct reminded her about the unfamiliar wood, in possibly hostile territory, with no one to protect her now.

She hadn't thought to bring any sort of weapon. She sat up and wiped her eyes, trying to see the cause of the noise.

Fully alert now, she rose to her knees and lifted the nearly burnt up candle from where she had placed it between two rocks, turning left and then right, trying to illuminate the area.

Something glimmered in the darkness beside a withered tree. Whether she saw light from another candle or the light from the sliver of the moon, she couldn't say.

"Who's there?" she called out, her voice throttled by tears.

"Why are you crying, little girl?" a soft feminine voice asked.

"Who's asking?" Now she scrambled to stand, Pappy's box at her feet. The urge to run came over her.

A woman with an oval face and slanted eyes moved out of the tree line into the light of the candle. She wore a long heavy gown covered with a moss-green cloak and made no noise as she approached on her bare feet. "Only a passerby. I heard your sobs and became concerned."

The stranger held out her hands placatingly. "I will not hurt you, little one."

Alyssa relaxed a little. "My Pappy…"

Then, without being able to stop them, the tears began anew. "Something's wrong. He ain't answering me." She lifted the box, shook it, and cried, "Pappy, oh Pappy."

The woman came to her side and placed a gentle hand on her shoulder. "Who is Pappy?"

Alyssa waved at the tin box and cried.

"Is this your toy box? Is it broken?" the woman asked. She ran her hand over the top of it.

"No," Alyssa finally answered. "My grand… a grand wizard lives inside. He ain't in there now. I think he's gone. F-faded away." Even as she said the words, she knew she sounded crazy. This stranger could not possibly understand how anyone could get into a tin box, let alone die in it.

"I'm sorry for your loss," the woman said, soothingly, squeezing her shoulder and then letting her go. "Shall I make a fire for us to sit by? Perhaps the wizard is hiding inside away from the chill?"

Alyssa shrugged, unable to speak. The woman moved, wraith-like. So much so, Alyssa didn't follow her movements and didn't know where to place her.

"Who… who…" she asked the empty air.

"Who am I?" the woman deciphered from behind her. "I am called Rylee. I live in these woods."

She draped her soft cloak over Alyssa's shoulders, flitted off again, and then returned with a small pile of wood that she stacked into an organized pile with dry tinder on top. "May I use your candle to light it?"

Alyssa nodded, touching the cloak. "Thank you for this," she said. "It's soft."

The woman didn't shiver at all, and Alyssa marveled at this.

Rylee smiled at her. "It's good for keeping warm and staying hidden. You may keep it."

Alyssa, grateful for its warmth, viewed the cloak more closely and her gentle touch revealed a tightly woven natural fiber softer than a goose's down.

"It's made from the moss of trees," Rylee explained.

Then the stranger tipped the almost burnt-up wick to the dry tinder. It flashed into a flame. She said a few words and bowed her head.

Finally, Rylee said, "Thank you, spirits." Then, turning to Alyssa, "We cannot burn it for long and cannot make it too high, as the woods are terribly afraid of fire in their weakened state." She handed the guttering candle back to Alyssa who blew it out and left it on the ground.

She stared at Rylee, confused. "You speak like you know how the trees feel about things."

Rylee pulled a log over to Alyssa and encouraged her to sit on one end of it. Then she sat beside her.

"I do. Of course, I do. I am a dryad."

"Dryad? What's that?" Alyssa asked, curiosity overcoming her sadness.

"Tree spirits. Did you know trees have spirits? We take care of them, keep them safe from fire and danger. We live inside of them, sometimes. I have been doing this lately, also singing to them songs of hale and hearty health. But alas! These poor creatures are sickening unto death." She waved at the withered branches nearby.

"We can sometimes intervene and bring them back to health, but these, I am afraid, have gone beyond even my medicine."

Alyssa raised her eyebrows. "You think it's the drought? Ain't had any rain in a long while. Wish my granny was here. She'd know what to do for them."

"Yes, the rain has disappeared," Rylee agreed. "But there should be rain by now. There has always been rain during this season. The weather is changing. Is your granny a healer?"

"Yes. She grows medicinal plants and herbs and can make up a poultice to fix pretty much anything."

"Do you know how to do this as well?"

Alyssa nodded. "If I have the right materials."

"You are indeed a friend to living creatures, then. We carry a strange bloodline, you and I."

"Sure do," Alyssa agreed. "And this is surely the strangest place I've ever been to. First, I meet a siren, and now you." Alyssa released her death grip on Pappy's box and set it beside her leg next to the log. "Maybe this is a dream after all."

"I do not consider meeting with a siren as dream-like. Those are water spirits. Perilous, if one is not careful. Such a meeting here in the Heightlands? Surely a sign of more evilment afoot, I'm afraid."

"What evilment?"

"The elements have turned wicked to all living creatures and the rains do not come. Our tree-brethren are dying from the lack of water. The water spirits are restless, swimming out of their homeland in search of food. I cannot even imagine what the air and fire creatures have done in defense. Something is wrong in the world of Daegries."

"Oh, yeah," Alyssa replied. "Same back home. Plants are dying from lack of water, animals won't eat. I don't know what to think."

Rylee smiled at her and stretched out her legs, flexing her bare toes to the fire for warmth.

Alyssa stuck her hands out in front of her to warm them. "At least it feels like autumn here. Back home you'd think it midsummer."

"What were you and the wizard doing out in the woods on such a night as this?" Rylee asked curiously, but with no malice.

"Going back to find the siren again," Alyssa answered. "If Pappy Oh has faded away, there's nothing left for me to do now. Go back to Half Moon Manor and wait until morning, I guess."

"Were you going to magik her?" the dryad asked.

Alyssa stared at her, filled with trepidation. "How did you…?"

"All magik users know other magik users, of course. I witnessed the trail of your magik throughout the trees, but most especially where your tears fell. They show up as moonlight and stardust." Rylee gently wiped a finger down Alyssa's cheek and collected the wetness yet to dry. Then she held it out until the droplet shimmered on her fingertip in the firelight like a wisp of liquid silver. "A mage's tears are twinkly lights for other spirits to see by."

"I'm not a mage… not like Pappy."

"But you must be, and a powerful one, for us to see your tears." Rylee motioned to the toy box. "I believe this Pappy to be special."

This reminded Alyssa of her loss and created another wave of silent tears. Big fat ones rolled down her cheeks. "He was. He truly was."

"Oh, now," Rylee said, patting her shoulder. "There's nothing to lament about. Your friend is only missing for a time. All things get reunited in the end."

"I'm not so sure. I magiked him into coming back home after he died the first time. Don't guess it would be right to repeat it. He said it sort of stretched him. He told me he might fade away. I guess he's really gone. Oh, Pappy." Another tear slid down, and she scrubbed it away with the back of her hand. "Guess going to the stream is a waste of time now."

"Why did you desire to speak again with the siren? Perhaps I can help…?"

Alyssa realized how she might have told the strange creature of the woods a bit too much already. "Oh, um. Personal business. I had a sort of run-in with her earlier this afternoon and wanted to make amends."

"Ah! You mean she fought with you, and you lived to talk about it?" Rylee said with a laugh.

"Well, yes. In a manner of speaking."

"Why did she attack you? And you may safely speak to me. I have no disagreements with water spirits."

Alyssa shrugged and stood to warm her backside at the fire, careful not to get too close and catch the cloak on fire. "Don't know. Guess she thought I wandered on her land or something. She pulled me in and tried to drown me."

"Hm, yes. They are territorial. Or she could have been hungry as I mentioned. But in this case, I cannot say for certain. She may simply have been sunning herself and you startled her.

Sirens are possessive creatures. They hide things and keep secrets to themselves. Anyone who tries to take from them does not end well."

"Pappy said they had treasures."

"This is true. But most encounters end badly with water spirits. You must be a strong magik-user."

Alyssa sat back on the log and wrapped the cloak tighter around herself. "I sure don't feel strong. I feel small and scared and alone. About ready to give up on this misdirected adventure if I'm being honest."

Rylee nodded her head and leaned toward Alyssa, pinioning her with mystical eyes. "You are not alone, friend. You have the woods and all the dryads to sing to your health."

"Thanks," Alyssa answered, disconcerted. "I-I wish I knew what to do. Go ahead or give up and go back. Pappy wanted me to find the siren and ask her to give me… um… something to aid in my journey through this land."

Rylee still had her gaze riveted on Alyssa's face. She patted the box again, letting her hand rest on the closed top. "Ah, the journey. Would it be to accompany the master of the manor nearby on a journey into yon mountains?"

Alyssa glanced away and closed her eyes. Locking gazes with this creature made Alyssa wonder if she could read her mind. "Kind of," she answered.

Rylee stood and paced closer to the fire, staring at the trees beyond. "If you decide to revisit the siren—and I believe you feel duty-bound to your fallen kin's request to do so—please know you will be required to barter with her. Sirens do not give without getting something in return. And certainly not their blood."

"Oh, do you know about that? Well, I have one of her scales," Alyssa said. "Would that be something she might want?"

Rylee laughed, a tinkling sound that danced in the darkness at the foot of the nearest tree. "No, my friend. She would not want a scale. She has those in plenty."

Alyssa considered what possessions she had that a siren might want and came up with nothing.

Then, as if she had something important to impart, Rylee knelt in front of Alyssa and took one of her hands. "Friend, you do not know me nor my kindred, but you have ties to us. I sense a familial bond. I do not know the wizard in the box, but his presence in your life somehow has a connection to tree spirits. We are ancient and wise. You can always trust us."

Alyssa marveled at this. "Pappy is connected to tree spirits?"

"He is or you are, and likely both of you are. Yes. You and he are related, and therefore we also are related. This is a wonderment to me as well. Anyway, you should not fear this journey you are on, even to see the siren. You have more power than you know. This adventure, as you called it, is for your good. To edify you. To educate you in Daegries ways. Be of good cheer and sorrow no more."

She let go of Alyssa's hand.

"How do you know?" Alyssa asked, a little breathless at the dryad's words trilling through her.

"Wood spirits know more than most would believe. For example, I know your name is Alyssa, and your friend in the box had been your grandpapa. Dryads have ancient bloodlines and have lived many lifetimes. We for certain know our kith and kin. There is a bond with you. I must see to the needs of my brethren in these woods now, but I will seek answers to this riddle."

Alyssa stared open-mouthed. "I-I'm a dryad?"

"Possibly," Rylee replied. "I felt something when we touched. I felt something also in the box. This is true. How I know things... well, dryads hear everything in the forest. We noted your troop as you passed through. Heard talk in the woods."

Alyssa nodded, understanding seeping in. A strange mist surrounded them while Rylee spoke. Alyssa imagined the trees on the opposite side of the fire leaning toward them, listening.

"Dear Alyssa, friend of forests, you are young now. But soon, your youth will be tested, and your mettle, and perhaps even your powers. Once you come into the fullness of it, you will understand how magik, once released, can never be contained again. Go forth on your journey, Alyssa, and believe good will always win."

Alyssa's mind filled with visions of a smoke-covered dark place where she stood with a halo of bright light all around her.

"When will I get this power?"

But Rylee did not reply. Instead, the dryad stood again, ready to leave.

"What would a siren want?" Alyssa asked, mentally exhausted. "I suppose I am duty-bound as you said, to give this my all."

The mists grew thicker, and the dryad floated into the grove of trees.

"What does any siren want?" she called back to Alyssa. "Something no one else has..."

And then, without further ado, the dryad vanished. A tree branch snapped somewhere nearby, and Alyssa jumped. The fire guttered, and she had no idea how long she had been sitting in the cold woods, talking to the dryad, now like an apparition. If not for the cloak still wrapped around her, she would believe it had all been a dream.

"I have to get out of here," she said aloud. She took the remaining tiny candle, brought a burning branch in, and relit it. Not knowing what else to do about the fading fire, she scooped up handfuls of dirt and dumped it on the embers. She hoped this would keep it from flaring back up and doing any damage to the trees. She did not need to add dryads to her list of enemies.

She scooped Pappy Oh's box up and strode ahead, staying on the same course as planned, but with a renewed determination to get siren's blood.

"If a siren's blood works a spell to find things in a musty old castle, then it's able to find an old mage in the Otherworld," she said out loud, in case dryads or anyone else listened. "Guess we'll see, won't we?"

She hoped she did not have to go into the Otherworld to use the spell. In fact, she hoped she did not have to go any farther than the siren's stream for help. As she trudged through the glade, she noted the sky grew a little lighter. By the time she reached the other side of the trees, the sky became a softer shade of purple with tinges of pink on the horizon. The candle burned out then, and she threw a thankful glance up for such a small favor from the gods.

It took a while to find her way back to the stream. Solly the Sun had already risen from his bed and shone a light for her to see by. She kept a watchful eye out for the siren as she followed the stream from its weakest and driest point backward to where it flowed strong and deep. The creature might be out sunning early in the morning before humans were running about, ruining her chances.

Alyssa talked to Pappy Oh as though he still accompanied her. For all she knew, he might be only more like a shade or spirit instead of a disembodied voice.

"Pap," she said. "I'm going to leave you sitting on the bank while I take care of this siren business, but don't you worry. It won't take long. You sit right here," she said to the box, placing it high on the ledge overlooking the stream. She removed the cloak and her slippers and set them beside the box.

After double-checking the box's position, she strolled down to the stream and stood, hands on her hips, hoping to catch the siren slipping into the water or edging up to the bank.

She's stealthy, Alyssa thought. I have to keep my wits about me or risk an ambush like before.

She paused and cupped her hand over her brow to block the light. Something shimmered under a ledge on the far side of the stream. The cave! Alyssa's blood turned as cold as ice as she remembered it.

"I ain't scared of no fish woman. I ain't scared. I ain't scared. I ain't—"

"Scared. Yes, so you have said," a voice behind her drawled.

Alyssa turned on her heel so fast, she nearly fell. The siren sat on the bank, the tin jack-in-the-box in her grasp. The shimmering must have been a trick of the light.

"Hey, now," Alyssa yelled at her. "You put that down. It ain't yours."

"No, it isn't. Yet."

"How'd you get over there without my seeing you?"

"Water spirits. We can appear as water or not, whatever we choose to do. You weren't expecting that and so you didn't notice." The siren tilted the box. "We also have our own magik. And this box could be helpful with it."

"No. It ain't never going to be yours; it's mine. And my grand pappy's," Alyssa told her, scrambling forward in the sandy soil, determined to take the box away from her.

"What if I require it in replacement for the items you have come for?" the siren challenged.

This stopped all forward movement. Alyssa stared into the mysterious eyes. The siren flipped her tail, and the scales glimmered and shone in the sunlight. The creature had massive seashells sewn together for a bodice, and when she moved, they clinked musically.

"How did you know I came back for something?" Alyssa asked, standing straight. Her feet sank into the sand of the stream bank.

The siren tapped the box with one long nail and then waved at the frail-looking willow bending over the bank nearby. "The dryads in the trees around this river told me this morning. You should not speak with night creatures so much. They are strangely dangerous and with a touch can know things about you."

Alyssa's memory of the conversation with Rylee seemed like it had happened a long time ago. In fact, she had nearly forgotten about it, like one would forget a dream from the night before.

But she recalled the dryad's touch as she had held her hand. Had it given the creature some strange power over her?

She pondered for a moment and then frowned at the siren. "Well, she had some choice things to say about you, too. But back to the present. Let's get one thing straight. I ain't giving you Pappy Oh's box."

The siren considered this and set the box back on the ledge. "As you say, but I would like something exotic from you. You should tell me what you want from me so I can decide on an appropriate exchange."

Alyssa hesitated, not even sure how to go about telling the creature what she wanted or why she wanted it. Pappy hadn't told her the details of the spell he would make, and now, as she replayed the conversation, she considered if he wanted the blood to find the gold rather than aid in their search for the scarf.

Finally, she opted for a delaying tactic. She figured out how to do this when dealing with Granny.

She pulled the dryad's cloak up from where she'd left it and threw it over the jack-in-the-box, hoping out of sight and out of mind would deter the siren.

"Before we our talk wanders off, can we at least share names or something? I mean, I think we got off on the wrong foot, so to speak," Alyssa said.

The siren tilted her head, and a slight smile lifted the edges of her mouth. This action reminded Alyssa the creature's teeth were like a barracuda's, all fang-y and sharp.

"I know your name already, Alyssa Chance, and I know both your kith and kin. You cannot hide on land or sea now."

This took Alyssa by surprise. "How can you possibly know me or any of my folk? Did the dryad tell you something about us?"

"Oh, you are a breath of fresh air, Alyssa. I should like to witness when you unleash your own powers. The answer is simple. *Magik.* Magik enables one to know more about nature, about living creatures, and… oh, so much more. Sometimes this knowledge binds us to things we do not even wish to know."

Alyssa trembled from head to toe. These people up here in this section of the Greater Daegries did not need to know all about her or her business. The dryad knew more than she would have ever told her.

I've been magiked!

Shaken, she asked, "Should I fear you or the dryad? I'm a little off kilter here. Y'all have me at a disadvantage. You know me, but I don't know you."

"No disadvantage, Alyssa. You have as much ground as we have. Besides, fear is a useless emotion for magik-users. And after all, what is there to fear? You have… magik," she said, pausing for effect.

This truth struck Alyssa more than anything anyone had said to her in a while. Why did she fear being alone? Being in the woods? Talking to a siren? If she had the tools, she'd throw a spell together and fight them, bring Pappy Oh back, and save the world, all in a day's work if she really tried.

Except…

She didn't know how magik worked yet. And she had no tools with which to enact any magik. Maybe, if what these spirits of water and trees told her held true, then a day approached when she would understand it all. She sure hoped so.

"Fine, then. I ain't scared of you. Are you scared of me?"

The siren threw her head back and laughed a deep hearty laugh. Tears of mirth sparkled in her mysterious eyes. "Why should I be? I have magik, too!"

Alyssa joined her in laughter.

I must be spellbound. I cannot stop laughing!

Then, when her water-loving new ally took a deep breath and righted herself, Alyssa resumed her discussion. "Well, we're even, I guess. Let's get on down to business. What do you need from me to get some of your blood?"

"Blood?" the siren asked, merriment completely gone. Red-hot color appeared from the top of her head to the tip of her tail. Her eyes, twin slits of flame-blue, flickered and flashed.

And then, she faded from view.

Alyssa blinked and blinked again. Nothing. She peered at the stream. The siren swam hard for the other side toward the black opening to her cave. It occurred to Alyssa that a siren shouldn't be living in a cave, but her thoughts scrambled as she realized the siren could disappear into it soon.

"Wait!" Alyssa yelled to her. "I wasn't going to hurt you none!"

When the siren reached the rock jutting out from the cave mouth, she pulled herself atop it and squeezed her hair out, angry eyes watching Alyssa's every move.

"Siren lady, come back. I swear I ain't going to do nothing mean. Your blood's good for—" She stopped and took a deep breath as she realized her mistake. "I can't yell my business across the world. Can you please come back?"

Control your mouth, she told herself. You don't know who is listening. If dryads can listen in and sirens are lying about, who knows what all might get in on this?

"You will never get my blood," the siren shouted, stretching out to sun herself.

"If you come back over here, I'll explain it. There're too many ears listening," Alyssa answered, peering around at the trees nearby.

"You come out to me."

Alyssa walked toward the water. "You'll drown me."

The siren flipped her tail fin like a cat. "Fine, do as you will. I cannot help you."

Alyssa debated her choices, each one terrible.

"Pappy, you sure took off at a bad time," she muttered. To the siren, she said, "Okay, give me your word, your soul promise, you ain't going to attack me and try to drown me if I come out there."

The tail flipped again and again like an annoyed parlor cat would do. "Fearful creature, I give it. You likewise promise not to attack me to get blood."

"Promise. And you can't magik me by singing either," Alyssa replied.

"Fine, fine," the siren agreed, waving her hand dismissively.

"What a crazy plan. This water will be the death of me. Colder than ice even in the midst of a dry spell." Feeling utterly silly for such an agreement, Alyssa pulled her shift off and waded out into the cold water in her gown. She muttered, teeth chattering, "How can I trust a sea creature who's already tried to kill me once?"

Gods watch over me.

She cheered the fact she could swim.

The movement will keep me warm. She recognized the lie even as she thought it.

The stream's current flowed gently, enabling her efforts, and she thanked the gods silently. She swam to where the siren sat. When she arrived, she pulled herself onto the rock, slipping, and falling a few times from the slime growing up the sides of it. The siren had made it seem effortless.

Once seated, Alyssa examined a scrape on her knee where she had clung to the rock, fingers digging in, her knees and toes hugging it until she got a better handhold.

"Okay," she said, teeth chattering. "I'm here. You and I have to work fast."

"You want my blood." The siren studied her, black hair shining in the sun like the feathers on a crow.

"Yes. Maybe just a drop." She glanced around and lowered her voice. "It's for an incantation."

"Yes. I know."

"You do? Then why did I swim all the way over here? You could've given me what I needed over there." Alyssa pointed at the far side of the stream. "And boy howdy, you sure got mad. Why did you lose your temper so fast if you already knew?"

"I thought for certain the nasty tree sprite jested about such a thing. They can touch one and learn great things. Then they communicate to all of their family about it. To hear it from your own mouth angered me. But this should be a lesson to you. You must be mindful of your words. Even asking for a favor should be done with thought and care. To ask for someone's blood is a very dire thing."

Alyssa inclined her head. "Okay. I'm sorry if asking you for blood sounded thoughtless."

The siren continued. "You must prove yourself, Alyssa Chance Oh. Life will test you many times. Nothing will come easy to you. You are a magik-wielder. Someone who others will turn to in times of need. Your ability to do as told now will ward off many troubles in the future. You are still untried."

Alyssa trembled. "Untried? Interesting choice of words. The dryad said something about my youth. Sort of the same thing." She marveled over the fact that she remembered the dryad's words. She barely recalled her face.

The siren patted at the water as if it were a beloved pet. "What will you use my blood for? And don't lie. I will jump into the stream and be gone if I catch you in a lie."

Alyssa squinted at the sun for a moment. Granny Gert always knew when she lied. She launched into a retelling of the journey thus far. Most of it did not surprise the siren at all. In fact, the siren relaxed and crawled behind Alyssa to braid her hair while she listened. It disturbed Alyssa that the dangerous water creature sat behind her with her long hooky nails threading in and out of her hair. Eventually though, she relaxed and retold her side of the battle in the water from yesterday; she felt compelled to apologize.

"I'm sorry if I scared you. I didn't mean no harm, I swear it. I didn't even know you were around this old stream. I'm going to say that I felt like a bit of fish bait while we tussled. Why did you act so mean toward me?"

The beautiful sea creature held out her green-tinged hand. "I accept your apology. My name is Lorelei. I'm sorry I attacked you. When you encroached upon me, I had to protect myself.

Instinct took over. In my defense, I recognized another magik-user and let you go. Most of my catches don't get away."

"I've heard." Alyssa shook her hand, gently. Once the siren had her hand captured, she would not let it go.

"Give me something in return for my blood."

Alyssa pulled back on her hand. "First, let loose of my hand; I'm going to need it."

"Ah. Holding your hand... it's like digging in dirt. Ugh!" Lorelei said, releasing Alyssa's hand and wiping it on her fin. "You're filthy with it."

"What?" Alyssa asked, flexing her fingers. Curiosity filled her at what the siren found so disgusting.

"Ask the dryads," Lorelei replied, washing her hands in a small pool that gathered on the backside. "Land magik is dirty and stinks. Wait and see. You'll find out in time. Know this, Alyssa Chance Oh. Many who test you for your magik will fall by your hand. It is the way of the land. The sea is far more forgiving. Life has ebbs and flows, a continuum of itself. Anyway..." she paused, glancing at her. "Now, what are you using my blood for?"

Alyssa took a deep breath. "Pappy faded away last night. I need your blood to bring him back again."

"No. You should not use my blood for such! This is worse than saying you wanted it to find the contents of my purse."

"Pappy said if we got some of your blood, we ought to press you for gold. I said no to his suggestion."

"I'll not give you my blood for a doorway into the land of the dead either, Alyssa Chance Oh. You of all creatures should understand how blood magik is most sacred. Mind yourself, young one."

Alyssa shook her head. She did not understand Rylee or Lorelei. They were always talking somewhere over her head.

"I'm dumb about blood magik or land magik or seafaring magik or anything else. The only thing I know is I need my Pappy back. I needed him when I brought him forth the last time, and I need him even more now. I ain't sure your blood will help me bring him back. I thought—"

"You thought you would take a precious item, like siren blood, and play with it to see what happened? Didn't this behavior get you into trouble before?"

"Maybe so," she conceded. "But I would do it again if it gained me my old Pappy."

"What if it doesn't bring your Pappy back? Will you then want to come back for even more?"

Alyssa thought that a fair question. She wondered if the siren might give her enough to use for two purposes.

"No. Unless… well, what if I needed it for a spell to locate magik items? Pappy planned to teach me a conjure to find the scarf. Which is why I'm out here you know. That blasted scarf."

"The dryad might have mentioned it." Lorelei preened herself by running her long nails down into the tough fiber of the seaweed. "I do not think you should use my blood in magik at all, unless used by me. I suppose the loss of this Pappy of yours could be an extenuating circumstance. But I am forewarning you, prepare to give me something of great value in trade. I am not doing a ballet over this."

"I reckon giving up blood wouldn't be something to be all giddy about. But I don't think I need too much." She paused. "But listen, what do you want? I don't have anything of great value to give for your blood. I mean, isn't blood the most powerful thing in the universe?"

"Yes," Lorelei agreed. "Absolutely the most powerful. I want nothing more than an item of value gotten at great cost. It must be something another siren does not have. Else, what is the reason for having it?"

Alyssa struggled to come up with anything. If she only had the scarf… But how to give it to a siren when the Gryphon King required it?

"I can bring you something back from the journey. Not sure what, but I'll keep a sharp eye for it along the way. I think I'll know it when it shows itself," Alyssa said.

"No. I have something specific in mind."

"Okay. What?"

"A tooth."

Alyssa stopped herself from laughing out loud. "What? A tooth?"

Lorelei gazed at her, eyes slitted. "Yes, a tooth. I can make it into jewelry. It will be the envy of all my sisters."

"What sort of tooth?"

"A nice large one. A fang."

Alyssa feared asking where she would find one, but Lorelei saved her the trouble.

"I've always fancied a Yeti's tooth. They live in cold mountains, a place to which I cannot travel. But your journey takes you there. Promise me a Yeti tooth, and my blood is yours."

"What if I can't get you one? Yetis are mighty big creatures. Even if I saw one, they might not let a stranger yank a tooth out."

"Then, I will take *your* blood as a swap." At this revelation, the siren bared her own fangs, and Alyssa threw her arm up, nearly falling from the rock.

Lorelei laughed at her.

Alyssa lowered her arm, and her heart thrummed in her ears. Then in a small voice, she added, "You don't *really* want my blood, do you?"

"Of course not. Did you not hear me say how land magik taints your bloodline? It's nasty, why would I covet any of it? Creepy things."

Alyssa relaxed, crossed her arms, and peered into the water over the side of the rock. The siren, although treachery personified, convinced her when she said she didn't want her blood. For the first time, she rejoiced to know she had a magik bloodline.

"How do I get a Yeti tooth?"

When she turned back to her companion, the siren lifted an eyebrow. "I know not. You must find these answers, girl. But you must swear to bring it to me, even though the getting of it may bring personal disaster or loss. Fair?"

Alyssa closed her eyes. What had she been thinking? "Okay, then. Yes. For your blood, I will bring it… somehow." If the siren knew she had land magik inside of her, she hoped she knew about her honesty streak. Her sworn word remained the only thing of value she could offer at the moment.

Lorelei pulled a medium-sized shell from her waistband and used the jagged edge of the shell to cut her finger. She squeezed out a few drops of blood onto the shell. Then she pulled out another shell and fitted it together with the first, bit it with her sharp incisors to make a tight cup and sealed them closed with her saliva.

When convinced they would hold it together, she pulled some of the seaweed from the side of the rock, tied it around the shells, and crafted a necklace.

Finally, she handed it to Alyssa. "Done," she announced.

Alyssa thought the whole transaction had taken place about as smoothly as barter for corn back home.

She placed the necklace over her head and around her neck, commenting on Lorelei's shells, when something about the jack-in-the-box on the bank of the other shore caught her eye.

The tin toy box shook violently.

Chapter Nine

Half Moon Manor

The shaking also drew the attention of the siren. She splashed into the water and swam toward the cave, disappearing beneath her own wake.

Alyssa swam hard to the other side, picked up the box and stared at it. "Pappy Oh?" she whispered.

She didn't know if it could be him or if, once again, something magikal and strange would unfold.

The crank turned and the clown's head popped out. "Howdy do!"

"Pappy!" Alyssa cried, hugging the box to her. "Oh, Pappy! I thought you were dead again."

"Whatever made you think that?" he asked.

"You haven't been talking to me," Alyssa said in a rush. "I thought you had faded away."

"Oh," he said. "I guess I did sort of give you a scare, huh? Well, I'm fine. Just took a break."

"A break? What do you mean a break?"

"Well, Lys," he said slowly. "There's something I didn't tell you about this box."

She stared at the clown's face. "What? Oh dear. What have you not told me?"

"See, it's like this… I ain't exactly stuck in this contraption. I can get out."

"You can do what?" She shook the box. "Get out? You mean out here where I sit?"

"Yep. Kind of like that."

"Well, where have you been then? You let me roam around at night with critters like dryads and sirens all over the place. What if something had happened to me?"

"Now, Lys, I would've known if something bad were happening. You're sort of like my maker, you see? When something happens to you, I feel it. Besides, you're smarter than you know. I took off on a jaunt to see the road up Needlemount way. Then I skipped to the house to check on your Granny."

"You did?" Alyssa's eyes widened. "How in Daegries did you do that?"

"Guess I'm mostly spirit these days. With a wish, I can fly like the wind to wherever I want to go."

"How is Granny Gert? Is she okay? What did she say?"

"Well, see, that's the problem with my being out of this tin thing. I can't talk or make sense to nobody. I can observe stuff. That's about all I can do."

"What did you see?"

"It ain't nothing good, Lys. Which is why I came back. I think I better pack myself up and head on to the house, permanent-like. Your granny ain't faring so well with old King Hubert. He's even bossier than me, and you know, that's saying something."

"But Pappy," Alyssa said. "I need you here. I mean, if you can't do anything or talk to anybody outside of the box, then what good could you do at home?"

"Oh, trust me. I can create a ruckus to keep that old gryphon busy. I'll make myself heard if I have to body-snatch to do it. But don't you fret none. I ain't leaving you until we get this spell finished. You're gonna need it."

"Why? What did you see at Needlemount?"

"Didn't exactly make it all the way there," he replied. "The weather is strange all the way up through the northern country. That's another reason we need to get your spell finished, set you on the road, and let me get on back to my lore books. I gotta find out what's really going on."

Frustrated, she said, "I got the blood from Lorelei, the siren." Then, she held up the necklace in front of the clown's face. "She swam off when you rattled the box. I had about decided to use it to bring you back from the dead again. Mighty glad that ain't needed now."

The clown's face turned toward the siren's rock. "Ain't that a blootie bloo? I wanted to meet her too. Let's get a move on then, gal. Sands in the hourglass are still slipping through. That old gryphon won't take to waiting none too kindly."

Alyssa wanted to say goodbye to the siren and thank her, but she didn't know who else might be listening, so she whispered instead.

"Goodbye, Lorelei. I'll be back with your tooth."

She waited for a moment to see if the siren returned or answered.

"What tooth?" Pappy asked.

When Lorelei never came back, Alyssa gathered up Pappy in his box, and they set out. She ignored Pappy's question, thinking to fill him in later.

When they returned to Half Moon Manor, the guard at the bridge lifted his eyebrows as they approached. The sun loitered in the sky, not quite overhead. Sir Hyer, the night watchman, had been relieved. Alyssa waved hello and hurried past. They had important business to do and the less talk the less delay.

Alyssa left word for Lord Bryon that she spent a sleepless night and would not be available until afternoon. After a quick, dream-wracked sleep, where she drank tea with dryads and sang bawdy songs with sirens, she woke ready to get the spell going.

Inside their room, Pappy Oh gave her the list of what ingredients he needed. "I found the incantation I want to use while down at the house. Your granny kept watching the pages of the book when I turned them. She thought some mysterious breeze floated through. I tell you, Lys, I'm going to have some fun when I get home."

"What do we need, Pappy?" She yawned and stretched.

"Don't take much. Run and ask that young fellow what owns this place to get you a pure metal bowl, some clear spring-fed well water, a little cinnamon, and a dab of salt. And this is important now— we might need something green, too. Maybe a frog? Or some ferns? Something green... I got it. How about grass? Get the newest, greenest you can find. I know it'll be a little hard with the drought and all, but maybe some that grows around that moat. And dig it deep enough to get the mud, too."

Alyssa nodded and crossed the room to exit. She'd studied enough spells out of his collection of books to know that when a sorcerer had a spell in mind, it usually depended on timing. Better not linger around asking questions. As she descended the stone stairs, she could hear Pappy Oh muttering to himself.

"Green as the grass that grows on the slopes in the summertime." Then, his giggling followed her down the stairs.

"Why do you need such as this?" Lord Bryon asked. He led them toward the kitchens, a squat wooden structure apart from the main manor.

"Pappy's plan." She didn't elaborate, certain that Pappy Oh would be unhappy if she should give away too much of his business, but also because she really didn't know how to answer. Thankfully, Lord Bryon didn't need explanation.

"His plan, eh? I'm glad about that. Well done, I say. It would please my lord father to know a plan on his behalf is at hand. Soon we shall be away, and I will be after his murderer. That cowardly snake."

Alyssa assumed he meant Madrid, the evil lord of Needlemount. She shivered. *Am I really going to go nose-to-nose with a murderer?* Her journey was taking her to places quite unthought of.

Bryon waved to a man dressed in a leather jerkin and leggings to come forward as they neared the kitchens.

"Crone, find these items, moat grass and mud. Bring it all to me here." Without a word, the man jogged off to do his bidding.

They continued into the kitchen where pleasing aromas of stews and baked bread filled their noses. Lord Bryon handed her a dull golden bowl from the kitchen's collection.

"It's pure, I can assure you," Bryon commented. "My father… I… own nothing less."

Finding a pure metal bowl turned out to be less troublesome than convincing the cook to let go of some of his salt, a prized spice in the manor kitchen.

"The salt, she is a mighty warrior at table," the cook argued at the request, waving his hands around for emphasis. He had an accent that lilted musically to Alyssa's ear. "If I should run out, how can I make the bread?"

Lord Bryon said roughly, "You will hand it over to Lady Alyssa at once. Be quick, time is of the essence."

The cook inclined his balding head. "As you say, m' lord." He took a wooden salt cellar from the shelf over his fire pit and gave it to Alyssa, refusing to meet her gaze.

"And the cinnamon," Lord Bryon reminded him. The cook added a long strip of spice to the nearby mortar and pestle and ground it into a powder. He poured it into the bowl Alyssa held out.

She curtsied. "I'll only use a little salt, I'm sure. And bring it right back, quick as a squirrel. Thank you so much."

The cook turned his broad body away and attended to his kneading, saying no more. As she followed Lord Bryon into the yard, she remembered learning bread-making from Granny. Alyssa missed the therapeutic release of pent-up tension by kneading dough, and punching it down made her feel powerful. She could imagine the cook doing so and felt a twinge of envy.

The manor's well stood in the center of the yard, tended by a youth with golden yellow hair that touched his collar. Alyssa had also seen him exercising horses from her window in the solar, her bedroom for now.

He drew up the wooden bucket at Lord Bryon's curt hand motion. He offered his lord a long drink from a ladle. They silently waited under the warm, late afternoon sun for Crone to return.

In a little while, he galloped up on a small pony carrying a bucket. He handed the wooden container and its contents to the stable boy while he dismounted. Then Crone took it from him and presented it to Lord Bryon. Next, he pulled from his pony's saddle a water skin with a thong around its opening. He filled it with water and placed it in Alyssa's hands.

"I'll thank you to return my water skin to me once you've finished with it. My mother made it for me, and it's one of the few things I've got left."

She nodded and thanked him.

Crone backed away and gave over the reins of his horse to the stable boy. Lord Bryon handed the bowl to Crone and instructed him to take it to where Alyssa and Pappy were staying. She hoped Pappy was sleeping. Crone would be terrified if he were to hear a disembodied voice.

Alyssa waited on Lord Bryon for instructions on what to do next.

"I will see this," he nodded to the bucket, "to your room myself. Your grandfather will consent for me to take part in this, surely?"

Alyssa dropped her gaze to the browning grass beneath her feet. "I suppose so. Do we have another option?"

Lord Bryon smiled and said, "No, you do not."

Alyssa fell into step beside him as they made for the room where Pappy waited. She took over the lead once they were on the stairs, the bladder hanging heavily from her hands.

When they arrived, Pappy Oh sat silently as all normal jack-in-the-boxes usually did. Alyssa breathed a sigh of relief. The bowl sat on a side table.

The box shook to life once they settled the items on the floor before him.

"Lys?"

"Yes, Pappy. We're back." She turned the crank and the clown's head popped out. "Were you quiet while I was gone?"

He made a yawning noise. "Yep, had me a good nap."

"Here 'tis," Lord Bryon said, waving at the odd collection. "What's the plan, Sir Oh?"

"I ain't exactly a sir, Sir," Pappy replied. "I'm just a mage. A simple man, no need for formality. And as to the plan... an illumination spell is in order, I believe."

"We need to do this in a room where your daddy kept the scarf. The remains of its powers might still linger there."

Bryon lowered his gaze and pulled on the ends of his mustache. "That's impossible."

Alyssa frowned. "Why?"

"Why? My lady mother is there. She is quite an invalid these days. Prostrate with grief, of course, but she has been ill in bed for a long while." His face blanched.

"You're afraid for her?"

He nodded, brow furrowed. "Something happened to her after she went riding one day. She became weak and developed strange dreams. With my father gone, she's only grown worse."

"Have you sought the *physishone*?" Pappy Oh asked. "There may be sorcery at work here. First your mother, then your father."

Alyssa thought hard about an entry in the book on follygrass and its magikal properties. "Did she ever wear the scarf? Maybe its powers affected her in a bad way. I recall reading that folks with weak immunities can be struck ill by the powers of some herbs and such. Maybe it made her sick? Could we help her out with a poultice or something, Pappy?"

Bryon cleared his throat. "I have misspoken. He kept the scarf on himself except for when he gave it to my mother. I saw her with the scarf wrapped around her shoulders when she trotted out of the stable that night, certain my father made her wear it for safety since it had been reported to protect its bearer. I thought little of it until now."

"You couldn't know. So, Lys is right. We'll have to find something to winnow out the worming in of the powers, although too much magik in a body might be too much. Couldn't be any worse than the lingering effects she might be suffering from, though." Pappy muttered more to himself than to them. "We'll cross that river when we get to the bridge," he finished. "Lead on, your lordship. We need to get started."

Bryon picked up the bucket with one hand and the bladder with the other. Alyssa lifted Pappy Oh and the bowl of spices. Bryon led them out of the solar and down a corridor until they reached a stone stairway going up. He turned and began the climb, finally stopping at a landing to catch his breath.

"This is the tower. She's in the last room on the left."

Alyssa took the lead, lifting the heavy door latch, and pushing open the wooden door. It creaked on its metal hinges, warning the inhabitant lying within that someone approached.

"My son?" a weak voice called out.

Alyssa set Pappy Oh down on a cushioned chair beside the door. Bryon settled the bucket on the long table in the center of the massive room. Alyssa set the bladder down beside the table leg.

"Yes, Mother, I've come. I've brought a visitor as well. She's Lady Alyssa, a healer from the Grasslands. A… *physishone*. Will you permit her to examine you?" Bryon shot Alyssa a grimace, apologizing for the lie. "She thinks she may have a cure."

The pale white hand fluttered weakly, and they crossed over to the giant bed. The woman who greeted them had once been beautiful. Her long auburn hair fanned out around her head, streaked now with gray.

She offered a garnet ring and Bryon kissed it, smiling weakly at her.

"You smell like dank water and dirt," the woman whispered, her nose wrinkling.

Bryon glanced down at his water-spotted clothing and frowned. "I've been doing some work around the moat. My apologies for not smelling… pleasant."

She smiled at him.

Alyssa moved closer beside Bryon and, when the woman saw her, she flapped her hands and developed an inability to remain still.

"You!" she whispered. "You've tainted my dreams for untold nights. What is it you would have of me? Bryon, why have you brought this creature here?"

"Your dreams?" Bryon asked, incredulous. "I've never met this girl before, and you most certainly haven't. How could your dreams be touched with visions of her?"

"She motions me to follow. We float over fen and field, yet we never arrive. I've woken so many days to confusion and exhaustion. What does it mean, Lady Alyssa?" Her voice weakened into a plea. "Please tell me." Her head moved side-to-side slowly, eyes downcast.

Conflicted, Alyssa spoke with the only reply she could think of. "Dreams are powerful reminders of things past, and sometimes things to come. If your dreams told you to follow me, then you should probably listen to what I tell you. I'm not here to hurt, but to heal. Your dream is like a kind of letter, written to get your journey to health started. There's power in the world we don't know about, including ones attached to names. You just used mine, which is a little bit of power you now have over me. In order to be equal, can I have yours?"

She nodded. "Pianna. I am Lady Pianna."

"Lady Pianna, you're sick because of the scarf your husband put on you the day you went out for a ride. Do you remember?"

She stared for a moment before nodding.

"Good. Knowing why we get sick is the first step to our healing. What we're going to do is make up a tea to put in you. It should pull impurities out of your body. Once that's done, you'll be able to get around again." Alyssa considered what else could be going on with the woman. "Only thing is, you're what we call magik-excessive. That means overloaded, like a basket too full of apples. You can't be around much stuff that has been attached to magik right now. And maybe forever. I think it might be a good idea for you to be in a room where there are some windows and light. Sit in the sun a few hours a day, rest, and eat good food."

To Bryon, she added, "Put her in the room we had. It's perfect. I'll build up the fire in here too."

Bryon listened intently and nodded. "I'll take her there straight away."

Alyssa pulled him away from the bed and out into the corridor. "Get her out of this room as soon as possible. The scarf's power may still be in there, leeching, bleeding her a little each day. I'll send the ingredients list down to the kitchen to get a tea worked up. You may find she doesn't need it, though, once she's moved away from this room."

"Aren't you worried that the scarf's power might make you ill as well?" Bryon asked.

Alyssa smiled and said, "Nope. I've been around magik too much. If I were magik-excessive, I'd know about it by now." She thought about that as they moved away from the room. Since her failure at reanimating Pappy all the way back to human, she might even be magik-deficient.

Later, once Pianna had been moved, and her tea had been ordered, and the items for the spell had been sorted out, Pappy Oh instructed them on the next steps.

"Lay out the grass and mud that's sitting on that table over there, Lys. Put it on a piece of clean linen. Mix up the spices in that water real good, and make sure the salt is in it. And light a few candles; it's too dark in here. Need lots of light to make sure it's working."

Alyssa hurried to do as he said but realized she did not have any linen. "Um… linen?" she asked Bryon.

Bryon inclined his head and strode out of the room. In a few moments he came back, a white linen pillow sham in his hands.

"My lady mother's maids will be annoyed about missing linens, but do carry on," he told her, handing the sham over.

"Thank you." Alyssa spread it flat and dumped the contents of the blanket onto it. Grass and mud seeped out over the white sham turning it into a dirty mess. Alyssa ensured the refuse had not flowed over the edges of the table, and she poured the water from the bladder into the golden bowl with the cinnamon and salt.

"What now?" she asked Pappy.

"First, let me tell you a few things all apprentices should know. One, clear your head of all nonsense. You got to focus on what you're doing. Second, we need something of value to set the deal which is why we needed that siren's blood. You got that, right?"

Ashamed for forgetting the valuable shell's content, she exclaimed, "Oh! I forgot about the blood!"

She struggled to pull the shell necklace on its dried seaweed chain over her head. "Drat this thing!"

Pappy interrupted. "Leave it where it is. It should be on or in the magik-user's body."

Alyssa gasped at his words. She did not want to consider what might transpire to permit siren's blood to be *in her body*.

"Lord Bryon, you going to be a part of this?" Pappy asked.

Bryon nodded, then cleared his throat and said, "Aye. Indeed."

Pappy Oh took in a breath. "All right then. You'll need something valuable too. Uh, preferably something green."

The young Lord hurried out of the room.

Pappy spoke to Alyssa with a bit of trepidation in his voice. "Listen to me now, Lys. You've studied spells for a bit now, and I'm confident you can do this. But if you have any doubts, any whatsoever, you need to speak up."

She thought for a moment. "No. I think I can do it. I've helped Granny make poultices and healing balms, and I've read heaps. Didn't worry about the spell to bring you back. Only how foolish I felt when it failed. I'm… I can do this, I think."

"Get your mind set."

"Yes, sir, Pappy." She closed her eyes and took a deep breath.

Lord Bryon returned carrying a brooch. "It's my mother's. It is made from emeralds dug from the depths of the mountains. Quite old and valuable."

"Well, good then. Now you pin that on your person and keep it pinned on. This might take all the powers we can get. Emeralds might be a mighty talisman at that. Good choice, little lord."

"What else, Pappy?"

"Take some of the grass and wrap it over your hands and then plaster it into place with the mud. Make it like your hands don't even exist. Become the grass and mud."

She started out well enough, making the first hand into a glove of grass and mud. But when she took on the task of covering the other hand, she struggled.

"Oh, permit me," Bryon said, realizing at last that she could not do it alone. "Sir… Pappy— will it matter if my hands work with hers to accomplish this?"

"Are you going on this little adventure, Sonny?"

"Aye, I plan to."

"Then get in there and get dirty."

Bryon hid a small smile and covered the other one of Alyssa's hands with the concoction. She kept them both over the already sodden pillow sham.

Finally, with a nod from Bryon, she said, "We're ready, I think."

"Put that bowl with the water and spices in it under her hands."

Lord Bryon complied.

"Let me say a few words. Just a tiny incantation, but an effective one. When I say green, stick your hands in that bowl and move them around, mixing up all the ingredients from off your hands into the water and spice."

"Yes, Pappy."

"Moss of fountain, fern of field, mud of river, bowl of gild, salt to bind, spice to yield, power now, her own to wield."

The water in the bowl shimmered slightly with a green tinge.

"Um, Pappy…"

"Not to drink, but to find, objects hidden, left behind. Without eyes, sight unseen, turn them all a violent green!"

At the word green, Alyssa shoved her sloppy hands into the bowl and sloshed them around. The water became a brilliant green that glowed out into the room, stealing the light from the candles.

"Now we own the brightest light, any object can be found, go wherever you need to be, your magik light is hereby bound."

And with that, the goopy mess in the bowl rose into a peak and soaked into Alyssa's hands and arms until nothing remained in the bowl except a tiny green droplet.

Bryon touched it with the tip of his finger, and it soaked into his skin.

"Pappy," Alyssa said. "I think it's done. The ingredients went into my hands and up my arms. I don't see anything now though. What happened?"

"It's inside you, Lys. When you need to find anything, all you have to do is call it forward."

Bryon stared at his fingertip which now showed nothing but flesh. "How does one do such a thing?"

"Well, that ain't hard, young fellow. You just tell it to show itself."

Bryon lifted the fingertip to inspect closer. "Show yourself," he muttered.

Nothing happened.

"Come out," he said, more determined.

Nothing.

"Sir, I believe you've left something out of this work. I've seen nothing happen."

"You seeking something?" Pappy asked.

Bryon stared at the toy box. "No, not yet."

"Well, it's a findin' bindin'. You use it to find stuff with. When you seek something, it'll be there when you need it."

Alyssa smiled at Bryon. "My grandfather is a powerful mage. He's never failed at any spell."

"I'll trust that when I see it." Lord Bryon sighed and turned to leave. "I'll send my squire's mother around to cleanse this room. We've left a mess on that sham."

"No!" Pappy and Alyssa said at the same time.

"We don't want anyone to know anything about this. We'll have to burn the sham, and Lys can return the rest of the stuff to the kitchen later. Better off if no one knows our business," Pappy Oh finished.

"I see," Bryon said hesitantly. "Perhaps I can find a sham to replace this one." He turned to leave and added over his shoulder, "We'll leave at first light. Better prepare." He gave her a curt nod and departed.

Alyssa tidied up the mess in the room. She threw the sham in the fireplace and saw it burn down until it no longer threatened to send flying embers out. She trudged down to the well and washed the bowl clean, then returned it and the spices to the kitchen. The cook's face broke into a grin when she handed him the salt cellar.

"I do not think you used any!"

"Not much. But… would you please remember to send a bit of tea leaves and a little ginger root, grated, and steeped in water, for the Lady Pianna's breakfast tomorrow? She's going to feel much better for having it."

He nodded, a slight frown between his brows. She patted his thick arm and departed his domain. Alyssa peeked in on Lady Pianna before retiring. She would like to place a soothing balm on the sick woman to speed up the healing process, but she didn't want to upset her again with her presence. Especially now that night had fallen.

She returned to the room where her grandfather in his toy box waited.

While Pappy chattered on about going to find the castle and where the scarf might be now, she gathered her belongings and refilled the pack to accommodate the jack-in-the-box.

Finally, she flopped down on the bed in exhaustion. Pappy, in a conversational mood, made her decide to bring up a few things on her mind. Since he had said he might leave her, it might be a good idea to get a few answers now.

"Pappy, what happened when I cast the spell to bring you back? You didn't make it all the way, and now that you've given me the illumination spell, I'm worried I might not get that to work right either. Do you think I might be a little magik-deficient? I need to know, because if so, I ought to try to remedy that."

A few moments of silence ensued. She rose from the bed and moved closer to the box. "Did you hear my question?"

The box rattled so violently, it nearly tipped over, startling her. The clown's head came up and Pappy cleared his throat.

"Now Lys, you're my grandbaby. You got my bloodline in you through your daddy. You can't start giving up on magik at one little hiccup. Magik doesn't always work like we want it to. Sometimes the spell has a humorous side. It's sitting out there laughing at us while we thrash around like a fish on a line. You'll get the knack of it, eventually. You're still a little bit of a *betwixt* and a few months from a *between,* so there're loads of time to learn magik."

She crossed her arms at his description of her age. Young ones were *betots*, her age group were called *betwixts*, and those over sixteen years were called *betweens*. She felt sure she was as ready as a *between* for the next step in life. Maybe more, after all she had been through.

She sniffed and let out a large sigh. "I'm better trained as a mage than most *betweens*, Pappy. You've been teaching me, and I've been reading up and doing stuff on my own. Why, those girls in their freshly pressed pinafores at the schoolhouse don't have a clue how to set a spell based on moon phases. I'll bet they can't even make moon water."

"Muddenfolk are not magik-users like that, Lys. You've been plenty busy studying, for sure. But how's that been working out for you?" he asked, voice brusque. "You already know that it's never-ending if a mage wants to be better than best."

She wished she could see his face and know if he teased her. His voice gave nothing away.

"So, do you even know what happened during the reanimation?" she asked. "There had to be a bit I left out, or something that got added in."

"I don't. I confess it, pure as snow."

"So, I *could* be magik-deficient, is what you're saying?"

He evaded the question. "Only time will tell, girl. Only time will tell."

"But you said I am half of your bloodline and you—"

"Magik ain't a specific science sometimes, Lys."

"Pappy, time ain't our friend right now. Hubert is expecting me back with the scarf. If I'm doomed to fail before I even get started, well, I think I need to know. Might as well go on back to Mudden without the scarf. Let the chips fall where they fly from, that being the case. You know how magik-deficiency can make a lot of things go wrong—Pappy?"

The box top closed quietly, and the voice within fell silent.

Chapter Ten

Travel – Kinsmen

Alyssa had everything ready to go even before the first rays of sun struck the manor and seeped into the windows. Pappy Oh had not popped out yet. Conjures often took the starch out of a body, and he would be more easily a victim of that.

The journey ahead, as unknown as it could be, might be even more taxing on the partially reanimated. Alyssa couldn't even think about herself. She knew her own unpreparedness, regardless as to the encouraging words from dryad and siren alike.

She wore the cloak from Rylee over her tunic and new pants, a gift from Lady Pianna to ward off the cold on the snowy trek north. Pianna had also given her soft gloves made from a lamb, but she didn't wear them, preferring instead to have her hands free to wield her weapon if needed.

The rising sun burned golden over the far hills, and she stood in amazement at how the daylight overtook the shadows. The topmost turret of Needlemount Castle stood serene and innocent in the haze of the distant horizon. But Alyssa's heart hardened at the treachery she felt certain lived within its walls.

She fingered the shell necklace, still around her neck. The spell now cast left no need for a sirens' blood. She grasped the dry, fragile seaweed rope and, with a slight tug, it came away in her hands. She shoved it down in her pack. What could she do with it now?

Maybe when she came this way again on her travels home, she would return it to the siren along with the Yeti tooth, if lucky enough to find one.

Not like finding anything would be hard now.

It bothered her that the "findin bindin," as Pappy Oh had called it, lived *inside* of her. At first, she had felt nothing after the spell finished. Now, hours later, she felt a fluttering in her arms and hands every so often that made her imagine the magik of the spell moving around like a living thing. Far more than a simple binding spell, for sure.

Just waiting to be released.

She paced, picked up an item on a small table, replaced it, walked to her pile of belongings, touched the rough wood of her bow. Her mind raced to everything that had gone before and what remained ahead. What good could a spell inside of her be if she had no courage to call it forth?

Alyssa steered her mind away from such thoughts. She would not be afraid. To go on, this adventure meant a fight for her family, much like Lord Bryon planned to do for his. He sought answers and revenge. She sought only the Gryphon King's scarf, but for that, she would accept whatever came.

All done for Granny Gert.

Her grandmother needed her to find the scarf. Pappy Oh needed her, too. She stood a bit straighter and mentally shouldered her burden.

At some point, she needed to uncover that special magik she held inside according to the dryad and siren. She sure hoped that would enable her to bring Pappy all the way back. Having him halfway here wearied her.

She sighed. And according to the recent revelations from Rylee and Lorelei, she would be in even higher demand in days to come. Someone else's needs might be put in front of hers or her family's. Although she couldn't imagine who else could be more important.

When a light tap sounded on the door of the tower room, she hefted her pack, slung her bow and arrow quiver over her shoulder, picked up the jack-in-the-box, and opened the door.

The squire stood there, his brow furrowed in question. She replied with a quick nod. He took her pack, and they descended the stairs and made for the courtyard where the horses stamped impatiently. Their nostrils spewed warm moist steam as they snorted in excitement.

"Hail, my lady. We ride to the foothills," Bryon said, a broad smile on his face. He leaned forward, planting his fist on his thigh and pulled a bundle from his pack. "My apologies for a lack of amenities such as breakfast. You did say our journey was urgent in time. Cook has sent you something to keep the hunger pangs away."

He waited for his squire to help Alyssa with the mount she was riding before handing the bundle to her. He wore a heavy tunic under his woolen cloak, and his pants were tucked into thick boots.

She looked down at her own footwear, scuffed and worn, but otherwise usable in the mountains, she hoped.

Lord Bryon's sleeve bore a dancing lion embroidered in gold thread, and a matching steep mountain glittered on his breast.

She smiled at the sight of him. He wore the part of a lord today. "Yes, time is not on my side. How far is it?" she asked.

"Only a few hours' ride. After that," he said, "we will be on foot as the terrain is too treacherous for the horses."

She permitted the squire to hold Pappy Oh for her while she climbed up on the wooden box used to aid short riders onto their mounts. The bow and quiver of arrows slipped down, hampering her attempt. She finally slung her bow over one shoulder and the quiver of arrows over the other, mentally commanding them to stay put.

"I hope you've trained as well with that bow and arrow as I have with a sword," Bryon commented as he observed her struggle.

"I've shot a few rabbits," she told him, trying to appear brave and formidable as she accepted her pack and threw it on her back, arms thrust through the slings. The squire took the bundle from his lord and stepped onto the box. He juggled the bundle and the toy box for a moment, then he tucked Pappy Oh into her pack, and handed her the bundle. It smelled wonderful. She felt her insides rumble as she peered at the chunk of cheese wrapped in a cloth.

"For the journey, my lady," he told her. "Cook sends gratitude for your care of Lady Pianna. He said to bid you well on your trip and to let you know he will ensure she gets the tea she needs on the morrow as well."

Alyssa thanked him and handed it back to be placed in the pack. She was amazed that the cook had been so happy about her attending Bryon's mother. And she celebrated the food as she had not even thought of breakfast.

Bryon grunted his thanks and nodded for the young man who worked with the horses to give her the reins. "Let us be off."

The squire implored him, releasing the reins, "My lord, please let me accompany you. You should not be without someone in attendance. I know that your liegemen are in turmoil now, many on a journey with the lords of neighboring lands, but…"

Bryon smiled down at him. "Axel, that is unnecessary. I will manage splendidly with the company at hand. You can prepare for my men to join me as soon as they may. Clean the manor rooms, prepare leatherworks, and contact my man, Lando, at the market. Have him take all my swords and metalworks into the manor. Preparations should be made at home as well as abroad."

"This sounds like plans for battle, my lord."

"If the aristocrats find the rumor of portals are true, we may face addressing many of them. If things go badly at Needlemount, there may well be war. Be of good cheer and mark my words."

The squire nodded and stepped away to let them pass.

The manor road wound long and unyielding through silent woods and often open plains. For the first hour, they didn't talk. She viewed the landscape as it went from rolling hills with a clear path to flatlands with more rocks strewn about in the way of the travelers.

Lord Bryon rode alongside, silently. He had thoughts to work out that concerned only him. Even Pappy did not make an appearance to interrupt.

In a wider stretch of the path, Alyssa reached down to pat her horse's neck and coo to him. Not a bad day to ride, she decided. And even though her unused riding muscles would ache tonight, she felt hopeful for the journey.

"You sit a horse well, my dear," Lord Bryon said, breaking his silence.

"Funny you should say that. I haven't ever ridden one before."

His mouth gaped open. "Never?"

She shook her head. "I rode an old decrepit mule once. He plodded from the barn to the water barrel. That's it."

This struck Bryon as funny, and he chuckled. "Sitting a horse is not so hard as long as he behaves. But should he startle at something—a bee, a flower, what have you—and bolt, well, that's the tale that tells all."

Two things happened at that exact time. One, music rolled from the tin box, and it shifted in her pack, causing the clown's head to pop up; and two, the horse did not like it.

The poor frightened beast shot down the path like someone had set his tail ablaze, nearly throwing Alyssa off. She clutched the reins and a handful of his mane, yelling for him to stop.

"Whoa! Whoa!" Lord Bryon shouted as he galloped to her side. He grabbed the reins and pulled back hard. The horse reared and stopped.

"As I was saying," he said, fighting laughter.

Alyssa, scared witless, could not speak. Pappy Oh had no such problem.

"Don't you love it when the air blows through your hair? That really felt good." At these words, Bryon guffawed and encouraged his horse to move ahead to hide his laughter while Alyssa readjusted her bow and arrows and tried to appear unaffected.

Another hour passed without incident. Alyssa asked Bryon about news of the aristocrats who had been out digging into the mysterious portal legend. He shrugged and admitted that no one had returned yet, and Sir Galdron, who had met them on their return to Half Moon Manor, had received no word from anyone, either.

"A portal opening up now would be a troubling incident," Bryon added. "If it is even true."

"How so?" Were the Putrid Plants on her family's farm hiding such as that?

"Madrid and Ragon would love nothing more than to have a means to move armed assassins around Daegries. A portal, or several, would suit their purposes well."

"Aren't portals protected by… something?"

"Or someone. Legends say portals can be protected from entry by anything from man-eating tigers to—"

"Man-eating plants," she finished for him.

"Yes, those too."

She fell silent. The ugly plants on the farm had popped up from nowhere. She still had no confidence that her spell had not created them. The spell had misfired, certainly. And if a portal opened in the southern parts of the Daegries, and she assumed it had, hence the Putrid Plants' eruption. It could certainly have openings in other places as well.

And if the Needlemount men had realized such an occurrence in the northern section of the realm and utilized it for their own purposes, well, she would have to deal with that sooner rather than later.

"I am uncertain as to what you know about some of the Greater Daegries history," Bryon said. "But during the olden days, the Dark Master discovered powerful magik. He learned lore by stealing into the wizards' keep to read books kept there. Now these were no simple primer books, mind you. It called forth a terrible time of destruction as he tried to wield spells from such."

"Aye, 'twas," Pappy said. "History bears out your words."

Then Pappy spent a good deal of time telling Lord Bryon about his travels as a young man and how the tall tales had popped up surrounding the Dark Master. The concept of a great evil overlord only made Alyssa yawn. She cared little for faery tales. In her opinion, they were meant to keep children from getting lost and from creating a ruckus.

When hunger pangs forced a brief rest, Alyssa slid from her horse, settled her pack on the ground and pinched off bites of cheese. She absorbed the conversation between her two companions. The lord's knowledge of magik seemed limited. It sounded like his region had no magik-users at all, and Pappy filled him in on Mudden and how the folks there had chosen using tools over using magik.

"They sound very advanced to me," Bryon said.

"Maybe, maybe not. They quit using their talents," Pappy replied. "Magik has its place if you can control it. You ain't going to get no man to fall in love with you by hoeing the garden. A love spell though? Works every time."

Alyssa tuned out. No wonder Pappy didn't want to encourage her to go to a Mudden school. Too little applied magik learning for him. As she bit into a nice-sized chunk of cheese, the young Lord laughed at something Pappy Oh had been saying.

"Ain't that true, Lys?" Pappy Oh asked.

"Sorry, Pappy," she replied. "My mind's wandered. What did you say?"

"I said your Granny Gert is one of the most famous gardeners in our region, until she got tangled up in that crazy vine that she grew somehow."

Alyssa nodded. "That's true. She can make anything grow. You should see her sunflower patch. And it wasn't only one vine, I think more like a bunch of them."

"What exactly is the vine of which you speak?" Lord Bryon asked.

"She called them portal protectors."

Bryon stared at his hands for a moment before asking, "*Putridaconacus*?"

"Something like that," Alyssa nodded. "But when you say it, it doesn't sound pronounced correctly." Her Granny Gert had a deep Lesser Daegries accent and when she said it, there seemed to be more music to the name. "I think it's longer or something."

Bryon mused silently, then said, "You may be familiar with the official name of it, as a gardener would call it by such. Those plants do not grow here anymore. Eradicated, killed off, as being too dangerous for the populace. I would imagine that your grandmother has had a terrible time healing from such."

"Well, she would have, except for those gryphon tears," Alyssa reminded him.

"Ah yes," he said. "Right." He cleaned up his food leftovers and helped Alyssa to remount. "Remind me to tell you a tale about those vines you were speaking about."

About then Pappy Oh decided to let Alyssa know his intention to leave. "Well, Lys, I guess I'm going to run on back home now."

She stared at the box. "Now?"

He answered, "Yep. I reckon I've come as far as I can come with you for now. I need to take care of a few things back at home, and well, we'll see how it goes."

"Pappy Oh, I need you. I can't do this by myself," Alyssa pleaded.

"Yes, you can, girl. You don't know it yet, but you're about the bravest Mudder in all the Daegries. You got a lot of your mama in you, Lys. She had a different sort of world about her. Made her pretty strong and powerful too."

"I wish she were here. She wouldn't be leaving me alone facing who knows what." She crossed her arms and thrust her lip out.

He fell silent for a moment, then said, "Okay, okay. I'll ride along at least as far as the climb up to Needlemount. But then you're on your own. You've got to face your own music. I can't do nothing stuck like this, anyway. Not without help. You have all your faculties and use of your limbs. You really don't need me."

She uncrossed her arms as hope sprang free. "Oh, thank you, thank you!"

Pappy grew silent again as they rode toward the foothills of the Heightlands, which were now bathed in sunlight. Alyssa enjoyed the sun on her back and even became a little sleepy. Pappy's sudden shout brought her back to alertness.

"Oho! What is that?" he asked, the clown's face turned outward.

She shaded her eyes with her hand and followed the direction his painted-on face pointed in. Dust rose from a group of travelers coming straight at them.

"Friend or foe?" she asked Bryon, who pulled his horse to a stop.

"This close to the foothills, I suspect foe. Prepare to get your arrows dirty."

She shoved the clown's head into the jack-in-the-box and told her grandfather to be quiet. She slid an arrow out of her quiver with a quiet swish and held it at the ready to nock it. She squinted at the riders. If assaulted in the open with no help or cover, the three of them wouldn't last long. Her mouth went dry.

"Hold. Hold," Bryon advised, holding his hand up to halt any activity on her behalf. He brandished his sword, breath held. The sun glinted off the blade. Then, with a great exhale, he cursed and expertly slid his sword back into its scabbard.

"What's happening?" Alyssa asked, but he had kicked his horse's sides and took off directly toward the scraggly group.

"Must be friends," Alyssa told Pappy, resettling her bow, and placing the arrow back in its holder. "He's clasping hands with them."

She clucked to the horse and eased the reins gently to encourage it to walk forward. On her approach, she could see the gathering contained four men and Bryon.

The men wore torn, blood-stained, clothing, and they carried wounds from head to toe. The ragged banner they carried declared their allegiance to the young Lord, as it bore the same lion and mountain that Bryon wore on his tunic.

"We thought you were captured, or even worse, dead!" Bryon kept saying over and over to the group. He finally focused on a young man standing with a hand on either hip who moved forward to speak.

"We pretended to be dead," he replied, grinning through the mud and muck on his face. "Then, when the demons who killed Lord Pryon took their leave, we found these ponies grazing, asked if we could have at least one from the owner. When he realized whose banner we carried, he gave each of us one of the finest."

"A kindness done out of revenge for the taxes exacted by Madrid. They were very angry, by the by. So, we followed the trail of the marauders until the snow caught us, then started back for home. All this time dodging through backwaters and bracken to stay as hidden as possible. Took us much longer than we intended."

Bryon smiled. "I will reward this horse owner handsomely, then. May the Gods smile on him!"

"What news, my lord?" the fellow asked.

"Strange news I bring. But first, I would have the entire tale of how my father perished and by whose hands," Lord Bryon replied, waving for Alyssa to come closer.

"Deveon, this is Lady Alyssa, a healer from the Lesser Daegries. She is riding with me to parlay with Madrid or his mouthpiece, whoever is chosen. I am calling for an account of my father's spilled blood. My lady, this is Deveon Purhart, my father's former banner man, and members of his company."

Deveon stepped close to Alyssa's steed and grinned up at her. Stained teeth showed beneath his overgrown mustache, and he appeared more bedraggled than the others.

"Pleased to meet you," she told him.

"At your service, my lady. Any friend of Lord Bryon's is a friend to me," he said.

He turned back to Lord Bryon. "I would beg my lord not to go on this fool's journey. Some evil magik beguiles Madrid and his men. Mindless souls who plunged into the snow. You would be safer with a better plan. A parlay and accounting of your father's blood will return little."

"I have another plan, only… it remains difficult to explain." He peered at the mountains in the distance.

Alyssa frowned, listening. A journey for fools after all? Would she end up embroiled in a war with the Needlemount men? How would such a thing delay her return? King Hubert had given her a timeframe. What if she didn't make it?

As she pondered this, Bryon turned to her. "My lady, could you tend their hurts? We would all be in your debt."

Alyssa nodded mutely, feeling as if she were standing on a hill with the wind slamming into her. She didn't know whether she should be afraid or calm. Focusing on tending wounds created a good diversion at any rate.

While she pretended to retrieve something from her bag, she privately conferred with Pappy on the best way to go about this task.

"I ain't got anything in the way of herbs," she said, tapping the toy box.

Thankfully, Pappy had stayed on alert. "Try it without. See what happens."

"But how, Pap? Granny always handled the hands-on stuff. I made poultices and picked herbs. I don't even know what she did in all that."

"She put her hands over a sickness or a hurt to see if it acted deadly, didn't she?" he asked.

Alyssa thought about this. Her grandmother always put her hands on someone she performed a healing for and determined what they needed from that.

"Yes, yes, she did."

"Try it," he replied. "You got a lot of her in you too, gal."

She took a deep breath and turned to the man, Deveon, hoping against hope that her ability to heal would prove stronger than her ability to perform a necromancy spell.

He gave her a knife that was passable for clean, and the white linen sheet that they carried as a flag of surrender.

"That will have to suffice for bandages," he said.

"Sit over there," she instructed, pointing at a large alder tree with low-hanging branches, but enough room underneath for someone to sit or lie down.

He complied, and she followed him over. Once comfortably seated, she put her hands over various cuts and bruises and closed her eyes, waiting for she knew not what. Then, for no reason, she felt a cleansing come over her, refreshing as a spring shower.

She placed her hands over an area of his leg without a visible wound. Nothing happened. She moved back to a deep slash on his side, and the warm feeling returned. She continued this way until certain of what she needed to happen.

Her heart swelled with pride and filled with assurance as the redness of the wounds faded when she laid hands over them and focused all her attention on healing.

None of his wounds were life-endangering, but upon a closer visual inspection, she could see that some of the deeper cuts would have to be treated by someone with a needle and thread. She bandaged those carefully.

Finally, she sat back and said, "I have healed the ones I can, but there are a few that will need to be stitched up. A *physishone* can tend to those."

She smiled at Deveon and helped him to his feet. They walked back to where the others waited.

"Lord Bryon, I think Deveon has some wounds that someone with tinctures and salves should tend. I suggested a *physishone*."

Deveon bowed respectfully, and she stepped away to move toward the others. They dismounted, as she explained that she came to help them.

As she watched them pass her on their way to the alder tree, she heard Lord Bryon, still atop his horse, speak to Deveon. "Why is it I failed to find you when my father and his page's bodies were discovered? I assumed the marauders took you. The news that the attackers were madmen surprises me not, knowing how skilled you all are. Your tale and my father's loss bow one to the other."

"This is a long tale, my lord, and a strange one. I would not have you hear it from atop your horse." He waved for Bryon to dismount.

Soon they were all gathered, either on the grassy mound near the alder tree, or directly beneath it. The alder stood alone amid dried and dying grasses. Unhealthy, but faring better than others Alyssa had seen. She stared at it curiously, thinking about dryads.

The company replenished themselves with water from bladders that Bryon had carried.

Alyssa went from man to man, treating injuries as she was able. None so much as winced in pain, which made her heart soar with confidence. When she finished, Alyssa wiped her hands on the cleanest part of a dirty rag Deveon had pulled from his pack, and she strode to her horse to whisper to Pappy Oh to listen but not say anything.

She left him in the pack on her horse and returned to the gathered troop. Taking a seat, she glanced Pappy Oh's way and saw the clown's head peeking out. Whether he had escaped the box and floated freely amongst them, she did not know.

When Deveon and his two comrades could once again speak about their ordeal, they told how Lord Pryon had fallen at the evil hands of Ragon, the son of the self-proclaimed king, Madrid.

"He assaulted with no warning, no cause," Deveon said. "Our Lord Pryon had been attending his page in the night and raised the alarm for us, else we all would have perished. In truth, his shouts were the only way we knew to pull our swords."

"Ragon, son of Madrid, King of Needlemount, or so he says, according to the… b-butcher," snarled a gray-haired man with a bloody bandage around his hand. "I slew as many of his henchmen as I could."

"King!" Bryon spat. "He needs to inform our true king. How can he even say such?"

"Rumor has it he thinks our good King Thalon cannot dethrone him. If he even has a throne," said the third member of the party, who had limped to where he sat. "Madrid has lost his mind, quite literally. And as all know, Ragon has always been a cruel and devious duke, leaving nothing but mayhem in his path."

Bryon took a moment to either collect his thoughts, snuff out his anger, or refocus on the story that had been told.

Finally, he asked the question burning in her mind. "What has happened to my father's sash? He wore it on his person at all times, but it did not appear anywhere near when I found his… remains."

Deveon replied. "Lord Pryon may have draped it around his page. Did you find it with him?"

Bryon shook his head. "No. Nowhere near. I do not think my father ever let it remain far from his side, if not on him. Why would he put it on Lure?"

"Perhaps for the lad's protection? Your lord father said the boy seemed too vulnerable to be in our company."

The company all murmured that they had heard him say as much.

The gray-haired man cleared his throat. "My lord, Lure had become ill. Lord Pryon thought it a fever, and in his great wisdom, decided the boy would be warmer with the scarf."

"How do you know this?"

"I tried to treat the fever with my own herbs," the man replied, shrugging. "I have failed him. And you. The sachet that I carried got lost in the battle."

"You are not to blame for the attack or loss of life," Deveon told him. "Nor losing a sachet of herbs. Do not blame yourself."

The other man clapped him on the shoulder. "That's true. We were taken by surprise. Not of our doing."

"None could have known the scarf had been magiked," Bryon said. "It may well have drawn Ragon to it. I asked to make sure no one had taken it off my lord father."

"Magiked?" the men asked in unison, before turning as one to gaze upon Bryon's face. When he glanced at Alyssa, their gazes followed.

All three heads nodded as understanding finally dawned.

"A sorceress?" Deveon asked Alyssa, voice hushed. She shook her head. More a simple healer to her mind, but she let the unanswered question of her identity remain open.

The third man, much younger than the other two in Alyssa's estimation, spoke in a hoarse voice, "No matter, we offer our swords in this endeavor to exact revenge for this crime. You have our condolences, my lord. For myself, I would single-handedly hunt down this murdering band and kill them all. Your lord father honored Lure by giving up the scarf, magiked or not."

"Yes," Deveon agreed. "Truly meant for no harm."

Alyssa's gaze went to the jack-in-the-box. Pappy Oh had it bouncing up and down. She shook her head to dissuade him. He did not need to make an appearance now!

She inserted her (and possibly Pappy Oh's) opinion hoping to hold him off. "I think the scarf decided it needed to change owners. It's had a brief history of doing that."

"But why would it choose the page?" Deveon asked. "Why not one of us?"

"Did this battle event fall during a full moon?"

They all consulted each other.

Deveon finally nodded. "Yes. Lord Pryon wanted to use the night's light to guide our travel. Time of the round face, easy enough to do."

"Most magik peaks during that time. Might pick the nearest person to it to switch bearers. Did Lure travel close to his lord?" Alyssa asked to any who might answer.

"Aye. His youngest son," Bryon replied. "And my brother."

Alyssa couldn't stop the gasp that escaped her mouth. "Oh!"

Bryon gazed at the trees around them. "Yes, I stayed home to tend my sick lady mother. Father feared that, as his successor, I should not go on the journey. Someone might slay me if the battle went ill."

She didn't respond, letting all of those gathered to make their own conclusions. Obviously, the scarf had chosen down the bloodline to the closest kin present.

"The magik may have caused our late lord to give it to Lure, but no such thing sent it with the likes of Ragon the Red, surely? What sort of magik could a scarf wield that would make its bearer give it away?" the gray-haired man asked.

Alyssa did not answer. They had taken the scarf from a corpse. Magik had not been needed.

"We still don't know everything but can only assume a potent kind of magik. A kind that would protect its bearer in ways unseen until it saw fit to make a move to another bearer," Bryon told them. "Which is why, with the scarf in the hands of Madrid and his ill-begotten son, we are all in dire danger."

Alyssa heard the springs of the jack-in-the-box snap as it landed on the ground beside the horse. The top popped open and the clown's face, with Pappy Oh's eyes, gleamed in the sunlight. Then the head went down, the lid shut tight, and it rolled toward them with an unsteady wobble because of the square corners.

Horrified, Alyssa ogled its eventual arrival by her side.

"Ho! What is this?" exclaimed the younger man when the box stopped between Alyssa and himself. He clambered to his feet in fear.

The eerie music crackled. The top popped open.

"Well, isn't this an amusing gatherment?" Pappy Oh said.

The men scattered, rushing for swords still in scabbards on their mounts.

Alyssa snatched up the toy box and clutched it to her chest. "Sirs, before you pounce on it, let me explain."

The men warily eyed her and her enchanted box, but Lord Bryon waved for them to return to their places.

"Alas, Deveon, 'Tis an even stranger tale the lady brings. Give her leave to tell it."

Seeing their liege unmoved stayed their hands. They gazed at Alyssa, expectant eyes as one. Then they returned to their seats. All carried swords with them, just in case.

"Meet Pappy Oh," she said. "My grandfather. A... a... mage from our place in Mudden," she said, swallowing hard. But not much of a mage in the situation they currently found themselves. She considered it a better outcome if those gathered here didn't know too much too quickly.

"He's inside this toy box because of a misplaced spell. We have reasons to parlay with Madrid, or Ragon, or whoever else will talk. It's important that we do this as soon as possible, as our farm and my dear grandmother's life swings in the balance." She ducked her head and moved closer to Lord Bryon. The misplaced spell comment had made her feel self-conscious again.

"Before you judge Lady Alyssa too harshly," Bryon added, "know that she has provided healing relief to my lady mother. I have given her leave to pursue this fool's journey, as some call it. Yes, and I will accompany her as well. Our paths are the same, though the purposes are different."

The gray-haired man knelt and laid his sword before Bryon and Alyssa. "I am Cerius, and I will pledge my sword to this cause, if my liege will consent."

Lord Bryon stood and nodded. "Yes, I consent. I permit it for you all; if you would care to join, your sword is welcome."

The younger man who called himself Fletch joined Cerius in pledging. Bryon stopped Deveon before he could voice his allegiance to the cause.

"Your wounds need more than we can do here. I would prefer you return to Half Moon and find a *physishone*. And stay with my lady mother, Sir Deveon. It will give me great peace to know you are there."

Deveon frowned at this. "But my lord, you need every man of us. Believe me. These madmen will be more than this few can withstand."

"I know this, and more. Which is why I will send you back to Half Moon. I left a puzzlement at home. See Sir Galdron and my liegemen to find out what has happened. I trust you to stand in my stead on that. And to warn my men, set a watch over my lady mother, and return to us here. Bring others if there is anyone left to send."

Alyssa listened to this conversation and struggled to contain Pappy Oh who jumped up and down in the toy box.

"Sir, Lord Bryon, we don't have time to wait for your men to come join us here," she reminded him. "The gryphon still waits on us. We have to hurry."

"Aye, I recall this unreasonable demand," Bryon replied. "Deveon, send your fastest rider to find this usurper and have him stand down."

Alyssa did not want to be impudent, but the young lord didn't understand the situation. "Lord Bryon, you can't do that, sir. That old gryphon sits at my farm, waiting for trouble. He's likely been reinforced by now, even though the place is hidden from anyone stumbling up on it by those plants we were discussing awhile back.

"Also, your folk couldn't get to it for a massive hedge maze that blocks the other way in. I would be the only one who could lead them through, and of course, I need to be here. Or there," she added thoughtfully, staring at the mountains.

Bryon paced around the mound where they gathered. "Did he say why quickness is so important?"

Pappy Oh spoke, finally. "Good Lord Bryon, that creature said the magik of the scarf would create some changes during the full moon which happened mere weeks from the conversation. We're sitting here now, losing time."

"Changes, eh? Like, changing bearers?" Bryon asked, brightening. "As before?"

Alyssa shrugged. She thought that to be true but didn't want to be proven wrong.

"Yes. Indeed." Bryon smiled to himself. And with that, he waved to the men to remount and spoke quietly to Deveon before remounting himself.

Alyssa carried Pappy Oh to the horse and paused. She had no box to step up on. How would she get onto her horse now? She hunted for a stump or stone, but none were close by.

Fletch, watching her, came to lend her a hand. She sat Pappy Oh in his toy box on the ground by the horse. Fletch showed her how to step into his cupped hands and when she did, he lifted her up and she threw one leg over.

He waited until she situated herself, the pack, and her weapons before handing her the box. She tucked it into her pack, letting the clown's head stay out in the open. Then Fletch gathered his own reins and remounted, situating his longsword in a scabbard over his back.

The party said their goodbyes to Deveon, who turned his horse's head toward Half Moon Manor.

The first tugs of panic constricted Alyssa's breathing at what lay before them. Pappy Oh must have understood because he hummed a merry tune.

About an hour into their journey, the foothills rose all around them. Alyssa likened them to mountains since she'd never seen such tall land masses before.

"Are these the mountains?" she asked Fletch who rode behind her.

He laughed. "No, my lady. These are but foothills."

She squinted and tried to see beyond where they currently were. Needlemount sat hidden from view. When the clouds parted for a moment, she realized the massive difference between a mountain and a foothill.

"We're going up there?" she marveled.

Fletch muttered a soft yes, and when she glanced at him, she saw a frown between his eyes. He had faced the Needlemount men before. His face went from placid to tense, and his jaw clenched. She turned away, giving him his moment of fear or anger.

The snow glistened on the heights ahead. It ran down the mountainside like icing on a cake. The drought had only brushed the area where they currently traveled. The land, still lush beneath the wintry cover, would soon display the effects of the colder air in the countryside. She could see dead grass, even now, brown and withered. Whether from snow or drought she could not say.

Pappy Oh had long ago given up his cheery tune and spent his time peering around, black painted eyes shining in the midday sun.

"Lys, did you know there are critters up in these hills? I've seen their eyes and heard them calling," he told her.

"When?" she asked, turning around to follow his gaze.

"All the way back to when we went through that tangled mess of briars."

She thought to when they had spent a few moments fighting their way through some dense brush at the beginning of the slope upwards.

"What were they, these critters?" she asked, pretending to be unconcerned. "And why haven't you said anything before now?"

"Dunno, biding my time. Might have been Yetas. Didn't see their faces or nothing. Used to be Yetas hereabouts."

Fletch had been bringing up the rear of the company. He overheard this conversation and moved up to walk his horse beside Alyssa's.

"Did he say he saw a Yeti?"

She frowned at Fletch before nodding slightly. Pappy called them Yetas in his far south accent, but he meant Yetis. The old mage's observations could scare everyone, and they didn't need that. She didn't doubt he had witnessed eyes. What or who remained to be seen.

Fletch's gaze traveled to the higher ground. Alyssa suspected that after an ambush from Ragon, the men would be noticeably nervous, expecting it again. Might Madrid himself be on the prowl?

"I should tell Lord Bryon since he has the front."

Alyssa gripped her bow. "If you must, sir."

Fletch rode ahead of the company and spoke to Bryon.

Then things happened lightning fast.

The air moved overhead. A branch rained down on Alyssa. And then another. She gazed overhead as the crashing above her began.

The landslide caused Alyssa to shout and jerk her horse to the inside of the trail. The horse, spooked at the falling boulder, nearly sent them back down the path they had been climbing. Thankfully, no one close enough to her suffered a crushing blow. The massive rock continued its downward trek, splintering trees and snapping brush. The boulder made a terrible cracking noise as it fell, like giant bones being broken.

She cupped a hand over her eyes, peering into the area overhead, trying to make out a shape, but nothing showed. Then, ever so slightly, a blur of white moved against the snow. The creature's black eyes peered down, and enormous arms hefted another large rock over its head.

This one, smaller than the first, came somersaulting down the mountain, bringing grass, brush, and other smaller rocks along with it.

Terrified, Alyssa slapped the reins and pounded her heels into her horse's side to make him run.

"Avalanche!" Lord Bryon shouted as the debris fell. The men forced their horses to rush forward, and Alyssa stayed quick on their heels. The group nestled safely under a projection of rock, away from the dangerous drop off.

The crashes thundered against a sheer rock face. When the shower of rocks ceased, Alyssa slid from the horse, gently set the backpack with Pappy Oh in it on the ground and grabbed her bow and arrows.

"My lady!" Bryon called out in fear. But Alyssa had already reached the area of trail where the rocks had tumbled down. She climbed atop one, anger seething through her, and peered at the upper level of the mountain where the creatures worked to find more rocks.

She nocked an arrow in her bow and sighted it, but before she could release it, Fletch touched at her elbow.

"My lady, that would waste a good arrow." He put out a hand to stop her.

She lowered her bow slightly. "They tried to kill us, sir."

"True," he continued. "But the distance is too great. I fear it would only fall harmlessly to a lower level or get mangled in a tree or bush. The creatures are too far away for an arrow to be effective."

Staring into the whiteness above, she could tell his words rang true. The arrow would never make it so far.

"So, what should we do then?" she asked, climbing from the tumbled stone. Her anger melted beneath Fletch's better judgment. She'd let her temper override her intelligence.

He pointed at the group huddled beneath the rock overhang. "Let's defer to good Lord Bryon, shall we?"

Alyssa nodded, and they strode to where she had left her pack. She slung it over one shoulder and followed Fletch to where the others stood discussing their dilemma.

She heard Pappy mutter something about cooler heads prevailing.

"We cannot continue up the mountain without knowing how to dispense with those creatures," Bryon said.

"One of us could scout ahead and see," Cerius suggested.

"We could also go back to Half Moon and reorganize, gather men and supplies," Fletch added.

Alyssa pulled the toy box out of her pack and now stood holding Pappy Oh. Lord Bryon asked, "What say you, my lady?"

She stared at her feet and then paced with the toy box in her arms as her grandfather spoke to her in low tones from inside. Finally, she stopped, and the clown's head popped out.

"Pappy has something he wants to say," she said, waving to the clown's head.

"Good Lord Bryon," Pappy Oh said. "Them critters are protecting their property same as anyone would do. I get their plan: attack anyone who threatens you. If we could convince them we ain't aiming to do no harm, they might be of help to us. Can't imagine anyone better than one of them Yetas to show us how to get up this here mountain to that castle."

Bryon considered his words. "Do you think you could convince them?"

The clown's face stared at Alyssa. Then, Pappy Oh said two words. "Stone magik."

Alyssa asked. "Are you sure, Pappy? You ain't never had no occasion to do any of that before. Do you even remember such a thing as a stone spell?"

The clown in its box bounced up and down.

She shrugged and turned to Lord Bryon. "We will go as scouts and barter with the Yetis. Pappy Oh has something he thinks he can do to convince them to let us through."

Bryon turned to the others. "What say you?"

The others nodded, especially Fletch.

"I would feel better if they had someone else with them," he said. "She's just a girl, and it's just a…" She followed his thought process.

"Not so, Sir Fletch," said Alyssa. "Pappy Oh is way more powerful than you know. Y'all let us get this done. We won't fail."

Bryon raised an eyebrow. "Well, we won't be able to travel any farther on horseback as the trail turns more treacherous as we ascend. The snow alone will prohibit their abilities. I say we try to form some sort of shelter and get the animals headed down the way we came. They will either find their way to Half Moon or a sunny meadow. Either way, they will be safer away from us."

This declaration met with some disgruntled muttering but ultimately became the best decision they could find, as the lord knew of what he spoke.

Alyssa reminded them all about the limiting deadline and how they had only a few hours of daylight left in the current day.

"The meeting ahead might cause such a time delay that we might miss it altogether," she said aloud.

"We shall move ahead with the utmost speed, my lady. Let us take care of the current crisis now," Bryon answered, handing her a blanket from his horse's pack.

Alyssa propped her bow, quiver, and her backpack against the niche cut out under the ledge. She pulled her gloves out and then refolded the blanket into a smaller bundle. She placed it in the pack, took food and a water bladder from Lord Bryon to add to her pack, and situated the rest of her belongings around it. She tugged her pack onto her back, slung her quiver and bow across her shoulders, and picked Pappy Oh up to carry him in her arms.

Alyssa gazed upwards as they set out, scanning the mountains. Her tunic and breeches were thick and the additional layer the cloak offered would go far towards fighting the elements ahead.

The climb would not be nearly as bad on the current trail, but the icy wind higher up would be a different matter. She shivered and wished for the cozy warmth of Solly the Sun on her shoulders and a day free of worry.

Lord Bryon pulled out a heavy robe that he draped around her shoulders and pinned it with a clasp at the neck, covering her pack and gear. He pulled the hood of the cloak up over her head.

He examined her gloves and boots and tsked. "You are not prepared for the weather. Snow can be as bad as rain. This is all I can offer."

She gratefully accepted the robe that was much too long and large. She pulled it tight around her, pulled the hem up, and tied it around her middle effectively covering her belongings.

The men clapped her on the shoulder and patted Pappy Oh's clown's head and wished them safe passage. She could feel the fear from them as they touched her, but their faces remained stony.

It would be a great thing if their blessings would manifest into some sort of luck, Alyssa thought to herself. But then again, Pappy Oh had always been the lucky one, their current situation excluded. If his power as a mage and all-around lucky man in general could not exact a change in their current situation, then nothing could.

They trudged up the hill before them. Pappy Oh's clown's face looked out from the jack-in-the-box as Alyssa carried him in front of her. If they were to encounter something on the trail, Pappy would need to see it as soon as it approached.

To bide the time as they strode toward the white giants, Alyssa asked Pappy to educate her about Yetis.

"Well, they been up in the mountains all over this land for as long as I can remember," he told her. "My grandpappy and pappy and I seen 'em when I was a boy. Don't know why they settled this way, but they did."

"Did y'all ever fight them?" Her voice sounded scared, even to her.

"Fight Yetas? Nope. Them Yetas was friendly to humans back in the day. See, they are about as big as a house. Bears and she-cats and even an ogre or two wouldn't mess with them. And because of that, they kept the trade routes cleared out so goods could travel over the mountains. That's how our family learned about them. I came through here a time or two, as I might have mentioned."

"You did? Our family traded over the mountains?" she asked, somewhat amazed. "I always thought we were farmers."

"Well, it's like this, Lys. Every farmer must have a marketplace to get his goods to. Elsewise what's the point, aside from feeding your young'uns?"

She nodded, deep in thought.

"Yes, sir. Our people always needed tools and skins and such and the mountain folk needed some dried foods," he recollected.

Maybe Pappy knows more than he lets on sometimes.

At any rate, she hoped he could handle Yetis. Her ignorance about the mountain giants caused fear to ignite inside of her with every step they made, closer and closer to the lair.

Finally, they rounded a craggy outcropping, snow blowing into their faces until they could barely make out the trail. Alyssa asked Pappy if he could stay outside, or if he would rather duck inside the pack.

"Naw, I'm all good, Lys. Them Yetas' houses can't be far now. They sure have some wicked weather to deal with, though."

Alyssa hated having to fight her way forward with every step in the blizzard, but it might keep them hidden from the creatures on the mountain for a while longer.

The leaden-gray sky lightened, and the snowflakes thinned. The hills all seemed the same to her.

"Don't know where we are," she told him.

"Oh, don't you worry none about that. I have a bead on them Yetas," he said.

"Really? Where are they? I don't see anything." She stopped to look around.

Pappy let out a yodel and the hill that rose right over them moved.

"Grinkle?" the Yeti replied.

At least, that is what Alyssa thought it uttered.

"Grumkin," Pappy Oh replied.

"Do dohs dere?" The Yeti moved to the side of the cliff and stared down at them. His massive eyebrows like snowbanks rose and then crashed together on his face. He had thick tree-trunk arms and long fingers that ended in black claws. With those, he could slice open an ice-covered boulder and serve pieces of it.

"It's Alyssa and Pappy Oh, mages from Mudden, a realm on the far side of the Meadowlands. We want to parlay," she said. Her voice wavered, and she hated how fear poured from every inch of her being. She hoped the creature wouldn't seize upon it.

"Doh?" it said, blinking its long eyelashes in confusion.

"Des, Doh!" Pappy yelled in agitation. "Take us to your leader at once."

The Yeti understood the inflection in his voice, even if he did not comprehend the words.

The creature reached his long fingers down and scooped them right up, closing his clawed fist around them securely. It whisked them through the chilled air and into the darkness of a nearby cave.

Alyssa's fears solidified like the ice all around them. They were now captives of the massive beings, and their companions would never find them in the cavernous interior of the mountains.

Chapter Eleven

The Yetis

Pappy whispered to Alyssa. "They can be a little slow to latch on, but don't worry about it. They'll come through in the end. Don't struggle none. He doesn't know his own strength."

The giant stopped only long enough to light a torch from the dying embers of a fire inside the cave, and then he took great long strides toward a destination unknown to Alyssa.

Along the way, water splashed in the darkness. The sounds of guttural laughter boomed out. Alyssa felt unseen presences and it made her shiver.

Whoever's splattering water sounds happy, she thought.

The cave's air, although chilly, did not freeze Alyssa's body the way the air in the mountain pass had done. The massive area had a warmth to it, like the very land around it was heated from an internal source. The warmth made Alyssa relax a bit. She tried to make sense of their direction, but they turned and twisted through rock-hewn corridors until she felt she would go mad. Then they passed beneath bowers of rock and minerals. The stalactite formations looked to Alyssa like giant teeth.

Great. Now I'm thinking how one of the snowmen has to give up a tooth for the siren.

She shuddered, shrinking down to stay away from their jagged sharpness, although the Yeti simply ducked and plunged ahead, ever mindful of the human parcels being carried.

Eventually, the Yeti strode through an archway into a room where the ceiling simply vanished overhead. Alyssa didn't want to speculate how deep into the mountain they had traveled. She once again thought of Lord Bryon and the others. Hopelessness filled her.

Under a shaft of light that bounced from somewhere far above onto crystallized ice formations, an even bigger Yeti sat on a seat carved out of the minerals. He held a giant ice scepter in one hand, and at his feet lay a Yeti, moaning and writhing.

"Greekie, dondo do dis. De day dis dam oh," said the creature who held Alyssa and the box. He placed his torch in a stone sconce on the wall and set them down in front of the seated Yeti, off to the side of the injured one.

"Do dondo dis? Dis don de oh." The leader crossed his arms and pinioned them with a fierce stare. His eyes were dangerously black like he had no soul inside. Alyssa shivered.

Pappy Oh, ever vigilant, bounced up and down in his box. "Why, the very idea!"

Alyssa shushed him. "What's the matter? Don't make anybody mad, Pappy."

"He told this here Yeta that I ain't Pappy Oh. Oh, yes I am!" The clown's face glowed at his exclamation. "*Dis Dere De Oh*!"

Alyssa flinched.

The leader sat up straight and pointed at the toy box. "Grinkle?"

"Gringle," Pappy Oh said in his normal voice. "Grumkin."

At these words, the Yeti rolling around in pain ceased movement and struggled to sit up. "Do day dis dood de."

"Des day," Pappy Oh said. "I am the Oh."

Alyssa grew tired of the back and forth and the strange language. "Pappy, what are they saying? What are *you* saying?"

He muttered in a low voice. "They don't believe it's me. I'm arguing that it most assuredly is me."

"Well, can you conjure up some more light? That might help, seeing as how it's nearly as dark as a bat's wing in here."

"Don't say bat in a cave, Lys; that might get something started. I can get some light though, sure enough." The clown's head dropped deep into the box and the lid shut with a snap.

"Hurry. They're staring at me, and I feel like I'm their next meal."

Pappy fell silent. She hoped he had left the box to find light. There were many others who stepped forward from places along the cave walls. Yetis edged closer, and she stood all alone with the tin box for protection.

Terrified, without even her grandfather's voice to guide her now, Alyssa trembled from head to toe. She turned side to side, keeping the nearest ones in check.

Before the closest creature could reach her, pale yellow light radiated along the edges of the ceiling and floated down. The gossamer wings of light fluttered all around them. It turned out to be millions of fireflies, happily flitting about.

The box shook, the crank turned, and the clown's face hosting Pappy Oh popped out. "Dow, doet do dee?"

The Yetis all oohed when the lighted ones appeared, and when Pappy Oh spoke, they peered at him closely.

"Do. Doet dow deem undant?" the leader asked.

"They finally get that I'm enchanted. Finally," Pappy Oh told Alyssa.

"Des. Die dam," he said to the leader. "You can talk at me normal, Fred."

The leader tilted his head. "Who wit you, Oh?"

"This here's my granddaughter, Alyssa. She's my apprentice, so to speak. But she oversees me right now whilst I'm in this toy box. Say, Fred, what's wrong with Ted?"

The Yeti, who sat holding his head and moaning, lay back and grunted.

"Backfired rock," explained Fred.

"Anything broken?" asked Pappy.

"Don't know."

"Alyssa has some skills at healing. Want her to look him over?"

"If Oh will allow. Many thanks. Yetis no see Mudden folk long time. What happened?"

"Mean times up here parts," Pappy told him while Alyssa set her pack aside with her bow and arrows and then carried him over to the injured Yeti. "Folks down our way quit using these trails to tote goods across. Marauders got too bad. Started selling more to locals and started raising crops based on actual need instead of greed. Staying alive made more sense than making money, I guess."

"Harrumph. Yas. Old man and son on mountaintop like ice," Fred said. "Slippery, and not useful." He motioned to the Yetis standing around. "Go. Find things to break!"

This sent them all scurrying out of the throne room in different directions. All had doorways leading to unknown areas, Alyssa noted.

"Why don't y'all go up there to Needlemount and tend to them rascals proper?" Pappy asked. "You got the numbers for it."

"Many Yetis tricked and enslaved. Men put head on spike if resist."

Pappy did not reply at first, as he instructed Alyssa to run her hands over the injured Yeti as she had done for their companions. She complied, holding her hands slightly above Ted, testing with her senses for any broken bones in his hands, feet, ribs, or neck. Her hands hovered over his head. He had a bruise and swelling.

She nodded to Pappy. "Ain't nothing broke. It's just a busted head on old Ted here."

Fred, the Yeti leader, clapped his hands and instructed Dred, who had carried Alyssa and Pappy into the cave, to act.

"Busted head, good news. Dred take Ted home. Make sure wife puts snow-pad on hurt." Then he turned back to his guests. "Fred, pay Oh for attention to Ted."

Pappy whispered to Alyssa. "Now it's going to get good."

She took him in the toy box over to Fred.

Pappy's head bobbed. "You don't owe me nothing. I'm passing through here with some menfolk down around Half Moon Manor. We all have some business with the folk up on that mountaintop."

Fred leaned back against his rock seat. "Careful, Oh. Listen to Fred. No good can come."

Pappy continued. "We're here to make sure Yetas ain't got a problem with us crossing their land. See, either Dred or some Yeta from his tribe tossed a big old rock down on us as we approached. Twice, to be honest. Wanted to come up here and see if things are still all right with us. 'Cause I can for certain make them all right if I need to."

"Oh, no. Ted." He closed his eyes, frustrated. "Ted, mistake. He toss rocks. How got banged on head," Fred pointed to his temple with a long claw. "Too much power, rock go down wrong way. Backfire."

Alyssa, tired from travel and grumpy at the way the conversation had gone, asked Fred, "Sir, can we go through or not? We have urgent business with the Needlemounters. The Yetis of the Heightlands can rest assured we have no ill will. We need to travel… quick-like."

The Yeti leader combed his claws through his tangled beard. "Apprentice hasty like spring rain. Bad manners speak first."

About that time, Dred returned. Fred waved to him. "Come over, Dred."

The younger Yeti drew near and grunted.

"Send kin word along north road. These and those can pass. No Yeti, no stop. Understand?"

Dred nodded and shuffled his feet which were the size of the fat part of Pappy's canoe paddles, as close as Alyssa could measure. "Uh," he said.

"Take Shred. Go then. Let know."

Dred clambered out.

"There," Fred announced. "That make snowball roll. Want to know why Oh in box, but not now. Apprentice made clear. No time."

Pappy bounced in his box. "Yeah, Fred. It's a dirty business, but we gotta go get 'er done. You know, if your people are up there held in that castle, you have a stake in this here adventure, too."

Fred sat forward, attentive.

Pappy continued. "Yes! See, we're going to do battle royal with that Madrid and his son, Ragon. Magik has done entered their world and mixed stuff up. Look at how Yetas have been captured in ways they never would have before!"

At this, Fred grasped a pike beside his throne and shook it. "Master and son tie to Dark Master?"

"Don't rightly know. The Dark Master was either killed or exiled from the underground." He paused, adding fire to Fred's excitement. "I'm here to tell you Fred, there's lots of *mystikal* energy in numbers. Put your fellas in with the Half Moon men, and us, well… that force might be unbeatable."

"Yetis like fight. Good for heart," Fred said, nodding.

"I'd like to have some of your fellas go with us up to Needlemount. They can fight against the north men and set the captives free. Let 'em loose on their attackers. See what happens."

Fred's hairy face fell. "Yetis suffer many losses from evil. No more Yeti die. Need keep silent like sudden snow."

"Bah," Pappy Oh said, voice rising. "Ain't gonna let nobody get dead, Fred. I might be stuck off in this tin can, but I can still conjure. And my gal here, she's going to be fully in control of her own powers and mine. Unbeatable, I'm telling you."

Alyssa, seeing that Pappy Oh might be onto something with getting the Yetis to aid them, added, "Yes, sir. The sheer bulk and size of your tribesmen along with our friends and all the skill combined…" She nodded to Fred. "Like Pappy says, unbeatable."

Fred rubbed his black claws across his furry belly. Finally, he said, "Give collateral. Will pay for Yeti if don't come back."

Alyssa stifled a grin.

"Well, I can offer y'all some stone magik, Fred. It's the least I could do. The leader we travel with is named Lord Bryon. You might know him. He's the son of that Lord Pryon what got himself killed up here somewhere. His kin and bannermen will swear loyalty to protect your folk. They'll all be safe as a baby Yeta in its ice-pen."

Fred's massive eyebrows clamped together like snow clouds at the mention of Lord Pryon. "My tribe slip down mountain when hear war cries. Hurt Yeti ears," he explained and put his hand over one ear. "Tribe too late. Tribe follow murderers back up trail. Many brothers taken then. Many lost."

He paused and fell into a thoughtful stupor of sorts. Pappy Oh bounced up and down in his box. Precious time passed.

"Stir him up," Pappy whispered to Alyssa.

"Mr. Fred," she whispered. "We need to act one way or another. Night's falling."

He raised his eyes and focused on them like he'd never seen them before. Eventually, he spoke again.

"Stone magik help Yeti. Yes?"

Pappy Oh answered, "Right as rain. Would help y'all to make fire a lot easier and melt up the snow for other uses. Breaks rock too. Make it easier for old Ted to throw them without them falling back on him."

Fred's black eyebrows lifted all the way into his furry forehead. "Why didn't Oh say so? Yetis accept terms."

"Good news," Pappy Oh quipped. "I'll go out and get right on that. Please have your tribe knead up some Yeta food for our group. We're as hungry as horses after field-plowing Friday."

Fred agreed to his suggestion and blew a horn to bring help. The young Yetis who responded were dispatched for baked bread, and others went down the trail to collect Lord Bryon and company.

"Bryon, son of Pryon, needs apology from Fred," the leader said, crossing his arms. "No saving. Very bad."

Pappy Oh did not reply. Alyssa gathered her pack and weapons and soon they were back outside, thanks to a lift from a young Yeti going that way. The heavy snowfall had ceased, and the Yetis had begun to clear a path with their feet.

"Now listen, Lys," Pappy said. "It ain't real magik we're doing here. It's something they have had for a long time but they're simple folk and don't know much about natural resources or what to do with them. So, we're going to help them."

"Make it snappy, Pappy. Time's a' burning," she answered, heart pounding at the disappearing daylight.

"You're right. Okay, now shoot your arrow into that crack over there," Pappy instructed. "That big one. Don't worry, it won't get lost."

Alyssa did as he directed and saw the arrow fly exactly where she placed it. Black dust fell from the crack. And in a moment, the arrow fell out, too.

"Did you see it?" Laughter tinted Pappy's voice.

"I saw my arrow come out of the crack all on its own. What's that about?" She frowned. *What did he mean?*

"It's Danglebugs, Lys, *Danglebugs*! Found out about them as a boy when my pappy brought me through here. They live in the cracks of that age-old rock face in these here mountains. Anything that gets into their homes, they just push it right back out again."

She stared at the clown's face in amazement.

"Now, go scoop up that dust and put it in a pile. That's the stuff they need to use for fire. The rock crunching stuff will be a little different."

Alyssa scrunched up her face in doubt.

"Go on, you'll see," he told her.

She collected her arrow and scraped the dust from the crack into a small pile. She stared into the crack, hoping to see a Danglebug, but none showed.

When she returned to the tin box, she still had some dust on her hands.

"What do I do now?" she asked Pappy, showing him the residue. "It's sort of sticky and doesn't want to come off." She held her hands up to her nose to smell them but found no odor.

"Wipe 'em clean on one of them snowy mounds over there. I've got a little magik I can create from here."

She stalked to the trail and wiped her hands in the snow on the nearest boulder. She kept wiping until they were clean.

Pappy yelled out, "Fire!"

And the snow turned a strange red hue. She glanced again at her hands, fearing that she had bled somewhere. But, as she stood there watching, the snow developed long red streaks like bloody cracks and melted away. She took several steps back in fear.

"Rock!" Pappy yelled again.

A large-sized boulder glowed beneath the red snow. In seconds, the red had saturated the boulder, and it burst into pebbles.

"How in Daegries…?" She marveled at the fantastic occurrence.

She hurried back to Pappy to relate to him what happened.

"Even Yetas can say words like fire and rock and make things happen," he explained. "Stone magik is really easy up here."

"That's plain old weird and wonderful all at the same time!" she exclaimed. "They won't have to work hard to break up the boulders at all. But how does it make fire?"

"The friction from the rocks breaking creates sparks. They have to get it sparking good, feed it some tinder, and fire pits will appear. They can do it inside too. Most of this mountain is made of rock and stone. Burns a long time, too, if they keep it fed."

"Wow. That dust can break rocks and make fire. Pretty neat, Pappy. But what if they get the dust in their fur? Won't they end up breaking rocks they are holding?" Her wonder turned into horror. "What if it sparks and they catch on fire?"

Pappy Oh replied, "Good question, Lys. I reckon the spell ain't foolproof, is it? But then again, building a fire with sticks and tinder ain't either. A body has to be careful with anything like this. Yetas have plenty of experience with making fire and burning things. We're getting them started with a means to an end. They'll have to use it and figure out what else they need to do."

She recalled how she'd melted a pair of slippers by propping her feet too close to the fire in the fireplace back home. "Okay, guess you got me there."

She picked up the box and stared at the clown's face. "How did you learn about this so-called stone magik? Heck, how'd you learn magik at all?"

"Books, Lys. You got to read a lot to know elemental magik's power in the world. Even the stuff that ain't magik at all needs thinking about. You gotta learn what you can harness and what you leave alone. You gotta try stuff, girl. Don't be scared to try your hand. The worst that can happen is it doesn't come along like you planned. Nothing is set in stone. You can always try again," he answered. "As for stone magik, Danglebugs make an enzyme when making their holes that melts rock. It heats up, the colder it gets. Discovered the bugs, as I mentioned, as a lad. Found out about the enzyme way later."

She placed him on the ground and wiped her arrow on some snow in the path. It turned red and a wisp of smoke flew away from it, but with the rock of the mountain far below it, nothing further happened.

"Well, I failed with getting you back here," she said. "I can't stop thinking about failure and homing in on what success might be like."

"Well, stop it. If I didn't think you could make it to that castle and get that scarf, I'd never have let you leave home. Besides, you're doing fine with your healing skills."

She smiled and pointed at the red snow. "Are you going to send this stuff along with us, too? I'd fancy a hot fire."

"Might do, Lys. Might do."

"Well, now that we know it works… shouldn't we make more dust to seal our bargain?"

"Yes," he replied. "Let's make an enormous pile of dust for the Yetas. I need enough to keep them happy until our journey is through."

Alyssa shot her arrow into the crack of the stone and dust fell as before. She repeated this process again and again until quite a large pile of dust collected. In the snow drifts, she cleaned her hands off and created a massive pile of broken rock, too. Nothing occurred since Pappy didn't trigger the magik with his words of fire and rock.

On a trip to collect her arrow, she saw a rather large black bug with a red stripe on its back peer out of the crack. It had pinchers and waved at her angrily with them.

"Pappy," she said. "I think that'll hold them. The Danglebugs are about to go to war with me over the crack attack."

Her enchanted grandfather bounced up and down in his toy box. She scooped up a bit of the dust and put it in her tunic pocket. Couldn't hurt to have it with them. There would be plenty of snowy rocks on the road ahead.

She carried Pappy's box back to Fred, the Yeti leader. Together they explained what the pile of dust meant, where it could be located, and what the users should do in order to use it.

"They gotta say when they want it to spark with the word fire. Likewise, they gotta say when they want it to work on the rock by saying rock," Pappy told him.

Alyssa added, "A pile of broken rock is waiting for them to get them started."

She also warned Fred that dust in their fur, along with sparking rocks, might be a dangerous combination and they should take care not to get any on them.

Fred nodded in understanding.

Alyssa didn't wait for the Yetis to rush out and try to make fire or break rocks. Instead, she sat by a small fire in the throne room enjoying the warmth. She ate some Yeti bread offered to her and listened to Pappy Oh sing a silly song to Fred:

Yetis to break rocks on the hilltop.
When the dust settles, fire comes from said rock.
If the snow mounds up, boulder still breaks.
And you will have a campfire for taters and steaks!

It sounded like a nursery rhyme from her childhood, but she said nothing.

Late that night, after Alyssa had fallen asleep by the fire, the Yetis escorted Lord Bryon and his men in from the storm, fed them, and gave them permission to lay out bedrolls and sleep by the fire as Alyssa had done.

When she awoke before dawn, she counted several lumps all around the still-burning fire, some as tall as she. Yetis, she thought. The immense creatures lost a lot of their horror when asleep, mild as sludge, calm and even-tempered.

Only once did she see young Yetis baring their teeth at one another. No one could be anger-free all the time, not even her, so she knew these massive snowmen could, and likely would, fight to the death if encouraged.

She couldn't imagine what it would take to keep even one of them fed. A lot more than poor old Tony back home, she mused.

A twinge of homesickness and worry came over her. What had gone on back there? She felt no closer to having the scarf than when she started.

Had Granny Gert been behaving? What about King Hubert? Could a falling out have occurred that resulted in some disastrous event?

Pappy Oh would leave soon and, although she would miss him terribly, she had come to terms with it. She had seen a modicum of success with her healing powers, as he had reminded her, and felt certain she could bring the illumination spell forth as required.

Getting to that scarf remains the challenge, she thought.

To have her grandfather back at home felt like having a looking glass close by. She could see ahead and discover what lay behind at any given moment if he kept his word on coming to her aid if she needed him.

While trying to go back to sleep on the hard floor of the cave, she comforted herself with estimating distance and thinking that today would see them somewhere around Needlemount. Maybe with good luck, even at its doorstep.

With the Yetis helping them, travel should go much quicker. They had broad legs that could devour distance better than a horse.

When light flickered down into the cavern room and sent darkness into corners, Alyssa dug around and found some salted meat in her pack. Delighted, she stretched it out on the hot rocks of the fire. Her memory went back to the squire of Half Moon Manor. He had given her cheese, too.

She would be sure to thank him when she returned… if she did. Soon, a savory odor issued out and brought the men out of their sleep.

"What is that smell?" Fletch asked, rolling over, rubbing his eyes.

"I'm heating up a bit of beef." She pulled off a slice." "Want some?"

He nodded and threw his bedroll back.

Soon, Lord Bryon and Cerius followed suit, and she gave each of them a slice of the meat. Pappy Oh remained quietly in his box. Or maybe out of it, she couldn't know.

Soon, Fred's head cook named Bred, an immense lady Yeti with kind brown eyes, set to stoking the fire in the central fire pit. Food preparation time had come.

Bred settled a cauldron of stew directly into the fire. The rising scent brought hungry Yetis filing in.

Bryon suggested to his group that they move away from the dining fire so the Yetis could get their fill. They complied but remained close enough to feel the heat and hungrily eye the pot of stew.

When the Half Moon gang settled in a quiet nook where shadows from the firelight danced, Alyssa sighed at how the place transformed into well-lit and cozy surroundings. She sat Pappy Oh in his box beside her and listened to the raucous chit-chat of the Yetis as they broke their fast. None of the Heightlands men had ever witnessed such a throng of big creatures before and might not again.

Pappy Oh finally came alive in the box, and the clown's head turned back and forth, listening. Every so often he would grunt in agreement or snicker in amusement.

The Yetis spoke in their native tongue which sounded like gibberish to Alyssa, who wished she could understand the guttural language like her grandfather did.

When the gathering thinned out, Bred motioned to Bryon and his troop, and spoke in her throaty voice. "Come. Come, eat."

Alyssa glanced at Cerius, who gazed at Fletch, who looked at Bryon.

"Let us not offend our hosts," Bryon told them, striding forward.

Alyssa put Pappy Oh in a niche where the rock formation created a sort of corner. "Pappy, I'm going to try out some of that stew. You stay put and don't get into any mischief."

He grumbled but did not argue. She took that to be a positive sign and made her way to the fire. The smell of the cooked meat and potatoes made her mouth water, and she waited to be served with some impatience. Her hungry companions shifted on the seats of cold stone.

When the food came, Bred served it on curved slabs of rock, a crude form of bowl. She gave them utensils made for baby snowmen, much like a fork and spoon beaten out of unidentified metal. As Alyssa studied them, she realized that even baby Yetis were nearly the size of a grown man. She gratefully accepted the utensils and supposed traders had come through to provide them to the Yetis. This type of metal would be scarce in the mountains.

In fact, as she thought about it, most of what the Yetis had for food, or tools, or most anything else, had to be provided for them. Nothing in this snow-crusted wasteland of a mountain could provide sustenance for them in such a way.

Her curiosity got the better of her and she turned the fork over to examine the prongs. "How was this made?"

Fletch, seated next to her, replied. "I am curious myself. And how did the Yetis get them?"

As Bred spoke to Alyssa, she gently poured a massive ladle full of food into all of the bowls. "Mindel, doer deppel dade dis."

The girl gaped at her. Pappy and his knowledge of the language sat too far away to help. And if he had escaped the tin box, he could not communicate to translate. She smiled at Bred and devoured the stew.

Cerius, next to Fletch, responded. "No matter how they came by it, I am grateful for it. Oh, it smells heavenly!"

Lord Bryon nudged Cerius to eat from his plate first. "If tainted, I would prefer not to eat it."

Cerius spent no time gathering a bite of meat, potato, and broth into his mouth from Bryon's plate.

"If tainted, sir, I cannot tell. It tastes as it smells," he said, after he swallowed the bite.

"Aye. I will wait a moment to see how it settles," Bryon said staring at the others' plates. Alyssa scooped another spoonful into her mouth and closed her eyes, savoring the flavors.

"Good enough," Bryon said, digging into the fare. No one else spoke for a moment as they tucked in to appease growling stomachs.

Bred viewed them calmly, before being called away by Fred, who had finally arrived for a meal. His position required that she serve him immediately.

He sat across from them and bared his teeth in greeting. Alyssa assumed Yetis had too many teeth to smile properly.

"Dere Grinkle?" he asked.

Alyssa remembered him using that term about her grandfather and realized that must be the Yeti name for him.

"Oh, he's over in the corner," she said, pointing toward where she had left the box.

Fred stretched his neck to peer over them and saw the glimmer of the toy box. "Dah, des dere."

She blew on her spoon to cool another bite and scooped it in. After taking her time to savor the taste, she asked Fred her question about the utensils, hoping he would have an answer.

He paused mid-bite, and she could see him translating his language into hers. "Utensils, utensils?"

She held up the fork and spoon. "These," she told him.

He nodded, understanding finally. "Thorock. Live in mountains."

She raised her eyebrows. "Not familiar with them. Who are they?"

Bryon, listening quietly to the conversation, answered. "The Haldor. The Ironmen of the Mountains. We know them as Thor's Rock, or in short, Thorock. They live in uninhabitable places and are possibly descendants of an ancient god. History says they were used by the Dark Master for evil purposes until they revolted."

Alyssa frowned. She had never heard of them before, nor any of this history. She ate another bite of the stew and chewed a piece of meat as she considered his words. Perhaps the Thorock had connections to food stuff, maybe even in the Meadowlands or the realm around Half Moon Manor.

A rattle and creak signaled Pappy Oh had decided to join them. She turned to see the box rolling on its side, jerkily, and not in a straight line. She left her seat to help him along.

Once she had him situated beside her, she tapped on the top, and the clown's head popped out. "I heard what you said, Fred. Wondered what in tarnation you meant. Them Thorock folks ain't been seen in ages. Only talked about in books now. They vanished when the Dark Master disappeared. Ain't that right, Bryon?"

He nodded. They all stared at the utensils with more interest. Alyssa reassessed her former opinion about where the food came from. Perhaps the Yetis traveled from the mountains down into lower lands to hunt.

Sadly, Fred replied. "Like eagle hides in aerie nest no one can see now. Thorock hidden. These diggers," he said, brandishing his utensils. "Last of Thorock work for long time."

Unable to contain her interest, Alyssa asked. "Why? What happened to them?"

"Mountain fall outside in. Yetis on outside. Have good luck, do Yetis. Nevermore see Thorock."

Alyssa mentally went through his retelling. What could make a mountain cave into itself?

"Mr. Fred, did y'all get food from the Thorock? What do you do now for food? How long has it been since the cave-in?"

He shoveled food into his mouth and frowned. "Few days, few weeks, Fred lose time. Wolves bring meat and share sometimes. Sometimes Yeti hunt for goat meat. Rocks make strong head-breakers. Sometimes travelers share for warm fire. Yetis eat bread when white powder is given as gift, but most often eat berries and herbs like hungry bear."

Pappy Oh, a bit taken aback at his story whispered, "Tsk, tsk. We're being given the best of what they have. They are kind to strangers."

"Yeti no interested in Thorock story. Tell story of Oh."

Alyssa could not let it go. "Do you mean Yetis didn't go in to see about the mountain men and find out what caused the cave-in? You don't know that they all perished, do you?"

Fred grew annoyed. "Yetis keep alone. No try to find. Thorock gone."

Pappy Oh softly told Alyssa to mind herself.

She let the matter drop, but her overactive imagination hoped to see signs the Haldor, or Thorock, still existed along the way to Needlemount.

The Yetis were stealthy, even for their large size, Alyssa thought. They could get on top of massive rock cliffs, mostly covered by snow and ice, and not slip or fall. Their large, flexible feet had long claws like their hands, and they could perch with nails dug in like a bird. The giants blended in so well in the snow-covered terrain, Alyssa believed the enemy ahead would be hard pressed to see them.

When she strolled along behind one of the four accompanying them, she noted the thick pads of their feet, like cow hide, only thicker. Of course, the icy weather did not bother them.

The day they set out from the Yeti cave held an unusual silence. Mostly from the snow that had fallen quietly during the night, but also from a lack of animal or human activity.

A narrow trail leading up a slant awaited them. The ground looked hard and unbroken by hardy scrub which grew up from the mountain slope lower down.

Soon, Solly hid his face behind heavy gray clouds that threatened more snowfall before night. Alyssa hoped they were at their destination before then. The thought of being caught in a blinding snowstorm with the wind whipping around them until they were faint from its onslaught made her shiver. Sudden drop-offs were common and hidden in the gloom.

When she asked Pappy what he thought of their travel time, her heart fell at his reply.

"Not gonna make the time limit the old bird-lion gave us," he said.

"What? Why not?" she asked, alarmed.

"First, we ain't even close to Needlemount. Don't know what is waiting up ahead to slow us down, either. Second, ain't figured out a speedy way to get you back to Mudden. Even if this little journey only took one day, getting back to that creature in the pasture will be hard, next to impossible."

"Can't you conjure up something?"

"Now, Lys. You know same as I do a conjure like that would be complicated, and conjuring without aids won't go nowhere. I need my stuff to make something like that happen. We ain't got no candles, no spell books, no nothing."

Thanks, Pappy. My worst fear.

"I ain't as young as I used to be, and I worry what might come out of a half-hearted attempt. So, I think I'm just gonna go on home. Think I can be more useful there than here. Gonna try to slow up that old gryphon. Keep him occupied, so he'll forget about you and that scarf."

"What do you mean by 'what might come out?'" Alyssa asked, chewing on a nail.

"You know how you got only some of me here? Same thing. Say I tried to bring us a giant Roc to get us home. But ill-prepared, I might bring a fleet-footed gecko, not a Roc. Wouldn't be much help to us."

She set her jaw. "Well, we'll work together. Two conjurers are better than one. Ain't that what you said back home?"

He closed the lid on his toy box and did not come out again.

Alyssa fretted. They had to get back and give the scarf to King Hubert, with no delays. Maybe Pappy had been right in his thought to go on home to Mudden. She might need all the dallying he could get the Meadowland king to muster.

A grinding noise brought her attention back to the present. She peered around for the cause. Nothing struck her as out of place, yet nothing she could think of could make such a noise.

When two of the Yetis they had brought along went scrambling up the hill beside her, she changed her mind. Something lived up there, even if she couldn't see it.

Evil thoughts darkened her mind. What if the Yetis were in cahoots with someone else on the mountain? What if they planned to ambush Lord Bryon's party?

She knocked on the toy box. "Pappy, come out here. Something's going on."

The crank turned, and the silly tune issued out. The lid popped open, and Pappy, inside the clown's face, eased out. "What's up?"

"Something has the Yetis disturbed. A couple of them took off like goats up the mountain."

"Did you see anything?"

"No, but I heard something that sounded like Granny's coffee grinder. All whirly and loud. Then the big hairy fellows took off."

Bryon halted the trek. "Where did those Yeti-men go?"

Cerius replied. "They didn't say. Quiet as field mice."

Fletch, who had not spoken since leaving the Yeti cave, said, "Someone's up there, I'll bet, and only two guesses who it is."

Alyssa settled her bow and quiver across her lap for easier access. "What's our plan in case of attack?"

Lord Bryon waved to her to cease talking. They all listened intently. A small avalanche of snow overhead rumbled down on top of them. They all shuffled to the inside of the trail to avoid being hit.

When it diminished to a trickle, they waited to see what had made the ruckus. Straight overhead, perched on a ledge, stood the Yetis lined up beside the most wicked-looking wolves any of them could ever recall seeing.

With coats of white and gray, brown and black, the beasts had yellow or amber eyes. Their muzzles stretched open revealing large, vicious fangs.

Alyssa had never seen a wolf up close, but she had seen drawings in books. "Way more dangerous looking in person," she muttered.

"Grundle," said a Yeti with them.

Pappy Oh, vigilant now, growled and yelled up at the one above them. "Grinkle, grundle, grimkin."

The Yeti nodded and said something to the nearest wolf, who backed away from the ledge.

Bryon asked Pappy to explain.

"Told him to get his hairy hide back down here. That rockslide wasn't meant to happen. The Yetas knew these here wolfies were around. They thought it would be a good idea to get them involved."

"We do not need wolves," Bryon answered. "They may even slow us down.

"Not hardly," Pappy replied. "They can go long distances quick. Don't require humans to provide food or water, most times. Got keen eyes and senses. Those critters can smell things way before we even see them."

Bryon thought it over. "As you wish, Sir Oh. But those Yeti-men must keep them in line. I can spare no one for that task. We must keep moving, and even more rapidly now than ever."

Alyssa listened with some trepidation, only relaxing at Bryon's last words. Finally, the need to hurry had gotten through to him.

The party moved forward, ever vigilant for rockslides, avalanches, and Madrid and his son. Their senses on high alert, one man or another jerked to a stop at the slightest sound every few moments.

"Fear of the unknown is going to be our undoing," Bryon said to the nearest Yeti. "Please, would you carry us?"

Alyssa agreed. "Fastest, safest way to carry out the journey."

The Yetis complied, carrying them where necessary. Soon, they climbed upwards, and Alyssa marveled at how the terrain changed. Everyone groaned as Yetis fought against the steepness all around them. Many found themselves thrust out in front of their Yeti carrier and sometimes dangled over far-flung precipices.

It had been a good idea to let the horses loose. Beasts laden with men and packs on such angles would have been cruel and terrifying.

After an hour of climbing, the region leveled off. Large boulders thrust through the ground and giant cracks appeared.

Alyssa had never seen so much snow. "Like grains of sand on shores of the seas," she mused aloud. "This must be where the Haldors' homes fell in," she mentioned to Pappy.

"That's what I'm thinking. Feels weird around here to me. Can't put a finger on it. My spiritual side is divining like a rod seeking water," came the voice of her grandfather.

She nodded and kept a watchful eye. The aura of the area held a definite *something*. She could feel it, too, and likened it to eating a breakfast of bacon and eggs. You didn't see the food once eaten, but you could still smell the aroma in the air.

"Wait! Wait!" Alyssa cried. "It's the aroma! I smell burning wood… campfires!"

The company stopped, and even the Yetis stared at her curiously.

"Yes. I believe there's someone around here. Perhaps the Haldors still live," Alyssa said, waving at the surrounding area.

Bryon thrust a hand through his hair and tapped his Yeti's hand. "There is no time for stopping to see if your suspicion rings true, Lady Alyssa. As you have said, time works against us."

Big snowflakes fell harder now, and darkness crept over the mountain. Alyssa pulled the hood of the cloak she had received from the dryad over her head and waved to the others to move along. Someday, maybe on her return to Mudden, she could come through here and do a deeper inspection.

Because of the worsening weather and fear of being crushed in a sudden fall, the Yetis let the humans down to manage on their own two feet. The snowmen trudged behind the troop, close enough to keep them in sight, and soon four wolves padded alongside. These travelers would occasionally rush forward on the trail to see what lay ahead. Their pink tongues lolled out like they were hot beneath their fur coats.

Once, a frightened snowy hare almost became one of their dinners as she hopped out to blink at the troop. The wolves charged her, and she darted back into her warren where they could not get to her.

After a while, this became a regular occurrence with the wolves. They would jog off in pursuit of an animal and come back moments later. Once, after a longer jaunt, they did not come back empty-handed. A poor red squirrel dangled lifelessly from one of their mouths.

Alyssa tried to block out the sounds they made as they stalked into the snowy mound off the trail and tore the flesh and crushed the tiny bones. Such violence, even for an animal, disturbed her.

Bryon called for a rest, and Pappy cleared his throat, as he sometimes did before speaking. "Lys," he said. "I think I'm going to take off now."

Alyssa gaped at the clown's face. He couldn't be serious. "Now? I mean, we're almost to Needlemount now."

"Yeah, I know," he said. "But you got this. The Yetas and their furry friends will be here to help y'all out... but your Granny Gert ain't got nobody in her corner. I need to go."

Lord Bryon stepped closer to the box, surprise on his face. "What did he say?"

Tears welled in Alyssa's eyes and slid down her cheeks. She wiped at them with her sleeve and didn't answer Bryon. "Pappy, are you sure?"

"Yes. Now, I told you. You can do more than you know, Lys. You know enough magik to keep yourself out of trouble. That illumination spell will be there for you to find that scarf and maybe other things you need. You can already heal hurts, seen and unseen, which is more than most healers can do. Try to tap into your powers if the need comes. I have faith in you, girl."

She nodded, shoulders slumped in defeat, as she realized his intention had not reverted. The others glanced at one another, and they shouldered their gear as the reality of their part in her journey came forward for them all.

Alyssa fought down her emotions and said, "Go on, then. But you better come back here if there's even a drop of trouble.

Let Granny know I'm coming back, quick as a squirrel. And you let King Hubert know I'm working on this situation as fast as I can. Keep him from letting down his end of this bargain, Pappy."

"I'll find a way to keep everyone on task. Now give me a kiss and I'll be off. You are going to be just fine, child."

She gave the clown's cheek a quick peck.

The toy box shook, and the clown's face went down. Alyssa knew her grandfather had gone because the box felt different somehow. Lighter, even. Tears streaked her face, and she sat down hard, gripping the box.

Cerius patted her back in camaraderie, and Bryon paced a few feet away.

Fletch spoke soft words of encouragement to Alyssa who finally let him pull her to her feet. Soon, they all moved ahead once again.

True to the Yetis' word, the pull in the muscles of their legs worsened as they approached another sharp incline. Here, trees were not simply winter-worn, they stood bent, withered, as if death had come upon them without warning. Alyssa studied them before being urged along. They had burnt bark on one side, and Alyssa feared the outcome if dryads had once inhabited them.

The snow drifted higher and became more difficult to trudge through. Alyssa lifted her feet higher to step into and out of the mounds. The trail, almost obliterated by the snow, turned unexpectedly and Lord Bryon fell a few feet down an embankment. Unhurt except for his pride, he posted a Yeti in front of the company after that.

Ice crystals clung to their boots, pants, and scabbards. It coated beards and eyebrows. The sun gave little warmth as it blazed its way down the sky toward the far horizon.

Pappy's empty toy box clanged against Alyssa's back in the backpack, and she sighed when she felt it. Loneliness overcame her. She wanted his silly songs to lilt out of the toy box.

Then, the land softened with rolling hills and less rock as the elevation flattened. They rounded a bend in the trail, and they recognized signs that this area had been tended. The tall grass came back, its tops poking out of snowbanks, and trees popped up, healthy-looking, even in the snowy weather.

Shivers and trembles shook Alyssa's arms, and she clasped them with her hands. Then the shaking traveled over her entire body. No chill from the cold felt like this. Something was wrong with the weather here, too.

And something evil lay ahead. She knew it with a knowing as old as magik itself. Now, with Pappy gone, she shouldered the dangers alone to protect the ones who traveled with her against whatever this evil might be. Rylee and Lorelei's words came back to her. In the days ahead, her comrades would lean on her.

"Who lives in these parts?" she asked through chattering teeth.

Bryon bowed his head a bit. "Needlemount men, their allies, and all who would do us harm if they knew why we came this way." His voice faded, and she knew his thoughts of bravery wavered. Perhaps he could feel the evil as well.

"It's okay, Lord Bryon. Don't forget you have magik in you now, too."

Only a tiny drop, she thought, but it would give him comfort.

He nodded and stood a little straighter, staring ahead.

She closed her eyes and thought of her own hearth and home far away to the south. She sent a loving thought out to her Pappy, at home and warm and safe, she hoped. Reopening her eyes, she searched the horizon and found small, thatched cottages dotting the area.

"We should stay as far away from them as we can," she told Bryon. "Who knows where their allegiance may be."

He agreed and waved for the others to follow them on a more northeasterly route.

When the sun lowered behind the peak of Needlemount, they called a halt to the day's march. They needed to make a fire, eat, and plan for tomorrow. But before all of that, a shelter must be created.

Lord Bryon chose a sturdy tree with branches nearly touching the ground and asked Cerius to hack off limbs from another for building a fire.

Alyssa stopped him, worried that the dryads would come after him tonight while he slept if he did such a thing. "No, Sir Cerius. I'll handle this. You go on and get together some food for us to eat."

She handed him her bow and arrow. "Not sure what you might find, but those wolves can help you find it, I'll bet."

He hurried toward the animals and went off for a hunt.

She strode to a tree on the other side of the trail. As if it had ears to hear, she stood close to it and whispered. She hoped the men would think she summoned a fire for them.

"Now, if y'all dryads are in there, just know we wouldn't be doing this without a need. I know y'all don't like strangers popping up unexpected-like. Now, for me to make a fire, I need some dry wood. I promise to keep it low, and away from your homes as much as I can. Will somebody please help me out with that?"

Either a sturdy breeze shook the tree she trailed near, or someone invisible shook it. Either way, dry broken branches pelted the surrounding ground. She gathered them in her arms, and softly said her thanks.

She laid the branches over a pile of rocks, pinched a bit of the dust in her tunic pocket, and sprinkled it over. Soon the rocks sparked as they crumbled into dust and the branches caught fire. She had a sizeable pile and knew they would be fine through the night.

Cerius and Fletch joined her, accompanied by Yetis and wolves. The creatures had flushed out rabbits and squirrels, and the men caught them easily.

"Nary an arrow lost," Fletch told her as he brandished her bow before setting it, along with her quiver, next to her pack under the tree.

"Good! Well, this fire is about ready to put some meat on. I wish I had something to put over it to cook on." Seeing her dilemma, Fletch pulled out a few of the branches and with his dagger soon had a ragged spit set up. Delighted, Alyssa speared a rabbit onto it and watched him place the whole contraption over the fire. They continued doing that until there were squirrels and rabbits dripping fat renderings and filling the air with delicious smells.

Lord Bryon had seated himself under their sheltering tree, and Alyssa could hear a slight snoring. Cerius and Fletch, eager to help, brought smooth-sided stones at her request. Alyssa situated them near the fire away from the burning wood.

The Yetis alternated standing around the fire with Cerius and Fletch, but the wolves had left, out for nocturnal howling at the moon.

Alyssa gazed skyward. The clouds hid Luna's face, but even partially visible, it became clear she saw the quarter moon. Her time for this adventure waned.

As she rotated the meat, she considered her plan. She would never make it back to meet the Gryphon King at this rate. Tomorrow, she had to get that scarf. But how to get home in less than a day's trip? Hopelessness filled her and she lifted a silent plea to Pappy to bridge the gap.

The young healer served the hungry company, silently aloof. While they ate, the men told the Yetis stories of hunting trips around the Heightlands. The snowmen didn't seem to understand much of it but nodded at the friendly voices. Alyssa ate and listened and wondered about the men's lives. She had never been so far from home before, and the tales amazed her.

When the talk died down, the area around them seemed to come to life. Invisible creatures cracked twigs, but there were no insects to bother them. Alyssa kept watch after seeing movement every so often. Whether animal or dryad, she could not say, but she knew they were there.

With bellies full and eyes drooping, the men called it a night. The Yetis dug into their places under the tree away from the fire, their thick fur keeping them comfortable. The men remained seated or reclining near the fire, snoring, and talking for a short while before rolling up in their blankets and bedrolls to keep warm. Cerius took the first watch, accompanied by a fat Yeti named Jed.

Alyssa, cold, tired, and worried, fell into a fitful sleep wrapped in the cloak Rylee had given her with Lord Bryon's blanket tucked over her. A few hours later, the moaning and creaking of the trees awakened her.

The fire wavered, and the two watchers were missing. Alyssa, alarmed for their safety, moved away from her blanket, and strode to the fire, stirring it with a branch to bring it back alive. She threw a stone into the fire and took a tiny pinch of the Danglebug powder to throw on it, and sparks turned into flames once again.

The trees waved and branches broke off and fell all around the area.

What manner of evilment is this?

She heard a faint cry somewhere in the distance. "Cerius?" she asked aloud. Then she yelled out his name as she caught up a stick in each hand, lit it in the fire, and ran toward the sound.

It may have been her imagination, but it seemed as though the trees shrank within themselves, and their branches drew upwards, away from the flames she carried. Some of the more supple branches seemed to point out a way.

She hurried down the icy pathway, realizing it might be a bad idea to go off alone, but she feared losing her friends while waiting to alert everyone. "Cerius! Jed!"

She paused, listening. Faintly, she heard another yell, this one low like a Yeti voice. They were together, but they were moving away from her. She yelled their names again and headed for the sounds.

By this time the others roused and sprang into action. Fletch found her first, thanks to her firebrands.

"My lady," he said, breathless from running. "What has happened?"

She didn't know how to answer. "Stay here with the others. Be on guard against attack. Cerius and Jed are out there somewhere; I heard them. But now nothing. I'm going to find them."

"You cannot go alone," Fletch urged. He took one of the burning branches. "Lord Bryon will know what to do in our stead. Let's go."

He led the way, and she followed, listening for any sound of the missing duo. She also considered where the wolves had gone. At least one stayed by the side of each of the four Yetis who had accompanied them.

She hoped the one with Jed would stalk their attackers. If she could locate Jed's wolf, she would also find the mighty Yeti.

Then, as if beckoned by her thoughts, the remaining Yetis and their wolves came crashing through the trees. They carried or wore the company's packs slung over their great forearms. Not burdened at all, they swooped around Fletch and Alyssa and bounded down the pathway, carrying large sticks as weapons and yammering to themselves. Alyssa noted, with some fear, that they also carried her quiver and bow.

Lord Bryon was shortly behind them, out of breath at their rushed pace. He had another thick branch in his hands, unlit.

Fletch took Bryon's branch and held the flaming stick to it, lighting both. Then, together, they lifted them overhead and saw the Yetis disappear ahead in the darkness.

"They need no light," Fletch mused. "Used to living in caves."

"No," agreed Lord Bryon. "They hardly need air, food, or anything else. I insisted on their carrying our packs. Once I discovered everyone missing, I relayed to them the trouble we were in. Let's hurry along. Maybe we can catch them. There is safety in numbers."

Fletch nodded and started off once again, leading them. They listened to the crashing and crackling that the Yetis made as they went through the snow and down the path. Alyssa winced at the damage they created to the land, but it made following them easier. Bryon collected another branch along the way to replace his which had burned down to a stump.

As they paused, Alyssa thought of some way to aid them in their search.

"I've got it!" she cried out, startling the two.

They stared at her. She handed her firebrand to Fletch and closed her eyes, lifting her hands over her head, and said, "Illuminate these woods; find Cerius and Jed, and the wolf."

As she waited briefly, the green glow traveled up her arms and sparked out of her fingertips, filled the tops of the trees, and spread before them.

"Follow that!" she told Fletch, taking her fiery stick back and waving for him to go. Lord Bryon lifted his hands to his face, and she could tell he considered whether he could have also done such a thing.

"Likely not," she told him, as they hurried off again.

Soon, they overcame the Yetis and wolves who stood staring up at the green cloud that floated over their heads.

"Don't stop!" Alyssa commanded them. "Go find our friends!"

They might not have understood what she said, because they hesitated, panting up at her in fear. But when she and the others passed them and kept rushing down the path, they caught on to the plan, and she could hear their rumbling voices somewhere behind her.

Soon, the green glow brightened, and Alyssa felt as though they may come upon the missing. Their gaits slowed in case marauders emerged first.

At the bottom of a hill, a frozen stream of water crossed the path and the missing wolf paced alongside it, as if afraid to go over. He had fur mottled with gray and black and stared at her with golden eyes. Jed's wolf, no question.

Alyssa eased to a stop beside it. "What is it, friend?"

She spoke to it like one of the hounds at Tony's shack. She had befriended them and knew how dogs of all kinds would bite if frightened. A wolf, even more so, she figured.

The wolf whined and paced along the edge of the water. Fletch lifted the flaming branch higher and stared down into the ice.

"Could it be that there is something in the ice that he's afraid of?"

Alyssa shrugged. "Not certain. Wolves are smart enough to know not to go over ice that won't hold them, I guess. We should take his advice and try to find a way around it. See now, the green glow has moved ahead."

The fog they had followed thinned, now that they had found the wolf. It floated ahead into the distance.

Fletch nodded and waved for her to turn right. "Let's go this way and see if there is an end to this icy patch."

The wolf howled. His brothers howled back behind him. They trotted down the trail and he sat and waited for them, rather than joining Alyssa and Fletch and Bryon.

"You show them the way," she instructed the wolf.

He whined again as though to say he would.

She held her branch up and motioned for the men to stand back. She took a few tentative steps off the trail and found it solid enough to hold her. She waved to them permitting Fletch to lead, and Bryon in the rear. Soon they followed obvious signs of someone else's passage.

Fletch plunged through the snow mounds, warning her of deep spots as he went.

The drifts slowed them down, and the Yetis and wolves caught them in a short while. Alyssa recovered her pack and ensured Pappy's box remained unharmed. Her bow and arrows were intact as well, and she adjusted them on her shoulders. The men recovered their packs from the big snowmen and put them on, their weapons also intact.

The Yetis stood, waiting, making guttural noises of impatience. Alyssa lifted her hand and addressed the men.

"Lord Bryon, I'm sorry for taking over like this, but with the spell being my own working, I reckon it has to be this way for a minute," she said.

He shrugged. "As you will my lady. I have no designs on this journey aside from arriving there in one piece."

"I guess we should ask what everyone's mind is," she continued.

She looked at the others. "Do we face whatever waits up there? Or stop for the night and follow the signs, or whatever is left of them, in the morning?"

Bryon and Fletch peered over at the Yetis. They didn't seem to understand nor care either way. Decided, Bryon said, "My lady, the snowmen will go if we go; they may even go without us, as they have a man missing as well. I say forge ahead. There's nothing keeping us from finding the marauders except darkness and snow. And you have eliminated one of those." He glanced up again, marveling.

She nodded. "Okay, just wanted to make sure we were all together in mind. We could fall slap into a trap if we're not careful."

Fletch shook his head. "We must try. Cerius would do this for us."

Alyssa turned to face the direction the magik took them. "Lead on, Fletch. Follow the light."

In a snow mound, Fletch snuffed out the burnt-up branch he had been carrying. Bryon and Alyssa did likewise. The glow gave all the light they needed now. Soon the land leveled off and, although snowy, became much easier to travel. The farther the company went, the more like a well-traveled road it became, hard-packed and flat. The Yetis made their own path and veered to the left, bouncing along the terrain, their yammering growing fainter and fainter. Alyssa knew well she and the men from Half Moon could not go that way and gave them passage. She and her company stayed on the road.

In a short while, the magik brightened again, and they came out on a ridge where the land dropped off into tiers, like stacks of books, each lower than the next. Beyond the final level, the ground stretched out into a plain dotted with campfires that glittered in the snow.

"Like a city of fireflies," Alyssa muttered.

"Worse," Bryon answered. "Buggo fires."

She stared at the sight before them and asked, "What in Daegries is a buggo?"

He moved around to the other side of her to stand beside Fletch, who shifted his feet.

"Something out of your nightmares, my lady," he whispered. "You might know them as bugbears."

She had read about those in a child's storybook. Evil that snatched babes from their cradles and ate them with wicked fangs.

The castle glimmered darkly in the moonlight as it broke free of clouds. The glow floated over the gathering on the plain, slithered onto castle walls, and dipped inside a window slit.

"Needlemount," Fletch said, awed.

Soon, they stood shoulder-to-shoulder with the Yetis and wolves and stared at the towers before them. They were ridiculously outnumbered and had no plan for what to do next.

"Our friends are there," Alyssa said to no one in particular.

"Yes," Fletch answered. "Alone and in need of us."

While they stood there, the pounding of hooves rumbled in the ground.

"And so, it begins," Lord Bryon sighed, brandishing his sword. Fletch followed his direction.

Bryon turned to Alyssa and said, "Lady Alyssa, you are the most valuable member of our company now. Your quest remains more desperate than my own. Dispense with the spell immediately; the enemy is following it. Run as fast as you can. Distract the buggos. Get to the castle. Do not worry about us. Go, now!"

"I can't leave you!"

"Danger comes. The only way out is ahead!"

And he pushed her hard on the back, sending her over the ridge, terrified words on her lips.

Chapter Twelve

Buggos and Needlemount

Somehow, Alyssa managed to right her position into a seated one. She skidded down the slope of the ridge, pebbles sliding beneath her feet, scraping her legs and palms as she thrust her hands out behind her to slow her fall. At a small outcropping of saplings, she came to a startling stop. She stood and assessed the damage and found nothing broken or mangled too severely in her fall.

Terrified, she peered out at the dangerous territory before her. Then she heard men shouting, and her heart fell. Her friends were in grave danger, and she could not help them.

She searched for the glow and faintly saw it lingering around the castle. Her placement on the highest level below the ridge felt still too close to the battle going on, so she moved toward the next drop off. Then the next, always keeping an eye on the castle and her magik. When she finally reached the last level, she could no longer see the glow.

I have to end the spell!

But Pappy Oh had not told her how to stop it once it started. She could not remember ever reading about a spell recall either.

Well, they do what they're sent to do, and they stop doing it when they finish. *But how do I make it stop?*

With her mind otherwise engaged, she slipped on an icy spot, nearly losing her quiver when it caught on a squatty bush. Her heart in her throat, she scurried back up the slippery hill a short distance to collect it.

When she felt safe enough to act on the spell, she shrugged the pack and quiver off her shoulders and decided.

Nothing tried, nothing accomplished.

She lifted her hands overhead and closed her eyes, focusing only on the illumination spell she had sent out. "Come on back now. Your search is over."

The green glow slumped from the sky and narrowed into a thin stream that flew toward her hands, finally drizzling down her arms until it completely faded away. The feeling of it returning drained her energy as though the spell itself wearied of activity.

She gazed out over the camp of buggos before her, much closer now. The shadowy figures moved back and forth in the firelight.

Buggos appeared as big as Yetis, only hairier and noisier.

She replaced her belongings, quiver in front now, and crept along listening to guttural sounds that could pass as laughter in front of her. She found a niche in a snowbank and hesitated to move for a time as she considered her options, which included danger on all sides.

Her limited knowledge of Bugbears haunted her. They were not a danger to the southlands. They didn't live near there. And no one mentioned them. Fear turned her mouth dry.

Better get a move on.

She drew closer to the creatures' camps. She could only guess at what had brought them there. Crushing a rebellion from the men of the Heightlands and especially Half Moon Manor came to mind.

Breathing deeply, Alyssa considered how to stop that from happening. A spell against these creatures? What kind of spell? She had nothing with which to summon powers against them. She wasn't even sure she could do such a thing.

The buggos' rotten body odor floated to her nose on a light breeze, making her pinch her nostrils closed.

"Me belly's curling into itself from hunger," the nearest one said.

"Aye. Fancy a bite of horsemeat, meself," replied his companion. They both chortled at that.

"Times is hard," the first said.

"Horseflesh will do in a pinch," the other admitted.

Alyssa marveled they spoke in a tongue she could understand, even if it sounded peculiar.

Nearly on hands and knees, she slunk along, putting distance between herself and hungry buggos. Soon she crouched behind a group of animals sheltered under a small grove of trees. These would be the horses of which they had spoken.

Only… they looked nothing like horses, and soon she discovered why.

Great snuffling and growling came from the animals, and then one stood on his hind legs, like a man. The firelight illuminated his snout, and she witnessed large teeth gnashing.

Bears!

The buggos rode bears? Her fears flamed at this new terrible danger, and she moved away from them as fast as she could. If one of the creatures decided to eat his trusty steed, he'd have a grand time of fighting it.

Beside a thick stack of firewood, she pulled Pappy's box out and placed her hand over the lid. "Pappy Oh, come to me fast, or the breath I breathe may be my last!" she whispered.

To her horror, nothing happened. The box did not rattle or bounce, and the jack-in-the-box head remained tucked inside.

"Pappy Oh, come on now, I ain't playing!" she hissed. But the box remained cold and silent in her hands. Her grandfather did not come to help her out of the current mess. His lack of allegiance made her want to throw the box as far as she could.

I knew this would happen!

Then, a cheer went up from the buggos.

Now what?

She rose slightly from her stooped position to witness the Needlemount men, on horseback, shoving her friends on foot before them, hands tied, heads down in defeat.

Friends held captive, no help coming to her, and arrows too few to do any good. Her determination flagged.

She had nothing. Nothing except magik, and she didn't even know how to get that to work. If she could distract the lot of them, get them divided and away from their camp, she could plunder a way to the castle. But how?

They herded Bryon and the others through the camp and beyond toward the darkness of a drawbridge. Her heart lifted into her throat. They were truly captives.

At that moment, something leapt onto her cloak sleeve and crawled up it. She gasped, startled. Then, she gently brushed it off and peered at it. A hornet. She considered the insect only a moment before returning her attention to the buggos.

They poked a Yeti in the back here and pulled a wolf's tail there. White-hot anger rose in her until she wanted to rush into the camp shooting arrows into the chests of every enemy gathered there.

If only I had that many arrows.

Then the hornet buzzed from its place on the ground, and she glanced down at it, her temper flaring.

Oh, if only I could send a million hornets like you to attack them!

And within a second, a mighty roar of wings flapping at magnificent speeds sounded overhead. She peered up to see the brilliance of millions of fireflies in the night sky.

They gathered into a massive hoard and swarmed the camp. She had never been so glad to see anything in her life. But why fireflies and not hornets?

Don't waste time worrying about that; this is your chance!

She stuffed Pappy's box down in her pack and ran straight for the outermost edge of the camp, one eye on the fireflies and the frantic buggos, still peering up.

Then, their mouths flew open. Long fangs and sharp teeth glittered in the firelight. And, joyfully, they feasted on the insects who dived at them.

So busy were they at their feeding that they were oblivious to anything else. Alyssa took advantage of the lull in their attention and followed the path where she had last seen her friends disappear.

Alyssa had no trouble getting to Needlemount Castle. She pulled the hood of the cloak over her head and used it to keep herself hidden. No one cared that she crossed the drawbridge, which in her estimation should not be down.

The guardhouse stood empty as did the courtyard beyond. This felt strange to Alyssa, even though she had no experience with castles or their operation. Such a large place *should* have a force of people. And most of them would be for protecting the lord's property if nothing else.

Where were all the people?

The deeper into the castle grounds she crept, the reason became apparent. On the other side of the courtyard, the barbican, an arched entryway, stood darkened except for burning torches standing on either side. Beside them patrolled the guards for the castle, and no wonder the Needlemounters believed them to be enough.

Four massive buggos, armed with maces, menacing spiked clubs, stood before the entrance, shields at the ready, helms gleaming dully in the night.

Alyssa paused beside a small garden with a dry fountain in its center. She slipped behind it to view the guards and consider how to advance.

With Pappy Oh gone and her friends somewhere within the castle, there would be no help forthcoming. And even she knew there remained no way to get around the guards except to climb the castle walls—an impossible feat.

No longer caring who saw the light from the illumination spell, she lifted her hands and said, "Glow, find my friends."

This action sent the illumination spell streaking out over the heads of the buggos and down the short tunnel behind them. Her hiding place lit up from the spell, and she had no choice but to stride forward, challenging the armed buggos.

If they wanted to kill her, they would have to catch her first.

"Get out of my way," she commanded, advancing, arms in front of her now. The buggos, whose faces went slack at the tiny figure commanding the strange light, made muttered noises of confusion.

She threw her cloak back, and she came at them, the magik flowing in front of her.

"Wight, wight!" one screamed in terror. The others, too shocked to say anything, stood with clenched fists as their brave comrade threw his club at her. He only succeeded in stabbing it into the ground a few feet away.

Alyssa had heard tales of wights told in the same vein as the will-o'-the-wisps. They were spirits that haunted graveyards. She choked back a laugh.

"Don't let it touch you!" another yelled, following his friend in pitching his club. Alyssa stopped movement as their attempts to harm her were failing. She raised her hands overhead again. The glow regrouped.

The buggos tossed their remaining weapons to either side of the barbican and fled down the tunnel screaming for their lives.

Before she recalled the spell, she remembered where it traveled and made her way in that direction. Now that she knew how to start and stop the spell, she marveled at how it followed her commands so easily. It existed inside her, a part of her. As natural as turning up or down the wick of an oil lamp. She grinned at the thought of the fireflies. Magik definitely performed when called upon.

With a slow gait, she followed the guards. They might attack at any time if they were lying in wait. Upon reaching the inner courtyard, she became even more stealthy, staying in the shadows, and putting a hand on her pack to quiet the contents.

The cloak protected her in the gloom of night. She stayed close to the walls of the gatehouse for as long as possible and then ran as fast as she could across an open area until she had arrived at the kitchen.

The smell of bread baking made it easy to tell the kitchen from another place. The aroma drove her stomach into rumbling fits.

When did I last eat?

She must have lingered a moment too long over the delightful scent floating on the night air, because when she turned to go toward the next building, powerful hands gripped her. And suddenly, someone yanked a cloth bag over her head, stripping her pack and quiver from her.

Her captors twisted her arms behind her and tied her hands with rough rope. Then they pushed and shoved her along a dank pathway, into the castle. They forced her to march a long way, turning left and right from the entrance.

She struggled and fell a few times. They hauled her back to her feet and forced her to continue forward. She constantly tried to come up with a plan but knew that she had no options.

Finally, they released her from the rope, and she rubbed her arms and hands to get the aching to stop. Then they pulled the bag from her head.

The man standing in front of her wore a chainmail hauberk. He said, "You are free to roam this room, but mark me, if you try to escape, magik or no, I will kill you." And then, to emphasize his words, he tapped the hilt end of the sword he carried in his gloved hand.

"I want my toy box," Alyssa commanded.

The man stared at her in surprise. "Your what?"

"My toy box. It's in my pack. I want it or I'll scream and scream and scream."

At her direction, the man found her pack and pulled out the box. "This? Why this is nothing more than a toy."

"Indeed, it is," she agreed, relief filling her. "And I want it."

"Perhaps it has magik?" one of the companions with him asked.

"No," she said. "It's my prized toy, and I don't want to lose it."

The man in a hauberk lifted it, flipped it around, and checked it over. He turned the crank and the strange music issued forth. Finally, the clown's head popped out, but the eyes were dead, with no Pappy Oh in it.

Satisfied, the man tossed it to her, and she caught it, clasping it to her.

He motioned for his armed companions to follow him. They strode back through the doorway from where they had entered and blended into the darkness beyond.

Freed from her captors, Alyssa found herself in a great room. Her friends greeted her warmly with smiles and back pats. Except for Cerius who was still missing along with the Yeti named Jed. That was when she realized none of the Yetis or wolves were with the others.

She wandered over to an outer wall where window slits normally gave sunlight and fresh air room to enter. But heavy tapestries covered them and created a gloomy atmosphere. As night deepened it became more dismal. Even the banners draped from the pillars in the middle of the room displayed dull colors and drooping ornaments in the dimness.

This large gathering place had not been used in a long time. Despair struck her. The place stood as silent as a tomb, and as bone-chillingly cold as one. Even the fireplace sat somber and bare.

Alyssa stood holding Pappy Oh's toy box in front of her like a shield as she considered their options. When she asked where the Yetis and wolves were, the men shuffled their feet. Fletch told her what had transpired.

"The snowmen rose up when entering the courtyard, sweeping the legs of two horses out from under their Needlemount riders. The horses fell on riders, crushing them. The Needlemounters were unprepared for resistance. So, after their initial encounter, the castle men let the Yetis and their wolf friends to scatter and run back toward the buggo camp.

"One of them said something about the buggos having a Yeti stew tonight," Bryon added, brow furrowed in anger.

"The Needlemount men made the Yetis carry our packs so they could bind our hands. All the dry clothes and food are with the creatures," he said. "Wherever they may be."

Alyssa fell silent, hoping that the Yetis got past the camp of buggos. Perhaps those firefly-eating animals would be asleep. She hoped her snow-loving friends had headed back to their caves and would return and bring help… and their belongings. How this would transpire, she didn't know. Fred had not been happy about sending the four Yetis to begin with.

Fred and his disinterest in saving the Haldor flitted through her troubled mind as well, and hope dimmed. He didn't have a history of getting people out of trouble. She could only hope his association and friendship with Pappy would give him a push in the right direction.

Magik would now be the only weapon the little group had, and Alyssa, as the only magik-wielder, hoped it would be enough. She couldn't imagine attacking the powerful Madrid or his son, or both, with spells that she cobbled together on the fly. And the pair of them had the scarf. That alone gave them a distinct advantage.

She wandered a few steps, staring at a wooden table and row of scratched chairs lining the wall. They had been moved aside, as if the master of the castle had asked someone to clear the floor for dancing. Alyssa set Pappy Oh's box on one chair and pulled out another one to sit in. No reason to continue to pace the stones until she drooped like the hangings overhead. She placed the jack-in-the-box back in her lap. Better to keep it close.

She wished Pappy still remained with them. He would know what to do right now. She could only assume. Would they meet with the fake king, Madrid, or his son soon? And then what? How could they get the scarf? Well-armed men guarded the castle grounds. Maybe Lord Bryon had expected this, but she had not. She didn't know what she expected. Perhaps that the scarf would appear and want to go with her.

Like it would know your intentions are pure. But what about the scarf's intentions?

This train of thought brought on its heels quite another one. A thought more devious. More deadly. What if the scarf had *wanted* to be stolen?

When she considered all she knew about the scarf and how it had shifted from hand to hand, it seemed to have a purpose for the person chosen to take it. Surely no magik item would desire to be an item in the gryphon's collection of treasures.

What if it left the previous owner on purpose instead of being taken? Why would it want to remain with a manor lord and be taken out of the world of Daegries? What kind of magik did the scarf have, exactly? Certainly, the ability to protect its bearer while reason to do so remained.

This meant that the magik in the scarf worked and purposefully moved ownership all the time.

It wants to be in the hands of someone else. This possibility set her back on her heels. Before she could focus on what that meant and how she could use it to her advantage, the man dressed in chainmail entered the great room. He pushed a bedraggled man and a Yeti in front of him.

"Cerius!" Bryon said.

The guard shoved the man and he fell, practically at Bryon's feet. The Yeti had shackles on his hands and feet and could only growl and bare his teeth at the man.

Lord Bryon clenched his fists. "Are you a drunkard, man? You dare to treat the son of a nobleman this way? And unchain this creature. How unchivalrous!"

The man only laughed and turned on his heel, heading back the way he came.

Alyssa knelt beside Cerius and put her hand on his back. The power unleashed on him zinged up her arm, blurring her vision. This magik felt like nothing she'd ever touched before.

Cerius tried to rise, but she encouraged him to stay put. "You've been magiked, sir," she said.

Then to Bryon, she added, "Lord Bryon, this man is plumb eat up with magik. He should lie down. I'll try to see where the spell took root. Maybe with a little luck, I'll be able to heal him."

They put a table upright and another beside it to accommodate Cerius. Then Fletch and Bryon hoisted him atop it so Alyssa could treat him.

While they were doing this, she walked over to Jed, the Yeti, and spoke gently to him. "Jed, you've been ill-treated by these men. You're a little scared to be with us now since we all seem the same to you. But I give you my word, my promise in Pappy Oh's name, that I won't hurt you, or mistreat you. Do you understand?"

He grunted. "Grumpkin?"

"Grinkle." She didn't know what it meant but remembered Pappy saying something similar.

The Yeti bared its teeth at her (his version of a grateful smile) and sat on the floor.

She ran her hands lightly over his hairy body, first his back and then his arms. She felt nothing out of place.

And no magik at all.

"Jed, did the men who hurt Sir Cerius do anything to you?"

Jed shook his head.

Relieved, she stood taller and asked, "Do you speak my language at all?"

He inclined his head and nodded. "Deetle."

Alyssa exhaled. "Okay, good. I don't think the magik that is making Sir Cerius sick has affected you. That may be a good thing, for more than one reason. But in case it is a delayed reaction to magik that comes without warning, you stay here and rest. And if you feel anything strange at all, let me know. Understand?"

Jed nodded. He rattled his chains. "Dan do date dis?"

She thought he asked her to remove his chains. She handled them. They were heavy, thickly looped and bound by a strong padlock. She would have to have a key or unlock it by magik.

"Let me figure out a way to get those off. Just rest now," she told Jed. As she passed Fletch, she said in a low voice, "Wherever they were kept, the jailer has the key."

Jed must have overheard her because he slumped and put his hands in his lap.

Alyssa said over her shoulder in Jed's direction, "I promise as soon as I get Cerius out from under the magik that's making him sick, I'll free you."

She gave Fletch a sharp nod and returned to Cerius.

She didn't ask if she could put her hands over him; she just did it. What she felt made her yank them back as though flames licked them.

The magik flowing in Cerius's body issued out like a foul odor. It repulsed her.

She stepped back and tried to remember all she had been told about people and magik and how sometimes it could make them sick.

Poor Lady Pianna's sickness from magik had been different. She made a weak vessel for the stream of magik that came from the scarf. That sickness had been like a candle melted to the bottom of the holder, depleted.

Cerius's affliction felt quite different. His body and mind were wrestling with the magik, as if trying to best it some way. Instinct told her the wrongness of it. Magik could not be repelled once absorbed. She knew this from the recent incident with the illumination spell. It seeped into her body and mind and rested there. She could call it up, send it out, and call it back, but she couldn't rid herself of it.

As the conjurer of the magik spell, Pappy Oh could call it out. He could remove it from her. But he alone had that power. Then, too, her magik used items from the land and acted straightforward in its intent. Simple, pure land magik.

She touched Cerius's face, and he opened his eyes, wicked as a wildcat. They darted back and forth and refused to focus on her.

What beguilement is this?

She didn't know what type of magik she dealt with nor where it came from. Not land magik, for certain. She didn't have any experience with much else to compare it with. She thought she'd know water magik or air magik. It couldn't be or feel much different than her magik, she supposed. Definitely not fire magik. She sighed, stumped and staring at the man before her. Pappy would know. Pappy could fix it.

Oh, Pappy, where are you?

When she captured Cerius's head in her hands to hold him steady, he convulsed. "Hold steady, Sir Cerius," she said softly. It didn't help. Vibrations shook his body. Determined, she didn't let go. She could only do what she knew how to do. If it released him, wonderful. If not... well, she had to try, didn't she?

She closed her eyes and gripped his head, fighting against his desire to thrash. "Magik, you must leave this body. This body is fighting you. This body doesn't want you. Get out!" Alyssa said as she pictured the magik in her mind. To her, it acted like a bat beating itself against the front porch posts at the farm. "Go back to your maker," she cried out.

She felt it leave Cerius and bang around in the room, trying to escape. It rolled itself up into a puff of smoke and wafted overhead, eventually dissipating, until it faded altogether. She had the taste of blood in her mouth after that, but it dissolved quickly.

The others did not see or react to it at all. This was the most curious thing to her. But maybe the powers she had sought were finally released in her, as the dryad and siren had foretold. For the first time, she could now command someone else's spell.

Refocusing, she closed her eyes and placed her hands over Cerius's chest until she could feel his heart racing, slowing, finally beating normally. He lifted a tired hand and patted her arm.

Alyssa smiled down at him. He closed his eyes and fell into a snoring sleep. Lord Bryon stood at her elbow. She was surprised at his presence, unaware he had joined her.

"You are a great healer, Lady Alyssa. They will write your name in the annals of time as the greatest healer," he murmured.

Fletch, who had been standing apart keeping watch, now strode to the other side of his sleeping comrade. "You defeated it. He no longer lies spellbound."

She nodded and felt behind her for a chair to seat herself. "Yes, but I don't feel so springy. Guess healing can make some of us a little weak." This weakness after healing became the only familiar thing she could focus on. Granny had always taken to bed after healing someone.

Fletch grabbed a chair, and Bryon helped her into it. They stood watching her, as if she too would fall victim to the magik that she had exorcised.

"My lady?" Lord Bryon asked, concern in his face.

"I'm fine, just a little faint. Give me a minute."

The two men stepped back a bit to allow her to be comfortable. They ogled their current surroundings.

"Get something to break that lock on Jed's chains. I don't think I'm quite strong enough to undo them with magik right now," she told them.

Lord Bryon moved to where a raised dais stood at the head of the great room, obviously where the master's table would be for a gathering.

An ornate pair of chairs, more like thrones, perched there, and Alyssa remembered that Madrid had touted himself as king. Lord Bryon walked around on the dais searching for something to break Jed's lock.

"How about the other Yetis?" Fletch asked, his serious brown eyes going from Alyssa to Bryon. "They ran from danger at the first sign."

"Not ran, Fletch, escaped. I would not discount them," Lord Bryon said, returning empty-handed. "The creatures are not fools. They understood how to win a battle with the armed men of Needlemount. Take out their mounts and doubts will strike at them. Something we missed. My lady, I find nothing to free Jed."

Fletch persisted. "Do you believe the creatures will return in numbers and with weapons to free us?"

Bryon shook his head. "I no longer know what to think. My plans have changed. This has been a fool's game from the start. I can only lean on Lady Alyssa and her skills to have a plan and execute it now."

The conversation stopped at that. Alyssa shifted on her seat as she realized they relied on her to save them from whatever awaited.

"Let me see what I can do," she told them, rising. As she walked back to Jed, a swish of cloth and tiny whoosh of air reminded them all that a time of reckoning approached. Indeed, had now arrived. Three sets of eyes met in consternation as someone strode toward them.

Chapter Thirteen

Edegast the Green

Surprisingly, the footfalls echoed from a corridor behind the raised dais at the end of the room, not from the direction the man in chainmail had departed.

Alyssa turned. She had sensed no such area. Had a hidden room been revealed, and they hadn't seen it? Suddenly, the lack of feeling in the room made sense. It had been hidden until such time as it might be needed.

They had been magiked.

If only she had known, she could have tried to hide them in the cold, uninviting hall. She wracked her brain to recall what Pappy had told her about blocking spells. One where a spell-caster could enchant an area to keep other magik-users from taking control, but that would never work when magik already reigned. And she did not have a spell book or any magik items with which to conjure anything.

The footsteps came closer, getting louder with each step. She focused on the sound, trying to imagine the gait. Someone with impatience...

They did not have to wait long.

The man wore a long forest-green robe tied in the middle with a yellow rope, with long ends that dangled down to his booted feet. He carried a staff of red oak. Alyssa gaped at him to see if he wore a scarf, but he did not.

Lord Bryon stood and glared at the man, who stopped on the dais to assess the group.

"So," the man said. "This is the raggle-taggle band of adventurers who have interrupted my evening."

"Who are you? Where is Madrid and his demon-spawn, Ragon?" Lord Bryon asked. "I would parlay with the man who holds sway over Needlemount."

The man's silver eyebrows drew together over his beak of a nose as he perused the group. His age could have been old or ancient. Even more than Pappy Oh. But hard living sometimes created that sort of countenance.

Alyssa shrank back, hoping he would overlook her. She fixed her attention on the aura of the room, the essence of which would show her the magik.

Her gaze went to the rafters overhead. Aside from the forlorn nests of some long-gone birds who had sought refuge there, nothing appeared out of order.

She peered at every pillar, every window slit, every tapestry. The last one, closest to the dais, had a yellow wisp of something floating in its tassels.

There! That's where the magik is hiding!

As the two men assessed each other's mettle, Alyssa moved slowly toward the pillar with the strange woven banner, Pappy Oh's box loosely held under her arm.

The robed man banged his staff against the ground and got the attention of all, especially Alyssa, stopping her in her tracks.

"You shall not come near," he told her, his emerald gaze piercing hers.

"I beg pardon?" she asked.

"I refuse your attention to my magik. You may not continue."

She gaped at him. "I'm sorry, I wasn't trying to—"

"Yes. You *were* trying to, but I rebuke you." The tiny yellow cloud faded away like mist in the sunlight. "See? I have removed what you were seeking so curiously."

Her vision blurred with fear. How could he have known she sought magik in the hall? How did he remove it so quickly?

"I am a wizard. I hail from the northern mountains, the Snowclids," he stated. Then he took a step toward her, holding the staff out in front of him. "And you are?"

"Alyssa Chance Oh from Mudden," she said with a tiny curtsy. A meeting with a wizard might not call for such actions, but it couldn't hurt to be nice. "I'm a healer, sir."

The wizard took a quick step backwards, nearly falling over the hem of his robe. His staff lit up with a golden light, and his face fell into hard lines once he recovered.

"No," he answered, with a bit of disdain. "You are far more than a simple healer. A third-degree mage, perhaps?"

This shocked Alyssa, and she whispered to Lord Bryon, "Wizards are the most powerful of mages. He's asking if I am as powerful as a wizard."

Lord Bryon took a step forward, permitting Alyssa to move away. "Who are you?" he demanded.

"My name is Edegast the Green."

Bryon crossed his arms. "Where are the lords of Castle Needlemount?"

"I've taken good care of them, never fear." Edegast moved to the leftmost chair on the dais but did not sit.

Alyssa sidled toward him, feeling the air with her senses to see if traces of magik surrounded him. Would this magik be sickening, as it had been to Cerius?

"And do not come any closer, young Castling. That is quite close enough," Edegast told her.

Alyssa stopped. *A Castling*? This had to be some sort of acknowledgement of her abilities. Something that she still had to come to terms with. She gripped Pappy Oh's box tighter. "If I may ask, sir, what is a wizard doing here in this place?"

Bryon nodded and added, "Aye. Wizards north of these mountains have not been south in a long time."

"It is a simple matter, really," Edegast replied. "I am seeking answers from the Haldor."

This revelation made Alyssa's mouth fall open. The Haldor! Her curiosity about the missing tribe of Heightlanders sprang to life once more.

A wave of heat struck Pappy's box and ricocheted upward, smacking Alyssa in the face. She struggled against the unexpected assault, worried she might pass out from the intensity. She almost dropped Pappy Oh's box right where she stood.

"Oh!" she cried, bending over in pain. "What in Daegries?"

Edegast coughed. "My apologies. I see your magik is as strong as I suspected. I wanted to get into that box. Apparently, an enchanted one. My mistake."

Alyssa straightened and rubbed her reddened cheek where it had burned. "How rude!"

Edegast pointed his staff at her. "You took liberties; so, did I."

She stamped her foot. "Your men took us prisoner, made my friend sick, and chained this Yeti. We mean no harm to you, Edegast the Green, but foul are the intentions of a wizard who acts like this. Clear your magik from this room, unchain my Yeti, and act like a civilized high mage or I'll—"

"My apologies, most sincerely," Edegast replied, cheeks reddening at her rising temper. Be gone!"

And with his words, the room cleared of the stagnation that had it spellbound, and Jed's chains fell away. Cerius woke mid-snore and grunted.

"Now, if I may ask," Edegast drawled. "What is your business at Needlemount?"

Alyssa recalled the gryphon's words about not telling all to strangers. "It ain't smart for us to come into this hall under arm-twisting tactics and tell a perfect stranger about our business.

Especially a wizard, who has just attacked me. Maybe I'll tell it, and maybe I won't."

Edegast smiled. This did nothing to make his face kinder, however. Crevices smoothed from between his eyes but deepened around his mouth. He stroked his mustache. "I apologize once more. You may tell of your own volition. Whenever you are ready." Then, he sat on the chair on the dais and stared at them, waiting.

"Best do as he asks," Fletch whispered. His eyes never left the wizard. Alyssa could sense Fletch coiled, ready to strike if necessary.

"Did you feel a touch of that heat?" Alyssa asked in a low voice. "That hurt! He's got my ire up."

She doubled her efforts at conversation with the wizard, thinking how she could draw him out and trick him if he subtly conjured something.

"I want to tell you now, if you bring magik against me again, I bet your Order will be pretty dang interested in hearing about it," she said, hoping he belonged to a part of the Order of Magik-Users that she'd heard Pappy Oh talk about. Her grandfather had always wanted to be a part of it.

He solemnly nodded. "Very well."

"Fine," she added, giving him as much of a focused stare as she dared. "Our business, Edegast, lies with Madrid and his son. On the way, we stopped and chatted with the Yetis for a bit, and they tagged along with us out of friendship. They disappeared mighty quick once they got the chance. Funny how they all scattered. Your men might be a little sore from that run-in with them. You'd think the Yetis know you or something. Except for poor Jed here. Would you care to expound on that any?"

Edegast stretched out his legs and nestled his staff into the crook of his arm. "Yes, that is true. The Yetis and I have not been on good terms in some time, I regret to say. My fault, really. I have not been down this way for a few years. It took me quite a while to learn what happened at the Haldor seat. No one in Yetiland knew anything about the cave-in. Or, should I say, no one would relate it. A disagreement ensued from that meeting that is still being felt."

"Pretended not to know, you mean? Well, that just ain't right," Alyssa added. "What with you being such a mighty wizard and all."

This compliment made him relax. "True," he agreed. Jed had moved away from his chains and sat as far away from the wizard as possible. He grumbled at the wizard's words.

Alyssa said, "You ain't made them feel much friendlier with chains and magik bouncing off their heads."

Lord Bryon, idling nearby, shuffled his feet a moment before asking with the utmost politeness, "We have business with Needlemount's master and his son. Could you produce one or both of them, please?"

"No," Edegast replied, amused at the man's discomfort in his presence. "I cannot. The father and son are my prisoners. They have knowledge of the Haldor, and I will not release them until they share it with me."

"They have more than a knowledge of the Haldor," Alyssa interjected, half under her breath. Then, louder, directed toward Lord Bryon as a ruse, she said, "I bet they had something to do with the destruction of the Haldor homes."

At this, Edegast sat up and gripped his staff. "Ah, so you *do* know something."

"Uh oh," Fletch said, fists clenching. "Better set him straight, Lady Alyssa."

The faint yellow mist showed up again, near the tapestry. Alyssa could not believe that the wizard would release his magik again in such a short time, the equivalent of flexing his muscles to show his power.

As if I would forget him.

Alyssa carried Pappy Oh's box forward about five steps and set him down by the pillar she wanted to investigate. She put a hand on the banner and gripped it while the magik struggled to get free.

At the same time, she pointed her finger at Edegast and said, "See here, Wizard. We don't know nothing about the Haldor other than what the leader of Yetiland told us. I was only supposing when I said that. I mean, think about it. If those folks up and vanished after the mountain caved in, it may have been a big old accident. End of story."

She felt the magik racing through the material and clung to it. "Right now, we need to see these menfolk that live here. My grandmother is in all manner of danger back where I'm from. I've come a long way, through meadows, mountains, and mayhem, to get here to take care of some business with them. You ain't going to keep me from it. No sir, you ain't."

And she shook the hanging, her anger flowing into it as if to tell the wizard's magik a thing or two.

Her friends were taken aback at the ferocity of her words, and the anger stamped on her face, but did a double take at the riotous laughter that emanated from the wizard.

His laughter bounced along the stones of the floor, against the walls, and even stirred the banners in the room, before finally echoing down the corridor behind him. Alyssa tried her best to thwart the magik that surged down her arm from the tapestry.

"Let it go, girl," Edegast gasped through his mirth. "You are not a good match for its power. But your attempt has amused me considerably."

Embarrassed to be held in such hilarity, she did as he requested, rubbing her hand and arm from the wrangling it had received.

Alyssa could not understand what happened. His magik became an afterthought for him. She had given everything she had, attempting to control it. The wizards were powerful and dangerous, and she should have known better. She could hear Pappy Oh fussing at her. She fussed at herself even more. Her power might have begun developing in her life, but it remained a fledgling still.

She slumped as she waited for the wizard to speak.

He wiped his eyes with the hem of his robe and took a few deep breaths.

"You have done something many have never done. You made me laugh. For that, I will grant you your wish."

She turned to stare at the others. Bryon shrugged in confusion. Cerius rubbed his eyes and stared at the sight before him. Jed growled and Fletch relaxed his stance but remained guarded.

All eyes turned to Edegast and waited.

"Yes, your wish for an audience with my two prisoners, I will grant. But before that, I will tell you what I am doing here, and why this room has been magiked, and how your man there got caught in it all."

Cerius gazed around, a bit unsteady even now.

"And why didn't the magik affect Jed? I'd like to hear that tale now," she told the wizard.

"Well, the short tale is this: your man there rested in the dungeon thanks to the guards, who are not my men, by the way. I issued something forth, not directed at him or his Yeti friend, mind you, but he caught it anyway. My focus must have strayed a touch."

Lord Bryon sighed. "This magik spell business causes a lot of difficulties, doesn't it? It's a pile of horse manure with butter on it."

Alyssa stifled a giggle. It sounded so much like something Pappy Oh would have said.

They sat at the long table pulled into the middle of the great hall. A serving woman, the first that Alyssa had seen, brought soaked rushes in and lit candles. Some nested in sconces on the walls, and some sat awkwardly in dishes on the table. This action alone made the room warmer and more welcoming. The men with weapons came and went from the room attending to this bit of business and that. They were busy, Alyssa would give them that.

Edegast had become friendly with the Half Moon Manor men after his show of might with magik. He hinted that, although an apprentice, Alyssa's skill must be controlled, and she should be mindful of that. She disagreed soundly, remembering how effective Pappy Oh had been in life. His skill rambled around, untried as a newborn colt.

"My Granny taught me a lot about healing, and my Pappy used that healing in some of his magik. I know something about both worlds and how to make them work together. But controlling it? Ain't so sure about that," she told him.

Edegast sent Jed, who paced in boredom, to find a guard and encourage him to come to the great room.

Soon the armed man who had brought them to the castle's inner room arrived with Jed. Edegast told the man to order his regiment and the buggos to loosen their guard. "Tell them that unless they wish to face the same fate as their lord, they should stand down and not impede any of this party." He used his staff to circle the air around the table, indicating all gathered. The man nodded and bowed to Edegast, spun away, and left. Jed followed him out, and Alyssa hoped it was to find his brothers.

Then, Edegast disappeared behind the dais for a short while. When he returned, serving men followed with trays of venison and pheasant, roasted and glistening with fat, followed by steaming potatoes and other root vegetables. They brought loaves of hot bread arranged on platters with apples and chunks of cheese. Soon, heavy goblets of winter wine arrived to quench their thirst.

After watching the wizard gobble on a pheasant leg and guzzle some of the wine, the company and Alyssa grew silent for some time while they ate their fill.

With the meal set aside and everyone's stomachs full, they assured their host it had been the best they'd ever had. Then Edegast wove the tale to explain his present situation. In that story, they learned how it fell in line with their own.

"Last summer, as I traveled through the forests of Genmyar on one of my infamous jaunts, I discovered a mysterious light leading off into the deep woods. Though inadvisable to part from a trail in such places, it intrigued me," Edegast told them. "The radiance didn't appear and disappear like swamp gas, and, in truth, the area felt not wet at all. But I could not imagine anything else that could make such a light. After several yards of my following the glow and observing its behavior, I realized my mistake."

Soon, all heads tilted toward the wizard and every eye became riveted. Alyssa had seen firsthand how easily words could weave a binding spell, but even she was captivated.

Edegast continued, "In the twinkling of a starburst, a band of Iefyr overcame me, fully fortified and treacherous. I consented to them without incident. They took me deeper into Genmyar. So much so that the path they chose will forever be lost to me as it dipped and bobbed up hill and over dale and through trees, a way only they could know."

Alyssa, ever curious, asked, "Who or what are Iefyr?"

Lord Bryon coughed softly and murmured, "Fables."

Fletch shook his head. "No, not so. They are as real as the aristocrats on your manor-lands. My Papa tells tales about them. They used to make seasonal appearances down below the Heightlands in the time of midsummer."

Cerius nodded, seeming to feel himself again. "My folks have said that, too."

Edegast noted the far doorway leading out of the great hall, as though he expected the Iefyr to come through it. "Yes, as real as we are. I never believed it until I saw for myself."

Alyssa sat back and thought about this. "I've only read about many of these people who live outside of Mudden. Bugbears, the storybooks say, are creatures of woodlands who sleep all winter and are kind of dumb with small brains. The creatures I met were not like that at all. Oh, and their love of eating fireflies? Not in any book." This drew a chuckle from her companions. "I saw it with my own eyes. The reason I could make it onto castle grounds—they were feasting on fireflies."

She continued, "Now, the Haldor are unknown to me, except for the things they crafted and what has been described in a book. Well, I got to see some of those items firsthand from the Yetis. Heck, we even used some of them, right?"

She glanced around at her company, and they all nodded.

"Now, you're talking about Iefyr, and none of the books I've read talk about them or what they're known for. At least, I ain't ever read that part yet. Are they wizards, too?"

Edegast laughed. "I confess, the bugbears are my companions. I brought them along to the castle out of the woods, as I knew not what I faced. They are good as guards and protectors, but they have little motivation. Except to eat. They will follow anyone for food. I will release them soon to return to their homes."

"About the Iefyr?" Alyssa asked. "Are they wizards, too?"

Edegast, brought to the present by her question, answered, "Yes, and no, young Castling. The most powerful of all magik-users, natural magik too. Unlike wizard-magik, gleaned through practice and spell work, elven magik is old and comes from the land, from Daegries herself. That is why to be captured and given admittance into their inner realm seemed unusual. They protect their ways strongly."

"But if they are magik-users, why haven't I read about them in any books on magik or spells?" she persisted.

"Iefyr don't mingle with men anymore. I doubt that they ever allowed anything to be written in any annals about them either. Their history passed down through oral stories such as have been told at campfires," he explained. "Only the wizards know their ancient history now. I never believed I would see Iefyr, let alone walk amongst them."

He reflected. "But, as you will see, it turned into a great thing. In the end they gifted me with a magik item as a way of thanking me for helping them with some difficulties they were having with… erm… something, and that item is why I have come here seeking answers. The Haldor know a bit about it. The men of Needlemount are the missing link between the making of this magik item, and the troubles of the Haldor and Elves."

Alyssa lifted an eyebrow at his hesitation. *He ain't telling us everything, either.*

She chewed a bit of bread and casually asked, "It wasn't a magik scarf, was it?"

Edegast took the goblet from his lips and silently, slowly placed it on the table while never breaking eye contact with her. "Why yes, as a matter of fact. How did you know that?"

She took a deep breath. "I'm searching for it, too."

The wizard snatched up his staff, now sizzling with power, and pointed it at her. "Are you my enemy then?"

Chapter Fourteen

Troubled Tales

Alyssa stared deeply into the wizard's eyes and saw no deception there. Her words truly alarmed him.

"Now hold up a minute, Wizard. I ain't your enemy."

"You come here, unannounced, powerful magik at your command, and say to me that the scarf is something you are seeking. How can I take that for anything less?"

"Well, first off," she said raising her hand in peace, "I don't want to fight you for the scarf or nothing. I need it to serve a purpose. Maybe once you hear my story, you'll understand."

He pointed the staff at the others at the table. "Are you aiding this girl in this endeavor? Are you my enemies?"

They shook their heads. He sat again, pulling his robe closer. "There are evil ones afoot, who knows where these days. I can take no chances."

Bryon said, "I am here with my kinsmen to exact blood money for the murder of my father and his page, my brother. Their spilled blood is the fault of Madrid and Ragon. The scarf has played a part, yes, but I have no designs to forcibly take the scarf. I've been unaware the scarf is magiked until recently."

The wizard lifted his brow and stared at Lord Bryon as though seeing all the way through him. "But you do desire it."

Bryon shrugged. "Only because it once belonged to my father. If Lady Alyssa's need outweighs my desire for the scarf, then so be it."

Edegast relaxed. "Indeed. We shall hear your family matters as related to your desire for it in a moment. But first, Alyssa, please continue your tale. With the scarf, there is always one to tell."

Alyssa took her time. She didn't need to rush through this story and make a mistake in the retelling. The wizard would see through anything she invented, anyway. She treated him as though she were speaking to Pappy Oh.

The room grew ever darker with the lateness of the evening. When Alyssa finished the story of the scarf as far as she knew it, with Bryon filling in his father's part, she ended by saying, "Sir Edegast, I don't mean to be harping on the same subject again, but we're in a real pickle about getting back to help my Granny Gert."

"I see. And Madrid and Ragon are the ones with the answers," he mused, digesting the idea.

"Yes. One or both knows something. And if we don't get that scarf back real soon, that old King Hubert is going to seize my family farm and do something horrible to my Granny. We have to get it to him before the full moon."

Edegast frowned at this. "The face of Luna waxes full already. This is a grave situation."

At this, worry welled up in Alyssa, and she rubbed at her lips. Fletch offered her a small smile, which didn't help matters, but she appreciated the gesture and accepted it gratefully.

Edegast stood and motioned for them to join him. "You shall have your meeting then. But if they should give you the scarf's locale, know this: you cannot take it."

Everyone stopped moving, and Alyssa held her breath for a moment. Finally, she found her tongue. "But why not? I'm taking it to the rightful owner. I thought you said you felt the situation grave… like you… would give it to me."

He waved his hand dismissively. "Before they took it from the gryphon, he took it from me. The scarf you seek is mine."

"Well, stretch my legs and call me a froglet," Alyssa said, eyes widening.

The company stood facing the wizard Edegast with disbelief on their faces.

"You mean that blasted scarf is the magik item that the Iefyr gave to you? And it's tied to them as well as the Haldor?" Alyssa asked, gooseflesh rising along her arms. "Something ain't right in all this."

Edegast nodded. "Yes. Worse, this scarf is one of the most powerful items in our land. My brothers in the Wizard Hall want it entombed there for safekeeping. I have to take it back north."

"Safekeeping from whom?" Alyssa asked.

"I cannot speak yet on that matter, as it is still being uncovered at this time. I give you my word that there is a desperate reason."

"What about my kinsmen murdered at the hands of these Needlemount men?" Bryon blurted out, waving his arm wide to indicate the castle. "That scarf was stolen from my father, Lord Pryon of Half Moon. How can you say the scarf is yours when it left your hand and has gone to others since?"

Edegast rubbed the back of his neck as he contemplated the dilemma facing them all. He paced a few times and thrust his staff onto the table.

He addressed Alyssa first. "I give you my staff as collateral in this matter. If you help to retrieve the scarf, I will act as your witness to the gryphon, who is not the true owner. He and I have unfinished business as well. How dare he steal it from me! Nevertheless, the scarf must go north."

Alyssa chewed on this thought.

Edegast then turned to Bryon and company. "If I do not satisfy your urgent matter with Madrid and his son, you may have my cloak, which is… er … a magikal matter of its own."

"I have no use for such an item," Bryon replied, aggrieved. "Blood money is in order. Or revenge. I would see these murderers hanged."

"Oh? Will money satisfy you?" Edegast asked, lifting an eyebrow. "A magik scarf would serve you far better against the hounding of a land baron."

"I have never hidden my feelings on the matter of taxation by these herein," Bryon admitted turning to Alyssa. "But before you doubt me, know that I would not take the scarf from you, whatever its value. I have only thought of it as a keepsake. I have no intentions. But if it were to be sold… perchance Lord Gryphon King could receive a portion of the proceeds? And others who have been damaged by it, certainly. Monetary compensation would serve as justice for all."

Now she understood. The scarf existed as little more than an advantage to the manor lord. But he didn't know that Hubert the Gryphon King had no use for money. He wanted power. Just as Lord Pryon had wanted. Just as Madrid and Ragon had wanted. Just as the wizard wanted… and in truth, Lord Bryon could also be seeking power. Was he? Could he be lying?

She lowered her gaze before addressing Edegast. She would have to tread lightly. "You sure are giving away stuff easily. First your staff, then your cloak. Are you expecting to die soon or something?"

Edegast came forward, stopping in front of her. "No. And you will not either, I suspect. But they are the only things I have with me that will suffice as a pledge of my word. Perhaps in the future we can find something more appropriate. The scarf must go north."

This made her stare at him directly, expecting him to wear a challenge on his grizzled face. Instead, it was placid, even kind.

"Only if my problem is solved first. South," she said.

Edegast ignored her. He placed his hand on Bryon's shoulder in a fatherly clasp. "As for your need for spilled blood to satisfy your family's losses, have you not heard it said that revenge for death with death will only result in a lower population? You surely cannot be of a mind to exact your own revenge on the men of Needlemount?"

Bryon lowered his shoulder to ease away from the wizard's touch. "You do not know the ways of men in the Heightlands, Wizard. We scorn magik on most days—your cloak will be of no use to me. We believe the way to settle matters is face to face, at the end of metal."

"Yes," Edegast replied dryly, wiping his hand on his robe. "I see that."

Alyssa remembered how the dryad and the siren discovered something about her by touching her. Did Edegast also have such an ability? If so, then he had discovered something distasteful in Bryon.

"Your father didn't go to Needlemount to war with the men here, did he? He went to parlay, right? Perhaps with the scarf as the bounty?" Alyssa asked.

Lord Bryon sat up straighter and put his face into serious lines. "Yes, that is true. He may have wanted to use it with these, my enemies, in exchange for the taxes they wanted to exact. I have no way of knowing. At any rate, I have no desire for a scarf, especially a magik one, other than in memory of my father and brother."

"Fair point," Edegast said.

Fletch sat quietly, watching this, only briefly casting glances at Cerius. Did they agree with Lord Bryon? Was revenge the only reason to make this journey?

The wizard returned to the dais, speaking over his shoulder. "Well, my young lord, perhaps when you meet the men you wish to disassemble with sword and hatchet, you will change your mind. Perhaps you may find compassion."

"Compassion? Like the compassion shown to my father and brother?" Bryon sputtered. "I think not, good Edegast. At the least, I shall require them in chains and taken to Half Moon for justice before our king."

After a momentary pause, Edegast faced him and replied, "Vengeance should be your last resort, sir. These are my prisoners you speak of, don't forget." His voice sounded calm, but his face wrinkled with dangerous intent.

If the staff of Edegast hadn't remained at the table, Alyssa would fear for Lord Bryon's safety. She reached for it, placing her hand on it. "Don't threaten Lord Bryon, Edegast. I'm sure his intentions are good. He won't do anything to your prisoners, except question them. If he acts otherwise, then let me be the one responsible."

The wizard turned away, his face falling into lines of remorse. "You understand more than is expected, young one."

She relaxed at his words, feeling she had thwarted the dilemma for the moment.

Fletch drew close to Alyssa. "Lady, what say you? This has been your adventure more than ours. We have lost one lord and son. We cannot afford to lose another. Vengeance may not be our only recourse and mayhap not our first choice on this day. I am willing to find out. Can we trust this wizard?"

Cerius strode to stand on her other side. "Yes, Fletch is right. I have pledged my allegiance to you as well. What do you believe is the right course?"

Lord Bryon slumped in defeat at these words. His men were giving him hard stares. Perhaps they didn't sign up for cold-blooded murder.

Alyssa replied, chin jutting at Edegast. "He's right. Vengeance and bloodshed ain't the only way." A headache settled over her forehead. "You are men I have traveled with a long way. My feeling is this: if Sir Wizard wanted to do ill to us, we'd already be dead. But those Needlemount men… well, we'll see soon enough what's what."

She let the thought lie there. She picked up Pappy Oh's box, grasped the staff the wizard had offered, and strode to the dais to meet him. "I'll see Madrid and Ragon now, have a listen to their tale and decide whether they get to live, go south with Lord Bryon, or remain your prisoners. They ought to pay for their deeds, no matter what. Guess I'll decide that, too. The scarf business has to be handled right away, though. They have to give it over to us. We can't afford to wait another hour."

Edegast nodded. "Yes, I understand your urgency."

She pushed the staff out a bit in his direction. "You and I will have to figure out how I can get the scarf south and you take it north at the same time."

Edegast lifted snowy eyebrows, and his face smoothed with his smile. "I have a plan developing already, dear lady. Let us go forth." He motioned for Bryon and the other men to join them. "You will be quite the greeting party."

Pappy Oh's box remained still and silent. Alyssa feared leaving it alone, on the off chance that her grandfather would return. But he hadn't made an appearance when she had called him in the presence of buggos, when her need felt so great. If he hadn't made it back by now, knowing her involvement with wizards and evil men, then he likely wouldn't.

"What about Jed? What about the other Yetis?" Alyssa asked.

"I'll leave word that we have gone to the dungeons. He can move freely as he wishes, and if he can convince his friends to join us, then that is also permitted. I think the path where we will go will be difficult for them to follow, however."

She asked the company if they wanted to pursue this part of the journey with her, or if they would rather go to a place where they could sleep. No one wanted to sleep.

Each man wished to parlay with the Needlemount men. Alyssa would have preferred to find a spot to sleep herself if that had been possible.

She shrugged, and Lord Bryon and his men followed Edegast onto the dais, around the chairs, and into a wide corridor that showed behind it. The yellow mist followed the wizard and stood over the doorway to it, and they all had to pass beneath it. Alyssa felt strange, as if his magik spell awaited an opportunity to jump on her.

She quickly got over this as they went along, and the yellow mist became a light orb that floated overhead illuminating the way. Smells of food wafted through the corridor, and she calculated how close they were to the kitchen.

Edegast collected a globe from a side table in one hand and showed it as the source of the yellow mist. The orb of mist fluttered onto the globe and then slipped inside of it. The now illuminated object lit up the area around them as effectively as a firebrand.

The wizard strode down the hall, turning left into a different corridor. He met an armored guard and instructed him to find the Yetis and wolves and make sure they were taken care of. The guard raised his eyebrows at her when Edegast told him that the creatures were her friends. She did not take the time to explain.

When the wizard finished speaking to the guard and the man took off in the opposite direction, the group followed Edegast once more as he took another sharp turn to the right and down a steep staircase.

They all hurried to keep up in the dark. When she caught sight again of the globe's glow, Alyssa breathed a loud sigh of relief. Edegast had not left them in the castle's darkness after all.

She remembered the wizard had told them Madrid and Ragon were his prisoners. Now, she would get her first glimpse of a castle keep and the area where they were being held. She clutched the staff with one hand and Pappy's box with the other.

She wished she had her pack and her weapons, but the tall back of the wizard gave her some small feeling of security. He didn't strike her as one to be trifled with, and he behaved utterly calmly.

I wish I felt like that.

At the bottom of the stone steps, Edegast turned right again and down another short hallway. The barred door of the dungeon stood stoutly before them, dark wood glimmering in the globe's yellow light.

Edegast stopped and waited for them to join him.

Fear stirred in her gut, a strong instinctual impulse. Her thoughts went to a dark place inside. She tried to shake it off, but the possibility of danger kept her tensed. She grasped the staff, but she didn't know the first thing about using it. Edegast knew they had no weapons and were literally at his mercy.

What if this strange wizard intended on throwing them in the dungeon with Madrid and Ragon? She slowed her steps. Making prisoners of them all might serve him far more…

When Fletch bumped into her, she realized she had completely stopped.

"Oof," he muttered, putting out a hand to steady himself. "I beg your pardon, my lady."

"Why have you stopped?" Bryon asked, pulling up short to keep from colliding with Fletch. Cerius, behind them, moved a bit slower than the rest, and stopped in time.

"What is the matter?" Edegast asked. "Why have you stopped over there?"

"Let's make sure we're clear here. You ain't planning on making the dungeon a little more crowded, are you?" Alyssa asked, pointing at the door with the end of the staff. A wizard remained a wizard, after all. No simple spellcaster such as herself could saunter into a wizard's territory without a bit of apprehension and even preparedness.

Edegast's face darkened. "You have my staff as proof of my sincerity. But you as a magik-user, of all people, should know that my senior warlocks would roast me over the deepest pits of Ridom if I should do such a thing."

Ridom, Alyssa had read, remained the historical torture chambers of all the greatest warlocks. "That's true," she whispered to herself. "Warlocks don't play."

Convinced, she waved to Edegast to open the door. "Carry on. But remember, I'm watching you."

He complied and entered before them, moving aside to let them enter, as well. The dank room seemed much larger than from outside the door, almost like a solar, of sorts. It had a window slit, uncovered, and a pile of straw with torn material lying over it. No one else stood in the cell.

"What mischief is this?" Bryon asked, waving at the room. "Where are the men?"

"One moment if you please," Edegast replied. Then he stared into a dark corner. "Come along, my good fellows. Show yourselves at once!"

At his command, two enormous rats scurried out from behind the straw and stood on their hind legs, with whiskers twitching, black eyes blinking at him.

If she hadn't been paying close attention, Alyssa would have asked the wizard again what game he played at. But no rat alive in a castle dungeon would have long hair pulled into a braid or long beards. These two rodents had been magiked.

Oh, Pappy. I wish you were here to see this.

Bryon rubbed his eyes in disturbed amazement. "What? What am I seeing?"

She set the box on the floor and drank in the sight of the rat duo. "Meet Madrid and Ragon," she answered.

"Well, I'll… can it be so?" Bryon turned to the wizard. "What has happened? Did you magik these men?"

Cerius spoke up. "Yes, he did, my lord. He accidentally caught me up in the magik, as well. And that is why you found me in that state on your arrival. I stood in the corridor with a guard, and the magik bounced onto me some way."

"Indeed, it did. I confess, not my best moment. I should have consulted with another magik-user before doing such evilment, but I had no choice. They refused to comply with my demands. My apologies, sir," Edegast said, with a slight bow to Cerius.

"You turned them into rats?" Fletch asked, eyes round. "Rats! I have never seen… such… wonderment."

Cerius inclined his head to the wizard. "As you can see, I pulled far enough out of the way to only get a taste of the magik. It is a fortunate thing that Lady Alyssa came along."

"Well, now what do we do?" Alyssa asked, rubbing her throbbing head. "We won't get much information from them unless someone can understand rat-squeak."

Lord Bryon, ever the optimist, replied, "Can't be much harder to understand than Yetish."

She couldn't argue with that. "Sir Edegast. I need them to talk to us. What can you do?"

He blinked a few times, tugged on his beard, and finally held his hand out. "You do not have to address me with a title, Alyssa. I am plainly Edegast. My father was a much greater wizard than I. His name was Trudor the White. Our colors designate where we are in the grand scope of things. So, Edegast the Green is who I am and simply Edegast to my friends. As to this other, give me that staff and stand back."

Again, distrust pulled at her gut, and she hesitated, pulling the staff in closer to her body.

"I would never do harm to you," he said, stiffly. "You should tamp down your thoughts, little Castling, as I can read them far too easily. Besides, I've already explained my position in these matters. Do you think I desire to be disbarred?"

Disturbed that he could indeed read her thoughts so easily, she relented. "Here," she said, handing the item over. "But let us move out of danger first. Please don't kill anyone."

He drew himself up taller. "You really are ill-informed about magik, aren't you?"

"Don't want to learn the hard way, either," she added.

They moved back to the door and faced the room. Cerius stepped outside, at Alyssa's insistence that he should not expose himself. It would be dangerous to be tainted again so soon.

The rat-men squeaked at each other and scurried toward the cloth on the straw.

Edegast pointed the staff at the pair and said some unintelligible words. Smoke drifted from the end of it right before it sprouted a thin spark of flame that struck them as they attempted to burrow beneath the tattered cloth.

The rats squeaked in terror as the magik encased them and they could not make a run for it. Alyssa heard an intake of breath at the magik they had witnessed and realized it came from her.

"Speak," Edegast instructed the enchanted men. "We are all simply trembling on every utterance." Then he handed the still smoking staff back to Alyssa. She accepted it with a curious glance at the end.

"Wizard," the rodent with the long beard said. "You change us back to our normal selves right this minute!"

"All in good time. Please introduce yourselves," Edegast drawled. "No one has had the privilege of conversing with rats as esteemed as you."

"Why, I'll—" Rat Longbeard started.

"Stifle yourself," the rat with a braid over his shoulder replied. His black eyes stared at Alyssa, and his voice sounded calmer than normal to anyone in his situation.

"Why? Wha…" Longbeard clamped his mouth closed, his whiskers drawing to a point. "Oh."

"What have you brought to us, Edegast? Magik-users?" the rat with a braid asked. "They cannot do anything to us. Nothing that you haven't already done, that is." Then he stood on his hind legs. "Ah. The heraldry of King Thalon, eh? And so you are Heightlanders. Of course." His tiny voice grew softer. "What is this about? We will not cooperate with any demands while enchanted as rats, you scoundrel!"

Edegast stood staring at the pair for a moment before chuckling. "You have nothing with which to bargain, Ragon. And if you do not wish to be boiled meat in a stew, you should explain yourself soon."

Ragon, the rat with the braid, said, "Ah, but we must have something, or why have you come here with this crowd? A crowd who appears to be as hungry as those wolves I heard howling a night or so ago."

Alyssa spoke up. "Ragon, Rat-King and Madrid, Lord of the Rats, or whatever else you may call yourselves, we have come a powerful far piece to get a scarf taken from Lord Bryon's father. It's my understanding you have it, or know who does?"

"Lord Bryon, eh?" Madrid, the long-bearded rat mused, moving closer to have a look. "Ah, yes, I think I see a resemblance."

"That's enough peering and proclaiming," Bryon said, voice deepening with authority. "You two need to know nothing else. My lady, I would refrain from giving them any more information than is necessary."

Embarrassed to be caught in such a way, Alyssa said, "Sorry." She knew better than to give information to the enemy. They could use it against her.

"Do not give any other names either," Edegast added before she could say more.

Her headache worsened in combination with exhaustion. She tapped the staff on the ground, aggravated. "Yes, sir."

Ragon scurried to the edge of the straw, where he stood, sniffing. "I smell a smell that is old, and yet familiar to me."

Madrid tilted his rat head and said, "Ah. As do I. This is surely the thing long awaited."

This interchange between the two rodents piqued Edegast's attention. "Maybe you should inform all of us what you mean by that."

The two snickered and their whiskers twitched back and forth.

"Why, you are the wizard, are you not? How do you not know?" Ragon asked. "The walls in Knowledge Mountain Hall are thick, but news still escapes."

"Yes, Edegast, surely you can *smell…* it," Madrid added, scurrying to Ragon's side.

Then, to Ragon, he asked, "The scarf has brought it here, hasn't it?"

Ragon sat back on his haunches, thinking. He didn't answer, but his eyes glittered with evil.

Edegast pinioned the pair with his steely gaze. "Tell us where the scarf is and be done with this parry and thrust."

"You cannot force us to tell you," Ragon answered. "But we might if given our normal forms again. A bargain, perhaps?"

"I wouldn't trust them," Bryon said to Edegast.

"Nor I," Cerius agreed.

Alyssa's curiosity rose, but she remained silent. If Edegast wanted to make them men again, he was within his rights, as he had magiked them to begin with. She didn't want to get between a wizard and his captives, not without reason. The rats would either tell them the scarf's location freely and of their own power, or they wouldn't. Personally, she wouldn't care to be in their place. She offered the staff to Edegast. "Here, you might need this."

Chapter Fifteen

Confessions

"I will give you one more chance to tell us. If you choose not to tell us, then you will be meat in a cook pot. I understand Bugbears love mice." Edegast stood up as straight and tall as possible to tower over the two, waving the staff away.

"If you do that," Madrid chirruped. "If you do that you will—"

"You will never find out," Ragon finished, tapping tiny ratty paws together briefly.

Alyssa, tired of their delaying game, turned to Fletch, handed him the staff, and charged forward to scoop Ragon up before he could scurry away.

He squealed in a rat-caught-in-a-trap voice, before repeatedly spewing, "Put me down."

"Stop," she commanded, tapping his tiny head. "Act like a man, not a mouse."

Madrid paced back and forth peering up at Ragon, terror in his beady eyes. Then he stopped, sat up on his haunches, twitched his whiskers, and patted his beard. "Put him down. What are you up to?"

"Isn't it obvious? You two have all the answers when you're banded together. I'm going to remove the most likely mastermind and let the other starve," Alyssa said, hiding her face.

She loved the little animals and always turned them out of the barn when encountered, instead of calling the old tomcat that took refuge there. Those were mice, mostly. And they never talked to her, not like these enchanted ones in her presence.

Despite that, she wouldn't harm anyone, enchanted or not. But they didn't need to know that right now.

"Follow me," she instructed Bryon and Cerius, who stood closest. "Fletch, come along. Bring the staff."

They all made ready to depart the dungeon with her and the rat. He squirmed and scratched at her hands. "Let me go. Let me go, you fool!"

"No," Alyssa snarled. "You're either going to tell us where that scarf is, or you're never going to see your father again."

The rat slumped in her hands. "I will never tell you. You can torture me, you can run me through with a sword, but you will never get that information from me."

Her mouth lifted at the corners, and she remained silent. It hadn't been Ragon she expected to blab about the scarf. She'd chosen him to take out of the mix so that Edegast could speak to Madrid. She'd also left Pappy Oh's box there in case he returned. He would get the location of the scarf out of Madrid. If only he came back!

But, if Edegast couldn't loosen the tongue of a rat, and Pappy Oh didn't make an appearance, then they'd lost nothing. She'd be happy to give it a try.

Later, Alyssa touched the staff resting against her chair. It comforted her, something like having Pappy's box close to her. She had placed Ragon underneath a wooden bowl left on the great room table, and she encouraged her friends to partake of the bread and cheese left there also.

She still had the leftover twinge from her recent headache, and the lack of sleep had put her into a waspish mood.

Ragon kept up a constant stream of utterings, all mean and threatening. Fletch asked once if they could throw him outside for the ravens to find, but Alyssa shook her head and said nothing.

Everyone witnessed Ragon's squealing and chirruping and yelling. The men in her company shifted uneasily at the rat's threats. Every word the rodent chattered sent a new sharp pain through her head.

After washing down the last bit of bread on her charger with a swallow of cider, she strode over to the wooden dish and lifted it, catching Ragon as he darted to escape.

As she considered her next move, a loud commotion began in the front of the castle. She placed Ragon back under the bowl and sought something to use as a weapon. Her hand landed on the staff, and she gripped it tightly. With the others, she skulked toward the noise.

Before they got far, the Yetis and wolves and guards burst into the great room, pushing them all backwards toward the dais.

"Jed!" she cried at the sighting of the massive, hairy creature. "Where have y'all been?"

They bared their teeth and spewed their guttural words at the same time. She had to hold her hand up to quiet them. The wolves paced around, sniffing at the room, and finally coming back to stand with their friends.

Bryon, Fletch, and Cerius all scrambled to take their weapons and packs from the creatures who still carried them.

Alyssa motioned for her bow and arrow to be set beside her. "Please, all of you sit down. We'll get this sorted out in a minute. I need to know what's going on with y'all and hear about any news."

They did as she asked, plopping down onto the floor in a row like stone monoliths. The wolves wandered, panting, and then settled down beside their friends on the floor.

Alyssa set the staff back where she'd had it, and directed her questions to Jed, but sometimes the others tried to answer.

She didn't know what they said. "I'm lost. I wish I spoke your language, or you knew mine."

At that, one of the smaller Yetis lifted his hand and said, "I speak Mannish."

Shocked, she turned to the well-spoken Yeti to listen to his retelling of what had happened to them since parting.

"We did not run away. Once outside castle, Needlemen caught us in yard and put us in horse barn by bridge. Yeti too big to tie up."

"Are any of you injured, or... magiked?" she asked, voice hushed at the end.

He shook his head and, as she eyed each creature, none looked to be hurt; they were in good spirits.

"Guards came and brought us here saying all is well. We were—"

Just then, a loud shout came from the direction of the corridor.

What now?

Edegast shouted again, and he sounded desperate. The group of snowmen rose to their feet, and Alyssa slung her bow over one shoulder and her quiver over the other.

Presently, Edegast, carrying Pappy Oh's tin box, hurried into the room, red-faced, and breathless. "Gone! Vanished!" he managed to say.

"What happened?" Alyssa asked, nocking an arrow as fast as she could.

"Vanished? Has Madrid disappeared?" asked Bryon. He immediately acted. "Fletch, you and Cerius take your swords and search this castle, every room. He cannot have gotten far. Yeti-men, take the wolves outside, search the grounds. Let them eat the varmint. Edegast, call the guards to arms, man!"

Edegast exhaled, inhaled, and raised his hand to get attention. "Halt... Stop... Not him!" he huffed.

Alyssa stuck out her arm to end Bryon's charge. "Wait. Something's wrong here. We can't send out an army for one tiny rat. What are you saying, Edegast?"

Edegast collected himself. "Not Madrid," he gasped. "The scarf. The scarf is gone."

"Aye. It *is* gone," Ragon cried in a tiny squeaky voice from beneath the bowl. "And you'll never find it."

"Gone where?" Alyssa asked, setting her bow and arrows down in order to lift the bowl and grab the rat.

He clasped his hands together and chirruped, "I'll never tell."

Alyssa squeezed him between her hands, shaking him until his head went side-to-side. "Yes, you will, Ragon of Needlemount. You'll tell us where that scarf is, right now! Don't make me call on my Pappy."

The tension that had been building in her since the arrival in the castle reached fever-pitch, and she trembled all over. Her head felt like it was battered by a typhoon. Some terrible malady came over her then.

The man-turned-rat screamed when he peered into her eyes. "She's gone mad!"

Even Edegast threw his arm up in defense of her fury released. Magik whipped from her and spun like a twisted cloud overhead. Her hair flew upwards, pulled by an invisible force, and her eyes seemed like twin flames.

Strangely, Cerius, who had been quietly standing by, seemed unaffected. He stalked to her and took the rat from her as easily as taking a rake handle from a scarecrow.

"Tell us!" Alyssa demanded. Her voice sounded like the moaning of a ship under heavy seas and the entire room of Yetis and wolves bowed slightly under the onslaught.

Edegast recovered first. He drew his cloak from the chair on the dais and tossed it over Alyssa. Immediately the energy that came at them from all sides stopped. She crumpled to the floor. It took several moments to restore order amid the chaos in the great room.

"Cerius, her magik does not affect you since she healed you. Quite interesting," the wizard mused. "Something else to research once I return to my home."

He walked to Alyssa and gingerly lifted the cloak away from her face. "Are you well?" he asked.

"Yes." She blinked and patted her wet cheeks. "I've been crying. What happened?"

"Not entirely certain but, believe me, I will research this matter soon. You either came into power, or lost control of it. But for now, it appears your magik grew greater than your ability to wield it."

She couldn't decipher what that meant but sat silently while he conducted business in her stead. Her headache had vanished.

First, Edegast dangled Ragon by the tail and carried him to the nearest Yeti.

"Would you like to have a morsel? I can offer this one."

Ragon screamed and attempted to crawl up Edegast's wrist.

"Oh, so you do not wish to be in a Yeti's gullet?" the wizard asked. "Then you should explain to me how your father lost the scarf and where it is now."

"Why do you not ask him?" Ragon sputtered angrily. "He's been in charge of it."

Alyssa could sense Ragon's anger at his father about the matter.

Edegast shook the rat, limbs dangling down toward the Yeti's palm.

"In a moment you will be in this fellow's belly," he warned. "Tell us."

Ragon's black eyes darted back and forth from the drooling Yeti mouth to the angry wizard. "As you wish, wizard. I will tell you. But you must take me back to the dungeon first. I must find my father and make sure he is well. You want me to think it is well with him, but you could have vanquished him. Wizards are often liars."

Edegast closed his eyes and rubbed his forehead, taking a in a deep breath. *The whole situation tries his patience,* Alyssa noted from beneath the cloak.

Her strength had returned. She pushed the cloak from her, holding it out to the wizard with one hand and taking the rat by the tail with the other. She placed him back under the bowl on the table.

"Behave, Ragon, or I will bite you myself," she told the rodent.

Fletch sat at the table, grunted, and placed his feet over the bowl, crossed at the ankles as if he were at rest and the rat hardly a consideration.

Alyssa and the wizard walked a few yards away into the corridor.

"What do you think Ragon is about?" Edegast asked her, staring back into the great room. "I suspect he is up to no good. I am quite uncertain whether to permit him access to his father or not. Together they are a formidable enemy. You were right to separate them."

She ignored his question for a moment. "How do you know the scarf is missing? I have a little knowledge about it and how it can change owners. It happens around the full face of Luna. The moon ain't full yet. Why would it do so before then? And now who has it? And how did that person or persons get it?"

Edegast pulled on his beard and averted his gaze. "That, my dear apprentice, is where things get a bit more difficult to decipher. Madrid has gone quite mad, I'm afraid. He kept saying the giant bird had the scarf. And that the bird took it by force."

"Oh, great gods," Alyssa hissed, shaking her head in exasperation. "This ends now. I'll find this scarf myself." And with that, she charged back into the great room. Her hair once again swirled with static, making the ends snake around her head like an angry goddess.

"Bog devils take your tongue if you lie to me, Ragon," she said, pulling him out from under the bowl. "Where's the follygrass scarf that y'all stole from Lord Pryon of Half Moon Manor? I'm only going to ask once."

His whiskers trembled, and he tried to squeeze himself out of her grasp. "I don't know."

"You do know," she shouted. "You took it! Right after you murdered Lord Pryon and his son. That evilment alone will see you die bitterly at the hands of his kin. Don't make it worse now. You may find mercy through honesty."

"I tell no falsehood," Ragon answered. "I do not know where that accursed scarf is now."

"How can you neither know its location, nor who has it, when it sat clutched in your claws last?" Bryon asked, holding a curved knife tip at the rat's throat. "You killed my father and brother, by the way." He pressed the blade closer. "How does this feel?" The creature's eyes went wide and then moved from side-to-side. "Where have you hidden it?" Bryon demanded.

Ragon squeaked. "It's gone! Stolen from us as well!"

Alyssa dropped the rat into the Yeti's palm. "Don't eat it yet, friend," she instructed. "Since you won't tell us who has it now, Ragon, I will leave you in the care of this fine hungry snowman. Would you like to know how long it will take to chew off your little head?"

Tears rolled down Ragon's long nose and dripped off his whiskers. "Please! I beg of you. Do not let him eat me!"

"Then tell us where the scarf is," Edegast replied, moving closer. "We will take you back to the dungeon and you can be with Madrid. If you are good little rodents, I may turn you back to your former selves."

Ragon brightened a bit at that. He wiggled down the Yeti's hand and clung onto the fur of his arm. "Wizard's promises." Then, he screamed when the Yeti shook his arm grinning at Alyssa. "If you must know, a large, beautiful bird stole the scarf from us as it hung out of the window. It had been in father's solar drying from a washing, and the bird dove from the sky and took it."

Alyssa laughed aloud, but Edegast's brow furrowed.

"Ragon, a bird? What sort of bird?" the wizard asked, disbelief on his face. "It would have to be a noticeably big bird to carry that scarf. And if so, wouldn't the guards shoot it down with arrows?"

The rat lowered himself farther down the Yeti's arm, but the Yeti flicked at him with a long claw, playing with it like a cat does with a mouse.

Alyssa asked, "What sort of bird would a magik scarf take up with, anyway? And why?" Then, she turned back to the rat. "Ragon, are you lying?"

"I am not lying. A very big bird, a big, colorful bird with wings of fiery feathers," Ragon said, clinging to the Yeti tightly. "The scarf untwined itself and practically begged to be taken away."

As if lightning had struck him, Edegast shouted, "I have it! The bird is not a bird as we think it is, but a magik phoenix! A phoenix would be the only bird that a magik item would seek. They have fire-colored wings. The scarf knows the phoenix can live a long time and even return from death."

The air left Alyssa's lungs.

Back from the dead? Resurrected! Like Pappy Oh.

"Where does this phoenix live?" she asked, excitement filling her.

"In the wellspring of the Haldor," said someone from behind them.

Chapter Sixteen

Rats Have Nine Lives

Red, the Yeti who spoke imperfect Mannish, scratched his splotchy auburn fur and bared his large, yellowed teeth as if he had something to say. Alyssa waved to him to speak.

"Haldor have bird with big tail. Much long beak. Dangerous to Yeti. Red's brother attacked one time. Much scary."

"Well, if that don't beat all," she said, amazed.

Alyssa used this information and slight interruption as an opportunity for Ragon to struggle while the Yeti considered his next snack.

She took her time removing him, but finally retrieved him from the unnamed Yeti, shook him a few times by the tail, and flicked him behind his ear to make him behave before she marched toward the corridor.

"Where is Madrid?" she asked Edegast, searching around for something to put the rat in. Cerius offered a drawstring bag. Ragon squirmed and wiggled, tiny rat claws scratching as she dropped him into it.

"In the dungeon, of course," Edegast answered. "Why?"

"I want to return Ragon there," she replied. "He told us the truth about the scarf. Why not let them be together?"

"As you wish, young Castling," Edegast said. "Let me enable the staff to light your way." He picked it up and pointed a rather long bony forefinger at the end of his wooden stick. It burned hot red like a fire-stoked ember. "Whilst you do that, I will gather those who will accompany us on this journey to the Haldor seat. I fear the Yeti will decline."

Alyssa, burdened with too many things to carry, said irritably, "It would be nice if they were going. They at least know how to travel over snowy mountains."

Edegast grunted. "I wouldn't be worrying about the outside of the mountains as much as the inside."

She stared at him.

"The Haldor are underground dwellers. Cavemen to the end. Not hairy and smelly like Yeti, but same lifestyle."

The soft-spoken Yeti who had told them about the Phoenix's nest in the wellspring of the Haldor raised his head and glared at the wizard, old troubles rising to the surface again.

Fletch, ever vigilant, said, "My lady, I will accompany you to the dungeon. We should not travel alone anywhere."

Alyssa smiled, relief flooding her face. She would appreciate someone else traipsing through the dark and dank castle. With a sword.

And the two set out.

When they were on the stairs leading down, Ragon made another attempt to get away. He bit Alyssa hard on the skin of her inner thumb, right through the bag.

Alyssa tried to touch the walls to balance herself on the steep stairs, use the staff for light, and carry the little animal at the same time. She suddenly couldn't keep him contained, and he fell away bouncing down the stairs, with the bag coming untied in the tumble.

He twisted tail over whiskers before he scrambled back onto his four feet and fled down the rest of the stone stairs into darkness beyond.

"Beggardom be on that rat!" Alyssa hissed, pressing her injured hand to her mouth and her back to the staircase wall. She only bled a small amount, but her vanity screamed at the misfortune. Bested by a beast. Pappy Oh would cackle with amusement when he heard this.

Fletch jumped from a step above her to get to her side and snatched up her injured hand to examine it.

"Lady Alyssa," he said, turning it over gently. "I truly need better light to see what hurts you have."

She nodded and brought the staff down to burn red over the bite.

He gazed at it for a moment before letting it go. "I think you will live this day."

She checked the sputtering illumination of the staff. "Let's go on and get to the dungeon. I'm sure Mr. Ragon Ratman will be there, too. He wouldn't leave his Papa behind."

Fletch bent closer, peering into her face. "If you should feel faint…"

She laughed. "I'm not a fainting girl. I've tended to worse injuries than this." The memory of her grandmother's legs after the plant attack returned to strike her in the heart. "We have got to move on. Time is of the essence." And then to herself, she added, "Hang on, Granny."

Fletch moved aside for her to take the lead. As she went from step to step, she had a sense of urgency without explanation.

No way to avoid intuition. Something is pushing me to hurry and find those scalawag rats. They are up to nothing good.

Alyssa stopped in front of the dungeon door, Fletch stepping to her side, mouth open in amazement.

The door stood ajar. Well, what remained of it. She stared at the charred remains of the entrance and at the wizard's shattered orb scattered across the stones. An ill wind blew through her hair, causing it to whip at the ends, as if angered.

"Oh no," she said, heart sinking. A terrible spell fluttered around the dungeon now. She could sense its undeveloped nature. More like a baby spell, seeking nutrition to grow. She didn't want to be there when it came around full circle and decided it needed her power to gain strength.

"Fletch, we have to go back. We have to get out of here. Right now!" Alyssa turned on her heel to head back to the stairs. But Ragon and Madrid stood there, shoulder-to-shoulder, wholly men once again, blocking the way.

"So glad you could join us," Ragon drawled, his braided hair gleaming in the light from the shimmering staff. His face was smooth except for the angry red slash that ran from his hairline to his right eyebrow. A scar that Alyssa did not miss and wondered if it had been from a recent knife wound.

"How… what…" Alyssa stammered, speechless at the appearance of the formerly enchanted men.

"You can never know what magik will do," Madrid said in his breathless voice. Much shorter than Ragon, he remained fidgety, as he had been as a rat. Perhaps enchantment spells left its victims with lasting symptoms. Alyssa could sense his indecisiveness and thought how she could use it. He pulled on his long beard and glanced at Ragon.

To Alyssa, the one in charge seemed obvious.

She gripped the staff and tried to keep the two men talking. "So, we're at a stalemate."

Madrid shuffled toward them.

Fletch drew his sword and wielded it two-handed in front of him. "Don't come closer," he warned.

Their evil eyes pierced through the darkness, aided by the staff's light. Alyssa inhaled sharply, certain they were both as mad as crows drunk on corn.

"Have you lost your wizard, little girl?" Ragon teased, his voice friendly. "Too bad he can't keep up with his magik-users. We'll have to punish him, won't we, Father?"

Madrid rubbed his hands together and giggled. "Yes, yes, we will."

Fletch whispered, "Mad as a court jester."

"How did you two escape the enchantment?" Alyssa asked, frowning, considering what to do.

"Father broke the orb, and it reversed the spell. You can never know what magik will do." Ragon repeated his father's words, sidling to the left, curiosity in his eyes.

This revelation made Alyssa worry even more. Why hadn't the wizard removed the orb from these fools? They were crafty, she had to admit.

How could she warn Edegast now that the rats were out of their cage, literally?

"What are y'all up to now? Y'all ain't magik-users, and the scarf has moved on," she said to Ragon.

"But you'll get it," he answered. "And bring it back to us."

"Why would I do that?" she asked, tapping the staff with her fingers, nerves twanging.

"Because you… are… a doer of good deeds!" Ragon said, lunging at her to sweep the staff out of her hands.

She yelled in pain when he twisted it free from her grip. "Give that back!"

Fletch tried to bring the sword down to cut Ragon's hands from it, but Ragon jerked out of the way and the sword sliced thin air.

Terrified, Alyssa put her hand out to stop his next strike. "No, Fletch! Stop! There is magik about."

"Foul play!" Ragon shouted at Fletch. "You missed, but you will pay for that mistake, mark my word." Brandishing the staff, he turned to his father. "Now we will see who a rat is."

"Rat, rat… who's a rat," Madrid sang out.

Fletch, disgusted by the two, moved back a step, probably to give him better odds with his swing.

"You will be a ribbon of yourself next, Ragon," Fletch threatened.

Ignoring him, Ragon lifted the staff aloft and said, "You will now serve me, girl. Make this staff brighter."

She laughed out at his words. "Sorry, Ragon, I'm not your apprentice, and I don't know how to make a wizard's stick work, any more than you do. I may be a doer of good deeds, but I ain't no fool."

Alyssa saw Fletch out of the corner of her eye. The sword swung slightly back and forth as he struggled with which man to slice through first.

"Watch Madrid," she told him. "He still has some rat in him, I think."

Ragon tapped the end of the staff and shook it hard. "Light, blast you!"

Alyssa rubbed her twisted wrist and said to Ragon, "I wish I knew where that scarf went. I'd wring your neck with it."

The strange surge of power she'd become familiar with went through her, and she examined her hands as the spell flowed from them. Her hair danced atop her head. Her magik!

"Find the magik in this castle," she commanded it, extending her hands in front of her. More and more green light spilled from her, shooting about the area like a great green flame.

The glow danced up to the ceiling high overhead and back to the floor, dipped into corners and nooks and swirled over their heads. Alyssa marveled at its increase in amount and power.

This activity startled Ragon and Madrid into silence, and they stared at how it sought every part of the area.

Fletch blinked twice, amazed. The glow illuminated the dark corridor, its ebb and flow mesmerizing them all.

It landed ever so lightly on the head of the two men, coating each hair and making it appear like string. Then it circled Ragon's shoulders in a mimic of a scarf.

He realized he had the magik on him and pointed at Fletch's sword. "That's utterly useless in your hands," he said, matter-of-factly.

When he said that, the sword fell from Fletch's hand and curled into a silver ribbon.

"My lady!" Fletch shouted, hands now empty.

Alyssa brought her hands down and said, "My magik melded with the magik from the orb. It does his bidding now." She stepped forward a moment too late.

The evil Ragon had picked up the ribbon and put it into his pocket, leaving Fletch unarmed. "As we have already seen," he gloated, "one can never tell what magik will do."

"You used my magik to work your own evilment!" Alyssa said, stamping her foot. "Good thing you're not a member of the Wizards Union and Guild."

"A fortunate accident," he muttered. "Nothing more. But do not think I will forget about it. You should know that others can use your magik when you are careless with it. Didn't your mother ever tell you to pick up your toys?"

The green glow dissipated from around the two men as if it knew its powers were going to be used against its owner. It rose to the ceiling and clung there like a spider, changing from yellow to green and back again.

Alyssa realized the truth of Ragon's words. It was *her* magik. It came from her. She could send it where she wanted to. And she should do so before he summoned up another "accident."

She didn't know how to separate the two magiks but figured she could recall her own easily enough. If the other came along, well, so be it.

Alyssa stared at him, and then at the staff he gripped in one hand. A staff of power. Her heartbeat increased. Pappy Oh had a staff. She remembered it well, as did her somewhat still sore nose. It had hit her and drawn blood. A mage's stick became charged with their power, which is why the spell required it to bring Pappy back from the dead.

She focused on the wizard's staff gripped in Ragon's grasp. *Find Edegast the Green*! She threw her arms wide and blew her breath at the staff, sending all her focus and thought toward it.

The action took the light from the staff, expanded its reach outward, and pushed it against the walls of the castle. Then the light corrected its path and flew up the stairs to search for the wizard, leaving them in darkness.

Her spell faded from where it had become tainted with the yellow mist. She thought the yellow mist might have followed the staff's light up the stairs as it sought its maker, as well. She couldn't be certain.

The staff, cold and dark now, became of no use to any of them.

"Not exactly what I had planned," Alyssa sighed. Fletch nodded to her. At least she thought he did. In the darkness it was difficult to tell.

Ragon, realizing that he and his father were in the dark with a magik-user and a skilled warrior, shouted at Madrid to follow him. He threw the staff at them in one last attempt to inflict injury, and the two men fled the area.

"Like rats," Alyssa grumped, feeling in the dark for the staff. The stick had sailed through the air like a javelin and landed somewhere beyond them.

"My lady," Fletch said, softly. "Use your magik."

"If it still works," she muttered. She focused on her hands once more. "Find Edegast's staff."

The green glow faintly ran across her hands. Weak and indistinct, it misted out of her fingers. She didn't feel a surge of power as before. The drizzle shrouded her in a haze of color, and she glanced around for the staff. It appeared beneath her magik.

She collected it and turned to see where the rats-turned-men could have disappeared to. She took a few steps, and the wall in front of her shined.

"Find out what this is," she said. The glow that had been surrounding her flew to the wall and outlined a hidden door. Alyssa recalled the spell and waved it to stay overhead. She wanted to see if they could get through the doorway, but when she put out her hands, the powerful vibration that came through them caused her teeth to chatter. She gave up the idea of entry.

"There's a corridor hidden behind that door," she said, flexing her hands. "And there's a spell on it to prevent us from following them. Ragon must have more magik up his sleeve."

"Of course. They really are like rats," Fletch replied. "Still, there is more to them than meets the eye."

She decided not to follow the Needlemount men. They could escape easily in their domain and might even trap her and Fletch.

Instead, she grabbed Fletch's hand with her free one. "We have to find the others."

They scrambled for the stairs leading up to where they had left their friends.

"Sorry about your sword," she told him as they climbed.

"Fortunately, Lord Bryon has some of the finest blades in the realm. I will not lack for a sword," he reassured her. After a moment, he laughed and added, "I hope that old Ragon does not bring the sword to life whilst it still sits in his pocket."

She joined his laugh, and they trudged up the stairs.

They met Edegast and Lord Bryon hurrying down to find them. The wizard raised a torch high, his yellow mist over his head like a cloud, long beard tucked in his belt, and cloak floating out behind him. He pulled up short when she shouted at him.

"Edegast!"

Relief smoothed the worried lines in his forehead. "Alyssa! So glad to see you in one piece. My mist spell confounded me. I didn't know whether to follow it or extinguish it."

"The Needlemount men have run away," Alyssa told Lord Bryon and Edegast. "They used your orb to destroy the door to the dungeon, breaking the spell you had them under. Or else they used your magik to remake themselves. I suspect they're halfway to Needle Flats by now." She passed the staff back to its rightful owner. "Here, I guess I'm done with this."

Edegast chuckled, handing the torch to Bryon, and taking his staff. "Drat my thoughtlessness. I never believed they would be clever enough to use it. I see they are, or else they have had help from a magik-user's handbook. Something else to be dealt with. My brothers will not be happy to hear that these foolish men are playing at magik."

Alyssa tilted her head back. "Have you considered they're big fat liars and still have the scarf?"

Edegast blinked down at her. "I believe them when they say the scarf is gone. I have sought it out with my seeker mist and never found it. Didn't you use your magik? Did it return a scarf to you?"

She shook her head. "I didn't try, but… it would have already found the scarf if it was nearby."

"Then the obvious answer is, it is no longer here."

"Well, just so you know," Alyssa said. "Ragon at least knows how to harness magik. He used mine."

Edegast sighed. "An unfortunate reason to file a report when I return home. Oh well, a problem for another day."

"Yes, another day," she said. "We should be on our way to where the Haldor live right now, this very minute. But we are all too tuckered out to even think of another trek in the dark. Personally, I'm falling asleep on my feet."

"Tomorrow will bring a great many things. You and the others should sleep soon."

Exhaustion had set in. Alyssa yawned, before adding, "That scarf is being naughty, and it may leave the phoenix before we can get to it. I don't have time to chase it all over the Greater Daegries. We have to find it soon."

"You are right, my dear. Although the full face of Luna approaches, it appears it has little to do with the scarf's ability to choose its bearer."

"I ain't losing hope," Alyssa said. "I have to get it back to the Gryphon King by the full moon day. He'll be waiting for me, and I need it to save Granny. I'm not going back without that scarf."

Edegast tapped the tip of his staff, illuminating the stairs. He headed back the way he had come, waving for all to follow. "I'm working on a plan for that. I am hoping you can help me."

Curiosity piqued, Alyssa asked, "Help you how?"

"What if the gryphon got his scarf back, only one not really his?"

She paused a half-step. "Beg pardon?"

Edegast peered over his shoulder at her. "Yes, well. I can see the dilemma written on your face. But if we could somehow create another scarf…"

She tilted her head and thought about it. "With follygrass? Where does that grow? What if we can't find any? Could we get it to look the same? Would we be able to fool him?"

They reached another landing and Edegast lifted his hand to stop her questions. "I have nothing in mind for certain yet. Let's see what our journey brings us. I would like to keep a few other options open, though."

Alyssa nodded. "The gryphon ain't the sharpest shovel in the shed, I'm thinking. I bet he could be fooled by a fake follygrass scarf."

"It would only be temporary, until I could have a parlay with him. He owes me, a registered member of the Magik-Users Congress, an explanation on why he stole the scarf from me, the true, rightful owner."

"I don't think any owner, former or present, has control over that scarf. It's obviously looking for something and keeps going to a new owner to find it."

Edegast digested this. Finally, he said, "Yes, it seems that way, doesn't it?"

They moved ahead.

He continued. "I'll research more about the scarf. Perhaps something in the making of it needs investigating. There is something about it that doesn't add up."

Fletch, who drew closer, asked, "What doesn't add up?"

Edegast shrugged. "Very little concerning the scarf. I've learned about it the hard way through misadventures and the tales of others, such as this party with us. I will find out though. Even if I must go back to the Iefyr and ask."

After that, they fell silent and went into the great hall where the company fell asleep in front of a roaring magik fire in the stone fireplace. Edegast set a watch inside with Yetis until the stars came out. Outside of the castle, the wizard had sent word to the buggos to remain in place and to be on watch for the pair of escaped men. Before sleep claimed her, Alyssa considered how to prepare for another long journey to the halls of the Haldor.

Chapter Seventeen

Follow the Wolves

The next day, the company departed Needlemount, still wary and silent, but this time with horses, food, and warm clothing. The Needlemount guards and cook and other assorted working staff had sent them on their way in style, but it didn't matter. Fear and danger filled their minds.

Alyssa wore a worried frown as she realized the short time she had to get the scarf and make her way back to the gryphon. The company traveled southwest across Needle Flats, down a slippery cliff face (the Yetis and wolves had no trouble) and into an adjacent mountain chain next to the Yetis' home. Edegast said that after the cave-in, the Haldor had moved to another mountain range. If this was that certain mountain, then what went on in the area where she had felt a strange magik or power? Even Pappy had felt it. Her jaw clenched at the thought of a magik under every mountain, some of it unknown.

The company kept a lookout for Ragon and Madrid, but plainly they had gone into hiding. Not even one set of tracks had been found. Edegast fretted over this for some time, saying what a mistake he'd made to underestimate the pair of former rats. Lord Bryon echoed his fears. Dejected by this new deceit of the Needlemount men, he planned on coming back to find them.

"They still must answer for their crimes," he declared.

Edegast moved stealthily on foot, stopping now and again to peer at tracks in the snow. Alyssa rode with Pappy Oh's box in her pack again, still and silent. She ruefully wished he would reappear, if only to entertain her with his silly songs. But if he remained with Granny, keeping her safe and somehow thwarting the Gryphon King, then she would have to be satisfied.

Fletch rode behind Cerius, carrying the banner of Half Moon Manor, and Lord Bryon rode alone, his anger causing him to speak roughly to his men. The Yetis had no need for horses, and their long legs kept pace with the riders without issue.

Nothing directed them to the home of the Haldor. No signs, no houses, no trails. Only Edegast's memory of a time when he had been there.

"What you do in halls of Thorock?" asked Red, watching the wizard curiously. He and Jed were brothers on their mother's side. Jed seemed not as versed in the language as Red, however. And Jed had dark brown spots, rather than the amber colored ones.

Edegast replied, "The last time I came here, I helped them craft rune-casts to be placed on swords made for the men of the Greater Daegries before the last war north of the Blighted Vale."

Red bared his teeth. "I no understand," he said, and kept walking.

Edegast shrugged. "Soon I will give a history lesson, as many of us are not aware of the happenings of the entire realm."

Lord Bryon, listening to the exchange, muttered, "I understand, as my family still harbors some of those blades. We were a part of that battle, I believe. Do you think the Haldor still exist?"

"Still exist as far as we know," Edegast told him. "Now, because of the cave-in, their fate is still to be determined. They were last seen going over the mountain we have recently exited and forging a trail this way. I will add it to the annals in the Wizard's Hall no matter what has befallen them. I am greatly delayed in my duty."

Cerius asked, "Are you saying that we could ride into a massive burial place?"

Edegast inclined his head slightly. "Let's ride on. The daylight is burning."

Alyssa tried not to think about the end of the journey being the end of an entire race of people, but such a momentous occasion as a mountain cave-in could not bode well for the inhabitants.

The land in which they traveled sloped up and down and became grim and empty. Black rocks with jagged edges like rotting teeth showed all around them, and they missed the annoying call of the crows who had trailed them that morning.

They went on and snow began to fall. Now, nothing moved, and the silence deepened as if even the wind kept her breath away.

Fletch pulled hard on his reins, pointing at a giant dip in the mountain. "Look!" he cried. "I'll wager it is here!"

The riders dismounted and stood with the wizard, the Yetis, and the wolves. They gaped at a massive curve downward in the landscape. The snow deceived the eye, and one could not tell where the curve began and where it ended.

"Red," Lord Bryon said. "Can you send a couple of your wolf brothers down there? We need to know if that land is solid or if we are all going to sink down into the famed halls of the Haldor."

The Yeti nodded and grunted some strange guttural thing to the wolf with black markings. He yelped and bounded down the sloping mountain. He disappeared for a while, and Alyssa worried about his safety but then glimpsed him climbing slowly upward. He reached a level where the others could not see him again, but, after a while, he reappeared climbing along a lip of stone on the far side, a little dot of blackness against the snow.

Alyssa exclaimed and pointed at the animal.

Fletch waved the banner and said, "Yo ho!"

The wolf stopped where he stood, almost at the top of the far side. He howled a lonely sound, and his brothers set off to join him. Alyssa, about to turn and jog for her horse, saw the wolf disappear.

She blinked and rubbed her eyes. Gone, as if swallowed by a snowbank.

"Edegast! The wolf!" she said, pointing.

"I saw that. We know it is safe up until that place. We will have to find out what has happened once there. Look! The gray ones have gone after. Let's follow before the snow blights out their trail." He climbed onto his horse and watched Fletch help Alyssa get onto hers.

"You do not have to go with me if you do not wish to," Edegast told her. "It might be unsafe."

"No, Edegast, we will go together," she answered quickly.

"Very well," he said as he gave control of his horse to Fletch.

"We can travel faster on one horse," he said as he handed her the staff and pulled himself up to sit in front of her. He grabbed the horse's mane and prodded its sides with his heels before shouting, "Go, go! Ride forth!"

Alyssa only saw a blur of white as they rushed down the slope and through the crunchy snow of the former mountaintop. Her pack with Pappy Oh's box in it slammed hard into her back. Soon, the terrain fell into disarray with mounds of snow-covered rock and stunted brush that the horse could not hurry over. Edegast let him have his head, only touching his sides occasionally to keep him headed in the direction he wanted.

The wolves had made it seem easy. The human journey took several hours.

Once they neared the other side, Edegast again walked alongside to see the paw prints of the wolves and in what direction they traveled. Alyssa handed the wizard his crook and took over the reins.

Here, the wind picked up again, touching their skin with icy tentacles. In a short while, the tracks bent upward. Edegast pulled his hood low, leaned on his staff, and drew his cloak closer. They trailed the wolves as best as they could, sometimes losing the tracks and having to go back to find them again.

Now they approached the ridge where the wolves had disappeared. The wolves had not returned, either. Edegast left Alyssa on the horse down below the ridge for the sake of safety.

"Hope springs in my heart, Alyssa!" Edegast shouted back to her. "A cave! There is a cave here."

Alyssa, only hearing the word cave, smiled and cupped her hand over her mouth to enlarge her voice. "Do you see the wolves?"

He cupped his ear to hear, as she repeated the question a second time, but the distance between them stretched out too far, and the blowing wind snatched the sound with it as it blew by.

The wizard waved for her to wait for further conversation and climbed back to where she waited. "The paw marks ended on a stone cliff jutting out from the side of the collapsed mountain, virtually invisible from here. There were many tracks jumbled together like they had paused there and couldn't decide what to do. But there is a cave, and they've obviously gone inside. I see no other sign of them, just the paw marks outside the cave."

Alyssa chewed her bottom lip nervously.

"Don't be afraid," he told her. "The Haldor are friends to wizards. If there are any left, that is."

She dismounted, pulling her bow and arrows with her and adjusting her pack. "And what if there are no Haldor, only something evil waiting inside this mountain?"

Edegast frowned at her arming herself, and said, "There will be no reason for weapons, Alyssa. Not that you need any. Your magik ability waxes like the face of Luna. Aside from that, there will be little room to use them. The cave-in will make traveling difficult and arrow-shooting impossible." He reexamined the ridge overhead and added, "The cave once had a massive throne room, the ceiling so far above you couldn't see it from the cave floor. All gone now, I suspect."

She nodded. He made sense. She slung the quiver and bow over the pack and left all of it sitting by the horse. She eyed Pappy's box, wearily. "The others will wonder why we left it all out here."

"We'll explain it when we meet them again," he answered, looking at her strangely. "This very well may prove a trial for us all. Do you wish to accompany me still?"

"I'll be joining you," she insisted. "This is my journey, ain't it? The reason I left Mudden to begin with. That is if the scarf hasn't left the phoenix for somebody else. If it's run off again, I'll be madder than a hungry buggo."

Edegast sighed, peering into her face. "As you wish. But you must stay close beside me. We do not know what we may encounter. I can illuminate our way with the staff. Keep your finding spell handy."

She nodded, almost laughing at him. The spell lived inside her and remained always at hand. Literally. They tied the horse to a shrub so that it wouldn't wander off, but out in the open where the others would see it.

They walked together into the cave mouth, partly covered over by a low-hanging thorny tree. The wizard used his staff to push the branches back, but they resisted. Finally, he threatened it. "Be gone, blast you!" and it shrank back at his words.

Alyssa marveled at this. A wizard's magik should never be taken lightly.

The tall, front room of the cave had dead vines and grass in it, but some animals had smoothed the dirt floor for sleeping. They could see paw prints from the wolves in the dirt.

The cave tapered as they traveled deeper into it. Inside the narrowed area, Edegast squatted and moved along in a sort of duck-walk. Alyssa, much shorter, simply kept her head down and stooped slightly. The temporary tightness widened out eventually into a small room with mud walls and floor.

Tracks from the wolves circled round and round in the room, as they had sniffed and scratched at everything they wanted to know about.

"They're not here," Alyssa said. "What happened to them? I don't see any way out."

Edegast commanded the staff to give them light. He held it up and moved it side to side to illuminate the wall they faced.

"Well, this is unexpected and unpleasant," Edegast said, finally.

"There must be a door. The wolves are missing, and we haven't passed them."

"I do not see a door," he answered, striding forward, peering closely at the wall. He inched back and forth, feeling it as he went. "Nothing."

Alyssa thrust her hands out. "Find the opening."

The glow issued forth from her hands. Much more powerful than the last time she'd used it. It floated to the top of the cave and misted down to the mud floor before it covered the wall like a green slime.

A round doorway appeared like the top on a large barrel. The mud had dripped and run down until it disappeared under the coating of it. It stood barely ajar but perhaps enough for a wolf to wedge its head into and open.

Extremely low to the ground, it had escaped Edegast's inspection.

"Why," he exclaimed, "the person who made that had to be a small person indeed."

"I doubt you'll fit through it," Alyssa agreed. "But I will, and the wolves did apparently." She moved to open the door, but a tremendous rumbling deep in the mountain caused the door to open, invitingly, of its own accord.

Edegast pushed his hand out to stop her. "I dislike the sound of that. You cannot go alone through this doorway. There could be danger on the other side."

She glared at him. "Didn't I say that? Too late to go back for bow and arrows now."

The wizard squeezed his eyes closed in thought. When he opened them, he said, "You can only go to locate the wolves. If you find anything dangerous, you are to come back to me. With the others, we will find a way."

"Well, howdy, you sound like my Pappy. Listen, Edegast, if I don't do anything else, I've got to find the wolves. They're members of our company, too. I'm responsible for them. You figure out how we can get the others in here if it comes down to it. The Yetis won't fit through that muddy slide we came through— no how, no way— so good luck with that."

After speaking her mind, she slipped down to her knees and climbed through the hole attached to the doorway. "Find light," she told the glow.

The doorway opened onto a tight corridor tall enough for her to stand in. The grown men would have difficulty, she noted before trailing the light as it moved ahead, seeking light.

Windowless rooms appeared on each side, uninhabited with no furniture. The spell went into these and came back out again.

Alyssa moved ahead, down the corridor, which burrowed into the mountain. She stopped occasionally, peering down at the muddy floor for paw prints. Once she spied shiny stones with glittering minerals peeking up at her, she realized she would be unable to make out any prints of wolves or anything else.

"Find the wolves," she instructed her magik.

The green glow fanned out over her head, illuminating the end of the corridor where it opened out into a massive throne room; the entrance was tumbled down with broken rock and dirt from a damaged roof.

The darkness of the cave room dissipated as the magik shone across it. Mounds of glittering, gleaming jewels and coins of gold and silver glistened under its bouncing light. They sat in chests and poured out in piles.

The mountain's fallen rubble had been moved to the farthest edges of the room. And now a small opening appeared across the way, letting in a bit of light. The green glow, almost like a green flame, pointed to it.

The wolves had found some way to exit through there. Her gaze traveled over piles of gems and chests of gold and coins stacked high. The wolves could have leapt from stack to stack until they reached the opening.

She said, "Return." And as always, the magik obeyed. Commanding the spell had become so normal, Alyssa no longer even found it a thing of wonder.

She looked over the throne room again. The small opening let in enough light to illuminate the mounds of goods there. The Haldor had been rich beyond measure if their home existed therein.

The vista captured her attention so well she almost didn't see the movement. The massive serpentine tail swept through a pile of glittering diamonds, drawing her eyes downward to see his red scales glinting in the light.

The creature stretched its long neck, aware of her.

Chapter Eighteen

The Door into the Mountain

Alyssa's terror banished all thought of finding the Haldor or the wolves.

"Come now," the creature drawled, peering at her. "Would you not stay with Karnargul, the Shining One? You've spent so much energy seeking… and finding… me."

Alyssa made the mistake of staring into the jade-green blinking eyes. "I… I…"

"Do come closer. I have such a time seeing little folks up close. What is your name, humankind? For by your smell, I can tell you are not a dragon." Karnargul took its time, crawling around. "Names are so intriguing."

Alyssa, remembering the advice from the gryphon about giving away too much information to anyone, didn't answer. She knew a dragon when she saw one. She had to get away.

But when she quickly turned, her feet flew out from under her on the slippery stones of the corridor. As she tried to right herself, she found, to her horror, scorched stones beneath her.

"What did you do with the wolves?" she asked, as she rose to her hands and knees.

I have to get out of here.

Karnargul sniffed loudly. "Your smell is not familiar. You are both human and something else. Very, very intriguing. You do not smell like a wolf. Oh, but I have not had a lovely wolf meal in a long time. Where are your friends, the wolves? Not in my chambers, unfortunately."

Alyssa didn't know what to think. Sometimes he talked to himself, and other times to her. The wolves may have found another way out, or they may have been eaten and forgotten about already. Either way, she would not stay to be the dragon's next meal.

She crawled up the thin hallway, putting distance between herself and the creature. Satisfied, she took to her knees and tried to breathe through her terror. She had gone forward far enough that she would be able to escape harm if the dragon should decide to throw a flame at her.

Karnargul lifted himself and one seeking green eye peered into the corridor's opening. She could see the eye shimmer, staring at her.

"Very well, small person. I will think about you and decide what you are." He moved away from the hole. She didn't want to bring her spell forward again, but she had to hurry and warn the others.

"Light," she commanded. The green mist flew from her and led her down the corridor to where her friends awaited. She felt rather than saw Karnargul's glaring eye.

Heat burned her back as the dragon issued forth a breath down the corridor.

No fire, no fire, no fi...

Alyssa broke into a run, pursuing the magik, triumphant escape filling her. When she reached the doorway, she scrambled through it and slammed it shut. She crouched in front of it, heart pounding.

The men of the company stood with Edegast, surrounded by the packs and assorted goods that had come with them. They peered down at her. Fletch extended his hand to her.

"My lady," Lord Bryon said, watching her right herself. "You have turned as white as a gardenia bloom."

"No one, no one, can go in." She placed her hand over her racing heart. "No one. No one."

Edegast came to her side. "What is it? Where are the wolves?"

"No w—wolves, no H—Haldor," she stammered, closing her eyes. "Found throne room—"

"The wolves didn't go inside," Edegast interrupted her. "We found more tracks on the ridge. They must have gone into the front area and back out again, over the mountain. There may be more of them over that way; they run in packs. There is no way to know if the tracks we have seen are our wolves or not. The Yeti cannot come in here, as you noted, so they have gone back home to tell their leader that we have found a way into the Haldor's mountain. They were not interested in seeing the hall of the Haldor anyway."

Alyssa closed her eyes and collected herself. She took several deep breaths. Finally, she said, "Dragon. There's a dragon inside."

"A what?" Edegast asked, glaring at her with steely eyes. "Did you say a dragon lives inside?"

She nodded.

Lord Bryon and the others coughed and milled about, muttering about fantastic tales of dragons and dragon hoards.

"We can't go inside again," she warned. "It's alive. It's awake. And now it knows me. I'd have been a toast crisp if I'd stayed."

Edegast took her shoulders and gave her a little shake. "Slow down. You know this for certain?"

She nodded. "It spoke to me."

Lord Bryon stepped closer to her. "There have been no great dragons in the Daegries since the wars. We have recorded none in a long time. This cannot be so."

Alyssa jerked away from Edegast and pointed her finger in Bryon's face. "Are you calling me a liar? I'm telling you the truth. A dragon is in there. He calls himself Karnargul the Shining One, and he lies on a giant hoard of all manner of wealth. The wealth of the Haldor if they still live. They've abandoned it to him. And I don't blame them, either! I didn't see a phoenix, and I didn't see anyone else."

Lord Bryon's face went from disbelief to fear. "We must plan. This changes things drastically." He turned to Cerius and Fletch. "Do you still carry weapons?"

They glanced at each other. Cerius drew his blade, a two-handed longsword, from a scabbard across his back. But Fletch's gaze fell to his feet.

"My sword is lost, my lord."

"What?" Bryon asked, astonished. "Not you, Fletch. You're the best... how?"

"Ragon turned it into a ribbon and placed it into his pocket."

"How could he?" Edegast asked, curiosity making him move closer. "Ragon has no magik ability."

Embarrassed, Alyssa said, "I used my illumination spell, and it touched him. He knew to use words that would cause the blade to fall from Fletch's hands into something harmless."

"Interesting," the wizard said, lifting an eyebrow. "This will be yet another thing to research. Let me see your sword, Cerius."

Turning the hilt toward Edegast, Cerius handed it to him.

"No runes," Edegast announced after a quick examination. He gave it back and paced more furiously. "Runes would have been quite handy."

Alyssa, fear subsiding, asked, "Wizard, ain't no way for us to fight that dragon, with runes or without. Why are we even considering it?"

He stopped and gazed down at her before walking around her, glancing carefully at her person.

"What? What is it?" she asked.

He stroked his beard as he came to a stop in front of her. "Yes. I do believe so."

"What?" she asked again, feeling strangely like a butterfly right before the net falls.

"I cannot be certain. I would have to have proof from the annals. There is an old tale that speaks of a small but mighty warrior who slays a dragon under the mountain. The battle, one of good versus evil, has always been a child's tale to keep them in bed at night. But now… with this… perhaps there is truth in it."

"I'm only a simple apprentice. I haven't even entered upper-level school yet," Alyssa replied shyly. "Ain't no tales about me."

Edegast shook his head. "No matter. The dragon, if he is an old one, and I suspect he is, would know the tale. It's common amongst my brethren, and if we know of it, the dragon certainly does. What was said? Tell me now and do not leave out any of it."

She relayed all that had gone on in the dragon's cave.

"He called himself Karnargul the Shining One," she repeated. "I remember how I shivered when he announced it. He has this pleasant voice, one that makes you want to sit down and hear a story."

Edegast grunted and tugged on his cloak. "Harrumph. Good thing you didn't."

Cerius sheathed his sword again and said, "My lady, even the magik glow that you wield cannot fight a dragon. No normal-made blade such as ours can do any damage to one, either. I am uncertain about this, but I do not believe that Edegast with his supreme knowledge of wizarding could find a spell to dethrone a sitting dragon from its hoard. So, what do you intend to do?"

"Nothing," she said. "Except maybe finding out if the phoenix lives somewhere here on this mountain. I think Karnargul would scare off even a bird like this phoenix. I mean, if I were him or her, I would never stay inside the mountain." She pointed at the far landscape. "No, I believe it has the scarf in its nest somewhere nearby, outside."

Edegast pursed his lips and stared at Alyssa from under his bushy brows.

"What?" she asked. "I can tell you have something you want to say."

"Well, it is this. The phoenix lives in a wellspring. A place of water. Not a nest, like an eagle or hawk. There is only one such place around here. It is deep inside this mountain, where the Haldor had their great hall."

"You mean the throne room where the dragon sleeps is not the place we sought?" She thrust her hand on her hip.

He shook his head. "No. We have found a way in, but certainly not the only way, and unfortunately not the right way."

"I remember a hole in the throne room, maybe left from the cave-in. Maybe not," she told them.

"That is *certainly* not the way I speak of," Edegast replied.

Lord Bryon spoke up. "Then why do we stand here waiting to be charred bones? We should go immediately to the entrance that will lead to the great hall of the Haldor and get the scarf. Lady Alyssa is running out of time, and I am thin on patience."

Edegast nodded and bowed sardonically to the manor lord. "As you wish, your lordship."

Fletch leaned down and whispered in her ear before walking past. "We need a map."

She nodded vigorously. *If only… and when I get home, I'm going to make one.*

Edegast led them back out to the ridge where snow blew in great white whirlwinds that threatened to sweep them away. The horses stood with their heads down and as close to the cave indention as possible to ward off the weather. Soon, the intensity drove the company back inside the cave, pulling the beasts with them where less wind and snow could cover them.

"We are going to have to wait this storm out," Edegast told them. "Not certain what we will face when it finishes, either. Maybe so deep we cannot go farther on this journey."

"It's like some angry Yeti is pouring buckets of snow over the top of the mountain, trying to bury us," Fletch agreed, blinking up at the sky.

Alyssa stood still, her gaze locked on the door entrance to the corridor. "How did you get in there, oh Karnargul the Shining One?" she mused aloud.

Edegast idled nearby and answered. "No cave-in as we know them to be, apparently. This one likely occurred from a weakened place in the mountain where the dragon went to roost. His weight caused the mountain to give way and fall in."

She nodded. "He's a big one. Monstrous big," she said. Then, crossing her arms, she stepped forward toward the entrance to the dragon's lair. "None of you, except Fletch, maybe, will fit through that door. I'm the only one."

"What are you saying?" Edegast asked. He pointed a finger at the staff and said, "Light."

It brightened the cave. The door's iron studs gleamed dully in the faint light from where the wizard had taken the time to wipe them. He had perhaps put a spell on the door as well, Alyssa mused. *For what purpose?* There would be no way of knowing unless she asked, but wizards were not used to being questioned about their workings, and she didn't want to lose the friendship with this one when she needed it so much.

"I guess since the weather won't cooperate, with snow piling up to the point we can't go on... and no one will fit in this door but me... I'm going to go back in there and try to slip past that dragon. If I live, I'll try to find the wellspring of the Haldor by myself."

Lord Bryon paced for a moment before inserting his opinion on the matter. "My lady, you can take my banner with you to show the Haldor who you ally with. Perchance if they know that the house of Half Moon has approved your journey, they will accept you."

Before he finished speaking, Cerius pulled a sheath with a short knife in it from his boot and added, "Take my dagger with you, Lady Alyssa. You may find a need for it in the darkness of Haldor Hall."

She took the offered weapon. "Thank you kindly for your dagger. I hope I don't need it, but I'll use it if I need to." She added it to a slit pocket in her pack that she now slung over her shoulders. Pappy Oh's box bounced inside.

Edegast mumbled to himself at these proceedings. Then he peered at her closely and said, "Your company has agreed this is your path to tread, my dear. It will not be a simple task. I will send my cloak with you, for warmth, for protection, and to barter with the dragon if need be. Few of them possess a wizard's cloak. Greedy creatures they are, too. And terrible liars. Do not believe a single thing it may say."

Alyssa felt a shiver go over her arms.

Fletch stepped up and nudged Alyssa with his shoulder. "You cannot go alone. I've offered my allegiance. If you travel this path, then I travel it with you."

Alyssa didn't know what to say. His duty and honor could send him into a battle to the death. She couldn't do that to him, nor any of them. They all wanted to go, it showed clear on their faces, but none could take this path. She stared at each man and made her own decisions.

"Lord Bryon," she addressed him first. "I can't take your banner with me, dragging it through mud and mire. Look at my clothing! You keep that banner, sir. I'll be mighty proud to carry it homeward when I get back. If anyone in the Haldor halls wants proof that the House of Half Moon is with me, they can ask, and I'll gladly tell them. My word is enough. And Fletch, you cannot leave your liege like this. He needs you."

The young man let his head fall slightly and without another word went to collect her bow and arrows.

To Edegast she turned and bowed. "Sir, you're a credit to the wizarding world, and my Pappy Oh will be told of your bravery and your offer for me to take your cloak. I don't know how you had to earn that thing, but it must not be an easy feat. I'm going to decline your offer of it, however, because it would be a great burden to carry, and it's way too big for me to wear. While it would be handy to have, I think I'll be okay without it."

Fletch, who stood holding her weapons, smiled.

She said, "You've been with me all along, and I value this bond. The whole lot of you need to get out of this cave as soon as possible and find the way into the wellspring of the Haldor through whatever other door there might be. I'm sure it'll be a much safer journey but maybe not as quick as my way, and you already know about my limited time."

All faces dimmed with this reminder.

"If I don't show up, Edegast will have to find that scarf and finish my journey," she said, giving them long and hard stares. "I'm counting on all of you. Please don't let me down. My Granny Gert is counting on me. If I can't fulfill King Hubert's request, it's on y'all to do it."

Fletch sighed heavily, disappointment in every line of his body. "I promise," he said, turning away.

"Aye. You have it," Cerius said, and gave her a pouch of dried food. "Here. You'll need sustenance."

"Aye, yes, you also have my word, my lady," Bryon added, and he handed her his water bladder. "Water, until you find the spring."

Edegast tapped his staff on the ground a few times and cleared his throat. "I am unhappy about this. You should take my cloak or take this young man along. You are just a snip of a girl. Unprepared and untried in the ways of magik. Oh, that I could make this trek!"

She laughed at his assessment of her. She didn't feel too much like a "snip of a girl" any longer. No *betwixt*-aged girl in all of Mudden could say she had been through as much as Alyssa had in one week. And as for her untried status in magik, well, she felt better about that than she ever had. Her ability to use magik might have gone astray in various ways, but she had twisted it into something usable every time.

"Y'all go and find the other way in and meet me at the wellspring," she said, finality in her voice. "I'm going to do this. Alone. Dragon or no."

Fletch returned, handed her the bow, and helped drape the quiver of arrows over her body. Then he tapped on Pappy Oh's box. "Shall I keep it for you?"

"He'd be mighty upset if he came back for it, and I wasn't the one carrying it," she said. "I'll manage somehow."

Edegast pulled on his beard and walked her to the doorway obviously meant for Haldor.

"Alyssa, a few things I would have you know," he said, stopping at the entrance.

She stared up at him from where she stood, drawing courage from within.

"Magik can be temperamental. If it doesn't work the way you think it should, then rein it in and make it behave. If you live through this, I will see that you get the finest training, for a wizard you are meant to be. I am certain of it."

She smiled at him and patted his arm. "Thanks, Edegast the Green." Then her face fell into determined lines. "If I ain't waiting at the door, please come find me. Who knows what that old dragon will come up with to entertain himself. And that scarf won't waste time in becoming his new toy. You know, it wants someone with power. We have to make sure it ain't someone with a long tail, sharp teeth, blowing fire and shedding scales."

Edegast nodded, patted her head, and twisted his hands as she disappeared back through the doorway that led into the dragon's lair.

Chapter Nineteen

Meet the Dragon

The cold and clammy corridor chilled Alyssa as she eased along, this time without her spell activated. For a short while, she stayed close to the wall, creeping down the path, hardly breathing. But soon enough, a warm amber light shone out ahead.

She recognized the soot smell now as she stepped carefully with one hand on the wall. Karnargul had made sure no one would be alive to talk about him when he burned everything black.

The fear of his fiery breath made Alyssa hope he slept deeply, or better yet, had gone. But when she reached the wide-open space of the throne room, a puff of smoke alerted her to his presence. It blew from his nostrils every so often. Her heart thudded in her ears.

Please be a sound sleeper, she begged silently.

She peered down into a throne room from the fallen-away ledge. The distance appeared too high to jump off. She squatted down and leaned over the edge into the open expanse to see the area left and right.

A staircase remained on the right side, but she couldn't tell how sturdy it might be or if it would even hold her. On the left yawned open air, and below that, tumbled down rocks. Given that she had no other alternatives, she slid over to the right side of the doorway and reached out to grab onto what remained of the iron railing on the left.

The distance became greater than expected, and she would have spun completely into the air before clanging against the staircase if not for the pack she wore. It slipped sideways and ended up between her and the staircase. She shifted it back in place and caught the bow with one hand as it slipped down her shoulder.

Suspended there, sweat popped out on her brow from the exertion. It proved difficult to maneuver and be silent, but she managed as she got herself righted on the nearest step.

A slight creak issued out into the stillness of the cave, sounding extremely loud to her. The dragon didn't stir. She sat on the step and drew in a quiet breath to calm her racing heart. The orange-red light source came from lanterns the dragon had set on fire. They must have been magik lanterns, as they didn't burn up and they didn't blow out. Alyssa would have to remember to get one of those before she left.

Finally, she stood, holding onto the rail against the cave wall, and took a tentative step down. She tried not to put her full weight on the step until certain it wouldn't fall below with her still attached.

Then she lowered her other foot. Step by step, she continued with caution to the bottom and chanced another glance at the dragon. Karnargul, much nearer now, appeared even bigger and more dangerous. His lower jaw jutted out slightly, and his massive fangs gleamed white.

She shook uncontrollably against the terror that gripped her. *One foot in front of the other…*

Every step away from the dragon across the expanse of the cave became one step closer to the phoenix and the scarf. She only had to make it across the wide cave floor, around the dragon, and find a way out.

Alyssa tried her best to dodge the jumbled mess on the floor of the cave. Karnargul had piles of so many coins and jewels, it became nearly impossible to travel through it without making noise.

She went along gingerly stepping over this and that and made great progress for a time. Then she came up to a chest filled with gold coins, barring her way. Piled high, the coins had fallen over the edge of the chest and created a mound all around it.

As she stood there, debating the best course of action to get past it, something caused the mound of gold coins to shift. They clattered out of the chest and into another mound beneath them. The noise jingled like a bell in the night, but Alyssa did not feel joy at the sound.

The once-sleeping dragon issued a single flame out of his parted mouth, and it entered up the dragon's snout, until his eyes fluttered open.

"So, you have come back to play, have you?" Karnargul asked sleepily. "Your kind always does. Well, what do you want? I am busy."

"Y—yes, I see that, Your Majesty," Alyssa said as she did a small curtsy. "I didn't mean to disturb your repose… er… your Busyness."

"But you have. Give me your name again." The dragon propped his head up on a cask of jewels. "I have decided you are human mixed up with one of those nature-creatures. The ones who prefer to frolic in water and amongst trees and are not too fond of air and fire, unlike myself."

"My name is Katrina Maria Purina," she answered, giving another curtsy. "You can call me Kat." She'd spent the entire way traveling down the corridor thinking of what she would say if he asked for her name again. Karnargul might not be his real name either, since Edegast had said that dragons were liars.

"Katrina Maria Purina," he said, thoughtfully. "That sounds foreign. Where are you from, Lady Kat?"

"Oh, I don't live anywhere around here. I've been traveling for days and days, over mountains, under mountains. You know how it is when you travel."

"Yes," he answered, turquoise eyes drooping a bit. "I haven't traveled for a long time. The mountain falling in became such a boon for me to get my treasures. But now I have lost track of time and that has created a bit of a problem for flying out again." He pointed upward with his barbed tail toward the opening that Alyssa had noticed on her first visit. Snow drifted down, melting as soon as it touched him. "I'm not entirely certain I would fit."

"You haven't been out of this mountain since the cave in?" Alyssa asked. "You must be bored." Alyssa wiped sweat from her brow. She wanted to keep easing sideways, getting closer and closer to her goal of getting on the other side of the throne room, but she didn't want him to figure out her plan.

Keep him talking…

"No," he said. "I've been stuck here since that time. Those creatures, the Haldor, tracked my activities. They saw me flying about the mountain, and I saw them, long beards dragging in the snow, helmets shining in the sun. I hunted for days for a place to land. Their mountain fell in through no accident. They created a rift of some sort, and it ripped the top off, sucking me down."

Alyssa tilted her head at his words. "A rift? But how'd they do that? It's a mighty mountain, from what I can see."

"Nevertheless, they succeeded. I nearly lost a tooth because of it, and very luckily, I didn't lose a limb. I survived the fall only barely. It's been years of agony from the scratches and bruises. See?" He lifted his back leg, giant claws dangling, and showed her a long gash that faded white against his red scales.

She stared. The inside of that leg appeared thinner, more vulnerable. Did they lose limbs only to regrow them? Did they molt like birds, losing scales and limbs during certain times of life?

These thoughts went through her head as she turned away, moved to the side of the chest of coins, picked up a goblet of silver, walked a little way, set it down, climbed over the mound, and then picked up a large, jeweled hand mirror. "What a lovely looking glass!" she exclaimed. Maybe because of the way she said it, or maybe the dragon's vanity, but at her exclamation, he curved around and glared at her holding the glass.

His reflection shone darkly. She could see his eyes grow more slanted, and his nostrils flare. Smoke curled out as if he contemplated blasting her.

"What are you doing with that?" he snapped. She placed it carefully on the pile where it had been.

"Oh, nothing, Shining One. Simply admiring your hoard. Wonderful. Just wonderful."

"Yes, and it is mine. And I do intend to keep it. All of it," he told her, pointedly. Then he swished his great tail and sent more treasures catapulting to the left and right.

She moved farther away from him, now on the other side of the chest of coins and in the clear from it. "Oh, yes. I would expect nothing less from such a magnificent dragon as yourself. You should be proud of it all."

"I am, rather." He stretched his neck out, great snout and teeth coming toward her. Once again, he snuffled. "Something about you intrigues me."

She now had the bow in her hand, carrying it on the side away from Karnargul. Had he seen it? Did he smell her fear?

"That's just my tired body giving off its unwashed scent," she explained, making it sound like a normal thing. "As I said, I've been traveling a long while."

"No," he replied. "There is something about you. A scent of the ancients. Something that reminds me of my youth." He stretched closer.

"Come closer, human. I wish to see you."

She stepped away again, swooping up a beautiful ruby the size of a grapefruit. "Oh, how lovely this is, dear Karnargul!"

And she tossed it into the air hoping to catch him off-guard long enough to run for the darkness of the other side. He snapped at the ruby, not knowing exactly what she had thrown, but the action itself didn't make him happy.

"Why are you so fidgety, Lady Kat? I am trying to be friendly." He flicked a few coins at her. "Take these, I have plenty." And he gathered his legs under him.

She moved again, slowly, as if she were admiring the items before her. She glanced his way and knew, if he got his limbs in action, he could lunge at her and gobble her up in one movement.

"Thank you ever so much, Sir Karnargul, oh Shining One. Where did you get your name, if I may ask?" A few more steps.

Easy… easy.

"I am the son of Darnargul, the most auspicious dragon ever to fly across the Greater Daegries. He named me for my grandfather, Tarandal."

The other side appeared dimly, but she couldn't make out a doorway. What if she got over there and found no way out? The dragon would shoot her with his flame, and that would be the end.

She took a deep breath. "How could you be named for your grandpappy and not have his name? Wouldn't your name be Tarandal?" She weighed a heavy jewel-encrusted crown in her hand, the perfect size for her. She slid it over her arm.

"It is the way of dragons. We have our own way of naming. What are you doing?" He had both eyes open staring at her, and the long neck stretched toward her again, now on full alert.

"Who me?" She turned to face him, holding the crown up. "I fancy having this."

"No. It's mine." He raised up on his front feet and pulled himself into a sitting position. "You cannot have anything that I do not give you."

She pulled the bow back over her right shoulder and eased away from him, now in a perfect flame-spewing distance. She considered her chances.

An arrow would do no damage. His hide is thick, and scales cover every inch of him.

"Dear Karnargul," she said, voice dripping with sweetness. "You're so generous to let me see your riches. What happened that you should enjoy so much? Where in Daegries did it all come from?"

He lifted a front foot, sending a small hillock of emeralds and rubies tumbling to the ground before replacing it on the floor.

"Why, those Haldor had all of this. They were selfishly keeping it all to themselves. Not like they couldn't make more; do you see? So, I claimed it."

"But," she said, startled, "aren't they all dead? Didn't the cave-in kill them all?"

Karnargul lay himself down again and picked at his teeth with a claw. "Of course not, silly Kat. They ran far away over the mountain and into the vale beyond. The Blighted Vale, it is called. I shall lay it to waste if I ever get out of here. Then it truly will be blighted."

This news did not make her happy. Had the Haldor clan moved from here and gone in search of new homes? How would she ever find them?

Alyssa stood in the shadow of the far wall of the cave at last. Karnargul moaned and flopped his head onto his front arms. His dejection sounded so intense, she wanted to glance back. But common sense told her to keep going.

She ran as hard as she could to the far wall of the cave, dropped the heavy crown, and scrambled over rocks and debris until her hands bled from the severe chafing.

Wait until Edegast hears the Haldor live, wherever it may be!

"Come back out here, Lady Kat," the dragon drawled. "I cannot see you."

She kept climbing up and up, hoping somehow to find another staircase, or maybe even a doorway.

"I'm exploring your kingdom, oh majestic Karnargul," she sang out.

The sound of her voice, now faraway, clued the dragon to the fact that she no longer stepped amongst his treasures. He thrust himself up and stretched his neck out, sniffing for her. His tail flipped back and forth like a nervous feline, creating an intense crater of falling goods.

When she thought she could climb no higher, Alyssa found an opening in the wall. It materialized as a chasm left over from the mountain's destruction. She had no trouble getting inside of it and found it large enough to fit a small wagon in.

A good thing too, as Karnargul decided at that moment to unfurl his wings and flap them angrily. The wind became like the teeth of a gale. Alyssa moved to the far wall of the chasm, out of the direct blow. Then she sat and curled up with her knees to her chin for protection.

"You thief! You have broken into my kingdom, pilfered my goods, and escaped! I will find you and grind your bones with my teeth!" Karnargul screamed, gnashing his teeth together as proof.

Alyssa sat like a mouse in a hole. She felt around the area for something with which to anchor herself, in case he redirected the wind.

A stream of fire flew straight at the wall where he thought Alyssa huddled. Fortunately, it missed her hiding place by a few yards to the left and below.

She stifled her scream of terror.

The fire and wind stopped, and he was silent. Deathly afraid of what he might be up to, she contemplated venturing to the ledge to gaze below.

Before she could act, his claws scratched and screeched against the plunder, and she realized his intention to get to her at all costs.

Then she heard him sniffing for her and knew her scent would give her away.

I've got to get out of here!

She scrambled to the back of the fissure and sought an opening farther away from the monster. The light dimmed beneath the projection of crushed rock, and she felt with her hands and fingers for an opening to squeeze into.

When nothing turned up, she decided that using her magik wouldn't mean anything if incinerated by dragon fire, anyway. She turned to face the throne room once more, and Karnargul lifted his massive upper body to peer into the crack.

She called upon everything she had.

"Oh, magik firelight, find an opening so that I can escape!"

The magik issued from her fingers like a stream of green fire. And, as instructed, it went out of the opening she had climbed through. As it flew by, the magik struck Karnargul directly in his eyes.

"Blinded! Blinded!" he screamed, flinging his body back and folding his wings over his face.

Alyssa didn't wait until he recovered. She scooted out of the crack, followed the green stream where it went down the wall and beneath a pile of jewels directly below. She slipped and skidded going down, scraping her already aching hands, until she reached the bottom. The dragon wailed and clawed his eyes.

She stuffed as many coins as she could into her pants pockets, took a few jewels, collected the crown where she had dropped it, and clapped it on her head. A ruby, not as large as the first, gleamed up at her, and she added it to her collection. Her pants were almost falling off her slender hips from the weight she'd added, but she would not let that stop her now.

The green glow shone into the pile of glinting gold. She thrust herself straight into it, arms out in front of her. Without warning, she started falling, falling, falling and there were only gold coins to keep her company.

Chapter Twenty

Goddess of Kasu

Alyssa wound up on a stone floor. The impact rattled even her teeth, but she shook it off, flexing and bending her wrists and rotating her shoulders to make sure nothing was broken. A shower of gold coins and gems fell around her in a continuous drizzle.

She paused to take a few deep breaths, with no sense of time or space. Nothing to direct her steps to find the Haldor seat, the phoenix, the wellspring, or anything else. As she stared down at her feet, she realized she'd never harmed anything or anyone in her life, and it opened an ache in her heart.

She brushed tears away. "I'm not sorry I injured that dratted dragon. He earned those fiery darts." But saying this didn't make any difference. She squared her shoulders and started out again, putting distance between her regrettable action and her need to find the scarf.

The stone floor sloped downward into the cavern, and she went along it, taking care with every step. She didn't want to end up tumbling down it and finding something unexpected at the bottom. As she went along, she noted several abandoned carts off the path. Apparently, they had been used for transporting Haldor-mined goods from the area below up to the throne room before the cave-in.

She turned and glanced back. The hole from where she had fallen had been covered over with the dragon's bounty. Had that been Karnargul's doing or the Haldor's? She shrugged off the question and continued on. Either way, it stood open now. She hoped that the dragon didn't fall through it anytime soon.

It was too small for him, likely, but an industrious dragon would find a way.

When she reached the path's bottom, she found herself far below the mountain, and she could see the faintest touch of her magik. The sound of dripping water soothed her somewhat. The scent of green growth, like moss on a riverbank, reached her nose, and she understood right away that the landscape had changed.

"Find light," she said, waving overhead.

The glow brightened, illuminating the ceiling. Her gaze traveled upward, and she saw shiny stalactites far overhead. Water puddled in front of her, making the stone floor slimy and treacherous. Algae or moss or some other aged growth confirmed what she'd been smelling. The runoff curved in a jagged line into the distance.

"Well, water makes a wellspring, and this is water, so I guess I'm following it," she said out loud. "And that's that, good or bad."

After only a short trek, where she found herself slipping off the wet stone, the floor gave way a little. Alyssa fell, scraping her side and rattling the pack with Pappy Oh's box shifting inside. She flung herself upright, heat rising in her cheeks, grateful no one saw her misstep.

Walk slowly, take your time.

Burdened with the coins, the gem, and the crown, she removed her backpack. After tucking her bounty inside, she pulled the cord as tight as she could to secure it. Then, before thrusting her arms into the straps, she shook it a few times to make sure the bounty fell to the bottom, or as close as she could make it. She double-checked Pappy's box and sighed with relief. No dents, no damages.

Finally, settling the pack on her person once more, she started off again. Slick mud covered the valley where the water had winnowed it out. She picked her path carefully but easily kept her feet dry.

Her curiosity rose with every step. How far into the mountain would she have to go this time? And what would she find? She would love to see the Haldor in there, and she'd love to find the phoenix and the scarf even more, but her journey had not been easy so far. She didn't expect this leg of it would be either.

The path narrowed, and Alyssa found herself in a tunnel of sorts. A rock formation overhead arched into the darkness, but she could make it out in the dim light from her spell's weakening light. Even when she commanded it to brighten, it resisted. Edegast's words returned to her about making the magik behave.

It's tired and weak because I am.

Acknowledging her exhaustion, she stopped to dig into the pack for something to eat. She slid down the wall of the tunnel to sit on the stone floor, and she crammed bits of bread and dried meat into her mouth like some wild thing.

How long it had been since she'd eaten, she didn't recall. Too long, according to her growling stomach. Eventually, when her strength returned, she rose from her sitting spot covered in wet, mucky mud from water oozing over pieced-together stones. She groaned at her bad fortune and strolled forward, splashing as quietly as possible, trying not to think of her clothes and how they felt as they clung to her.

She hugged the wall as she went, not knowing what lay ahead. A place for her to sit and rest never materialized, so she kept going.

And on and on she went, berating herself for not going with her friends around the mountain. It certainly could be no longer or more difficult than this path she'd chosen. If she ever got the chance to relate this tale to her Pappy, she'd tell him that her strength never flagged, although her attitude surely did.

Soon her tired legs stumbled on invisible rocks and gullies in the rivulet she followed, convincing her to find some place safe, off the path, where she could curl up and sleep without risking peril.

But no place felt right for a long stop, so deeper into the mountain she went. Her exhaustion made her lose hope of ever finding the wellspring of the phoenix or seeing her friends again. For hours, only the dark tunnel around her, the water under her feet, and the endless slippery path through it served as her companions.

Finally, coming to a complete stop, she lifted her weary arms and extended her hands. "Magik, find the wellspring of the phoenix and let's get out of here." It might be fruitless, but she had to try. Striving forward endlessly had not gotten her anywhere.

The green glow drifted down from overhead where it had been misting along. It traveled up her hands, then up her arms, and then back down, finally issuing from her fingers as it always had. But now, it appeared puny and fragile. It meandered without a true direction.

The other side of the tunnel, opposite the wall she had stayed close to for so long, opened out into wide nothingness in places which terrified her as she thought of how she could have stumbled and fallen into the chasm.

In fact, she recalled walking a little close to that side sometimes and hadn't gone over by mere chance. This made her reconsider the tunnel. Had the Haldor made this? Did they know how to use magik, too? Had their magik been placed to thwart any other magik-user from invading?

Pappy Oh had tinkered with many spells and even used tiny ones to teach her how to play hide and seek as a *betot*. He would hide something from her with magik and she wouldn't find it until he broke the spell.

But why would the Haldor set up a hiding spell here? There had been nothing to see or care about in this whole long trip through the mountain. Simply a tunnel. Just a path through the cavernous area.

What if that was the entire problem? It had been hidden.

She couldn't *see* it. Unless she had been so tired she had missed the telltale signs of something important. "No. I couldn't have missed anything. I've been careful," she said aloud. "The Haldor created some sort of spell, and I'm just now realizing it."

Shocked at herself for missing something so obvious, she exclaimed, "That must be the case. Why, a hide-and-go-seek spell would prevent me from seeing anything and from even knowing if anything existed!"

She tried to recall what could remove such a spell, but try as she might, nothing came to her tired mind.

"What did Pappy say?" she asked aloud, now pacing back and forth. "He had to do something… no, it was something he said…" She paced some more.

She couldn't remember.

Frustration set in. What if…

Refocusing her illumination magik, she said, "Find the blocking spell and release it."

The spell started out fine, but when it bounced against the wall beside her and dissipated, she realized she wouldn't be successful. Her magik seemed ill, confused.

She had not been certain what Edegast meant by telling her to rein magik in and make it behave, but she had to try. It certainly couldn't hurt now.

"Come on, glow. Find the spell, please."

The magik covered the wall and dripped down it, as if she had thrown paint on it.

"That's it?" she questioned out loud. The wall *was* the spell. She couldn't imagine what that even meant. She touched the wall, and the glow re-entered her hands.

She decided to check for some sort of triggering device on it that would make it open like a door. Perhaps a door, or a fake wall, or many other things that could hide in a spell.

She started up as high as she could reach and brought her palms down the structure, using as little force as possible.

The entire process felt like putting her hands on the injured Yeti or Cerius. It became an intuitive sort of knowing, or an out of the way feeling. Something always stood out in the energy around the object she focused on. But the wall where she stood gave her no sign of anything wrong with it.

She sighed and slumped, letting her hands dangle at her sides. She glared at the wall and moved down a little, putting her hands on it once more. Lower, like the door to the corridor where the dragon's lair had been.

There. *There.*

A faint energy, but certainly different, it pulsated under her touch. She decided to give her magik another command.

"Show me the energy living here."

The green glow misted out and covered the wall. She had to take a few steps backwards to see what it showed.

A drawing of a window appeared with branches of trees outside of it, and a flame-colored bird sat on one branch. The sight made her inhale sharply. This drawing, what potentially lay beyond, brought her joy and relief.

"Find a way beyond the energy of this spell. Find the phoenix," she told her magik.

It hovered there, hesitantly, the image of the window fading.

"Don't resist me, spell. I'm the apprentice of a mighty mage, the same one who created you. Don't resist me. Find the phoenix, now!" she commanded, temper flaring.

The magik gathered itself like an unholy fire and burned into the wall. Sparks flew out, and she threw her arm up to shield herself against it. The sudden fear of being blinded by her magik, like the dragon had been, filled her. And she stepped backwards again.

This time, her foot's heel found the edge of the path and the weight of the pack pulled her backwards as her arms windmilled wildly. She went into the chasm, hit her head on something in the dark on the way down, and knew nothing else.

Unaware of how long she'd lain like a crooked rag doll on the bottom of the cave floor, she opened her eyes and peered upward. The air above her blew through tree branches.

And strangely, something rang familiar about that tree, but she couldn't remember through the pounding of her head. She tried to move but found herself wedged into a tight spot.

She tried to turn onto her left side, but her effort met cold stone there. She tried to turn onto her right side and found nothing there but more frigid stone and darkness beyond. Not knowing how close she might be to another more deadly fall, she remained still for a time.

Then, the shivering began. Her skin trembled from chilled air that wafted across her. She could be outside of the Haldor's cave. She could be on the other side of the mountain, for all she knew.

Gotta move. Gotta know where I am.

Flat on her back, she assessed everything she could feel around her. The pack remained under her, its bulk hard against her back. She patted her sides and tried to find the bow and quiver of arrows. They had disappeared in the fall.

Up high between the branches of the tree, the green glow glimmered faintly, waiting to be retrieved.

Movement stuttered above her in the branches like birds, silently watching, without twittering or sound. Perhaps only the icy wind blowing distant leaves, she mused. Then she marveled at how she had managed to avoid broken bones from the limbs that were hidden in the dark.

Exasperated, she twisted hard, side-to-side, and worked free from where she'd been stuck in place. When she could finally sit upright, she pulled the pack from her back and discovered Pappy Oh's jack-in-the-box missing as well.

"Return to me, magik. Don't fail me now." Her pulse thrummed in her temples as she realized her predicament. "Find my belongings."

The spell drifted down from above and painted the tree branches with light as it came. She stared up at the tree. One of the massive offshoots could have been what she had struck on the way down. She noted a large open area where branches thinned out, and she figured that must be why she had been virtually unharmed. She reached up and found the bump, broken skin, and source of her headache.

One branch cradled her bow. The crumpled quiver, with arrows sticking out in all directions, hung from another. And there, between two limbs, sat Pappy's box, upside down, the clown's head staring, as if questioning her.

"How in Daegries am I supposed to get that down here?" she asked, annoyed.

She slapped the ground on either side of her legs, anger taking over. The pain from her scraped palms screamed as she felt gritty sand beneath them.

Why did this have to happen now?

She gazed up again, thinking, If I've gotta leave all that behind, well, I just have to.

Her magik would have to be her weapon, and Pappy Oh, if he even came back, would have to take up residence in something else.

Right now, I need to get to that wellspring and rescue that scoundrel scarf.

She tried to gather her feet under herself, but the area curved up, bowl-shaped, making standing difficult. After several attempts, during which she became out of sorts, she commanded her spell once more. "Find light in this gods-forsaken place!"

The magik brightened, and she could see that she had fallen into a stone bowl with a lip around it. She stretched out on her belly, crawled to the edge of the lip, and leaned out to see what she sat upon.

The stone bowl sat atop the hands of a statue of the Goddess Kasu, the water-bearer. An enormous statue that she assumed to be the original. Her Granny hosted a replica of this statue in her garden. As a little *betot*, she had played around it. Granny would fill the bowl with seeds from her sunflowers to attract birds. Alyssa realized at that moment that the grit beneath her was not sand, but birdseed.

She sat inside the bowl that Kasu carried in her hands over her head. After another look, she estimated the drop to the ground below to be a great distance. It didn't appear flat, either, but dotted with gardens of some kind.

Alyssa rolled over onto her back and stared up at the tree. She must have fallen asleep, because when she came to again, the glow had faded and found its way back to her. She felt no need to call on it again. Instead, she focused on her choices and what to do.

The Haldor had created this place, and, like the wellspring, it had to have meaning. She thought hard about the Goddess Kasu, the water-bearer, the goddess of creativity and fertility, and all things good that she had learned from Granny. The water from Kasu's fountain had many healing powers. She didn't hear any water splashing even far below her. The fountain of Kasu was dry.

Certainly, from the little that she knew about the Haldor, they likely worshipped such a goddess. Since they were creators of all things metal, and stone, and gemstone-encrusted, the Goddess Kasu might mean a good number of things to them.

Alyssa sighed, rolling to her side, pulling off the pack as she went.

"Dear Kasu, please help me," she moaned. "I simply want to find the wellspring, the phoenix, and the scarf. I'll worship you forever if you can make that happen."

She reached up and found the bump on her forehead. Smaller than before.

How long have I been here? No one besides Edegast and my friends even know that I've been this way. I could die here.

Alyssa closed her eyes tightly. Those sorts of thoughts wouldn't get the scarf and save Granny, if indeed she still had time. She caught her second wind and struggled into a sitting position, determined to make this disaster work out in her favor. That scarf would not win this battle, not as long as she had breath.

Again, she tried to stand. The bird seeds slipped beneath her feet. She scooped some of it up to look at it closer. "Find light," she said. Her spell issued forth, brightening the whole area. Definite bird seed appeared.

"Ugh," she said, dropping it, and wiping her palm on her backside. Her hands had seen better days, and she grimaced at the pain. She'd scraped both palms on her tumble from the dragon.

Dejected, she gazed up at the tree. "If you want them back, you'll have to go and get them," she told herself. She drew her pack closer, stood on it to reach the lowest branch, and pulled herself up, limb by limb, pausing to collect each item she had lost. She placed the arrows—still intact, thankfully—back inside the quiver from where they dangerously dangled. The quiver easily fell into its normal shape once she shook it a few times. She slung it over her shoulder.

She placed the bow strap over her head until it draped across her body securely, then used both hands to get to Pappy's box.

Why it should matter so much to her, she couldn't say. But she couldn't leave it behind. Maybe when she got back home to the farm in Mudden, she'd put it somewhere for a keepsake. She'd have to get him all the way back to life first, though.

Thoughts of Pappy filled her, and as she rested against the tree branch, she called out to him.

"Pappy, where are you? Why don't you come back to me?" she asked the box.

It sat in her hands, still and silent. He surely had all he could handle back home. He wouldn't make an appearance to her under the mountain. Maybe he couldn't reach her down here, anyway.

While these thoughts plagued her, she made her way back toward the bowl. She realized below her the branches to the tree continued past the bowl of Kasu and, if crafty, she could climb from this tree to another one farther down. She scooped up her pack and moved to leave the bowl of Goddess Kasu.

At first, she felt like a squirrel going from branch to branch, hugging the trunk, but her attempt proved fruitful and in a short while she regained solid ground.

She paused, glancing overhead at where she had come from.

The bowl of the statue perched high overhead and, now that she had left it, birds were landing there to get the seeds. She'd been keeping them from their food source, apparently.

Happy to be on land again, she told them, "It's okay, birdies. I'm off to find the wellspring."

She readjusted everything on her person, making certain of its security, and peered around for some sort of trail. Things were growing in this section under the mountain. And then she saw overhead a sky filled with stars, twinkling far above her. She had fallen into the area where the mountain's top had disappeared.

But where did the Haldor go? They could conceivably have stayed here. But then again, they were seeking protection from a dragon. There would be little protection here. And Karnargul had said that the Haldor had gone to a place he called the Blighted Vale. She did not know where such a vale could be, or even if it existed. Karnargul had been under the mountain for a long time and might be lying, anyway.

She kept walking. The sky lightened before she chose a thin willow tree to rest under. Solly peeked over the far hill. She had been gone from her companions overnight at least, but she remained unsure how long exactly. Unable to see the moon, she didn't know what the face of Luna showed at the present time. She only hoped for enough time to keep the gryphon at bay.

Alyssa didn't mean to fall so fast asleep. She slept deeply and knew nothing until she awoke hours later, shaded by the tree and slightly chilled from the breeze that blew through the area. It occurred to her that the other side of the mountain had ice and snow, but this side showed snowdrops and crocuses like spring had arrived.

"Strange indeed," she muttered as she sat up and rubbed her eyes. Nearby a rock with shiny moss claimed her attention while she got her wits about her. She was too groggy to think.

Her stomach growled and she felt unmerciful hunger pangs. She pulled the pack over and rummaged through it, seeking something to eat. There were a few slices of meat that still appeared appetizing, and some dried bread that didn't.

She pretended not to see the mold and ate around it. Thirst hit her, and she pulled Lord Bryon's water pouch from her pack and drank from it until empty. This act caused her to begin thinking about water from the wellspring. Wouldn't there be water going to it?

Well, there must be… isn't that what the wellspring would be, a fountain of water?

Then she remembered the rock and moss. There had to be water somewhere.

She brushed the crumbs from her lap and stood, peering around. The trickle of a stream flowed from behind her. So, Kasu's stream or fountain wasn't totally dry. Carrying the pack again, she walked beside the stream for a long way ahead.

It wended beneath a bridge made from rocks, reminding her of Granny's attempt at such a structure back home. She sighed as longing rose within her to be done with this adventure and back at the farm.

"Nothing for it," she told herself, sternly. "Have to go on. Hang on, Granny; I'm coming back. Pappy, I sure hope you're able to keep everything in place until I do. Scarf, you better get ready. I'm coming for you."

Her thoughts went to her friends who were out there somewhere, trying to find her. She could only hope she strode in the right direction.

As she passed under the bridge, she admired the craftsmanship. The stones, specially cut and fitted, almost made a pattern in colors and design. If only Granny Gert could see how this had been done, she'd have a much better chance of building a bridge she could be proud of.

Oh well, I'll show her one day. Or I'll make it myself as soon as I set foot on Mudden land again.

She peered out beyond the bridge and saw a path that dove into the midst of wildflowers. Butterflies and bees floated around them happily. This side of the dragon's lair, as she had begun to think of it, had been virtually untouched by the drought that had seared all the parts of Daegries she'd seen thus far. It was as if it enjoyed permanent spring.

The thought of remaining here struck her. Her tired body would like nothing more than to sit down and not move again.

Her desire to pursue the flowered path away from the mountains and to discover more about this land pulled at her. But it fell short as she realized she had a bigger journey, a more important part to play. And who knew where it went? Certainly not to the Haldor, she decided gazing ahead at the mountain. She noted where it once again met the water she followed.

A trek into nature would have to wait. She moved ahead staying with the water in the hope it would lead her to the wellspring.

Before she entered the dimness of the mountain again, she saw the bright blue sky and knew that if she never had to walk beneath the ground again, it would not bother her. She preferred the sun and good land and all it offered.

Suddenly, overhead, a massive bird with long tail feathers of red and gold issued a mournful cry full of homesickness and loss. It nearly broke her heart to hear it, but she knew this must be the phoenix. It could be no other.

It flew away over the mountain, and the sight made her rush ahead. Her heart lifted at seeing the bird that would lead her to the final destination of her journey.

Chapter Twenty-One

The Haldor

The tunnel on this side still had a part of the stream, but the water source became thinner and less rocky as she went along. For the first time since leaving her company, she felt as though she truly was on the right path. Seeing the phoenix, brilliant in its plumage, like one of Granny's sugar maples in the fall, had been the jolt of encouragement she needed.

Soon the darkness became more than she could manage with her naked eye, so she called on her magik once more for light. The tunnel wound ever on into the mountain, a pathway to more of the same stone, mud, water, and darkness. The phoenix's mountain, she called it now, and hoped to catch a glimpse of the bird somewhere.

She saw that the tunnel had other paths cut out of it, and she wondered if her path, the straightest one, might be the wrong one.

These thoughts ended when she heard a great groaning and whirring and the sound of metal against metal. A light grew brighter at the end of her current path, and she slowed. If this was another dragon, she would be out of sorts in the worst way. She pulled her bow and nocked an arrow, keeping it pointed down as she slid along the wall for safety.

She peered into the room where the path ended. Though much like the dragon's hoard, no fire-breathing creature appeared. Instead, an actual fire, a mighty inferno, rose in the center of the room, turning the men who worked there into shadows. They carried melting ore from one place to another beside the fire, pouring the liquid carefully into molds.

The appearance of gems glittering in large urns and coins stacked high all around the room, neatly and precisely, sent her heart soaring.

Could this be the Haldor? Karnargul had lied. Haldor!

For it must be them. These short, squat men wore long beards and had helms of metal, as they had been described. They worked tirelessly, forging ore, and hammering stone into tools. They also tumbled crystals into gemstones in big metal tubes. The noise was deafening.

Oh, if only Pappy Oh were here, she thought. He would love to see these magnificent men at work. She stood there amazed and stared for a long time, until someone's head lifted and spotted her.

He pointed at her and shouted for the others to take note. Because of the amount of noise coming from the work at hand, he had a hard time being heard.

Finally, he got the attention of two other barrel-chested men. Alyssa's time to run away had passed. Not that she wanted to, anyway. If anyone could show her to the wellspring and the phoenix, it would be these men. Exhausted and running short of time, she replaced her arrow and her bow. Then she crossed her arms and waited for the trio of men, as they moved away from their duties and started toward where she stood in the doorway.

They arrived carrying hammers and acting annoyed. Two of them took an arm each, and the third took her bow and arrows. They led her back the way she had come, away from the hot forge area, and hurried her down the first side path they came to. And it went down, not up, making her immediately afraid.

In surroundings dark and airless, the stocky men didn't slow down to accommodate her small stride. Rather, they picked her up off her feet and let her dangle between them as they hurried along. It hurt being dangled under the arm like someone's loaf of bread, but she bit her lip and stayed quiet.

Once, when she attempted to explain herself, they ignored her. The turnings they made off the original path meant she would never find her way out again without help. But at each juncture, she saw a candle in a metal holder, and she tried counting them, hoping that would lead her back out again if they ever gave her the chance.

Finally, the men slowed and turned into a carved-out room with torches on either side, and a rather ugly Haldor man seated upon someone's version of a throne. It teemed with rubies and sapphires, and the lion's arms with claws that turned under at the end.

Obviously important, he sat and stared as they approached.

The men dumped her unceremoniously in front of him and tossed her weapons in a pile beside his feet.

"She stumbled upon the forge," the blond-bearded man on her left said.

"She didn't resist us, but came along agreeable-like," the man who had been on her right said. He had a long, black beard, braided with tiny bells at the ends of it.

The third man, hooded, with thick bushy eyebrows to match his red beard, turned to her. "You are in the presence of his Kingliness, Vernon the first, Lord of the Realm of Haldor. You should bow."

She raised her eyebrows at this. *Another ruler? How many will I meet on this journey?* But she did as he asked and bowed low.

"Your Kingliness. I am Alyssa Chance Oh," she whispered as she rose. Her ability to heed majestic instructions seemed to have been perfected through the days on her journey.

Vernon waved at the three men to depart. "I can handle this prisoner, thank you."

Alyssa relaxed when the Haldor royal spoke and understood her language, unlike the Yeti who spoke guttural gibberish.

"What are you doing in our forge?" King Vernon asked, clasping his hands in his lap. He peered at her from beneath a jeweled crown, but his voice sounded friendly.

"Simply an accident, kind sir. I came in through the throne room of the dragon, fell onto the stone bowl of the goddess Kasu, and ended up coming this way, hunting for my friends and—"

"You have been in the presence of that demon spawn, Karnargul?" he sputtered, interrupting her.

"Y-yes, by accident. I happened upon his lair, much as I stumbled into your forge."

He glared at her for a moment, reminding her of Granny Gert's face when she had caught Pappy using magik inappropriately.

"Pray continue. I would have the complete story of how you survived such an encounter, as rare as it is."

She walked up to the dais and sat on the edge of it next to where King Vernon perched on his throne. He said nothing, but she knew it was highly unusual to sit in the presence of anyone higher than a lord like Bryon.

"I'm sorry for sitting this way, your highness. I'm plain tuckered out from the trek here. Anyway," she said, slumping her shoulders in relaxation, "we, that is my party and I, were hunting for a way into the mountain to find you, that is, the Haldor. I saw this little door that none of my friends could fit into, as we—I mean your kin and I—are built a little on the small side. So, I was chosen to pop in and nose around the inside. Well, as you have guessed, the dragon piled in there, in all of his Shining One meanness."

"The cave-in destroyed that door, we thought," Vernon mused. "Finding out there is another way in still is news. Not entirely pleasant, considering."

She nodded. "Yes, well, there it is. And I went back out before Karnargul could fry me with his flame, to tell my friends that this most definitely would not be the way to go in."

"I sense an additional story within this one," he grumbled.

"Yes. *But*, they couldn't convince me not to try to get through the dragon's treasures and find a way to the other side of the mountain. I've been hunting for the wellspring of your people all this time. I didn't know any other way, and as I am on borrowed time, I didn't want to wait to travel all the way over to the other side and come through another door if possible. Not even knowing if one existed. So, I came through and here I am."

"Karnargul didn't try to stop you?" He raised an eyebrow as if she told a lie.

"Oh, yes, he did, but fortunately for me, he has poor vision for things right under his nose. I suspect if I had been a fat bunny hopping around a few miles below him, he would have had no trouble at all seeing me. But up close, not so much."

"We would like to know how to get rid of him. He sits in our parlor, lying on top of our people's wealth, and we cannot get in and he cannot get out."

Alyssa thought for a moment before answering. "King, I would be thrilled to help in that endeavor, but I'm behind on an adventure to find that phoenix you have living in the wellspring. It stole a scarf from men up Needlemount way, and I need it. Otherwise, I'd pitch in."

"If the Haldor aided you in this scarf hunt, would you help us with the dragon?"

"Sure, I mean, he thinks y'all live over in the valley on the other side of this mountain. He called it the Blighted Vale. He says if he ever gets out of the pickle he's gotten himself into, he will make desolation of that place and all of your kin."

"Oh, he does, does he? That is interesting to know. There is a village over in that vale, and it borders the Wine Sea. A few Haldor do live there. We should warn those men of trouble brewing. If we should ever be able to evict his scaly tail from our front room, he might decide to do such a thing indeed."

The King brooded, as if the decision to rid himself of a dragon would be a boon for his people but a disaster for others, and he would have to live with the outcome of such a thing.

"I do know folks, who, if we could get them over to the dragon's side of the mountain and into the throne room, might be able to fight him and win," Alyssa said.

"It would have to be a dangerous group of people who could do such a thing. Karnargul is an ancient and cunning dragon."

"Would you happen to know the Yetimen who live on the lower levels of the Heightlands?" Alyssa asked. "They would make a powerful enemy of the dragon, based on their size alone."

The king of the Haldor crossed his arms, annoyed. "Yes, I know the Yeti, and a stranger, less appealing family of creatures I cannot imagine. What on Daegries could they possibly do for us regarding a dragon? Their... fur... burns as easily as our beards." He pulled on his as if to emphasize his words.

"Y'all had a falling out, huh?" she guessed, watching his face closely.

He nodded. "They took advantage of us. We forged iron and stone goods for them. But then, when the trade route came right between us, they interfered with our buyers, saying our prices were too high and our goods not worthy. Then they sold them the same goods we had either given, traded, or sold to them, luring the buyers away. We quit dealing with them before the cave-in, and I doubt we will ever start anew."

"Yeah, my pappy told me about how his pappy and him used to bring farm goods from Mudden all the way up through here back in the day. Said the trade route had issues and they stopped doing business in the Heightlands."

Shock registered on his face, and he asked, "Your name again, my lady?"

"Alyssa Chance Oh."

The King tilted his head. "Would your pappy be Sir Pappy Oh?"

Alyssa's jaw went slack. "Well, yes, as a matter of fact. Although to my knowledge he was never knighted. Do you know him?"

"Yes, I know him," he told her, waving excitedly. "His father dealt with my own. Those were the most delicious vegetables and herbs we ever received. Such a terrible loss when they stopped coming here. Blasted Yetis." Then, he stared at her in amazement. "I cannot believe I am sitting with a relative of the great Oh. This is indeed a new day."

Alyssa smiled at him, considering this revelation about the Yetis. She thought maybe Fred, the leader, would be hearing from her. The two factions needed to patch up their differences. Maybe then Pappy could get the trade going again and benefit everyone, somehow.

"Perhaps you will convince Sir Oh to come back one day. It would be a joy to meet him again. He could come along with the Yetis, and we could parlay."

"My thoughts, too," she told him.

A journey through Yetiland on her return home to Mudden would happen for sure. She still had to get a tooth for Lorelei the siren.

"I'll be sure to mention it to him when I see him. And to the Yeti leader. It would be good for all of us, the way I see it."

She brushed her hair away from her forehead and touched the bump, still sore but not swollen. "I do understand how bad your situation with the Yetis must have been. But there ain't no doubt they are good at hunting, and from what I've seen, good at being quiet, mostly. I think Karnargul might have to think a minute before attacking them."

"Karnargul cares nothing for size. He will turn everything into cinders if it pleases him."

"What if the Yeti were to make a bargain with him to get him out of the mountain? He really wants to get out. If they could enable him to get out of there, then your people would have their home back."

"And then? That evil creature would go straight to the vale and destroy it. Simply for the sake of his own pleasure and nothing more. I am not sure that I want restoration of the Haldor in exchange for the destruction of another tribe," he said. Then, thoughtfully, he added, "He is truly an evil one."

"Well, think about it, your Highness. I reckon it's a big deep subject. The Yetis owe y'all though," she said, standing. "Now, to my own troubles... Can I get your permission to go forward and find that wellspring?"

He planted his hands on his thighs, stood to his feet, and waved at her to retrieve her bow and arrows. "The Haldor are at your service, Lady Alyssa. It would be a kindness if you helped us with Karnargul, in return."

She nodded, thinking. "Well, for starters, he is as blind as a cave rat when things get shoved up under his nose. He uses his sense of smell to find whatever's around. He has done this for a long time because he even knew how unusual my scent seemed. Now, don't ask me what that means as I ain't had time to figure it out yet. He could have meant I was a girl, and he hadn't smelled one of us in a long time. At any rate, I sort of put his eyes out for good, I think. At least he screamed about being blinded by the light I thrust in his face. So, he may be blind. Dragons talk in circles, don't they?"

King Vernon smiled at that. "Yes, they do. Even so, his assessment could be true. He could be temporarily blinded."

She crossed her arms. "Well, temporary or not, he couldn't find me after that."

He gazed at her bow and arrows. "It isn't often young ones come through this realm armed."

"That's no harm, there, King Vernon. That's something I use to put dinner on the table sometimes."

"Still," he added. "I suspect you could take the eye out of a chicken from a good way off."

"True enough. Well, I guess I'm ready to go on. I appreciate your kindness, and your listening ear about my troubles."

"I will consider your thoughts on the Yetimen."

"And I'll be happy to put your troubles on my list, too. As for that old dragon, a few of my company might be up to the task, if you need reinforcements. A couple of my friends are handy with swords. I'll have to ask them when we meet up again."

"What has happened to your company?"

"I sent them over the mountain to find another way into the wellspring. Do you know of one?"

"Yes. We were under these mountains for years before the dragon divided us. There are tunnels created by my grandsire, Morin the First, tunnels by my father, Gaylin the First, and so on. The front door once faced the sea. That would be the one your friends will eventually come upon."

She nodded, slung the bow over her shoulder, and turned to bow to him. "I thank you, kind King Vernon. I'd like to be shown to the wellspring now, and then out that front door, if possible. Otherwise, I might wander your Haldor halls for a long time."

He pulled out a golden horn draped over his chair's back and blew it in three quick blasts. Soon, two heavily armed and thickly bearded Haldor men appeared.

"You will show this lady first to the wellspring of our forebears and then to the door of Mervyn. Feed her first. I believe she is thirsty and hungry and would respond well to our kindness. While that is about, get her more food to take on her journey. Who knows when it may end?"

Alyssa could not argue his logic at that point either.

The men again took routes through the underground world of the Haldor that she would never understand, but eventually they came upon the stream and the bridge once again.

Alyssa sighed, relieved. At last, a place she recognized. It felt good to meet the mountain men and know they had not been exterminated.

Her companions traveled in the complete opposite direction that she had taken and instead went up and over the stone bridge. This annoyed Alyssa, as she remembered thinking about what the bridge led to. Oh, if only she had gone that way!

The wellspring of the Haldor was a beautiful garden set outside the mountain, surrounded by its majesty. The stream meandered there and ended in a large lake.

But to Alyssa's disappointment, the phoenix did not appear. She gazed all over the gardens, and even downstream a way, but saw nothing she had sought for so long.

Her heart fell.

"Sirs, the phoenix that lives here is supposed to be the current owner of a follygrass scarf. I've traveled a long way to find it. Has anyone seen such a thing?"

The men glanced at one another and one shrugged.

"Milady, the phoenix is a mysterious bird. She dives deep down into the wellspring to feed on fish, but she has never shown us her aerie. We always thought she lived close by, but you say she lives here. That is curious. Perhaps she has a treasure trove here, also."

She shook her head in confusion. That didn't sound right.

"But you have not seen this bird wearing a scarf?"

They both laughed. "No milady. We have seen no such thing."

She paced back and forth, staring at the lake and an ornate fountain in its center where gods and goddesses poured out water onto a stone mountain. The mountain had an arm that jutted out and ended in a moat. Alyssa felt this fountain portrayed what the mountain of the Haldor appeared like from the air.

She leaned forward, staring hard at what appeared to be the backside of the fountain. Stone figures there scooped up water and dropped it into the bowls of the gods and goddesses so that the water always moved, back and forth, from moat to mountain, endlessly.

"Does the phoenix come back and forth all day or all night?" she asked her companions. "I'm not sure how long I should wait here."

"The bird has no certain schedule, save her own."

She nodded. "Will you permit me to stay until she appears? I must find the scarf. She's my only hope."

"Yes, milady," the Haldor man replied. "Our liege has commanded us to do this for you."

"And then show you to the door," the other Haldor man added.

She smiled and thanked them. The afternoon sun shone down on her back as it made a slow trek across the sky. She appreciated the clear sky, even though the air turned rather chilly as the sun lowered.

"Miss the farm. Not going to lie," she said, rubbing her cold arms.

The three of them passed the time sitting by the fountain and eating food that the king had ordered given to her. She didn't realize how famished she'd been until her first taste of cheese.

If the Haldor men judged her manners by the way she crammed food into her mouth, they had the good grace not to show it.

Finally, full and satisfied, Alyssa curled up on the stone bench, closed her eyes, and rested. She didn't know how long she had slept until the taller of the two men shook her awake.

"Milady, the bird is about," he told her, pointing at the sky.

A dark speck in the sky, high overhead, circled and circled and circled before flying down to land on the tallest of the gods in the fountain.

The Haldor men, in awe of its beauty, bowed low, taking off their helmets, their beards touching the ground.

"Squawk!" the phoenix said. "Who are you?"

Alyssa, surprised that the creature could speak, stammered a moment before saying, "Alyssa Chance Oh of Mudden, in the lower Daegries. Oh my, dear Phoenix, forgive my ignorance of customs."

She did a curtsy and tried to appear humble.

The phoenix bobbed her head and preened her glorious flame-colored feathers. Then, as if it were of no account, said, "Yes, Alyssa Chance; I have been seeking you. You have been hiding under the mountain, keeping me waiting."

This surprised Alyssa into silence. She couldn't imagine such a lovely bird as this ever searching for her.

"I have been speaking to those who have seen you pass. The dryads have tracked your journey, and the wolves, and they know much."

"Why were you hunting for me, if I could be so bold as to ask?"

"There is the scarf to be reckoned with. I took it from the men in Needlemount, as they are not the proper persons to have it in their possession. Evil begets evil, and items of power have no place with evil."

"You have the scarf, oh beautiful Phoenix?"

"Squawk! Yes, I have kept it safe until your arrival. Powerful Elven magik is woven into the scarf, and it should not be possessed by anyone who is not a true magik-user."

Before this journey, Alyssa did not consider herself a magik-user, but only a lowly mage, still of an apprentice rank. Now, she knew the truth. Powerful, but still untried.

"Dear Phoenix, I've only recently used spells. My knowledge is new concerning magik. I plan to take the scarf to the Gryphon King in the Meadowlands. My family farm and the lives of my family depend on this. The gryphon did a kindness to my grandmother, and this scarf's return is my repayment."

"Some debts can never be repaid, Alyssa Chance. But items of power often have plans of their own. Nevertheless, my time is short. Why do we not take it out and see what it thinks?" the phoenix answered.

Before Alyssa could reply, she flew straight up, far into the sky, straight at the sun, and then spiraled down, down, down, dipping into the bottom of the fountain in the moat. She grasped something with her claws, tugging it until it appeared, and she could turn upward once more. Her wings flapped mightily, blowing air against Alyssa's face. She dropped the garment directly in front of Alyssa.

The scarf, at last.

At first, it seemed bedraggled and the worse for wear, especially since it had been under water. But to Alyssa's great surprise, its threads undulated until it seemed as though it had been made from strands of gold. The phoenix fluttered to the ground, picked the scarf up in her beak and lifted off once more in order to drop it over Alyssa's shoulders. It curled around her like a live thing.

Alyssa experienced a few moments of excitement, followed by relief. She had come so far, been through so much… and now she had the scarf at last. She touched the wet material, and a surge of victory filled her.

Don't you give up on me, Granny. I'll be back to deal with King Hubert soon.

As she sat there, her emotions going from one stage to another, the scarf dried, resuming its normal green-gray color. The phoenix perched on the back of the stone bench.

 Finally, the bird spoke. "That's what I suspected."

Oh no. What could be wrong now? "What?" Alyssa asked, lifting her hands and letting scarf fall. "What did I do?"

"Do? You have done nothing, child. This scarf has chosen you. It's wrapped around you like a second skin. I doubt you will remove that, gryphon debt or no."

Alyssa stared at the scarf where the ends dangled, and she pulled on one side to remove it.

It wrapped itself around her wrist.

She tried to disentangle her wrist, and it wrapped around her hand.

"No!" she shouted. "Don't do that!"

"I'm afraid you'll not be able to remove that scarf. It has chosen you."

Alarmed, Alyssa said, "The scarf has been doing this all along. Choosing who it wanted to be with for a time and clinging to them until it could pass ownership to someone else. You'd think the gryphon or Lord Bryon or Ragon or someone would have told me—that if it gets on you, it sticks to you like beggar's lice. Lady Pianna wore it. So maybe the attachment is only temporary. But I guess it isn't usual to let others wear it like this."

The phoenix squawked again and bent low to peer into her face.

"Alyssa Chance Oh, make no mistake; this is not a common scarf. It will not seem common, it will not appear common, and it will not *act* common. The others chose the scarf. It has chosen you. A distinction and one of high import."

"But I have to get it back to the—"

"Gryphon. Yes, so you've said. But as a magikal property, it can go or stay as it chooses. You may find that you cannot give it back. The scarf may not wish to be in that person's presence. A power item seeks power to fulfill itself. You are the one it chooses."

Despair filled Alyssa. *What if I can't give it to the gryphon?* "But I didn't come here seeking it for me! I came here to fulfill an obligation. The scarf doesn't even belong to the gryphon. The Iefyr created it for the wizard Edegast and gave it to him. The gryphon stole it from him. Then Lord Pryon stole it from the gryphon and then Ragon and Madrid stole it from him, and then you stole it from them, and now—"

"Now you are here at last. The scarf sought you. It traveled from the Iefyr to the Meadowlands before being waylaid from its mission. It didn't want Edegast the Green; it sought you, wee one."

Chapter Twenty-Two

The Bop

The trip to the door of Mervyn, also known as the front door, as Alyssa later learned, could only be reached by Haldor tunnels. She lost track of days and didn't know if time remained to get home before the gryphon would retaliate.

She touched the scarf around her neck. Not that he could take it anyway.

Gods be good. Pappy, please hold him for a little longer.

When the Haldor men flung open the massive door, fortified with iron bolts, hasps, and locks, Alyssa squinted at the sun-streaked landscape. She drank in the sight of far mountains and a vivid turquoise lake that flowed around the foot of it, straight into the sea. The vale that the dragon had called blighted seemed far from that.

It sported tiny houses, all in a row, facing the lake.

"Sir," she asked the nearest Haldor man, who was in no hurry to go back to the forge or wherever they had come from, "can you tell me which direction to go to find the door on the other side of the mountain? I have friends hunting for me and need to know which way to go to meet them."

He crooked a finger and motioned for her to follow him down a rocky path. It joined a wider way and led up, up, up. She nodded, however unhappily.

"Is there anything else you require, milady?" he asked.

She shook her head and thanked him and his friend for their kindness in seeing her this way. They did their duty according to the request made by their king, but she felt grateful anyway.

Before they left her there, she asked, "Also, kind sirs, would you know the current cycle of the moon? Is it the first quarter, third quarter, or full?"

The Haldor man who usually remained silent replied, "According to our calendar, which lies in Haldor Hall, Luna would be nearly full now, milady. She should provide a brilliant light to walk the path by."

Her heart sank. If it took her days to find the others, she would be too late getting home. The squat Haldor men closed the massive Mervyn door leaving her alone again.

She wished she could sprout wings and fly home! Then she remembered Pappy had done that, in spirit anyway.

Things would be so much easier if something simply fell out of the sky and enabled her to go home. But this journey had never been easy and wouldn't start now. Besides, what in Daegries could carry her that far that fast?

Then, she remembered the phoenix and her beautiful feathers and how she could fly straight at the sun and not be blinded or burned.

If only she could carry me.

Strangely, the scarf grew lighter, and loosened its grip around her slightly.

She spoke to it. "I would like to remove you from around my neck and put you around my waist, if you don't mind."

The grip loosened even more.

She pulled one side of it, and it came off easily. She wrapped it around her waist and tied it, making a jaunty sash of it.

"Much better."

Then as she adjusted her pack, now heavier with food, she turned to stare at the path she would have to tread up and over the mountain to find the others. Her bow and arrows felt like senseless extra baggage now that she had the scarf, but she didn't leave them behind.

"I may find a use for you yet," she said aloud. Then, with nothing but nightfall fast approaching, Alyssa took off to find her friends.

Overhead, a dark cloud covered the fading sun's rays, and Alyssa bent her head back. The phoenix flew over, and she had a few friends with her.

They settled on a hillock nearby and waited for her to get to them. She struggled to run with her pack banging into her back, but she finally made it, red-faced and panting.

"What… What…" she tried to say.

The phoenix, ever observant said, "We are here to help you, Alyssa. As you are the rightful heiress and bearer of the Scarf of Magik, it is only fitting that we honor you with our help. Also, time is important in my life. I have no time to waste. "

She bowed her head to Alyssa who curtsied to her in return. Then the phoenix lifted a wing and fanned it toward the other four giant birds.

When she could gape at the birds, she thought they were eagles, only they were far too immense to be normal eagles, such as she had witnessed while in the mountains on the trail through Yetiland.

"These are my friends. They are Bop, or in Mannish, birds of prey. They will not hesitate to eat a Yeti, so remember this. They are not discriminating in their tastes and have taken horses, and cattle occasionally. Because of your association with me, they will refrain from such in my presence. Your friends were taken captive by an Iefyr patrol two nights ago when they accidentally stumbled upon the Elves. Edegast has had conversations with them in days past and is renewing his friendship. It is well enough to take you there. Then we will see if these mighty wings will permit you and your friends to go home on their backs."

Alyssa, so shocked she couldn't speak for a moment, finally asked, "I thought the Iefyr lived north of the Wine Sea where the wizard's castle is? What would an Iefyr patrol be doing this far south?"

The phoenix squawked. "You can never know with the Elves. They make it their business to dabble in the affairs of men, Haldor, and others. I suspect they have heard of the movements of the dryads and sirens, which you know of, and are hunting the cause."

Alyssa remembered the discussion at Half Moon Manor about the mysterious portal and remembered Granny saying that the Putrid Plants hid a portal as well. She worried about the possibility that, by bringing Pappy Oh back, even partially, she had opened a rift in the world of Daegries and things would only get worse.

Would the phoenix know about that kind of thing? She glanced at the birds.

Better not ask too many questions right now.

She listened to the phoenix's instructions on how to get on the Bop's back. She went slowly and carefully until she sat right behind the massive wings.

To guarantee she didn't lose Pappy Oh's toy box, she shoved it deep into the pack and pulled the string tight. Her bow and arrows where tightly wrapped around her shoulders.

Once assured that Alyssa perched securely, the phoenix squawked at the Bop, and they lifted off the hillock. The Bop carrying Alyssa joined the phoenix, and the others brought up the rear.

The clutch of birds climbed higher and higher, making raucous clicking sounds to each other. And the whoosh from their giant wings added to the racket until it grated on Alyssa's nerves.

Every time the birds called out, they either dipped downward unexpectedly, or banked into the wind. Alyssa fisted the feathers and squeezed her eyes closed.

But after several of these occasions, she realized these creatures knew exactly what they were doing. The movement became as normal as standing on her own two feet.

She tried to relax and appreciate being so far above the land. From this height, she could see the bowl-shaped mountain she'd traveled underneath for so long, and the tiny dots of the towns along the Wine Sea. The center of the bowl had to be where the dragon slept. She shivered. If that dragon ever found his way out of the throne room, the access to the unsuspecting townspeople would be too easy.

The Bop soon swooped down and flew low over a wooded area and although not a large wood, it was large enough that Alyssa marveled at it.

"What is the forest called?" she asked the Bop.

"Shadows," it answered with a squawk.

She had never seen a map of Daegries, but she would like to one day. The forest of Shadows would be a dark patch on the northern slope of the Haldor mountains. *I'll add that to my map when I get home.*

Soon, the Bop slowed down to a flutter and settled into a murky glade. The others landed beside it, and the phoenix stayed atop a tree that bent under her weight.

Nightfall arrived, and Alyssa could hear the stirrings of the surrounding forest. Whether dryads peeked out to marvel at the gathering of the noble birds or the busiest squirrel, she could not say.

She gazed up at the sky seeking Luna's face. When she found it, she knew true despair. The orb shone down in its fullness already. If she didn't make it back before evening tomorrow, she would lose all hope of making the gryphon's deadline.

She carefully slid from the Bop's back and thanked it for getting her there safely. Then, she turned to the phoenix and asked, "Where will I find my friends?"

"Oh, never fear, wee one," the beautiful bird replied. "They will find you."

And then, as if summoned, a trio of armed Elves known as the Iefyr, eased from the trees. They wore deep forest-green and tree-bark-brown clothing, and their long pale hair hung down, untied.

They looked so much like trees in moonlight, Alyssa could only stare in amazement.

An Iefyr male took charge, sending the shortest of the group over to unburden Alyssa of her pack. She made sure Pappy's box nestled securely and let him have it.

"Is this the girl?" he asked the phoenix.

"It is," she replied, preening.

Had the bird of wonder betrayed her to the Iefyr? Alyssa frowned at the phoenix, who lifted off from her tree with a squawk before settling on the ground close by her.

"Don't scowl so, wee one. They will take you to Edegast. You can trust them. Edegast is an honorable wizard who will see you safely back to your land. And the Iefyr are the pinnacle of all that is good in this world; fear not."

Relieved, Alyssa asked, "Excuse me, dear Phoenix, but… what about the Bop? Will they take us all home?"

The Bop who had brought her whistled loudly. The phoenix bobbed her head. "Yes. He says they will. You may be asked to do something for them in return, however."

Alyssa slumped in defeat. She tired of the "I-will-do-for-you-if-you-do-for-me" game.

She cast a sideways glance at the Bop. "What would that be?"

The Bop flapped his wings and clicked three times.

The phoenix translated. "A token from the Farmlands where you live. Perhaps a fat calf?"

Horrified, Alyssa frowned at the thought of sacrificing one of the farm's animals, but she had to meet the gryphon soon, and this had become a fast way to achieve her goal.

"That's a bad idea," she told the Bop. "It's closing on fall there, and they will have already slaughtered all the animals that were marked for such. There won't be much available."

The Bop ducked his head under his wing and bit at something. When he lifted his head again, he talked in chirps and whistles to the phoenix.

Finally, the beautiful bird said, "They will need food for the long flight to and from. Can you suggest anything for them to eat?"

She didn't know if the Bops ate anything aside from meat, but she could only try.

"All I know is we have mighty ugly big plants on the farm that need to be destroyed. If they want to chew on some greens… but be warned, they are called Putrid Plants for a reason. They attacked my Granny Gert, and they might not be good eating."

The phoenix's mild reaction to this news surprised Alyssa. If she knew about portal plants, this would certainly raise her feathers.

But when the phoenix told the Bop what Alyssa had said, she did so with no reaction at all. The Bop, with his friends, hopped around, pecking in the rich soil of the forest, and did not answer.

Apparently, the Putrid Plants didn't appeal to them. Alyssa added, "The Meadowlands are on the way. The Bops could conceivably find good greens and small animals there to feed on. The Gryphon King rules over it all, so he might have to be consulted."

"Squawk!" said the phoenix. "The gryphon is of no concern to these birds. They are called birds of prey for a reason. They will eat him if he is not careful."

Alyssa shrugged. If the deal resonated with the Bops, she wouldn't concern herself with the outcome between them and King Hubert. The pompous Gryphon King might well set a sumptuous table for them all.

"What do you say?" the phoenix asked the Bop. "Is this acceptable? Will you find food in the Meadowland instead?"

The Bop chirped, and the other birds bobbed their heads. The agreement had been decided.

Now Alyssa had to accompany the Iefyr through the forest to meet up with her friends and head home.

The phoenix, satisfied with her finished task, came closer to Alyssa and told her something in a low whistle.

"Wee one, you will soon bloom into adulthood. You will find when that happens, you will need your mother. When you are ready to find her, send a word to me. I will help you."

"My mother?" Alyssa asked, shocked. "Do you know my mother?"

The phoenix bobbed her head. "Yes, and she is alive. As is your father. But that will be another journey for you when you are ready. Until such a time, train hard to learn all you can about magik. You already show great promise."

"You mean, I can go to where they are?" Alyssa felt tears welling in her eyes. "They are alive?"

"They live, that is true. But as I have already said too much, I will leave the rest of the telling to one who is wiser than I.

Edegast is your best resource for all things to do with mankind. Use your magik well, child. It is not a toy to be shown off to the youth in your circle."

And with that, she flapped her beautiful wings and lifted off the ground.

"You may speak Mannish to the Bops. They will decipher it in their own way," she told Alyssa as she flew away over the trees.

Alyssa could only stand there with her mouth open, marveling at the world she found herself in, a world that still contained her parents whom she had thought lost years ago, wrapped in a magik scarf that she couldn't remove, in a place most people would never see.

Chapter Twenty-Three

The Iefyr

The nearest Iefyr stood as slender as a sapling. They all bore weapons like her own. They let her keep hers, and she gripped the string of the bow tightly.

They led her through the deep forest where no sunlight or moonlight could find its way in through the heavy foliage. The journey felt like being under the mountain again, only now hot and windless. Strange stirrings sounded loud in the night-hushed woods.

The Iefyr came upon a place where they recovered torches. And with a snap of their fingers, produced flames on them. Alyssa inhaled sharply in surprise. She hoped she could learn that magik!

Then away they went, sweeping her along a difficult dirt path strewn with rocks and sticks that she sometimes stumbled over. The Iefyr girl who traveled behind her gripped her shoulder, pulling her to a stop.

The Elven face pressed close to her, and dark red lips said, "Beware. Animal tracks." Alyssa peered down at the ground between her and the leader who also knelt and sniffed the tracks. Something enormous had been through the woods. The Iefyr leader lifted his torch, moved ahead slowly, and then waved for them to follow.

"Gone now," the girl whispered. "Walk slowly, but do not leave the path."

A short time later when nothing sprang out of the woods at them, Alyssa relaxed. She even witnessed a squirrel skipping ahead on the trail, but it scurried off once it sensed someone coming. It watched the party pass by from where it gripped the side of a tree, chirping, and swishing its tail.

Alyssa loved to watch squirrels play in the trees on the farm but had no time for it now. The Iefyr, nimble on their feet, hurried her along, noting the path and adjusting their way as needed.

Eventually, lights shone out in the woods ahead, and they moved quickly toward them. The lights—torches fastened onto wooden poles—illuminated the gathering place for a small village of Iefyr. They had built a few huts made from grass and long wooden logs near a gurgling stream. The area also sported a few campfires.

Alyssa, uncertain if dryads lived here or nearby, hoped they constantly monitored the flames. Upon closer examination, Alyssa felt they could extinguish this tiny village in a matter of hours. Take down the huts, put out the fires, and the Iefyr could be in another glade quickly. She had a sense that the Iefyr were nomadic, and it gave her a great desire to be that way, also. The journey through the Greater Daegries had been enjoyable for her, and she wanted to do it again one day, without familial dangers from stuffy gryphon kings.

As she stood warming herself beside a fire and contemplating these things, Edegast charged out of a hut and came rushing toward her.

"Lady Alyssa!" he exclaimed. "So glad to see you at last! I feared you were dragon food after all. But as I told the others, you are more powerful than you know." Then he added, pointing behind him, "Lord Bryon had a nasty fall and is within the hut there. The others are not far away. Well, all but the Yetis and their friends, the wolves. They didn't care for the Iefyr's ways and left to go back home on foot."

She nodded, and opened her mouth to inquire what had happened when the wizard noted the scarf wrapped around her. "The SCARF!"

She glanced down at her waist. "Yes, I have gotten it. Or rather, it has gotten me."

Edegast stepped back to get a better look at her, then at the scarf again. "Something is wrong."

She tried to mask her feelings but in the end, a note of annoyance went through her. "I can't get it off. It chose me, the phoenix said. I am its chosen bearer or something."

He stroked his beard. "I see."

"So, when I learned I had to come here to find you, I figured I could get more information about the scarf. Find out what the Iefyr know about it. There's more than meets the eye with this one. There's a whole other story to be told, I believe."

"Hm. Yes," he mused, walking around her, gazing at the scarf. "As you say, it definitely has decided you are the one."

One of the scarf's ends lifted itself and turned, as if anticipating the wizard's movements. It patted Alyssa's hair and stroked her cheek like a kindly friend would do.

"It didn't do this when you had it?" she asked, removing the scarf from her face and replacing it where it belonged.

He shook his head. "No. Not at all. In fact, it kept sliding around so much I wanted to take it off. That is precisely how the Gryphon King got his hands on it. Or paws, I suppose I should say."

She nodded, deep in thought. How had the former lord of Half Moon Manor taken it from King Hubert? If the scarf was meant to switch owners, it wouldn't be hard, she guessed.

He straightened and waved to her. "Come along, young Castling. The others await you."

Alyssa trailed the wizard inside the hut to see her friend, Lord Bryon, sitting on the side of a wooden framed bed, cupping his right elbow with his left hand. His arm trembled from where it lay wrapped in bandages, and he frowned in pain.

"Lord Bryon, good to see you! But what in Daegries has happened?" Alyssa asked, concerned. She let her weapons fall to the ground and rushed over.

"Ah, my lady. 'Tis very good to see you, alive and well! As to this," he motioned to his hurt arm. "Confounded wolves led us through the forest, and a tree root tripped me."

She covered her mouth to hide the grin she found plastered on her face. "Oh. I thought you'd fought a bear."

"Fine, fine. Laugh if you must, but you try tracking a four-footed creature through the woods in the dimness of afternoon. That root must have been as thick as my leg."

"Well, I'm relieved to see you alive and well, even if a little worse for wear," she told him. "Would you like me to see what I can do?"

He nodded and held it out for her examination. She rubbed her hands together to warm them and placed them over the bandage. The pulsing from his wound felt like she had her hands on a live heart. She jerked her hands away.

Edegast, watching her, asked, "Is anything wrong?"

She closed her eyes and replaced her hands. "It's different."

Then, without warning, the scarf lifted its ends, and covered her hands. Alyssa ignored it, forcing her mind to clear and focus on the injury.

"The scarf… truly the one," Lord Bryon said, voice low.

Alyssa nodded and kept going. Her injured friend sat quietly although she could tell he wanted to talk to her about the scarf.

She could feel where the bruising was at its worst. She opened her eyes and stared at the arm, and then it seemed as if she could see through the bandage, skin, and tissue. The injury appeared dark in places, but the blood still pulsed, and the bones were solid.

The scarf flattened itself out and she focused healing magik into the bruising, noting how it lightened and the blood flowed more evenly. Once done, she pulled on her hands to remove them from under the scarf, and it lifted itself, falling back in place.

"Do you feel relief?" she asked Bryon.

He nodded, his brow relaxed. "The scarf is exactly as I last saw it, although it did not try to heal anything. You must truly be a healer, and the scarf must truly be magik."

She drew a deep breath and removed her hands. "You're sorely bruised, Lord Bryon. But I don't find nothing broken. I think a few days of light work using that arm will fix it right up."

He smiled and said, "That's almost exactly what the Elves said. They did not have your special touch, however. Or that scarf."

She returned the smile and moved away a pace or so. Edegast leaned down to peer into her face.

"Are you well, Lady Alyssa?"

"This scarf—" she began.

"What about the scarf?" he asked, tilting his head.

"Did you note how it acts alive? It's almost like it's miming my actions."

He smiled. "It is a magik scarf, nevertheless, and sometimes magik performs out of hand."

She nodded, pulling gently on the scarf's ends, as if that one act would show she wasn't scared of its antics.

"Is Lord Bryon well?" Edegast asked, moving away.

"Yes," she answered. "Just a little bruising. He'll be fine."

Then the hut filled with other members of her company, and she greeted them.

Fletch came bounding up to Alyssa, grabbed her by the waist, and swung her around as far as he could in the little space.

Her cheeks grew warm at his happy greeting, and he set her back on her feet. "It is so lovely to see you, Lady Alyssa. I have been angry at myself for letting you go without me on that journey into the dragon's teeth. You should not have done that alone."

"As it turns out, I'm pretty good being on my own," she replied, grinning at him. "My bow and arrows were never used."

"And the magik? Did it serve you?" he asked, his face relaxing at her words.

"Well, that's the fur of another Yeti. Maybe on the trip home I'll have time to tell you all about it."

Cerius approached her. "I would be most thrilled to hear that story myself, milady."

He shook her hand vigorously and told her how brave she'd been.

Then, all of them at once saw that she wore the scarf around her waist.

"It's the one," Lord Bryon told his liegemen.

"It is follygrass, indeed!" Fletch added, standing back to observe it. Thankfully, none moved to touch it. The scarf wound around Alyssa so protectively, she feared it might retaliate if touched.

"This is a tale in need of retelling," Cerius said. "Come, let us find chairs for us all."

Edegast interrupted. "Now, now, my good friends. The hour draws near for the Iefyr to make their nightly fire ritual to say goodbye to the day. As the moon is almost full, I think it would be good for us to join them."

Alyssa ducked her head shyly, grateful for the wizard's intervention. She understood the others wanted to hear how she came about acquiring the scarf, but she wasn't ready to go into it yet. And the personal way the scarf acted in protecting her made her nervous as to what it might do if anyone got too interested in her new friend.

As she made her way to the roaring fire, she pondered if the scarf had been so protective of others who had worn it.

Lord Bryon joined them at the fire in the center of the little village. They listened as the Iefyr sang about the great land they loved so well and thanked the sun for its duty done to all living things.

> *Let us sing to you the song of the wood,*
> *Ferns of green and dragon's hood,*
> *All filled with life and the kiss of fall.*
> *Sunlight bright and giving life to all.*

The wooden flute's music made Alyssa sway in the moonbeams that danced on the ground between the shadows of the trees where she stood.

Trance-like, she didn't know when the music hushed, and the folk focused on her and the glow in her feet that traveled up her body until it wavered over her head like a halo.

The scarf unwound itself from her waist and did a dance over her head, becoming one with the glow. Together, the magik that Alyssa carried within herself and the magik of the scarf became a part of each other. And together they bound themselves into a golden knot symbol over her head.

When the light from the two magiks blended and created its own sigil in the night, the crowd rippled with joy. Then, as if they had completed their performance for the evening, the scarf draped itself over Alyssa's shoulders and the glow faded completely.

This energy shift, from one to the other and back again, must have taken its power from the human wielding it because Alyssa fell in a heap and knew no more.

Chapter Twenty-Four

Healers All

When she woke again, she found herself on a straw-filled bed in a hut with her company standing around her, their anxious faces peering down. She tried to moisten her lips with her dry tongue and speak, but her vocal cords refused.

Then emerged one of the Iefyr, a lady elf this time, most lovely in her white linen shift tied with a golden belt around her slender waist. She seemed to Alyssa almost a vision as the torchlight shone down on her.

"Who… who… are you?" Alyssa finally asked.

"Oh, my dear," the elf answered. "I am Llaney. I am honored to serve you, Alyssa Chance Oh. You must eat and drink before you can go forward on your journey. Your life-fyre has dwindled near to death."

"And we cannot consent to that," Fletch said near her head as he patted her shoulder.

"You are far too valuable to dwindle to anything at any time," Lord Bryon added, and he bent down to whisper, "My arm is much healed; thank you."

Edegast nodded, watching her from the foot of the bed. Cerius stood beside him, his longsword resting in the crook of his arm. They all had a protective air about them, and this alarmed her somewhat. She recalled nothing after the fire-song at sunset.

Edegast waited until Llaney finished her treatment of Alyssa, with food, water, and a sweet mead elixir. Once Llaney took her leave of the hut, Edegast came to Alyssa's side and told her what had befallen her.

"The scarf of the Iefyr does not treat you the same as it has treated any of its bearers before. I have asked for counsel from Orton, the Iefyr leader here. I think he may enlighten us at least in a small way about the scarf and its history."

"Good," Alyssa said. She lifted her hand and then let it fall. "Find out how to get it to leave me and go back to the gryphon if you don't mind. I have to get back to the Meadowlands before nightfall tomorrow."

Edegast noted her fatigue. "Perhaps there is a way to avoid another long journey to that place. You are not in any way able to go anywhere now."

She tried to reply, but he had three heads when she gazed at him. The others who moved into view also sprouted multiple heads. She closed her eyes to refocus, but the effort to reopen them proved too great, and she fell asleep immediately.

The next time she woke, the sun glittered through the woven leaves of the hut. She tried to raise onto her elbows but had no energy to manage that. She rested a moment or two and tried again. Her grunting and groaning as she rolled over to get out of bed brought an Iefyr healer hurrying in.

"My dear, you must not do this," she told Alyssa, placing a restraining hand on her shoulder. "My name is Cerlyn. I am here to care for you."

"I have to get up and get out of here. I have a Bop standing nearby to take me home."

"You intend a bird to fly you away?"

"Yes," Alyssa answered.

"No," the healer replied to this. "You cannot. You might not have the strength to hold on. What if you fall? The world needs you, Alyssa Chance Oh."

Alyssa shook her head and slid her legs over the edge of the bed. "The world doesn't need me half as much as my granny does. I have to go."

Cerius passed by the doorway. He heard their voices and entered. "My lady?" he inquired, glancing from the healer to Alyssa.

"Help me up, dear Cerius. I'm ready to dress and face this day."

Cerlyn, the healer, stepped back, shaking her head in disbelief. Cerius sat beside Alyssa, allowing her to put one arm around his neck while he wrapped his arm around her waist. Then he stood, lifting her to her feet. He waited patiently as she leaned onto him for support and steadiness.

"All right now, Lady?"

She released her grasp on his tunic. "Yes, thank you."

The Iefyr healer frowned and pursed her lips in uncertainty, moving toward Alyssa and then stopping short.

"I'll be fine, Cerlyn. I'm a healer, also. I'll manage," she told the woman, waving her away.

Alyssa felt weak and wavering, but she refused to let the Iefyr woman know that.

"What's the news from Edegast, Sir Cerius? Has he talked with the leader yet?"

Cerius stepped away from Alyssa to check her steadiness.

"Yes, he sent me to see if you were well enough to have a parlay."

She nodded, glancing around for her clothing. The Elves had put her in one of their fine robes, the magik scarf in its customary place around her waist. When her hand fell absently to the scarf, the ends curled around her hand like a contented cat.

"I need my clothes," she said, staring at the healer.

Cerius and Cerlyn looked at one another before he nodded. "I will see to that, right away."

After assuring himself she would be all right for a moment, he strode from the hut in search of her clothes.

Cerlyn left the hut with many backwards glances at Alyssa, who stood stroking the scarf thoughtfully.

"So, I suppose you've decided that I'm the one you want now. Which is fine until tonight when Luna's face is full. You'll have to come untied and go to the gryphon for whom this whole adventure began," she told the scarf who curled around and around and up her arm.

"I mean to give you up, Scarf. I do," she said, hoping it understood. How would things be if she couldn't give it up to the Gryphon King in return for her family's freedom? She shivered at the terror that gripped her.

Soon, the Iefyr healer from last night, Llaney, entered the hut, joined by Cerlyn. The two Elves were gentle with her and helped her to take a bath in a wooden tub. The scented water made her feel much better. After the bath, they were determined to make her go back to bed. On a tray, she spied a goblet of mead elixir.

"I'm not going to drink any more of your tinctures," she told them. "I'll need all my wits to get back home. And homeward I'm going, no matter what."

They stood there, unsure how to proceed.

"But Alyssa," Llaney said. "This is unusual. You cannot possibly be well enough to travel. What if you fainted again as you did last evening?"

"I'm willing to take that chance," she told her. "I have to get back home as soon as possible."

In a short while, Edegast entered the hut with Cerius behind him, holding a nicely folded bundle. Cerlyn took it and handed it to Alyssa.

"When you are ready, my lady," Cerius told her with a quick nod. They all strolled out except the two healers. Llaney set the tray on the floor beside the bed, and Cerlyn busied herself fluffing the flower-stuffed pillow, which sent a soothing scent into the air.

Alyssa donned her freshly washed pants and tunic, coaxing the scarf to curl around her feet for a time. Then when finally presentable, she picked it up and wrapped it around her waist once more.

"Please enter," she said, loud enough for anyone outside to hear. She sat on the edge of the bed, smiling shyly to the women standing there.

Edegast led the way, another Iefyr man following him. Edegast waved to the Elven women. "Leave us," he told them.

The other members of the company did not enter the hut, but she knew from the sleeve that showed occasionally outside the door that they stood guard close by.

The Elven women took the tray and tub with them as they departed. The Iefyr leader that joined Edegast came to Alyssa, took her hand, and pulled her to her feet.

They stood eye to eye. She gave him a direct stare, never letting her gaze falter.

One corner of his mouth lifted. "Hm, yes, I see."

"You see what?" she asked him, finally breaking eye contact. "And who are you? Edegast, give me direction here."

Before the wizard could reply, the elf lifted his hand and said, "No need, young one. I have the information you seek."

Feeling weaker than expected, she sat and then shuffled around, propping herself up on pillows in more of a reclining position.

"I am Orton. I lead this party of Iefyr in this area of Greater Daegries. Our business is our own, but it may prove that your journey and ours crosses paths again. That remains to be seen. I know already from the power you showed last night, from the reaction the scarf had, from holding your hand, that you are a kindred spirit to us. That would explain many things."

"Kindred?" she asked. The words of the dryad and the siren returned to her.

"Yes. It is my belief that you are at least half-Iefyr."

She stared at him for a few moments, trying to understand. She frowned and turned to Edegast. "How? I'm so confused."

Edegast pulled out her grandfather's toy box and placed it in her lap. "I believe your grandfather might be able to explain the missing pieces. Can you call him, please?"

Alyssa stared down at the box, then back at the faces before her. "I don't think it works that way. He left us awhile back to go home. He wanted to oversee the goings on with my grandmother and the Gryphon King. I don't think I can simply say, 'Pappy, come on back here,' and have him appear. In fact, I tried that once or twice and nothing happened."

Orton grinned at her, and she noticed for the first time his woodland clothing and Elven ears. He had slanted eyes and white teeth that shone like stars. She blushed when she felt like she had stared too long, but something about him rang a memory in her mind.

"Try this," Orton said, holding his hand over his heart. "Dearest one, I call on you now. You must obey your mistress when she is in need."

Alyssa figured it couldn't hurt to turn the crank and try to get Pappy to pop out like he used to. She turned it and the happy music floated through the quiet hut.

She clenched her eyes shut. "I need this magik spell to go and find the man named Pappy Oh."

When she said that, the scarf wrapped itself around the box, and the clown's head popped out. She stared at it closely. The box shook in her hands.

"What? What do you need, gal?" Pappy's voice asked.

She burst into tears of joy, hugging the box to her bosom as if it were her lifeline.

It took her a few minutes to fill Pappy Oh in on what all had happened to her and the company since he left them.

To some of it, he said, "Uh, huh" and to some of it, he remained quiet. She wanted to hear his thoughts, but he had seen they were not alone.

Finally, she told Pappy the reason for her calling him back.

"This fellow here, Orton, is an Iefyr leader. He thinks I'm half-Iefyr myself because of my magik ability and the way the scarf attached itself to me. Also, a matter of a fire-song and me passing slap out, but I can tell you all about that later." She took a deep breath. "Do you know anything about my mama or daddy being Elven? Are you or Granny Gert Elven?"

The clown's face remained immoveable. When Pappy Oh finally answered, his voice sounded nervous. "There's strange blood in our family, but I ain't never heard of it being Elvish. Course now, that could come from your mama. Never one to talk much about her family around us, and we didn't think it anything to discuss around the dinner table, if you get my meaning."

"That's another thing," Alyssa said. "Mama and Daddy too, most likely, are still alive. The phoenix told me so. I don't reckon she'd tell a tale about that."

"Could be Lys, could be. Your granny and I have wondered for a long time if they were off visiting her family, or if something bad happened to them. We wandered into that area around the maze, hunting them. When we heard that old gryphon holler and saw how sharp his beak was, well, it made my blood run cold. They likely got hurt or killed, to our minds. Couldn't run off and leave you completely without kin, you see? Then, the townsfolk began nosing around and that set us right where we were. No more roaming. I tried to find a spell to bind that old bird-lion, but aside from killing him, there was nothing."

"So, you never knew for sure what happened to them?" Alyssa asked thoughtfully.

"No way for us to tell, really. We hoped for the best and believed in the worst. You were the most important thing for us to focus on. Figured they'd come along one day, if they could."

Orton asked, "Do you know what your daughter-in-law's name had been before marriage?"

Pappy grew quiet, thinking. "I wanna say Eggladris, but not sure how that is even spelled."

Orton's face didn't change at this news, and he glanced out the doorway of the hut. When he turned back to them, he nodded. "Yes, Egladris, E-G-L not E-G-G like the food, is a name known to me. Alyssa is part Elven, at least. This doesn't surprise me. I saw the way her magik and the scarf danced together last night." Orton shifted his eyes to Alyssa. "Believe me when I tell you that many of my homeland will be happy to hear of your existence. You should make finding your parents a chief concern when you can do so."

"Oh, I am," she assured him. "Or at least I will be. Quick as a bunny."

She stared at the clown's face. Pappy had indeed given them the missing information. "Why haven't I heard about this before, Pap? Are you sure y'all didn't know about Mama's Iefyr blood?"

"Well, really, your mama stayed quiet, Lys. Didn't talk much about her life before coming to the farm. We assumed she had an awful childhood or something and let her be. She became a good wife to your daddy and took to motherhood really good when you came along. Sometimes you ain't supposed to know everything about a person, but you can love them all the same."

Alyssa shrugged. "I guess. But now, I'm sitting here with a scarf wound all around me like I'm its mama or something," she said, patting the scarf as it attempted to wipe her face free of drying tears. "It's got a plan and I'm it, and I don't exactly know what to do about things. If I try to give this scarf to King Hubert, it might not go."

"I believe there is another way," Orton said.

Alyssa waited for him to continue.

"Let me speak to the Iefyr here with me." He smiled mysteriously and took his leave of them.

Edegast and Alyssa stayed with Pappy Oh, and Cerius and Fletch peeked into the hut to see if they could enter.

"Everything okay, Lady?" Fletch asked.

She grinned and said, "Right as rain, Sir Fletch. We're getting ready to go back home. Are you two prepared to take a flight into the sky on the back of a bird?"

They laughed a little, glancing at one another. They seemed hesitant as to how the trip might go, but as always, they were ready to follow her.

Edegast showed no concern at the thought of flying on the back of a Bop, and Alyssa secretly believed he had already done so.

When Orton returned, the healers were with him, as well as a wizened old Iefyr woman with kind brown eyes and especially big Elven ears. She wore a long, misty-gray tunic, and soft doeskin shoes. She carried a bundle under her arm.

Orton introduced them. "Alyssa Chance, meet Darshee Zindi. Darshee is one of our greatest healers and seers. She foretold your arrival here and prepared something for you."

"How could she have known?" Alyssa asked Edegast.

"The Iefyr are incredibly wise and often know things before they happen. I might have had a thing or two to do with this, however."

Orton waved to the old woman to present her bundle. She shuffled up to Alyssa and held it out. "This is for you," she said in a raspy voice.

Alyssa set Pappy Oh's box aside and took it.

"What is it?" Pappy asked, bouncing a little "What you got there, Lys?"

Alyssa unwrapped the large leaves and beneath them lay a scarf that looked exactly like the one she wore.

"It's another scarf!" she exclaimed, holding it up for everyone to see.

Edegast smiled. "I thought maybe a duplicate might put off the gryphon for a time. We still need to know more about the scarf that you are so intricately connected with. Why it chose you, and what kind of power it wields, especially now that it has melded with your magik. The gryphon doesn't need a magik scarf such as that, nor do I, nor anyone who may develop it into a magik item for evil."

She sat straighter and stared at the fake scarf lying in her lap close to the real one. They were virtually the same. "I thought you intended to take it to the Wizard's Hall and have it entombed?"

"The Iefyr has warned against taking that action. The scarf has found its true owner. Keep it safe, though. I will be gleaning all that I can from the tomes at my disposal."

The fake scarf sat innocently in her lap.

"Do you think it will fool King Hubert?" Alyssa asked the old woman, Darshee.

"The material is from a tree where follygrass grows. It does not have any special powers like your scarf. It will appear the same, only it will not afford him any magik."

"So, it would not… say… protect the wearer in battle, for instance?" Lord Bryon asked from the doorway. He had remained outside, watching, and keeping guard.

Darshee, whose back was stooped over from age, turned her head to stare at him. "No. Made from no magikal substance, you see, its power is in its beauty."

He dropped his head to his chest. Alyssa felt the pain of a broken heart for him. This scarf with no power would be useless in battle, and unlikely to be sold for gain; two things the lord of Half Moon Manor had considered. Without her magik scarf, he would be virtually the same as any other warlord seeking revenge. Now, besieging Needlemount for retribution seemed his only choice.

"So, it has no magik in it?" she asked to be sure.

Darshee shook her head. "None."

"Is it possible to make another magik scarf for me?" Lord Bryon asked, hope tinging his words.

Orton tilted his head and closed one eye. "That would not be wise, I think."

Alyssa refused to gaze at Lord Bryon. She knew what his face would portend, and her heart sank. Evil filled the hearts of men sometimes. Especially when hatred entered their world. Lord Bryon had a bloodlust, and a magik scarf would not be good for him to have.

Edegast walked to Alyssa and took the fake scarf. It weighed little, and when he wrapped it around his neck, it fell into place.

"I think this will suffice," he declared, unwrapping it and handing it to Orton. "King Hubert will not know. We can accept this as a suitable replacement for the Scarf of Egladris."

Alyssa glanced at each of them. "The Scarf of Egladris? Is this something of my family?"

"We do not have a better name for it now. Until I can return to the Hall and get more information from the annals, it is what we will call the magik scarf."

Alyssa frowned. "I thought the Iefyr made this scarf for you? Do you mean you don't know where it came from?"

Edegast shifted his feet. "No, you are quite mistaken. The Iefyr *gifted* it to me. They didn't make it, albeit they crafted an excellent imitation."

Pappy Oh, who had sat quietly all through the proceedings, now spoke up.

"The Scarf of Egladris, eh? That makes it yours by name rights, Lys. You said you needed a magik item to practice with. Well, here you go, then." The toy box bounced happily next to her.

She smiled and patted her magik scarf at her waist. "Well, I guess I'm ready to go then. I have a meeting with a gryphon at sunset."

Chapter Twenty-Five

The Journey Home

Alyssa thanked the Elves for their kindness. She still marveled that they were kindred now. She promised to come to their homeland north of the Wine Sea as soon as she could spare a visit. Perhaps there she would find more information about her parents and what had happened to them.

Orton and the healer, Darshee, came to see her and the company off. Darshee handed her the bow and a new quiver of arrows. Everything felt different, and she noted how Darshee beamed up at her.

"I have restrung your bow and perhaps added a touch of Iefyr magik to the arrows. You should never miss," she said.

Alyssa's heart surged at this radiant place in the woods and the people full of compassion. She wished them all well and walked toward the glade where she'd left her Bop.

She longed for the little farm on the border of the Meadowland and her own soft feather bed. Her heart ached to see Granny Gert's eyes light up when she spied her return. She wanted to hear old Tony humming to the horses as he threw them sweet feed. Her tiny country home—she was more than ready to get back there.

The Bops remained where they had landed in the sunny glade. Had that only been yesterday? She could hardly believe it, so much had happened.

She spoke in a low voice to her carrier, telling him of a few stops she needed to make along the way. He squawked and said something in chirps that sounded almost like, "Yes at once," but she couldn't be sure.

She spoke quietly to Pappy Oh and tucked his box deep into the pack with the lid down, remembering that he didn't want to see the world rushing by. She climbed atop her bird and waited for the others to join them.

Then, like a strange skyward caravan, they all lifted into the morning sun, waving and crying out goodbyes to the ones left behind.

Soon the mountains rose all around them, and Alyssa pointed out one snowy mound. The Bop chirruped to his friends, who quickly lowered and found places on solid ground. She asked her Bop to drop her on the ledge. He complied, although he seemed unhappy about the small amount of room on that ledge for him. The matter of treacherous drops all around for his passenger made him twitchy, too.

But soon, Yetis poured out from the caves under the ledges, and she spied Jed and Fred.

"Hello!" she called to them, waving with all her might. She had to drop her pack beside the bird, along with the bow and quiver, then jump down, clinging to the Bop.

The Yetis marveled at her survival from the dragon's lair and at the scarf that wound around her protectively, warming her in the cold air.

When they stopped chattering in Yeti-tongue, she said, "Fred, I need a Yeti tooth. Someone requested it in a bargain I made. Can you get me one?"

He grunted and said, "Grundel."

The nearest Yeti, a youth it seemed, although he stood as tall as his father and equally as hairy, thrust out his hand. "I grow new teeth," he said, opening his mouth to show off gaps in front.

She took the tooth, a baby tooth for a Yeti, but still immensely large.

She wrapped it in soft pliable leaves the Iefyr healers had given her for this occasion and tucked it carefully into the pack.

"I thank you most kindly," she told the Yeti youth. "And you as well, Fred."

"Tell Oh we miss him."

Pappy Oh remained silent in his box, and she figured he had enough to think about right now. Her heritage and its mysterious turn had taken them both by surprise.

She patted Fred's hand and said, "Yes, I certainly will. Now, listen Fred, there's one other thing I need to tell you. A dragon lives down under your mountain here with no way out aside from a little hole in his roof. If he ever claws his way up there and opens it, this entire realm will have a terrible time. Put together a Yeti war party and go after him. Karnargul is his name, and he's fierce. Convince him to move on."

"Yetis have history books," the big Yeti answered. "Dragon Era in Daegries. Yetis know what one can do when left untended. Fred remembers this."

"Good. Well, better pull out those books and find out how to get rid of him. The Haldor might help. They are still around, by the way. I found them, too. Another story for another time."

"What about Haldor? Did they remember Yeti?"

She nodded. "Yes. Someday soon, you should get together with King Vernon. Once the dragon is gone, he would be interested in talking about opening the trade route again. You didn't present the best business practice by ruining his dealings with others. Pappy Oh's willing to be a part of that parlay, maybe to be a middle ground between you. But not right now, because the Haldor are too busy rebuilding the other side of the mountain. And also, too busy to test the dragon, or slay him. You could do it as a goodwill gesture to them, though."

He scratched his head and grunted.

Then after a few moments more of handshakes and a few guttural words from the Yetis, Alyssa took her leave of them.

She climbed aboard the Bop, and Fred handed her the pack and her bow and arrows, while the Yetis yammered on and on about her giant bird friend. They kept their distance though, as one could never know how far a Bop's neck might reach.

She waved goodbye, and they lifted off. The Bop's giant wings flapped powerfully, moving them through the air. Soon, the others joined them in the sky.

Alyssa heard the box rattle, and it worked its way up from the inside. Pappy turned the crank on the toy box and popped out. She reached around and pulled it sideways so she could see the clown's face.

Pappy said, "I ain't gonna come out here for long. It's downright chilly up here. I wanted to say that you have charmed them Yetas. Yes, sirree. You really have."

He had been listening in then, she thought with a smile. "Having them and the Haldor as friends might open up that pathway to trade again, Pappy. Something to think about."

He bounced up and down a little. "So, are we headed back to home now?"

"Just a few more stops, Pap."

"Okay, well, I'm gonna take a nap."

She nodded. The clown's head went down, and the lid shut. She adjusted the pack again onto her back, tucked her thumbs in under feathers, and tried to watch the landscape below.

She'd told the Bop about Lord Bryon's home in the Heightlands, trusting he would see it with his keen eye. Soon they dropped out of the sky and slowed over the grounds of Half Moon Manor. Dogs ran out and yapped at them as they landed in the courtyard, always keeping their distance from the wicked beaks of the flying creatures.

The men who lived at the manor, Lord Bryon, Fletch, and Cerius, dismounted from their birds. Edegast stayed atop his bird for a few moments longer, speaking low to the creature and then slid off.

The men patted the birds' necks, much like one would do to a horse, and strolled up to Alyssa, who had gotten off her Bop, as well.

"Are you taking leave of us then?" Lord Bryon asked.

She nodded. "Yes, I still have a long way to go. I'd like to see your dear mother, though. With the scarf on me, however, I don't want to take any chances with her health. Would you see if she could come to the window so we can wave?"

He said, "She will be grateful for your kindness. I am certain she would do this for you."

Alyssa smiled at all the men, and told them, "Y'all are welcome down in Mudden-town any time you like. Just come on by. Hopefully soon, I'll have gotten rid of those Putrid Plants, and the path from our place into the Meadowlands will be clear and ready for travelers. It sure would be nice to see friends coming to call."

Fletch and Cerius bowed low to her, promising to come south someday. They kissed Alyssa's hand and wished her well on trail's end. Fletch especially lingered over his goodbyes and vowed to see her again.

They patted the jack-in-the-box's top and said goodbye to Pappy Oh, who remained inside. The mage muttered farewell from his safe place.

Pulling the leftover food from their packs, they gave it to the creatures who had carried them home. The Bops gobbled the food, then lifted into the sky and headed back to their homes. Only two remained—the ones who would carry Alyssa and Edegast on the last leg of their journey.

When the great birds were only specks in the sky, Lord Bryon waved at the manor house where his servants approached. He instructed his liegemen, "Fellows, go meet them and tell them all is well. They should prepare a homecoming feast. We deserve it."

Fletch and Cerius strode toward the people from the manor, calling out greetings as they went. When they were out of earshot, Bryon placed his hands on Alyssa's shoulders and made sure she paid full attention.

"About the Putrid Plants, my lady. I believe they are portal protectors, for evil invaders. Every last stalk of them. We destroyed them in the Heightlands years ago, fearing entry into our part of Daegries from other places. Dark places. This was long ago, to be true, but not so long that I do not remember. Strange creatures showed up, and we wondered if it would end life as we knew it back then." He paused for emphasis. "Creatures came from the underworld, dangerous enough to strike fear in every strong man's heart. Many battles were fought. Fortune smiled upon us then, and we rid ourselves of them quickly. My suggestion to you is destroy those as quickly as possible. We certainly will do so if it is found the same in this realm once again."

She frowned. "What if they're growing again somewhere and no one has found them yet?"

"That is the fear of the aristocrats and my fear, as well. I will parlay with my men and send scouting parties to seek the truth of this matter."

She thought for a moment, pulled the toy box from her pack, and tapped its lid. "Pappy, come on out here and say goodbye to Lord Bryon. You're being a mite rude."

The crank turned, the eerie music played, and the clown's face popped out.

"Ho! Are we there already?" he asked, sleepily.

She laughed. "Not yet, Pappy. I wanted you to say goodbye to Lord Bryon."

While Pappy Oh chatted amicably with the lord of the manor, Alyssa dug around in the pack, pulled the siren's shell necklace out and put it around her neck. Then she hunted until she found the ruby she'd stolen from the dragon.

She hauled it out and presented it to Bryon. "Lord Bryon, I got this from the dragon's hoard. I figured you deserved something for this journey, even if not what you wanted. I hope you will accept it instead of the scarf, and as a payment for blood money from Ragon and Madrid. They are still up there in Needlemount, and maybe one day, you'll get your time in the sun with them."

The ruby glimmered darkly in the late afternoon sun, and Bryon took it with a hiss of pleasure.

"My lady," he said. "I am speechless. This is too much."

"No," Pappy added, tilting the clown's head. "It's exactly right. Good thinking, Lys."

Bryon thanked her again and left to ask his mother to wave goodbye.

Edegast, who quietly stood by during this transaction, stepped close to Alyssa to address her.

"Young apprentice, that was a noble thing to do. I am curious, however; how did you get the dragon to agree to your taking leave with his treasures? To my knowledge, dragons do not grant such without grave repercussions."

Alyssa ducked her head. "I just took it. He'll never miss it, there's so much of it. I picked up a few other things whilst there, too."

"Alyssa Chance Oh!" Pappy Oh exclaimed. "You didn't steal treasure from a dragon? Do you know what that means?"

She glanced from Edegast's storm-cloud face to the comical jack-in-the-box. "No. What does it mean?"

Edegast pulled on his beard and paced back and forth, anxiety written in the lines of his tall form.

"It means, silly goose," Pappy Oh said, "that our dragon friend will want to exact revenge on someone, and that means you."

"Not for a while he won't. I blinded him with a ricocheted blast of my magik. I didn't mean to, only trying to fend him off."

Edegast's face paled at her admission of guilt.

She frowned, and her voice rose. "It was an accident! And then, he couldn't come after me, so I took the treasure and ran to find a hiding place."

Edegast paced again. "He will recover, Alyssa. He will recover. I have known dragons to even grow new tails, they recover so quickly. And when he does, he will find a way out of that mountain cavern and will hunt for you." He pointed a bony finger at her.

"Well, he has to find me, now, doesn't he?" she snapped at him, now struggling with shame for her actions. "And I'm going to be far away from him, so that might take awhile. Besides, I asked Fred to send a Yeti party to call on him."

"Oh Lys," Pappy moaned. "You didn't!"

"Yes, I did," she answered. "Didn't you hear me when I was talking to them a bit ago?" Pappy cleared his throat. "I've been napping a lot. I guess I missed it. What made you ask them to do such a thing?"

Alyssa's gaze went from the toy box to Edegast. "They're the only group of people even close to being able to take on a dragon."

Edegast's face turned crimson, and he sputtered like an angry rooster, ruffling his robes. "He will trap them underground and kill them all! They will be perfect targets for dragon fyre!"

Unused to being reprimanded so harshly, she tried to control her anger by rearranging the pack. She left Pappy Oh in his box to go in last.

Then she told them, "I can't undo what's been done. I can only move ahead. The Yetis are strong enough to do battle with the dragon. If they can contain him, trap him, or even kill him, then all this talk is pointless. And if they can't, then they can call on the Haldor. King Vernon will come to their aid; he wants the dragon gone, as well," she finished.

Edegast stopped pacing, crossed his arms, and tapped his temple, trying to find an answer. Finally, he said, "I won't be coming along with you to Mudden after all. I must go back to the Yeti caves. I hope in enough time to stop such a dangerous plan."

And he ran to his Bop waiting nearby, climbed on its back, and shouted out to Alyssa, "Always keep the scarf on your person! I will return soon!"

They took off faster than Alyssa had ever seen before. She felt low after they left, worrying that she had created a terrible problem for her friends, the Yetis. And fretting about danger to her own life grayed the day, too.

She brightened a bit when Lady Pianna waved a pale hand in greeting and farewell from her sleeping quarters in the manor house. Lord Bryon stood beside his mother and waved goodbye too. When he returned, he had a private word with Edegast who didn't make any comment. Finally, the lord of the manor waved to them and said, "Fare thee well, Alyssa and Pappy Oh. May we meet again one day!"

They waved to him and watched him trudge toward his home. When they were alone and it became obvious no more goodbyes were to be said, Pappy asked, "So, what now? Are you ready to go on home then?"

She touched the necklace. "No. I have one more stop to make. I have something for the siren. A bargain we made for her blood."

He lowered the clown's head, and the lid snapped shut. "Let's go," he said, a little muffled.

She climbed aboard the Bop, situated her pack and weapons, and repeated where she wanted to go. He lifted off and soon the land below took on the woody characteristics of the forest where she had met the dryad. She waved to the trees in case someone peered out from there.

Then the Bop lowered again, right by the running stream. She slid off his back onto the sandy soil, and he went straight into the water, like a bird in a mud bath.

Alyssa pulled her pack from her shoulders, set her bow and arrows beside it, and took the toy box out. She set it aside and lifted the Yeti tooth wrapped in leaves out next. Then, she replaced the jack-in-the-box and carried the tooth with her, looking for Lorelei.

Pappy popped out of the toy box, warning her to be careful. "We gotta get moving, so don't dawdle."

She nodded, said nothing, and strolled along the bank. She stopped when she saw the big rock on the other side.

Soon, she heard a loud splash somewhere nearby. The siren, Lorelei, swam up to the bank but didn't get out of the water.

"Hail, Alyssa Chance Oh. Have you come back to give me my Yeti tooth, or are you back to require more blood from me?"

Alyssa laid the leaf package on the sand, pulled the necklace from around her neck, added it, and said, "I come in friendship and to repay my due. I've brought the Yeti tooth as agreed, but I'm also returning the shell with your blood."

The siren's dark eyes widened a little at these words. "You are different, Mudden girl."

"Reckon I am. I've been through Yeti caves, bugbear camps, and dragon lairs, and I've flown on the back of a bird of prey. And I survived it all," she told her. "I ain't afraid of much any longer. Not even you."

The siren crawled onto the bank and sat beside the bundle. She took the leaves in her hands. "Ew. They have touched this."

Alyssa didn't know who she meant. "They?"

"Elves."

"Iefyr. Yes, they gave the leaves to me."

"Nasty touchy things, Elves."

Alyssa crossed her arms. "That is your opinion, Lorelei. I found them kind and gentle and quite nice."

The siren peeled the leaves back, gingerly, so as not to touch them too much, and marveled at the Yeti tooth. "Ahh. Such a tiny one. Must have been a baby."

"Young, yes. Not a baby, I don't think."

Lorelei took her shell necklace from where Alyssa had placed it on the ground. "You didn't have to return this. What use of it do I have? I have more blood, and shells lie in abundance by the sea."

Alyssa smiled and uncrossed her arms. "Because I ain't happy being indebted to a siren nor any other creature. No sir. From now on, I take what I need, and I return what I want. We're even now." At such a definitive statement, the scarf became rigid and tightened itself around her waist.

"You cannot decide what the debt is, nor when it is or is not paid in full," Lorelei replied, dark eyes laughing.

Alyssa turned abruptly and trekked back to the Bop. Lorelei murmured loud enough for Alyssa to hear. "You'll be back, Alyssa Chance. You'll need me again someday."

Alyssa didn't bother telling her what she thought about such a prospect. Instead, she gathered up her belongings and climbed aboard the Bop. She lifted a hand in farewell to the siren, but the creature had already slithered into the water and neared the other side of the bank and her sunning rock. The cave shimmered darkly in the light.

Alyssa muttered under her breath. "Dumb portals! You don't belong in this stream, but I'm going to find out how you got here, one way or another."

She tapped the Bop on the shoulder, and he took off, flapping his wings to get lift.

"Take me to the Meadowlands, to where the Gryphon King holds court," she told the Bop. "There you will find food."

He ducked his head, keen eyes focused down at the landscape, and adjusted his flight pattern.

She leaned backwards and told Pappy the end of their journey neared.

"Good," he answered. "I'm getting tired of all this flying around."

Once they landed, a little bumpy, to be sure, Alyssa thanked the bird and arranged the scarf beneath her clothing. Then she put the fake scarf around her neck and tied it with a loose knot.

"There," she said, scratching at the itchy material touching her neck. "Egladris, you behave for a time; I don't need no mistakes while with this pompous king." The magik scarf gently moved as if to reassure her it understood.

Chapter Twenty-Six

King Hubert Holds Court

The distance shortened via Bop. It took no time at all to travel from the siren's sunning rock to where the gryphon had left them. The bird of prey settled, glad to have grass and bugs to eat, but always seeking something bigger to ingest. He ignored Alyssa as she slid from his back.

On the ground, she adjusted the pack, bow, and quiver comfortably. She took a deep breath and strode toward the area where she felt she would find the gryphon.

As expected, King Hubert lounged under a shady tree, twitching his lion tail and pecking at the feet of a goat to aggravate him.

"What do you mean?" he shouted at the goat. "You cannot have searched under every rock and between every branch. You lie!"

Alyssa coughed politely. The gryphon sneered at her and continued to berate the goat.

"You're inept. Get out of my sight." He waved to Alyssa to come forward. "You again?"

She laughed. "That's funny, King Hubert. I'm here because you told me to be here."

He blinked a few times, and then he must have had a recall of his business with her. "Oh, yes, the matter of a scarf, I believe?"

She nodded, pulled the fake follygrass scarf from around her neck, and held it out to him. He took it, winding it around his own neck. "You are a good and faithful subject," he told her.

"I'm not your subject, King."

"I speak to the scarf," he replied, dryly.

"There's peace between us for now," she said. "I thank you for your tears and for saving my granny's life."

Pappy Oh spoke up then. "Make no mistake, Gryphon. I'm a powerful enough mage to disassemble your kingdom. You would do well not to threaten my family, nor my family home ever again."

Alyssa added, "And if anything is wrong at my house, I'll hold you responsible. War or no war, I'll come hunting for you again, with my bow and arrows." She stared directly into his brown eyes. "And I won't come alone."

He gaped at her, judging her true meaning, her weaknesses, and her strengths.

"There is something different about you now, Sapling. You are almost fearless. You will find your farm and your grandmother quite intact. I would not have acted upon my threat. We do not believe in war or warmongering in this realm. I told you that." He sniffed, as if offended.

She laughed loudly. "Yeah? Well, excuse me if I believed you when you threatened them with harm. I'll remember not to do that again."

And with that she turned away from King Hubert and his pompous court, which she noticed consisted of a few cows and a few horses that had pastured there.

She carried her head high and walked back to the Bop. She climbed onto the bird with her pack and its cargo, never glancing again at the face of the lying gryphon king.

She directed the Bop to carry her to the farm over the Meadowlands by trailing Old Stony. During the flight, the scarf of Egladris worked its way out from under her tunic and flapped in the breeze.

The Bop landed them safely at nearly the same spot from which she and Pappy had left. She bid him farewell.

"Thank you, kind bird of prey. You may return to the Meadowland and feast at will. The puppet king, that old gryphon, will not do a thing about it. He is all talk and air bubbles. Have your fill of grasses and bugs and grow strong enough to fly home. Thank the phoenix again for everything and remember me to your children."

He warbled something that sounded like "And to yours," before departing, his giant wings blowing Alyssa's hair into her eyes. She blamed her hair for the tears that flowed down her cheeks.

Home!

She pulled Pappy Oh's box from the pack and told him to come out and see the place. "We're home, Pap!" she said, crying hard.

Then she tossed the pack over her arm and carried her grandfather in his toy box into the farmhouse to see Granny Gert.

"Granny!" Alyssa called. "We're home!"

Alyssa found her grandmother seated on the floor in her bedroom with items belonging to Pappy Oh or Alyssa in a circle.

"Granny? What are you doing?"

"Gert! You ought to know better than to do that. You ain't a mage." Pappy Oh sounded horrified. "You been snooping in my books?"

The old woman stood and glared at them. Alyssa wiped tears from her face.

"We're home, Gran," she repeated, twirling around the room, arms out, finally hugging the old woman to her in a tight embrace.

"And a good thing, too," Granny said, holding Alyssa a moment longer. "I was about to do the unthinkable and bring you both back from the dead, as I was sure you had been taken and killed somewhere."

Pappy had left his box, Alyssa assumed, because he didn't have anything to say to that. She saw items in the circle moving around, and she knew she wasn't doing it.

"Uh, Gran," she said, stammering. "I–uh–I… Well, I'm mighty sorry we left and didn't tell you about it. But well, we're home now, and we'll never leave you again. Because if we need to fight gryphons or dragons or Yetis, we'll do it together, right here in our own backyard."

Her grandmother started to walk out of the circle, but Alyssa stopped her. "You gotta open the circle to get out, Granny Gert. Like this," and she smudged a place to make an opening.

Then the toy box shook violently, and Pappy Oh's voice floated out. "Lys! Lys! What in tarnation did you do to the spell to bring me back? I need to know everything that you used and what incantation you called on. Everything!" he exclaimed.

She walked over to the desk where she'd left the Grimoire of Necromancy open. "Here it is, Pappy. Right where I left it."

The box popped open and did a flip in the air coming to rest on its side. Pappy never replied, but the pages of the book slowly turned. The items in the circle floated up as if examined, and then the box shook again.

"Alyssa! Did you shed blood in that circle?" he asked finally, tinny voice high-pitched.

"Well, yeah, I guess so. I cracked myself in the nose with your staff, accidentally. Oh, and I cut my hand," she showed him the almost healed nick.

The toy box bounced up and down and Pappy Oh said, "Oh, Lys. You not only brought me back, but you brought back other stuff, too. Didn't I tell you that blood has to be a part of any spell to make it go?"

She shook her head, certain that he had not said any such thing apart from the need for siren's blood. *The Grim* hadn't said that either as far as she knew, but Pappy was a powerful mage, and he likely knew things she didn't.

He continued. "Well, it does. And if it's like a reanimation spell, you must be mighty careful with it or you risk bringing back something else from the other side that you don't want."

Alyssa felt her heart flutter. "Like what?"

Granny frowned and thrust her hand on her hip. "Yes, indeed, Pappy. What could she bring back that has you fired up?"

"Them plants out there. Them plants are not of this world. They came from the other side. They guard portals of the Underworld. And until we figure out a way to get rid of them and shut the portal up, any number of nasties can come crawling out right into our backyard."

"Pappy, what in the goodness are you saying? How do you know this?"

"Well, first off, it was a mild fall when we left. Then a harsh winter approached as we were in those mountains a week ago. But now we are back here, and peek around you. Has winter even thought about arriving? It feels like springtime out there. Something is bad wrong with the weather. Portal magik is like that. It affects plants and weather and people. Gert, come here and let me have a gander at you."

She scoffed at him, and said, "How? You're in one of Alyssa's old toys. How can you even see anything at all with that clown's face?"

"I don't rightly know, Gert. But I know you need to be checked over for anything weird from that plant's attack. Other than the poisoning, what else was wrong with you?"

She shook her head. "Nothing, nothing at all. I'm right as rain. That gryphon's tears fixed the poison problem just like my book said it would."

"Did it say anything about the side effects of portal plants? I'd be feeling it out now, Gert. I really would."

Alyssa carried the toy box over closer to Gert and held it up. "Look real good, Pappy. Let us know if you see anything."

He replied, "I'm coming out of this thing. I can have a peek without this thing. I just can't talk to anyone."

The box jiggled and jumped in Alyssa's hands, then stilled. Granny stood like a statue not knowing what to do while her husband examined her. She didn't even feel anything.

When Pappy Oh spoke again, his voice sounded solemn. "Gert, I can't tell if there is anything wrong. Nobody can tell simply by looking. We need a sorcerer, a wizard, someone with greater knowledge than me. Lys, do you think Edegast would come?"

"I don't know Pappy. He tore off like the wind to save the Yetis from the dragon. I had hoped he would come to Mudden and maybe help me figure out how to get you here all the way."

"That's another thing, Lys. I been thinking about all this business with the spell. I don't think you could bring me all the way back because your blood is not all Oh. Since your blood has only a part of my blood in it, you could only bring me back partway. A wizard might know what's missing if we could get one here."

Alyssa thought about that for a moment. He sounded uncertain about what he said. "Edegast is likely going to be busy for a while, and he's the only wizard I know of. Can we watch Granny and holler for him if she starts acting off or sprouts something strange? And while he's here tending to that..."

He said, "I don't see that we have much choice. But you have your work cut out for you, girl. Go get all the books you can find on portals, plants, and side effects of magik. We need insight into this. Good education for you, Apprentice."

Alyssa grinned at him and set the pack on the bed to dig through it.

Granny, sufficiently certain they were not going to disappear, wiped her hands on her apron and declared she was going to make a feast for their dinner.

Alyssa's stomach growled appreciatively. She held out a hand to halt the old woman's movements. "Wait a minute."

She pulled the crown out of the pack and gently placed it on the healer's head. "You look real regal, Granny."

Gert, embarrassed at such frivolities, patted at the crown and pinched Alyssa's cheek. "You're a good girl, Lys."

Grinning, the young magician piled the dragon's coins on the dresser, stack after stack. Then without another word, she took off to collect the required books from a bookshelf to study up on plants and their side effects.

"How did she get so much money?" Granny Gert asked, astonished, staring at the piles of coins.

"Well, it's a long story, Lady Gert. Never let it be said that Ohs don't know a thing or two about a thing or two."

Epilogue

The Scarf

The eerie warm fall went late into the year, and not a drop of snow fell, to the point where winter never appeared. When true spring came, the trees shed their leaves completely, and new ones sprouted almost in the same day. This was far more disturbing to the townsfolk of Mudden and on Alyssa's family's farm than anything else. The weather became all anyone talked about.

Shortly after her arrival back at home, Alyssa, with Tony's help, burned the Putrid Plants down to the root, and when they withered away, the charred remains were dug up and buried out in Granny's sunflower patch.

The black hole behind and beneath the plants on the other side of the bridge remained a bothersome mystery. No one observed anything coming out of it, but Granny filled it in all the same. Sometimes it shed her filling detritus though, and that was when Alyssa began to patrol her family's land, cleaning up the goopy messes and keeping an eye on the hole more closely.

She watched to see if more Putrid Plants ever sprouted there, and she walked the rows of sunflowers, too. Just in case.

As Alyssa sat holding Granny's yarn for her needlework that winter, she pondered if she'd ever encounter another siren, see another dryad, and if the snow around the Yeti mountain ever melted in summer.

Pappy remained with them, still only a disembodied voice in a box until such a time as a wizard would happen by. But not one of them cared. Her grandparents didn't try to keep her from going into town or exploring any longer, but only told her to mind her manners.

The Muddentown folks seemed to keep their distance even more now. Tony must have blabbed something in town, Alyssa thought. But then again, her saucy attitude toward them didn't bring many seeking friendships either.

As for the scarf, she kept it near her all the time as it refused to leave her for any reason. One evening when she fluffed it up before stretching it out on her bed for nighttime, it floated into the air and hovered there.

"Well, smother me in gravy and call me a biscuit," she exclaimed.

The scarf expanded in two directions and lowered itself for her to climb aboard.

"You're a magik carpet, too!"

What's Next?

The story unfolds...

There is a drought in the World of Daegries and evil is stirring...

Yes, it is true. This is not the end... Book two is already underway. Be sure to follow MK at all the social sites and join the newsletter on the website MKBrowning.com